Dear Reader,

February 14 is *the* most romantic day of the year. It's a time to send chocolates, flowers and heartfelt cards. It's also a time to say "I love you" to the special person in your life....

Once again Harlequin is delighted to celebrate this day with a wonderful collection of short stories, MY VALENTINE 1992. Written by four popular Temptation authors, these stories capture the fun, fantasy and sizzle of February 14.

We hope MY VALENTINE 1992—our valentine to you—will bring you the love and laughter of this romantic occasion. And reaffirm that the spirit of St. Valentine lives on in our hearts throughout the year.

Happy Valentine's Day!

Birgit Davis-Todd
Senior Editor
Harlequin Books

P.S. We love to hear from our readers!

FOUR TEMPTING STORIES FROM YOUR FAVORITE TEMPTATION AUTHORS!

Gina Wilkins
Voted Best All Around Series Author for 1991 by *Romantic Times* magazine, Gina is well loved by readers. This talented author has written twelve Temptation novels; her delightful wedding trilogy begins in April 1992. Gina lives with her husband and three children in Arkansas.

Kristine Rolofson
Kristine is currently writing her sixth Temptation. Her trademark humor, warmth and sensuous writing style indicate she's definitely an author to watch. Kristine makes her home in Rhode Island with her hubby and their six children.

JoAnn Ross
Popular Arizona author JoAnn has written more than thirty-five books. Her stories are always imaginative and innovative—as in JoAnn's *Dark Desires,* a Temptation with a special Gothic twist, also available in February 1992. Coming in September 1992 is *The Knight in Shining Armor,* part of the Rebels & Rogues miniseries, Temptation's year-long salute to the hero.

Vicki Lewis Thompson
This two-time RWA Golden Medallion finalist has been writing for Temptation since it launched in 1984. Multitalented Vicki has also contributed to the Superromance and Intrigue lines. Her sixteenth Temptation novel, *Anything Goes,* is due out in May 1992. Vicki lives in Arizona with her family.

my Valentine 1992

GINA WILKINS
KRISTINE ROLOFSON
JoANN ROSS
VICKI LEWIS THOMPSON

Harlequin Books

TORONTO • NEW YORK • LONDON
AMSTERDAM • PARIS • SYDNEY • HAMBURG
STOCKHOLM • ATHENS • TOKYO • MILAN
MADRID • WARSAW • BUDAPEST • AUCKLAND

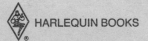 HARLEQUIN BOOKS

MY VALENTINE 1992

Copyright © 1992 by Harlequin Enterprises Limited

ISBN 0-373-83229-X

MY VALENTINE 1992 first printing February 1992

The publisher acknowledges the copyright holders
of the individual works as follows:

DENIM AND DIAMONDS
Copyright © 1992 by Gina Wilkins

THE VALENTINE RAFFLE
Copyright © 1992 by Kristine Rolofson

A VERY SPECIAL DELIVERY
Copyright © 1992 by JoAnn Ross

VALENTINE MISCHIEF
Copyright © 1992 by Vicki Lewis Thompson

Contents

Dedications

For my son, Ben, another Nebraska man
—Kristine Rolofson

To Jay and Patrick and now Lisa, with love
—JoAnn Ross

For Larry, my favorite valentine
—Vicki Lewis Thompson

DENIM
AND DIAMONDS

Gina Wilkins

A Note from Gina Wilkins

My husband of fifteen years says that he is not a "romantic" type of guy. He gives me candy every Valentine's Day (even when I'm dieting, unfortunately), but he's not one to poetically express his feelings, and he takes money much too seriously to spend it frivolously. Yet John once made a truly romantic gesture to help make my dreams come true.

We were going through that tight-money stage most young marrieds experience. We could afford food, diapers and formula, but few luxuries. A woodworker who doesn't like to buy on credit, John had been saving for years for a table saw. Harlequin had just requested a first, full manuscript from me when my secondhand typewriter suddenly died. Without a word, John took his savings—almost enough to buy his saw—and bought the most expensive electronic typewriter he could find. There was no guarantee Harlequin would buy my book, but John always believed in me—and wanted me to be able to write in style.

It wasn't Valentine's Day. It wasn't even February. But true expressions of love aren't always accompanied by flowers or candy or sentimental cards. Real relationships require hard work, deep commitment, frequent compromises and occasional sacrifices, which is also the point of my story, *Denim and Diamonds*.

John and I now have three beautiful children. We both work out of our home, so we're together all the time—and yet he's still my best friend and most loyal supporter. That typewriter has long since been traded for a computer, and with my first royalty check, I bought John the best table saw I could find. John still buys me candy on Valentine's Day—even when I'm dieting. And he still claims he is not the romantic type. I know better.

Chapter One

"HOW CAN YOU SAY Valentine's Day is nothing to get excited about?"

The woman's question caught Beau Harmon's attention. He looked up from the paperback Western he'd been reading as he sat on the concrete floor in one corner of the apartment-complex laundromat. Surrounded by the noisy machines, he hadn't heard anyone enter until the woman spoke.

The women hadn't spotted him yet. Beau usually chose this spot over the uncomfortable straight-back chairs for that very reason—he hated making polite small-talk while his clothes washed. He didn't always go unnoticed, but usually his location, along with the ever-present book in his hand, conveyed the message that he wasn't in search of conversation.

"Why would anyone get excited about a silly occasion like Valentine's Day?" a second woman demanded in response to the question that had drawn Beau away from his book.

Beau recognized both voices, but it was the second that made him close the book and eavesdrop more enthusiastically. Though he couldn't see them, he could clearly picture the two women who were loading machines behind him. The one who'd spoken first was Carole Lipton, a petite yet nicely curved blonde with an enticing walk and a boyfriend the size of a small building. She lived in the apartment two doors down from Beau's.

But it was the other woman whom Beau could visualize most vividly. Alison Tindall. Deep-set green eyes, a kissably full lower lip, a delicate oval face framed by glossy sable hair and a slender, graceful figure that looked great even in those Yuppie executive clothes she favored. He could even see her chewing her lower lip the way she did when she was in deep thought. That always drove him crazy. Made him think longingly of soothing those delicate nibble-marks with the tip of his tongue.

He listened closely as the women continued their good-natured argument.

"Silly?" Carole repeated indignantly. "Valentine's Day is so romantic!"

"It's so fake," Alison retorted.

"What about the flowers?"

"Cut flowers are a waste of money. They're ridiculously expensive, they wither in no time and you end up just throwing them out."

Beau winced at her response. Yep, that sounded just like Alison, whose voice he usually heard shooting down another tentative overture from him. He'd tried everything to get her to go out with him. His killer smile—the one that usually worked wonders with the opposite sex—flattery, even a rather offhand, nonthreatening, just-buddies invitation for pizza and a movie. Nothing had worked with her, though he'd had considerable success with those tactics on other women.

"Gosh, you're so unromantic." Carole, again. "Okay, so how about the candy? I adore all those expensive chocolates in the fancy packages."

"Cavities and calories wrapped in silly heart-shaped boxes trimmed with ruffles and plastic roses? Puh-leeze!"

The woman was impossible. Beau scowled, his closed book propped on one upraised, denim-covered knee. Not only had he begun to suspect that she was a bit of a snob;

now it seemed she had a heart of stone, as well. What *would* it take to soften her? Damn, but he wished he knew.

"Valentine cards, then," Carole suggested. "Surely you have nothing against those."

"Give me a break. Sickly-sweet messages written by strangers? Face it, Carole, February 14 is just another day, commercialized and romanticized by florists and card companies to generate millions of dollars in sales."

Beau wasn't even sure what he saw in Alison. She wasn't his usual type. He liked women who laughed easily, didn't mind getting a little dirty, understood that honest hard work needed to be balanced with equally hard play. Alison Tindall was the quintessential career woman—sleek, serious, and very ambitious. She wore the right clothes, drove the right car, worked late hours and weekends.

And she nibbled her lower lip and made him crazy, dammit.

He'd taken one look at her when he'd moved into this apartment complex three months earlier and had wanted her. Each time she rebuffed one of his friendly approaches, he vowed he'd never try again. And yet, each time he'd known he would.

Maybe he just wasn't accustomed to feminine rejection, he reflected wryly, wondering if his relatively easy conquests in the past had made him conceited. Or maybe he sensed that there was more to Ms. Alison Tindall than designer suits and leather briefcases.

He'd heard her laugh with her friends, admired her obvious competence in her job, had even once spotted tears of sympathy in her eyes when a child from a nearby apartment had fallen right in front of her and torn a thin layer of skin from his bony little knee. Beau had just stepped out of his own apartment when the accident happened and he'd helped Alison carry the little boy home.

Entranced by her tears, afterward he'd asked her out again—only to be politely, but quite firmly, rejected.

"Okay, Alison, let's have it," Carole said firmly, slamming the lid on a washer. "Tell me what you've got against Valentine's Day."

Beau pictured Alison bent over a laundry basket and had to swallow a groan. "All right, I admit it," she said. "I have a personal prejudice against the day. Some old wounds."

"I guessed. What happened?"

"A series of lousy Valentine's Days when I was a teenager. I was kind of chubby in high school—"

"You? You're kidding!" Carole's exclamation echoed Beau's startled reaction.

"No, really. I was painfully shy, and dedicated to my studies. Needless to say, when the cheerleaders and beauty queens were deluged with flowers and jewelry and heart-shaped boxes of candy, I was passed over. When I was in the eleventh grade, I had a major crush on a boy who seemed to like me, as well. I thought we had quite a little romance going. Until Valentine's Day, when the cute redhead next door showed me the nice box of candy he had given her. Turned out he was just being nice to me so I'd help him study for a calculus exam."

"Why, the sneaky creep! I knew guys like that in school—everyone did, for that matter. It shouldn't have put you off romance forever."

"It wasn't quite that drastic. It was just one incident when Valentine's Day proved more painful than pleasant."

"Name another example," Carole challenged.

Alison responded without hesitation. "In college, I earned a bit of extra spending money by working in the reception office of my dorm. On Valentine's Day, it was my job to call the various rooms to announce the endless deliveries of flowers and gifts for the sorority sweethearts. Someone usually managed to point out that there hadn't been anything delivered for me.

"During my senior year I was involved with someone, but he was the scholarly type who scorned 'romantic trappings,' just as I pretended to do. On Valentine's Day we attended a reading of antiestablishment free verse in someone's basement." She spoke with an ironic dignity that only emphasized the chagrin she'd experienced, and made Beau wince in sympathy.

Okay, so maybe he could understand why she tended to be a little prickly. Had all the men she'd ever known been total idiots? Hadn't they looked at her and been ready to chew furniture to have her, the way he had?

"Bummer," Carole commented. "You mean no one's ever sent you gifts on Valentine's Day?"

"My mother sent me a pink sweater when I was a college sophomore," Alison muttered, obviously embarrassed to admit her romantic yearnings. Beau thought she'd worked so hard to build her glossy, impervious shell that it bothered her to reveal the occasional crack, even to a close friend.

"Of course, I've long since outgrown those silly fantasies about Valentine's Day," she hastily assured Carole. "Even if I were seeing anyone special now, I certainly wouldn't expect a lot of phony trappings on February 14. Besides," she added with an attempt at humor, "chocolates aren't on my diet."

"Then how about a low-cal ice-cream bar?" Carole suggested, abruptly changing the subject. "I've got some in my freezer. We can watch TV at my place until these clothes finish washing."

"Sure. Just let me— Okay, there it goes. The coin thing was stuck."

"I hate it when that happens. So, how's the Hinson project going? Did you ever get . . ." Carole's voice faded away when the two women left the laundry room, allowing the door to swoosh closed behind them.

"No," Beau muttered after a moment. "It would never work, old son. She'd chew you into little pieces."

And then he smiled slowly. "Still," he murmured, "it might be worth a shot. It might just be worth it."

He closed his book and began to make plans for Valentine's Day, which happened to be less than a week away.

ALISON WOKE with a scowl on February 14. It took her a minute to figure out why, and then she chided herself in exasperation. Hadn't she only recently assured Carole that she'd outgrown her romanticism? It was just another day, right? No reason to expect any variation from her usual daily routine. Ignoring her lingering depression, she dressed in her best "power" suit and twisted her sable hair into a sensible chignon. After a moment of thought, she donned the flashy diamond earrings she'd bought as a reward for her latest promotion. She usually saved them for special occasions, but today she needed the reminder that she was successful and competent—totally self-sufficient.

Fully dressed, she studied her reflection with quiet satisfaction. This was no chubby, shy, dreamy-eyed girl, but a productive, intelligent and reasonably attractive businesswoman. And it wasn't as if no one noticed her these days. Thoughtfully nibbling her lower lip, she thought of Dane, the professor from the University of Arkansas at Little Rock, with whom she shared an occasional dinner or theater production. And she wasn't forgetting Jonathan, the computer salesman from Dallas, who called her to spend a pleasant evening with her whenever he was in town.

And then there was the man who lived in the apartment directly across the compound from her own, who'd been trying to talk her into going out with him for three months.

Beau Harmon. He was everything she did *not* want in a man. Tall, lean, blond and borderline gorgeous, he was simply too self-confidently attractive. It had practically stunned him that she hadn't immediately fallen for any of his well-practiced pickup lines. He was unapologetically blue-collar—he'd said he worked as a lineman for the power company—rarely wore anything other than well-worn jeans and flannel shirts, and drove a four-wheel-drive vehicle. He'd probably been a quarterback in high school. The kind of guy who wouldn't have given Alison a second look, choosing instead to concentrate on the cheerleaders and homecoming princesses. Not her type at all.

She preferred more sophisticated, more intellectual men. Men who were more interested in a woman's sharp mind and professional competence than in the way she filled a sweater.

So, why was she wasting time thinking about him, as she had done so many times in the past three months? She snatched up her leather handbag and headed for work, putting the persistent Beau Harmon—and Valentine's Day—firmly out of her mind.

Chapter Two

THE FIRST THINGS—the very first things—Alison saw upon entering the office were the red roses sitting on her secretary's desk, right beside an enormous heart-shaped box of chocolates. Mary Lou, Alison's secretary, was talking excitedly to two other secretaries, all of whom were busily admiring the gifts. "Isn't it the sweetest thing?" Mary Lou sighed. "The deliveryman told me Harry paid extra to make sure these were waiting for me as soon as I arrived."

"You're so lucky. All Donald ever buys me is a small box of candy, and then he usually eats most of them himself," a broad-hipped brunette said with an envious sigh. "He never sends me flowers."

"Charlie gave me my engagement ring last Valentine's Day," the tall black secretary from the office next door said. "I don't know what he's doing this year, but he's been hinting for days that I'm going to be thrilled. The rat's making me wait until dinner before he gives me my present."

Mary Lou glanced up to see her supervisor standing in the doorway. She immediately looked guilty at being caught gossiping during work hours. "Good morning, Alison," she said, coming instantly to attention.

"Good morning, Mary Lou. Carlene, Betty." Alison greeted the three. "Lovely flowers, Mary Lou. Did Harry send them?"

"Yes, he did."

"Very nice. Would you mind getting the Hinson file for me, please?"

"Of course." Mary Lou gave her friends a quick wave of dismissal. They left immediately. Alison could hear them returning to the subject of Valentine's Day gifts as they headed down the hallway to their own offices.

Alison stored her purse in her desk and reached for the stack of mail waiting for her perusal. Too bad her friend Julia was out of town. A partner with a local public-relations firm, Julia was dry-witted, ambitious, and contentedly single, though she acknowledged that men had their uses at times. A quick telephone chat with her would have provided a welcome relief from the Valentine's Day hysteria surrounding Alison.

Eight more hours of today to endure, she thought with a sigh. By Monday, everything would be back to normal. *Thank goodness.*

SHE WAS DEEPLY IMMERSED in paperwork when Mary Lou knocked on her door an hour later. "Come in," she called out, distracted from her work.

"Delivery for you, Alison." Mary Lou sounded vaguely awed.

Alison looked up from her report. Her eyes rounded when she saw her secretary carrying in an enormous, heavily-blossomed pink begonia plant in an elaborately decorated ceramic pot. "Did you say that's for me?" she asked cautiously, when Mary Lou set the plant on one corner of the desk.

"That's what the deliveryman said," Mary Lou assured her with a smile. "I take it you're surprised?"

"You could say that." Who in the world had sent it? she wondered, reaching for the tiny card held by a plastic clip. Mary Lou, discreet as always, returned to her own office to give Alison privacy.

The delivery hadn't been a mistake. Alison's name was printed quite clearly on the tiny pink envelope. Unfortunately, hers was the only name she found. The message on the card read only, "Happy Valentine's Day."

It had to be Carole. Alison studied the plant with a smile of somewhat embarrassed pleasure. Her softhearted friend had probably felt sorry for Alison because she wouldn't be receiving a Valentine. She'd even remembered that Alison didn't much care for cut flowers, sending a living plant, instead. It was a sweet gesture, of course, and the plant was beautiful, but Alison wished Carole hadn't done it. After all, she hadn't been whining or complaining when she'd expressed her experience-based distaste for this particular occasion. She certainly didn't want Carole to feel badly for her.

As if in telepathic response, Carole called not half an hour later. "Would you mind keeping an eye on my apartment for me this weekend?" she asked almost as soon as Alison answered the phone. "Ted and I are going to Hot Springs. He's made reservations at the Arlington and at Coy's for dinner tonight. We're going to the racetrack tomorrow."

"Sounds like fun."

"It does, doesn't it? He took me completely by surprise. This is my Valentine gift."

Alison winced, but spoke naturally enough. "Speaking of which—you wouldn't know anything about a beautiful begonia plant, would you?"

"Well, I know they have lots of flowers and they're relatively easy to take care of, unless you happen to have two brown thumbs, like I do. Why?"

Alison frowned. She'd been so sure Carole had sent the plant, but Carole had never been particularly talented at dissimulation. She sounded as though she had no idea what Alison was talking about. "You didn't send it?"

"A begonia plant? No. What makes you think I did?"

Alison reluctantly explained, knowing her friend would be delighted by the mystery gift. She was right.

"Alison, how exciting! Who could have sent it?"

"Dane, I suppose. Though it doesn't seem like him to send flowers. Still, it must be him. Who else could it be?"

"Well, I don't care, I think it's a very romantic gesture. Maybe Dane's not quite as dull as I've accused him of being."

"Now, Carole, don't start romanticizing. You know Dane and I are just good friends."

"So maybe he's trying to change that."

Alison hoped not. As much as she enjoyed Dane's company, she really wasn't interested in pursuing a more intimate relationship with him. Though she wouldn't have admitted it for anything, she secretly agreed with Carole. Dane was very nice, but just the tiniest bit dull. The college professor usually took her to the Repertory Theater or the Arkansas Symphony or the local dinner theater, followed by an in-depth discussion of the performance. She found their dates intellectually stimulating. Unfortunately, her intellect was the only part of her that found Dane stimulating.

She assured Carole that she'd keep an eye on her apartment. After promising she'd tell her if she found out who'd sent the flowers, Alison hung up the phone and returned to her work. Still, she found her eyes straying more than once to the lovely pink blooms of the begonia. *If not Dane, who?*

THE SECOND DELIVERY arrived just after lunch. Mary Lou didn't even try to hide her amazement when she carried this one in. Alison looked at the white basket full of exotic fruits in astonishment. "But I—" she began, then really didn't know what else to say.

"He's original, I'll say that for him," Mary Lou murmured with a smile as she headed back to her own desk. "Those fruits look wonderful. And so much more interesting than plain old apples and oranges. Where d'you suppose he found them in Little Rock?"

Since Alison couldn't even guess who "he" was, she didn't particularly care where the basket had been purchased. She was already digging for some clue to the sender. She found a card tucked among the fruit. One sinfully rich, heart-shaped chocolate in red foil wrapping had been taped to the corner of the card. "One piece of chocolate won't hurt that spectacular figure of yours," the card read impudently. "Enjoy."

It couldn't possibly be Dane. Even if he had ever noticed her figure, he'd never have mentioned it so whimsically. Her first impulse was to call him and find out once and for all if he was the sender. But what if it wasn't him? What would she say, then?

Could it be Jonathan, the computer salesman from Dallas? Grand gestures were more his style. The man was cheerfully, unapologetically materialistic, but Jonathan would want full credit for his extravagance. Alison went out with him occasionally because he amused her, though she sometimes lost patience with his obsession with money and status. He'd made it clear from the beginning that he wasn't interested in a long-term commitment with any woman, though he would like very much to carry his casual friendship with Alison into the bedroom. She'd made it equally clear that the bedroom was not now, nor would it ever be, part of their relationship. They were friends, nothing more.

She found it hard to believe Jonathan had sent the gifts. He wasn't one to waste money on lost causes.

"Who's *doing* this?" Alison asked aloud.

IT WAS VERY LATE that afternoon when the final delivery arrived. Mary Lou laughed in undisguised amusement as she tiptoed with exaggerated caution to Alison's desk, a beautifully-wrapped square box cradled in both hands. "It's marked Fragile," she explained when Alison only watched her in numb astonishment.

Another one? She stared at the box as though it were entirely possible it held something lethal, making her secretary laugh even more. "I think I like this guy," Mary Lou murmured, turning to walk briskly away. Alison was grimly certain Mary Lou would head straight for her friends' offices to discuss the unusual deliveries her normally no-nonsense supervisor had received that day.

Almost nervously, Alison slipped the white satin ribbon from the box, then peeled the silver paper away, wondering if this time she'd find the name of the sender. Her breath caught as she lifted a porcelain figurine from the white tissue paper that had protected it within the box. Perhaps eight inches tall, the little clown smiled endearingly at her as she studied him. He was dressed in baggy, brightly-colored clothing and his hair was a mop of bright gold. He held a battered derby in his tiny hands. It was impossible not to love him. And then she discovered the tiny metal key in his back.

Moments later the delicate notes of a music box played—what else?—"My Funny Valentine." Alison closed her eyes and groaned softly. She wondered if anyone would notice if she waved a white flag. She surrendered. She had never been so thoroughly, if reluctantly, charmed.

Who was sending her these things?

She found the card at the bottom of the box. Though it wasn't signed—to her intense disappointment—it was written in a bold, masculine handwriting that could only belong to the sender. "I'll pick you up for dinner at seven," it read. "Wear something elegant."

Her pulse unsteady, Alison studied the message. She knew that Jonathan was in Canada for the next week on a business trip. So it had to be Dane. Maybe he'd been brainwashed by greeting-card commercials and florists' jingles. Or maybe Dane wasn't as dull and unimaginative as she'd considered him.

Should she go with him to dinner? It was terribly arrogant for him to assume she was free on such short notice on this Friday evening—even for believing she wanted to go out with him if she *were* free. But, as it happened, she had no other plans for the evening and—she had to admit—she was flattered by the attention. If anyone had courted her this way a few years ago, before she'd put all that romantic foolishness behind her, she'd have been putty in his hands by now.

She wouldn't go quite that far now, but she decided abruptly that she would have dinner with him—at which time she'd tell him that it really hadn't been necessary to go to so much effort on her behalf. She really didn't believe in the Valentine's Day mating rituals.

"I'm leaving now, Alison," Mary Lou announced from the doorway. "Anything else you need first?"

"No, you can go. I'm sure you have big plans for the evening."

"I doubt that I'm the only one who does," Mary Lou replied archly, nodding toward the deskful of Valentine gifts.

Alison just managed not to blush. God, when was the last time she'd blushed? she wondered in bewilderment. She really didn't know how to cope with a day like this one. "Good night, Mary Lou," she managed.

"Good night, Alison. See you Monday."

"Mmm. Monday," Alison repeated, but her thoughts had already turned back to the evening. Just what *was* Dane expecting from her during this date?

AT TEN MINUTES TO SEVEN that evening, Alison stared at the same mirror she'd looked into with such satisfaction just that morning. Only this time, rather than a no-nonsense career woman, a near stranger stared back at her.

Valentine's Day hysteria must be contagious, she decided with a disgusted shake of her head. Her dark brown hair swayed softly around her face with the movement. Though she rarely wore her hair down, she'd brushed it until it gleamed in a silky curtain to her shoulders. And without really thinking about her choice of clothing, she'd dressed in a slinky black sheath she'd worn only once before, having decided it really wasn't her style. The dress was rather shapeless on a hanger, but when donned clung lovingly to every curve. The low neckline bared her throat to the top curves of her breasts. The sleeves were long but sheer, making her arms look pale and delicate beneath them.

She'd left the diamond earrings in place, adding a diamond pendant that sparkled enticingly from her partially exposed cleavage. Dark hose and high-heeled sandals completed the ensemble—and the transformation from career woman to seductress.

"Wear something elegant," the unsigned card had instructed. Well, this was elegant, but since when had she automatically followed any man's instructions—particularly when she wasn't even absolutely certain who had given them?

She couldn't quite believe she was doing this: getting ready for a date when she wasn't even sure exactly who would be picking her up. It must be Dane—after all, who else could it be?—but she still found an odd, unexpected excitement in the mystery he had created for her. Which wasn't at all like her.

"Honestly, Alison," she muttered. "This had better be just a temporary aberration."

Still grumbling at her uncharacteristic behavior, she turned away from the mirror to find her coat and purse.

The doorbell rang promptly at seven. Now, that was more like Dane. Always punctual. The thought helped soothe the unexplainable attack of nerves that had quivered in her stomach with the first peal of the doorbell.

Taking a deep breath, she opened the door—only to find her tall, blond, borderline-gorgeous neighbor grinning at her with what could only be called smug satisfaction. She'd never seen him in a suit before, but she had to admit—if only to herself—that he looked spectacular in one.

"Hello, Alison," Beau Harmon said, his voice whiskey-smooth. "Happy Valentine's Day."

Chapter Three

BEAU THOUGHT it had probably been years since Alison had been struck speechless. But now she stood in her doorway staring at him, seemingly unable to say a word.

He reached up to run a finger around the collar of his crisp white shirt, feeling as though it were strangling him. She looked beautiful—more beautiful than ever. He'd advised her to wear something elegant, but he hadn't dreamed he'd find her looking—well, like this. Sleek. Classy. Sexy as hell.

"Ready for dinner?" he asked. The trick now was to make sure she didn't back out before he got her in his Jeep van.

She cleared her throat. "You—"

He gave her no chance to refuse. "Good. I'm starved. Here, let me help you with your coat."

She frowned at the coat and purse in her hands as though she'd never seen them before.

Smiling amiably, he slipped the coat out of her tight grasp and moved behind her. She automatically lifted her arms when he held the garment for her. Only when he'd smoothed it over her shoulders, taking his time with the pleasant task, did she seem to realize what she'd done. "Look," she began heatedly. "I—"

He dropped his hands immediately, if somewhat reluctantly. "I've made reservations at Chez Colette. You've been there?"

"Yes, I—"

"I haven't, but I've heard it's very good. Door locked?"

Somehow he'd manipulated her out onto her doorstep, with the door closed behind them. She still looked rather stunned, so he used her disorientation to his advantage, chattering as if they'd planned this date for weeks. "Brr. It's cold tonight, isn't it? I may have to get one of those long wool overcoats eventually. Somehow my down ski jacket doesn't look quite right over a suit." He took her arm as he talked, leading her gently toward the parking lot.

Her shock finally wearing off enough to allow her usual independence to reassert itself, Alison shook his hand away and turned to face him. "Now, just wait a minute—"

"Beau," he supplied when she hesitated.

"I know your name," she snapped, though he'd have been willing to bet that lingering surprise had wiped it momentarily from her mind. "What I want to—"

"You know," he interrupted with a husky edge in his voice, "I forgot to mention how beautiful you look tonight. You take my breath away." It really wasn't just a ploy to take her off guard again. He was utterly sincere. Just looking at her tonight made it difficult for Beau to even remember his name.

Apparently he'd taken her voice away—again. He took advantage of the moment to touch her arm. "I'm parked right over here," he murmured, gesturing toward the metallic-blue Jeep Cherokee. He'd washed it, and the chrome glittered in the harsh light of the security lamps. He wondered if she'd noticed how much trouble he'd gone to to get her to go out with him tonight.

Maybe she had. She took a deep breath and nodded. "Fine."

He broke into a smile of sheer relief as he realized that she would be accompanying him without further resistance. Okay, so his methods had been somewhat underhanded. She'd just made it all worth it. Now, if only this evening went well.

"Just let me unlock the door for you," he said, quickly jamming the key into the lock. He was almost afraid she'd change her mind if he didn't hurry.

He steadied her with a hand at her elbow as she climbed into the Jeep. And then he loped around the front to hop into his own seat. Alison had snapped her seat belt, and was studying the stack of CDs in the console between them. Country and western, of course. Alison probably listened to classical music. Soft rock, maybe.

At that uncomfortable reminder of the distinct differences between them, he cleared his throat and started the engine. "I know it's not exactly a luxury vehicle, but it serves my purposes."

"It's really quite comfortable."

"Thanks. Twenty-six more payments and this baby's all mine." He pulled out of the parking lot, clutched and shifted. Out of the corner of his eye, he saw her gaze focus on the movement of his thighs, but she turned her eyes firmly to the road ahead before he could be sure.

Was the physical attraction really all on his side, or did she find him even a little attractive? he worried uncharacteristically. Most of the women he'd dated had made it quite clear that they liked what they saw when they looked at him. He only wished he could read Alison as easily as he had those others, whose faces he couldn't even remember at the moment.

"Beau?" Alison said tentatively when they'd driven maybe five minutes in silence.

"Yes?"

"I really didn't know it was you."

"I didn't think you would. Who'd you expect—the guy with the tweed jackets who brings you home early and leaves you with a kiss on the cheek? Or the one in the Italian suits who keeps you out later, then tries unsuccessfully to charm his way into your apartment?''

She frowned, and he realized that he'd just let her know exactly how closely he'd been watching her during the past three months. Maybe he should have kept his mouth shut.

Twisting one dark sable lock around a fingertip, she shrugged off his question. ''I just didn't expect you,'' she muttered.

''Are you disappointed?'' He'd tried to sound teasing, but the attempt had fallen sadly flat. He'd sounded all too serious. He waited tensely for her answer.

She kept her eyes turned forward, refusing to look at him. ''I guess I'll just have to let you know later, won't I?''

She didn't sound mad. He almost grinned in relief. ''Yeah. Guess you will.''

A moment later he reached for the radio power button. He paused with one finger hovering above it. ''I like having music when I drive. You mind?''

''Of course not.'' Like him, she seemed to realize the music would provide an excuse not to have to make stilted conversation during the drive. Now, if only they could find something to talk about through dinner.

The music blasted out at a near-deafening volume, the way Beau tended to play it when he was alone. Grimacing a wry apology, he turned it down, though he didn't bother to change the station. He was quite sure it wasn't Alison's type of music, but after a moment he noticed her toe tapping idly against the floorboard in time to the song.

Ignoring the available valet parking, Beau pulled into an empty space half a block from the restaurant entrance. ''I don't like strangers driving my wheels,'' he explained, reaching for the door handle. ''You don't mind walking, do you?''

"Of course not," Alison assured him, trying without much success to hide a smile. Beau almost grimaced at the thought that she found him an amusing change from her usual escorts. Why hadn't he just forgotten about trying to impress her and taken her to B.J.'s Barbecue, where he'd have been more at ease?

The restaurant he'd chosen turned out to be one of Alison's favorites, though she explained that she'd eaten there only occasionally. It was, after all, one of the more expensive establishments in Little Rock. She seemed surprised, though pleased, that it had been Beau's choice for the evening. Maybe this had been a better choice than B.J.'s, after all, he thought in relief.

They were seated at a tiny table lit with a flickering candle centered among fragrant flowers. Beau squirmed in the undersized seat, studying the menu and wishing again he'd selected a place with red-checked tablecloths and a pile of napkins to soak up barbecue grease. So he'd thought to impress her, had he? Hell, he didn't even know what to order.

Great start.

He looked up to find her watching him over the top of her menu. She immediately ducked back behind it.

"So, what are you having?" he asked.

The underhanded tactics he'd used to get her to go out with him might have tempted a lesser woman to repay him by ordering the most expensive items on the menu. Alison seemed to be above that. "The salmon sounds good," she murmured, closing her menu. "I've had it before. The chef has created an interesting sauce."

Beau cleared his throat. "Yeah? Well, maybe I'll try that, too."

"Wine, sir?"

Beau glared up at the sommelier for a moment before softening his expression. "What would you recommend for the salmon?" he asked the young man simply—and then glanced at Alison, "Unless you have a preference?"

"I'm not very good at choosing wines," she admitted. It didn't seem to bother her that he'd just admitted his own lack of expertise in that area.

He found himself liking her more by the minute. He wasn't crazy about this snooty restaurant, but he'd begun to notice the slightly envious looks he was getting from some of the other male diners when they saw him with Alison. He didn't blame the guys—to Beau, she was the most attractive woman in the place. Some of his usual cocky confidence returned. He smiled at her, deciding he may as well be up-front with her, let her know exactly what he was really like.

"I'm afraid I'm not really into the glamorous dining scene," he confessed. "A burger and fries are more what I'm accustomed to."

"Then I'm flattered you made an exception for to-night," Alison responded lightly.

"Are you kidding? I'm the envy of every other man here."

His intimate tone made her flush, to his secret delight. She reached quickly for her water glass. "I forgot to thank you for the gifts," she said when she'd taken a sip. "Though, of course, you shouldn't—"

"You're welcome. I like your hair down. Is that your natural color?" Incongruous comments had worked before to keep her off guard. He used the tactic again to prevent her from scolding him for sending the gifts.

Alison blinked at the question. "Yes, of course it is."

"Beautiful. What sort of movies do you like?"

Maybe she allowed him to change the subject to ensure a pleasant dinner. Whatever her reason, she let it go, choosing instead to answer his question.

Alison liked romantic-comedy movies, an occasional art film. Beau admitted to preferring action-adventure flicks—the more car-chase scenes, the better.

As he'd suspected, Alison favored classical music and soft rock. She told Beau that she really hadn't listened to much country and western. He wasn't surprised.

She'd never read Louis L'Amour, though she said she understood he'd been quite popular with his loyal readers. No, he told her in answer to her question; he'd never read any of the authors she listed as her favorites.

"You like sports?" he asked, searching desperately for something—anything—they had in common.

She nodded. "I like watching football. And winter sports, such as downhill skiing and particularly, figure skating."

He felt his eyes widen. "You like football? No kidding?"

Alison smiled. "Yes, really."

"Who are your favorite teams?" he asked, not because he didn't believe her, of course, but because he wondered just how closely she followed the game.

"The Raiders and the Bears. I always cheer against the Cowboys, though. I'm not a fan of theirs."

He grinned. "Me, either. So, what do you think of Chicago's chances for the Super Bowl this year?"

The rest of the meal passed quickly as they eagerly discussed the one interest they had in common. Beau figured they'd probably find other things if they kept talking. Maybe there was hope for them yet.

Alison cocked her head in question at the expression on Beau's face when he studied his empty plate. "Didn't you like the food?" she asked.

"Yeah, it was good," he assured her quickly. "But—well, they don't exactly get carried away with the portions, do they?"

She was surprised. "You mean you're still hungry? After all that?"

His grin kicked up one corner of his entirely-too-sexy mouth. "Honey, I could've eaten twice that and had room for half a chocolate cake," he admitted. "I've been told I have the appetite of your average elephant."

Ignoring the casual endearment that had sent her pulse to racing despite her best efforts to control it, Alison lifted an eyebrow. "So why don't you weigh as much as one?" she asked.

He shrugged. "Metabolism, I guess. My dad and my brother are the same way. Mama says she's spent half her life trying to keep the three of us fed."

Alison liked the affectionate way he referred to his family. She liked the way he shrugged. In fact, she was beginning to like entirely too many things about this man with whom she had so little in common. Maybe that was why she'd turned him down each time he'd asked her out before. Maybe she'd known she'd be getting into something she wasn't quite sure she could handle.

He'd been a very pleasant dinner companion. Amusing and considerate and unselfconsciously sexy. She tried to remind herself that she was still annoyed with him for his Valentine's Day deception. But now, even that seemed typically Beau—charming and slightly offbeat with a touch of thoroughly masculine arrogance tossed in.

"Do you have a family, Alison?"

"Of course, I have a family," she answered with a smile. "Two parents, three remaining grandparents, two sisters and a brother."

"I'll bet you're the oldest kid."

"Yes, I am. How'd you know?"

He only shrugged and smiled. "Where does your family live? Were you visiting them when you were gone for a week at Christmas?"

She frowned a little at this further evidence that he'd been watching her quite closely for the past three months, but she answered evenly, "Yes. I'm from Batesville. My parents and grandparents still live there, as well as one married sister. My other sister lives in Memphis and my brother attends Arkansas State University."

"How old are you, anyway?"

He continually caught her off guard with his personal questions asked in such a matter-of-fact tone. She cleared her throat and murmured, "Twenty-seven. You?"

He made a face. "Thirty last week."

"Belated Happy Birthday."

"Thanks. My brother's a couple years younger. He's been giving me a hard time about turning thirty."

She laughed. "Being the oldest of my family, I can identify with that," she admitted.

His blue eyes were warm on her face. "I like your laugh." And then, before she could make a response—whatever it might have been—he said impulsively, "Let's have dessert later. Somewhere else, okay?"

"Of course, if that's what you want." She realized she had tacitly agreed to extend the evening after they left the restaurant, but she was really in no hurry to bring it to an end. After all, she was having a very nice time, and her only alternatives for the evening had been a pile of paperwork or an evening of television.

Beau paid for the meal with a credit card—not gold or
platinum, just the regular kind, she noted. He waited until they were outside, walking toward his Jeep, before giving an exaggerated sigh of relief. ''Tell me I didn't eat my
fish with my dessert fork or anything,'' he begged humor-
ously, one hand just touching her elbow.

Funny how she could almost feel the warmth of him
through her wool coat and the sleeve of her dress. ''You
did fine,'' she assured him. It felt oddly natural to be
walking beside him, smiling at his teasing. How could she
have become so comfortable with him in such a short time?

''I have an idea.''

She had a few of her own. She sincerely hoped his
weren't along the same lines. She wasn't altogether certain of her usually unshakable willpower at the moment.
''What's your idea?''

''Why don't we relax a bit now? I know a great place.
We can dance, have a drink, talk some more. There's a really good band playing this weekend.''

''That sounds nice,'' Alison agreed, picturing an intimate little lounge most of her associates frequented on the
weekends. She'd heard someone mention a locally-
renowned band being booked there for this romantic
weekend, a group well-known for its own arrangements of
Glenn Miller and other big-band tunes. She wondered
what the odds were that Beau was thinking of that very
place.

Ten minutes later Alison studied the club Beau had
driven to and decided the odds were very slim indeed that
she'd be hearing any Glenn Miller pieces this evening.

Chapter Four

AN ELABORATELY-LETTERED sign identified the club as J.T's Place. Alison had heard it was a popular country-and-western dance club, but had never had the inclination to visit. The parking lot was filled almost to capacity, mostly with vehicles of the pickup persuasion. Couples strolled toward the entrance — the men dressed in jeans and boots, the women, in short skirts. Looking at Beau, she noticed that he'd already rid himself of his tie and unfastened the top two buttons of his shirt. She was beginning to feel distinctly overdressed.

He grinned at her expression. "Trust me," he said. "We're going to have a great time."

Trust him? A man who'd sneakily manipulated her into going out with him? Who'd spent the entire evening charming and romancing her over an elegant candlelight dinner? A man who had somehow transformed himself from an attractive, affable escort into a somewhat dangerous-looking stranger merely by removing his tie and loosening his shirt? Even his thick gold hair had suddenly developed a tendency to tumble rakishly over his forehead, though it had remained neatly combed during dinner.

Beau had been out of his element at the restaurant; Alison would be out of hers in this place. Deciding turnabout was only fair play, she took a deep breath and reached for the door handle. "Okay," she said bravely. "Let's go in."

Beau laughed at her expression and opened his own door. "This is really going to be fun," he repeated.

Alison chose not to respond.

By now she should have expected that the interior of the club would be a pleasant surprise. Hadn't everything else turned out that way so far during this unusual date? The decor was tasteful, following a blue-and-beige Southwestern theme. The bar was a massive antique, set against one wall, gleaming with brass and glass and mirrors and bottles. Couples swayed on a large dance floor. The country-pop band wasn't one she would have chosen, but they were quite good at their type of music.

An overweight woman in her thirties, trying to look younger by means of harshly-bleached hair and too-tight, too-revealing clothes, looked up from a table where she sat with a rotund would-be cowboy. Alison was vividly aware of the woman's minute scrutiny and obvious disapproval. "Wonder where she thought she was goin' tonight?" the bottle blonde asked her escort, not bothering to hold down her voice. "The friggin' opera?" And then she laughed raucously at her own joke.

If he'd heard, Beau ignored the comment. Alison gulped and followed him to a miraculously-available small table tucked into a cozy corner, feeling decidedly out of place in his element. Was this the way he'd felt at Chez Colette's?

A young waitress appeared at the table almost immediately. "Well, hi, Beau. How's it going?"

Beau flashed a lazy grin and nodded. "Just fine, Patrice. Looks like y'all are busy tonight."

Patrice rolled her eyes expressively. "We sure are. It's been like this since seven."

"Patrice, this is Alison."

Alison was the recipient of a long, appraising once-over. And then the waitress smiled. "Nice to meet you. What can I get you to drink?"

Patrice took Alison's order, then winked saucily at Beau. "No need to tell me what *you* want. I'll be right back."

Alison gave Beau a dry look when the woman hurried away. "Come here often, do you?"

He grinned. "Yeah. How'd you guess?"

As if in confirmation, a man on the dance floor nearby called out Beau's name. Beau waved a greeting before turning back to Alison. The movement ruffled the thick forelock tumbled above his eyes. Her palms began to itch, making her wonder if his hair was as silky to the touch as she thought it would be. She curled her hands in her lap. "You never told me where you grew up," she said quickly, needing to make conversation. "Here in Little Rock?"

"Close. I'm from Benton. My dad worked in the bauxite mines until they closed down a few years back. He was one of the lucky ones—had enough time in that he drew a pretty fair pension. My brother's with the Benton police."

"And your mother?"

"She wages a never-ending battle against waxy buildup and ring-around-the-collar and works in her garden when she's not in the house. You wouldn't believe the amount of food she cans and freezes every summer."

"Oh." Was that the type of woman Beau was looking for? Alison's cooking was pretty much limited to microwave dinners.

"What does your father do?" Beau asked, making himself more comfortable in his chair by swinging one arm over the back. The position stretched his white shirt over muscles earned through daily manual labor. Alison's mouth went dry. She wished Patrice would hurry with the drinks.

"He's a doctor—a general practitioner," she managed to answer casually enough. "My mom's an English professor at Arkansas College in Batesville."

He nodded, his expression hard to read. "You know, I'm not even sure what *you* do."

She squirmed in her chair and looked around for Patrice as she answered, "It's a bit of a mouthful, I'm afraid. I'm executive assistant to the vice president of human resource development for Lakeland Industries."

Beau winced. "Wow."

"It's not quite as complicated as it sounds," she assured him. "Mostly I do the paperwork Tim, the vice president of HRD, doesn't want to do. Occasionally I'm allowed to supervise an entire project."

"Very impressive." And then he smiled, and her heart tripped. "But then I've thought you were very impressive since the first time we crossed paths in the parking lot three months ago."

Damn, the man had a sexy smile. Trying to ignore a major hormone attack, Alison looked up in relief when Patrice returned with their drinks.

"For you," the waitress said, setting a tall, condensation-damp glass on a tiny napkin in front of Alison. "And a ginger ale for you," she added, thumping a second glass on the table with a wink at Beau. "Now, you two have a good time. I've gotta get hopping. Just give me a wave if you need anything else."

"Thanks, Patrice."

Beau looked back at Alison to find her watching him quizzically. "A ginger ale?" she asked in surprise. She'd expected him to be a beer drinker. Or bourbon, maybe.

"I like ginger ale," he admitted. "In fact, you might say I'm hooked on the stuff."

"I suppose it's harmless enough." She toyed with the plastic-sword-speared maraschino cherry floating at the top of her own drink.

"Yeah. I'm afraid I got a little too fond of beer when I was in my early twenties. I had to find something to replace it before it messed me up good. This is what I found."

Alison looked at him in dismay, her hand tightening on her own glass. She thought of the wine they'd had with dinner. "I'm sorry, I didn't know. Does it bother you that I'm having a drink?"

He chuckled and shook his head. "I'm not an alcoholic," he assured her. "I can tolerate an occasional drink and it doesn't bother me at all that you're having one. I just happen to really like ginger ale, okay?"

She couldn't help smiling back at him. "Okay."

The band returned from a ten-minute break and announced that they'd be playing an entire set of love songs in honor of Valentine's Day. Beau tilted his head when the first number began. "Want to dance?"

"Sure," she agreed, relieved it was a slow dance. She wasn't exactly current on the popular country-and-western steps.

It felt natural—a little *too* natural, perhaps—to move into Beau's arms on the dance floor. As they closed around her, Alison was reminded again of how strong he was. Though she'd never danced with Dane, he'd slipped an arm around her occasionally. His arm hadn't felt like warm steel. Hadn't made her shiver in decidedly sexual awareness.

There was a brief moment of awkwardness when she waited for Beau to take her right hand in standard dancing position. Instead, he smiled and placed it behind his neck along with her other hand. His own settled warmly at her waist. "Okay?"

Glancing around, she noticed most of the other dancers were in the same intimate position. "Okay," she agreed, well aware that she hadn't even been tempted to demur.

Beau gave her another of those spine-melting smiles and began to sway easily to the music. The top of her head came just to his chin; he rested his cheek against her hair. Alison wondered if he could feel her heart racing in her chest. She felt his thumping steadily, if somewhat rapidly, against her. Her breasts brushed his chest. She swallowed a moan when they tautened in response. His thighs were solid and warm where they pressed lightly against her softer ones. She tried to concentrate on the music to distract herself from the sensual pleasure of dancing so closely to Beau.

The lead singer's voice was smooth and mellow, the backup singers in perfect harmony. Alison had never heard the song before, but she thought it was lovely. It expressed the anguish of a heartbroken lover trying to hold on to a relationship coming to an end. He was even willing to hear a lie—a promise of lifelong love—rather than accept the inevitable.

"I like this song," she murmured.

Beau's arms tightened just fractionally. "It's one of my favorites," he admitted. "'A Tender Lie,' recorded by Restless Heart. It's a tearjerker, isn't it?"

She smiled and gave in to the temptation to rest her head on his shoulder. "Mm. Pretty, though."

That song faded into another. She and Beau continued to dance by mutual, unspoken agreement, neither in a hurry to move out of their comfortable embrace. It had been a long time since Alison had been dancing. Her eyes closed as she savored the moment. She couldn't rememher the last time. Couldn't remember any partner fitting her more perfectly than Beau.

"You feel good in my arms," he murmured as if he'd heard her thoughts.

She lifted her head to look up at him. "You're a very good dancer."

He smiled and guided her into a swaying turn. "I'm feeling inspired tonight."

She laughed for no real reason except that she suddenly felt wonderful. Happy.

Beau grinned, his eyes caressing her face. "I really like your laugh," he said again.

The song ended. "Don't move," Beau ordered, brushing his lips across her temple. "I may keep you here, just like this, all night."

"I may just stay." Heavens, was she actually flirting with him?

Another song began. They continued to dance. "Country-and-western songs seem to focus heavily on lost love, don't they?" Alison asked with a smile.

"Loving and fighting and beer drinking and truck driving," Beau agreed good-naturedly. "Ain't it great?"

She laughed and pressed her cheek against his shoulder, enjoying the way his hands slid up her back in response.

It was, without doubt, the best Valentine's Day she'd ever spent. And it wasn't even over yet.

Chapter Five

ALISON HAD NEVER thought she was the type to be seduced by quirky gifts and candlelight dinners, murmured
compliments and hours of slow dancing.

She'd been wrong. By the time she and Beau walked
hand-in-hand out of J.T.'s Place, she wouldn't have denied him anything.

She shivered when they stepped from the cozy warmth
of the club into the frigid February night. Beau wrapped
an arm around her and pulled her close. "I should have
come out first and let the car warm up," he said apologetically. "I didn't think of it until now."

"I'm fine, really," she assured him. "You're the one
who must be freezing. You're not even wearing a coat."

He smiled down at her. "You look adorable with a pink
nose," he murmured, then dropped a kiss on her nose before shoving his key into the lock of the passenger door.

Her heart fluttering from that all-too-brief touch of his
lips, Alison started to climb into his vehicle, only to stop
when his hand fell on her arm. "I'm sorry," he told her,
turning her slowly around to face him. "But I really can't
wait any longer for this."

Her eyes widened when his arms went around her, then
closed tightly as his mouth covered hers.

His skin was cold, his mouth warm and firm against
hers. She found herself unable to think, unaware of the
cold or the surroundings, unable to feel anything except
Beau's arms around her, his lips on hers.

Other lips had touched hers. But Alison knew that no
other kiss had ever been as powerful as this one. There

were kisses—and then there were *Beau's* kisses. No comparison.

She couldn't have said how long the embrace lasted. But eventually she felt the tiny shivers running through Beau as the frigid night air penetrated his thin white shirt. She drew back with a frown of concern. "You're freezing," she scolded. "Get in the car."

His grin was crooked, his breathing not quite steady. "Funny," he replied. "I don't *feel* cold."

"Get in," she repeated, unable to hold back her own smile.

"Yes, ma'am." He helped her into her seat, then loped around the front of the Jeep to vault into his own. "Damn," he said, his breath forming into a cloud in front of him. "It *is* cold, isn't it?"

"I won't say I told you so," Alison promised primly, fastening her seat belt. He chuckled and started the engine.

He hadn't turned the radio off earlier, so the music began to play. Alison knew it was only coincidence that the lyrics told of a cocky, self-assured man vowing that the woman he pursued had no choice but to love him. "No doubt about it," he sang, "I'm going to get you."

She cleared her throat and looked out the window at the passing scenery.

Beau said very little as he drove them home, though occasionally he hummed along with the radio. It was obvious that he really enjoyed music. So did Alison. Too bad, she thought, wincing at a particularly twangy number, their tastes didn't run to the same type of music. She'd liked some of the songs she'd heard in the nightclub, but she'd stick with Michael Bolton and Elton John.

Ignoring the radio, she concentrated on Beau, watching him surreptitiously through her eyelashes as he drove.

She'd noticed earlier that clutching and shifting caused the muscles in his thighs to ripple. Now she knew how solid those legs felt when pressed against her own. She'd admired the way his luxurious hair glinted pure gold under the passing streetlights. Now she knew just how silky that hair felt when it brushed her cheek.

She'd suspected the first time she'd seen him that the man was a threat to her orderly, uncomplicated life. Now she *knew* he was. He could turn her life upside down—if she let him.

Despite her better judgment, which warned that she and Beau had little in common, that they were all wrong for each other, that there couldn't possibly be a future for them, she wanted him. She didn't know when she'd first realized it—maybe when he'd smiled at her across the dinner table, his blue eyes warm in the candlelight; maybe during one of those long, romantic dances.

Or maybe she'd wanted him from the first time she'd seen him standing in the parking lot of her apartment complex, lean and beautiful in his tight jeans and shoulder-stretched denim jacket, one of his sexy companions giggling beside him as she'd helped him carry his possessions into his new apartment. Alison had sternly ignored that first flash of attraction, telling herself she shouldn't want him, wouldn't have him. Obviously, judging by the ease with which he'd manipulated her into spending this evening with him, she hadn't suppressed the attraction as well as she'd thought she had.

She couldn't help wondering again just why he'd gone to so much trouble to arrange this date. Though she knew herself to be attractive enough, she suspected she wasn't his usual type any more than he was hers. Was it only that she'd piqued his ego when she'd turned down that first invitation?

She had to admit that nothing in his manner during the evening had indicated he was the overly conceited type, despite his easy self-assurance; but maybe he simply couldn't accept that any woman was immune to his charms. She'd tried to tell herself that she was the woman who could resist him; now she knew better. She winced when he turned a smile toward her and caught her staring at him, and she quickly averted her eyes to the road ahead.

Great, Alison. Why don't you just tell him he's turned you into a breathless schoolgirl, wondering how far you should let him go when he takes you home?

"You seem very far away," Beau startled her by commenting as he turned into the parking lot of their apartment complex. "I suppose a penny's not nearly enough to offer for your thoughts."

"Not nearly," she replied lightly, grateful for the dim lighting inside the vehicle, which would conceal her faint blush.

Beau parked in his usual place and reached over the back of his seat for his jacket and tie. "Next time let's wear something that goes with my down jacket, okay?" he asked as he opened his door and hopped out to the pavement, shivering dramatically in the outside air.

Next time? Alison wondered about that as she opened her own door to join him.

He put a hand at the small of her back during the short walk to her door. She liked the feel of it. "Hey, you know what?" he said suddenly, watching as she pushed her key into the lock.

She turned the knob and glanced up at him curiously. "What?"

"We never had dessert."

She hesitated only a heartbeat before saying somewhat tentatively, "I think I have some cookies in the pantry. I could make coffee to go with them."

He smiled, but glanced at his watch. "It's pretty late. You're not too tired?"

Tired? He had her so wired with nerves and hormones that she wasn't sure she'd sleep for a week. "Of course not. Come on in."

His smile deepened. "Thanks. I'd like that."

As soon as they'd stepped inside, Alison tossed her purse on a wing chair and started to shrug out of her coat. Beau was behind her promptly to help her out of it. The man certainly had nice manners. He caught her off guard when he nuzzled her hair with his cheek and murmured, "I really like your scent. What is it?"

She wore only one brand, for every occasion. She liked to think of it as her signature. She couldn't for the life of her remember the name at the moment, though she'd been wearing it for years. "I—uh—thank you," she said instead, stepping quickly out of his reach. "Just put the coat over that chair. I'll hang it up later."

He complied, glancing around the living room as he draped his jacket over her coat. "This is really nice," he said, admiring her Georgian reproduction furniture, the burgundy and hunter-green accessories.

"Thanks. It's the same layout as yours, of course."

"Yeah, well, I'm afraid I'm not much of a decorator. I've got a lot of odds and ends that don't particularly match. My mom calls it 'Early Salvation Army.'"

She chuckled, though she wondered why none of the pretty women she'd seen him with during the past few months had helped him with his decorating. No taste of their own, perhaps? Or maybe he'd never kept a particular one around long enough to make her mark. Then, appalled at her atypical cattiness, she turned abruptly toward the kitchen. "Make yourself comfortable. I'll start the coffee."

She really needed just a few minutes alone, out of range of whatever magic he worked on her.

On an impulse, she turned on the radio she kept on her kitchen counter as she passed it on the way to the refrigerator, where she stored her coffee. An old Hall and Oates number was playing. *How refreshing,* she thought with a smile.

"Cleansing your musical palate?" Beau asked wryly from the doorway.

Alison dropped the coffee scoop. Mentally scolding herself for her foolish nervousness, she picked it up and rinsed it off, throwing Beau a smile over her shoulder. "I guess so."

"I'm flexible," he assured her. "I like C and W, but I listen to rock sometimes, too."

"You really like music, don't you? Do you sing?" she asked, desperately needing to make conversation. The kitchen was small and seemed to shrink even more when Beau joined her in it. She was suddenly very aware of being alone with him in her apartment.

"Yeah, sometimes," he answered. "I play a little guitar. Sometimes I join some guys I know who have a country band. They play some local gigs—the Eagles Club and the VFW, that sort of thing."

"I'd like to hear you sometime," Alison said lightly, because it seemed the polite thing to say. And because it was entirely true.

"I'm sure that can be arranged. But only if you promise not to cover your ears and run screaming from the building," he teased.

"You have my word." She turned from the coffee maker to find him standing between her and the pantry. In this small kitchen, he'd have to move aside to allow her to pass. "Um—I'll get the cookies out of the pantry," she hinted, taking a step toward him.

He moved, but not out of her path. Instead, he closed the small space between them and took her in his arms. "Alison," he murmured, lowering his mouth to within an inch of hers. "I've wanted to be with you for so long."

She sighed and rested her hands on his chest. "I'm not at all sure this is sensible," she responded truthfully, her eyes locked with his burning blue ones.

"Are you always sensible, Alison?" he asked huskily, his thumb stroking the corner of her mouth, his breath warm and soft on her face.

"I've tried to be," she whispered. "Until—" She sighed again when his fingers threaded into her hair, her eyelids growing heavy.

"Until?" The word was only a wisp of sound across her moist, yearning lips. He lowered his head just a bit more, so that she could almost feel the heat of the kiss she craved.

"Until now. Beau." She slid both arms around his neck, bringing his head down that last fraction of an inch until his mouth covered hers.

He groaned into her mouth—a sound of combined pleasure and relief. And he kissed her with an intensity she'd never known before, a hunger that seemed ready to consume them both. She discovered there were a great many things she'd been missing with her safe, intellectual, sophisticated dates. She was shockingly eager to find out what else she'd missed with other men.

Maybe Beau Harmon *was* a walking heartache, she thought dazedly. But how could she pass up the opportunity to find out for herself what it would be like to be with him, to be loved by him? She couldn't.

"I want you," he muttered, stringing hot, stinging kisses over her face and throat. "I've wanted you since the first time I saw you."

He'd been with another woman the first time he'd seen her. Right now even that couldn't bother her. "I want you, too," she whispered, uncharacteristically shy. She buried her face in his throat, her arms wrapped tightly around him.

He tilted her face up to his with one finger, his cheeks flushed, his smile crooked. "Why don't you show me the rest of your apartment?" he suggested huskily.

Torn between longing and common sense, she bit her lower lip. He didn't pressure her; simply waited for her decision. That as much as anything gave her the impetus to nod and step back. "There's not much else to see," she murmured, her own voice sounding half an octave deeper than usual. "Just the bedroom."

"That'll do," he assured her. "Believe me, that'll do just fine."

She smiled and took his hand.

Chapter Six

BEAU KEPT AN ARM around Alison's waist as they entered her bedroom. She didn't bother turning on the light, nor did he make any pretense of studying her English-garden decor. He stood beside the bed and cupped her face in his hands. His palms were rough, work hardened, but they felt good against her flushed skin.

She wondered if he could tell she was nervous, if she should mention that it had been a while for her. But he probably already knew, she thought, remembering his earlier comment about the usual endings to her dates with Dane and Jonathan.

His lips brushed her forehead—a butterfly kiss. Each of her eyelids received the same fleeting caress, as well as the end of her nose. Her chin, her cheeks, her ears, her temples—he touched his lips everywhere but her mouth. Murmuring her frustration, she sought those tantalizing lips with her own.

The kisses they'd shared earlier, which she'd considered spectacular, faded into insignificance behind this one. He tested the shape and softness of her lips, learning them thoroughly before his tongue surged eagerly beyond them, anxious to explore more of her. His hands slid leisurely down her back to the curve of her hips, then pulled her gently into the cradle of his slightly spread thighs. She trembled when she felt his arousal against her, awed at this evidence of how badly he wanted her.

He tilted his head to a new angle and took her under again with another long, drugging kiss. Sometime during it, he discovered the back zipper of her dress. She hadn't realized he'd unfastened it until she felt cool air against her skin. He slipped the silky fabric from her shoulders, smoothing it down her arms with hands as unsteady as her own. He was trembling, she noticed in wonder. Why? Was it possible that this meant as much to him as it did to her? That she wasn't just another conquest after just another date?

Suddenly impatient, she reached for the buttons of his shirt. Between kisses and caresses and huskily murmured words, they undressed each other. Beau swept out one hand to flip back the comforter from her bed, dislodging ruffled pillows, which scattered unnoticed at their feet.

The room tilted when he lay her back against the sheets. She clung to his forearms for support, then stroked her hands down his chest when he lay beside her, propped on one elbow. She'd never seen a more beautiful man. *Magnificent.*

He cupped one of her breasts in his hand, smiling when the soft mound just filled his palm. "Perfect," he breathed, lowering his head to taste.

She arched into his mouth, her heart racing. "Beau!"

"Easy, babe," he whispered, his breath hot on her moist, distended nipple. "We have all night."

All night? That wouldn't possibly be long enough for her to explore these feelings. She squirmed again when his tongue stroked across her nipple before his mouth moved in search of its twin. And then his hand slid down her stomach and into the dark curls between her legs and she shuddered, lost to thoughts of anything but Beau. Wanting only to give him the same pleasure he was giving her.

Their soft moans echoed in unison in the shadowed corners of the bedroom. Bedclothes rustled as two bodies shifted fluidly within them. Their breathing was ragged, their words disjointed; their skin sheened with perspiration. And still they lingered, savored, delayed the inevitable conclusion. By the time Beau finally shifted to lie between her thighs, Alison was almost in tears, need coursing through her in long, shuddering waves. She was drowning in desire and she clung to him, opening to him even as she begged him to end the torment.

"Alison. Oh, babe, it's so good," he groaned, sinking into her, sinking with her into the depths of passion, of frenzy, of avid impatience. They cried out in incredulous, simultaneous wonder when the crest broke over them, sweeping away thought, reason, the ability to speak. And then they floated, clinging tightly to each other, slowly—so slowly regaining their breath and their sanity.

"Oh, man," Beau said at last, exhaling in a gust as he rolled to his side, pulling Alison into the circle of his arm.

She buried her fingertips in the fine blond hairs on his chest. "I'm feeling rather dazed myself."

"Anyone ever tell you you're dynamite?"

"No," she stated simply.

He grinned, his disheveled hair tumbled boyishly over his forehead, a full-grown-man sparkle in his eyes. "Trust me," he said. "You are."

She propped herself on one elbow and looked at him, running the little finger of her free hand across his lower lip. "Is Beau your real name?"

"Mmm," he murmured. "Beau Edward Harmon. My mom was into old Southern tradition. My brother's name is Samuel Clayton. We call him Sam."

Hence Beau's very Southern manners, she thought with a smile. His mother had probably drilled him from the time he could stand upright, if not before.

He reached up to stroke her cheek. "You're so beautiful," he murmured. He touched one diamond earring. "Nice. Did the guy in the Italian suits buy them for you?"

"No," she answered sternly, though she could tell by his smile that he'd been teasing. "I bought them for myself."

"Good." With one finger, he followed the chain of her necklace from her nape to the pendant that lay between her breasts. "You look good in diamonds. They go particularly well with the outfit you have on at the moment."

"I'm—um—not wearing an outfit at the moment," she pointed out breathlessly, her pulse leaping when his finger circled one nipple. She was amazed when it hardened in response. How could she want him again already? she asked herself, knowing the question was rhetorical. Because she *did* want him. Again. And again.

"I noticed that," Beau replied, lifting his head to her breast. "You look spectacular just like this."

She cupped the back of his head with one hand, holding his mouth to her breast, closing her eyes. She couldn't remember what they'd been talking about. She decided it really didn't matter, anyway....

THEY NEVER DID GET around to eating the cookies. Nor did they have breakfast Saturday morning. Instead, they alternated between dozing and making love until early afternoon, when hunger finally drove them out of the bedroom in search of food. They munched on cheese and crackers and sliced cold cuts smeared with Dijon mustard. Until Beau decided to find out for himself how the spicy mustard tasted on Alison's lower lip. And on her throat. And the upper curve of her breast. They ended up making love in the kitchen—Alison sitting on the edge of the counter, her arms and legs wrapped tightly around him, the few clothes they'd donned scattered recklessly around them.

BEAU SEEMED DETERMINED to learn everything there was to know about Alison during the weekend, asking endless questions about her job, her family, her friends, her interests. Though she answered willingly enough, she wondered why he seemed so fascinated by everything he learned about her.

"I guess you have a college degree, huh?" he asked at one point, as they lay on their stomachs in her living room, a half-finished board game between them. A steady rain fell outside, which had given them an excellent excuse to spend Saturday indoors, enjoying their time alone together.

"I have a master's degree," she confirmed. "In business education, actually, though I decided to enter the corporate world rather than the academic one." Suspecting that he didn't have a degree, she didn't want to embarrass him by asking. She rolled the dice and moved her playing piece.

Idly watching her fingers move over the game board, Beau volunteered, "I've got three semesters of college credits. Went to UCA in Conway for a while, until I got tired of the grind of classes and homework and quit. I never would have lasted long enough to get a master's degree."

She propped her chin on her fists, supporting herself on her elbows. "Is that when you went to work for the power company?"

He nodded, the dice cupped in one hand. "Yeah. I like being outdoors, the pay's good and I work with some great guys. It's a good job." He rolled the dice, then made a sound of disgust when his game piece landed on a penalty square.

Her focus more on Beau than the game, Alison thought about what he'd said. She'd already figured out that Beau was intelligent and well-rounded, that he probably could have done anything he wanted for a living. Yet he worked as a lineman because he enjoyed it. *Why not?* She wondered uncomfortably if she'd been a bit of a snob about his work before. Not that she'd turned down his invitations because of his job. She simply hadn't thought they had enough in common to form a relationship, though she found herself liking Beau more with every minute she spent with him. And there was certainly no doubt that they were compatible physically!

ON SUNDAY, they went out for lunch, then returned to her apartment to spend the rest of the day together. They argued about music and movies, books and television programs, laughed at stories of growing up and first forays into the dating scene. They took turns choosing radio stations, switching every half hour. Beau didn't mind rock, but he proclaimed himself bored senseless by classical. Alison rather like country pop, but some of the music his station played made her cringe. It didn't matter. She was having a wonderful time. Beau seemed equally happy.

Both were reluctant to see the weekend come to an end. But Sunday passed and Monday arrived, and with it their responsibilities to their jobs. Beau left early Monday morning with long, lingering kisses and an invitation for a movie and a casual dinner that evening. Alison accepted with pleasure, then sighed when she was alone. She missed him already.

She left for work in her usual clothes, her hair neatly upswept, her mouth quirked into what felt like a permanently foolish smile—knowing she'd never again look at Valentine's Day the same way she had before Beau had turned it into a magical memory.

MARY LOU WAS ALREADY at her desk, as usual. She looked up at Alison with a polite smile that quickly turned into a look of speculation. "Well, good morning. Nice weekend?"

Alison blushed, wondering if it was really so obvious that she'd fallen head over heels in love in the sixty-three hours that had passed since she'd left the office Friday afternoon. Her blush only made Mary Lou smile more brightly. "The—uh—the Hinson file?" Alison asked, trying to concentrate on her job.

"On your desk."

"Thanks." Alison hurried into her office. She was able to wait all of fifteen minutes before she picked up the phone and dialed Carole's work number.

"So, who sent the flowers?" Carole demanded as soon as Alison identified herself. "I've been curious about that all weekend, and, by the way, my weekend was incredible."

"So was mine," Alison answered dreamily.

"Oh?" Carole sounded decidedly intrigued. "Dane turned out to be more interesting than we both thought?"

"It wasn't Dane."

Carole waited as long as she could, then squealed in frustration, making Alison chuckle. "Who was it, darn it?" she demanded. "I'm going crazy here."

"Beau Harmon." Alison waited anxiously for her friend's reaction.

"Beau Harmon?" Carole repeated in surprise. "The blue-eyed blond hunk with the great butt and the to-die-for smile who lives two doors down from me?"

Alison couldn't help laughing at the description, curious what Beau would have said if he'd heard it. She suspected he would have cringed in embarrassment, even as he'd grinned in reluctant pleasure. "That's the one," she admitted.

"Wow. Didn't you turn him down for dates a few times?"

"Yes. Fortunately, he doesn't give up easily."

"Fortunately? Does this mean you've been out with him this weekend?"

"You could say that," Alison murmured, thinking wistfully of dinner and dancing and two days of talking and lovemaking. Would there ever be another weekend quite like that one?

"Wow," Carole repeated. "I never would have expected—I mean, the two of you don't seem to have very much in common. He's not exactly like the other men you date, is he?"

"No. Beau is definitely in a class by himself."

"Uh-oh. I know that besotted tone, even though I've never heard it from you. You've fallen for the guy, haven't you?"

"In a major way." Alison sighed, pleased to have someone to confide in.

"Alison, that's great! Unless— He *does* feel the same way, I hope?"

"I think so," she answered cautiously. "I mean, it's too soon to start talking seriously or anything, but—oh, Carole, he's fantastic. I can't wait for you to meet him."

"I've met him, briefly. He seems very nice. I can't wait to see the two of you together. Imagine. You and Beau Harmon. Who'd a thought it?"

"I certainly wouldn't have," Alison admitted. "But— Who knows? Crazier things have happened, I guess."

"I've got to get back to work. I want to hear all about this weekend though, you hear? Let's have lunch."

"Tomorrow, okay? I have a lunch meeting today. And I want to hear about your weekend in Hot Springs, too. All the juicy details."

"This is going to be fun," Carole predicted.

Alison agreed wholeheartedly.

THE WARM AFTERGLOW of the spectacular weekend wore off for Beau sometime around noon on Monday. That was when he started to worry that eight hours in her usual work environment might make Alison regret the involvement that had developed between them Friday night. Would a day among the tailored-suit, silk-tie, college-degree crowd make her wonder why in the world she'd started sleeping with a lineman?

It wasn't like him to worry about such things, but then he'd never felt quite this way about anyone before. Never been as obsessed with any woman as he was with Alison, not even during his teens when all the other guys had been prey to the agonies of first loves. For Beau, romance had always been easy, amusing and carefree. Now he realized he'd never known what it was like to really be in love, to have his heart held firmly in two small, feminine hands. Hell, he'd probably loved her from the first time he'd seen her, though he didn't try to delude himself that the feelings had been mutual.

She could break his heart if she chose, he thought soberly, only half his concentration on his job as he worked thirty feet off the ground at the top of a pole. No other woman had ever held that power over him. He could almost resent her for making him that vulnerable. Almost.

"C'mon, Beau, get your mind out of your jeans and hurry up, will ya?" a coworker complained in a shout from below. "It's cold out here!"

Beau flinched. The guys he worked with had taken one look at him that morning and started ragging him about being "caught" by a woman. Maybe the rumors had been started by a couple of guys who'd been at J.T.'s Place Friday night and had seen Beau with Alison. He'd never even seen them there, which had only reinforced their belief that he was hopelessly obsessed. The signs were all there, they'd assured him gravely. Everything but a ring through his nose.

Or a ring on his finger. He spared a glance at his ringless left hand. It shook him to realize that for the first time in his formerly unfettered life he wasn't altogether opposed to changing that condition.

A blistering curse drifted up from below him when Beau fumbled a wire cutter, sending it tumbling to the ground. "Dammit, Harmon, what's with you today?"

"Sorry, Bubba. I'm nearly finished here." He turned his attention grimly back to the job at hand, futilely attempting to push thoughts of Alison to the back of his mind.

Chapter Seven

BEAU WAS SURPRISED to find himself standing nervously on Alison's doorstep late Monday afternoon, stalling for time before pressing the doorbell button. He brushed an imaginary piece of lint from his brand-new jeans, tugged at the cuffs of his down jacket, ran a hand through his neatly-combed hair. Why was he so nervous about seeing her again? Why was he afraid that eight hours at work had changed her feelings about him, whatever they had been?

And then she answered the door, looking absolutely gorgeous in a brightly-colored sweater and snug jeans.

"Hi."

She gave him a smile that almost stopped his heart completely. "Hi, yourself." And then she lifted her face for a kiss.

He pulled her into his arms and covered her mouth with his, deciding not to question his luck.

BEAU AND ALISON fell into a pattern of seeing each other every free evening during that week and the next. Even as their physical relationship deepened and strengthened, so did their emotional one. Alison was in love, though she couldn't have begun to predict the outcome of her impetuous affair with Beau Harmon. Nor was she certain about his feelings for her. Was his interest only temporary? Or did he have long-range plans he had yet to discuss with her?

It also bothered her that he seemed to have a chip on his shoulder about her associates and her friends—it seemed as if he were predisposed to write them off as snobs who'd have no use for a blue-collar worker like himself. She'd tried to disabuse him of that belief—though she'd known he was probably right about a few of the people she worked with. Not her real friends, of course.

On Thursday, nearly two weeks after their first date, Beau had to attend a party being given by some of his acquaintances to honor a coworker's thirtieth birthday. "The guy's not exactly a friend," Beau explained with a grimace. "But I couldn't think of a way to get out of going." He asked her to go with him, and she accepted, although the way he hesitated with the invitation made her puzzle over what she was getting into.

The party was held in a country-western club. Unlike J.T.'s Place, however, this club was an aging, noisy, smoky dive in a neighborhood Alison never would have driven into alone. Beau had assured her she looked terrific when he'd picked her up, but now she feared that her gray wool slacks and pink-and-gray cashmere sweater would be out of place. Beau wore his usual jeans and boots, though he'd paired them with a white turtleneck pullover beneath a blue and white geometric-print sweater.

"Yo, Beau!" a raspy voice called out when Beau and Alison walked into the bar, squinting to find his friends in the smoky dimness. Raucous laughter followed the greeting. Alison winced, realizing that the drinking had already begun—heavily.

"Beau!" Ignoring Alison, a copper-haired woman in painted-on black jeans and a partially-unbuttoned black blouse threw herself at Beau's neck. "Baby, where have you been keeping yourself?"

"Under a rock, Charmaine, just like always," Beau answered flippantly. He skillfully peeled her large breasts away from his chest and held her at arm's length. "Charmaine, this is Alison Tindall."

Charmaine pouted, but murmured a greeting, eyeing Alison's prim clothing with obvious derision.

Music blasted from overhead speakers, a taped rendition of a song that had been made popular years earlier by the movie *Urban Cowboy*. Even Alison recognized it.

"Come on, honey, let's two-step," a bearded hulk in a red-and-black flannel shirt bellowed, grabbing Alison by the arm. "I'm stealing your date, Harmon," he added, already towing her toward the minuscule dance floor.

"But I don't know how to two-step," Alison futilely protested, already whirled into two meaty arms.

"'S okay, sugar. I ain't too good at it myself," he assured her cheerfully, then proceeded to prove it by crushing half her toes beneath an enormous boot. Wincing, Alison peered around him toward Beau, who sent her a grimace of apology before the persistent Charmaine clutched his arm again for attention.

Alison had never been so relieved to hear the ending of a song. She was bruised, breathless and disheveled when the grinning hulk returned her to Beau. "We'll have to do that again sometime," he shouted before grabbing an equally reluctant Charmaine. "C'mon, baby, let's waltz," he yelled, whirling the redhead away. Alison could almost feel sorry for the woman.

"We'll do it again over my dead body," she muttered.

Beau muffled a laugh and slid his arm around her. "Having fun, babe?"

"You know it, *babe,*" she answered tartly, glaring at his sheepish grin. If he thought she would agree to any more evenings like this one, he was sadly mistaken.

"We won't stay long," he promised. "Want to dance?"

She sighed and agreed, relieved that the next number was a slow one. No evening could be all bad when part of it was spent in Beau's arms.

Alison definitely didn't fit into the group at the party, particularly when another hour and a half of drinking had passed and the conversation turned raunchy. She'd never thought herself a prude, but the language and jokes were a bit much—as far as she was concerned. She longed to be at home—with Beau. Was this why they'd fallen into the habit of spending so much time alone together? Had they known all along that neither of them fit into the other's social world?

The others at the party didn't seem to particularly care for her, either. She suspected they regarded her as a snob. It really wasn't that, she assured herself half guiltily. This just wasn't her kind of entertainment. She watched Beau during the evening, unable to tell if he was really having a good time or simply putting up a front for the others. Only with one man did he really seem to be himself—a tall, lanky, cowboy type Beau introduced only as "Tommy, my best friend."

Alison found herself liking Tommy more and more as the interminable evening wore on. Though he kept a beer in front of him, he wasn't drunk and he seemed to make an effort to talk to her whenever she felt particularly left out. She could understand why Beau liked the man so much.

A blonde in desperate need of a touch-up danced on the table at one point, knocking over someone's rum and cola. The drink splashed on Alison's leg. She managed a smile. A weak one. An unshaven drunk from across the room decided he wanted to dance with Alison—whether she wanted to or not. For a moment, it looked as though Beau were going to be forced to fight the man. Alison cringed, then sighed in relief when several of Beau's friends "escorted" the man outside with relatively little trouble.

She could have clapped her hands when Beau indicated that they could leave. "Finally," she murmured, stepping out of the loud, stale-smelling club into the fresh, crisp air of the parking lot. Even the gasoline fumes smelled better than old smoke and body odor.

"Sorry, Alison. I know you didn't have a very good time. That group's a little more—uh—earthy than my usual friends."

"I like Tommy," Alison said with an effort to be tactful as she climbed into Beau's Jeep.

Beau smiled in quick approval. "Do you? I'm glad. He's a great guy."

"Have you known him long? Tommy, I mean."

"Since we were kids. We used to ride in local rodeos together."

"You rode in rodeos?" She hadn't known that, though she realized she shouldn't have been surprised.

"Yeah, some. I finally got tired of breaking bones and gave it up."

Alison remembered a few old scars she'd found during leisurely explorations of his delectable body. So that was how he'd gotten them. He'd always laughed off her questions before—or thoroughly distracted her from them. "Does Tommy like that group?" she couldn't help asking.

Beau shrugged. "'Bout the same as I do," he answered. "They're just guys from work. We play a little basketball together on weekends, softball in the summertime. They're okay when they haven't had so much to drink."

Since she didn't want Beau, as well as his friends, to consider her a snob, Alison said no more about her uneasiness during the party.

ALISON HAD PLANS for Friday night—a country-club cocktail reception for an engaged couple she knew. The groom-to-be was an executive at her firm, she explained to Beau. It would look bad if she didn't show up at least for a little while, though she didn't really know the couple that well. "Office politics," she said apologetically. "You understand."

Beau had assured her he did, even offering to rent a tux. Pleased that he was going with her, she assured him that a dark suit would be perfectly acceptable.

Beau knew from the moment he picked Alison up at her door that it wouldn't be his kind of evening. She was wearing a slinky silver thing that looked as though it might have cost a week's pay—or more—and her diamond earrings again. She'd put her hair up, applied her makeup with flair. She looked absolutely beautiful—and somewhat intimidating. He ran a finger beneath the collar of his new white shirt. He was oddly relieved when Alison flashed him a smile and threw her arms around his neck for a kiss.

"You look wonderful," she murmured, sounding like the Alison he loved.

"Thanks. So do you."

She grimaced ruefully. "I hope you're not bored out of your mind tonight."

He chuckled. "I owe you this after last night."

"Yeah," she agreed fervently. "You do."

They took her car this time. Alison drove—and didn't hesitate to turn the expensive vehicle over to a valet for parking, Beau noticed with a grin.

Because it seemed appropriate, he took Alison's arm as they walked into the country club, in which the gleam of crystal chandeliers competed with the sparkle of the jewels worn by the women in attendance. *Yuppies,* Beau thought with a mental sigh, taking a slow survey of the room. *Oh, boy.*

"Alison! Darling, you look adorable." The patently insincere greeting came from a tall brunette in a sequined gown that glittered whenever she moved. She air-kissed Alison's cheek, making Beau have to bite the inside of his lip to keep from grinning. He nodded politely enough when Alison introduced him. The woman—whose name Beau didn't quite catch—gave him a once-over, murmured something vacuous and drifted away.

"The president's wife," Alison murmured as soon as the woman was out of hearing. "He's thirty years older than she is. Rumor has it she's sleeping with his son."

"Classy dame, huh?"

Alison chuckled quietly. "Uh-huh. Oh, here comes Tim—my supervisor. He's okay—a little stuffy."

Stuffy was not exactly the word he would have chosen, Beau thought as Alison introduced him to the fiftyish man who sported an expensive toupee and had stuffed an obvious spare tire into suit pants that should have been an inch or two larger in the waist. The man looked like a jerk.

"Very nice to meet you, Harmon," Tim Hunter said, offering a smooth-skinned hand for a halfhearted shake. "So you're here with Alison."

Beau nodded in response to the obvious question.

"So what do you do, Harmon?"

"I work for the power company," Beau replied easily.

Hunter's eyebrow lifted. "Management?"

"Lineman."

"Oh. I see. Well, enjoy yourself. There's a champagne fountain in the far corner, Alison. Er—perhaps you can obtain a beer at the cash bar, Harmon."

Beau forced a smile. "Thanks, but I prefer ginger ale."

Hunter eyed him quizzically. "How interesting." He walked away without saying anything more.

Alison's cheeks were flaming. "Why, that— Beau, I'm sorry. He was obnoxious."

Beau shrugged. "No big deal."

She seemed to feel an explanation was necessary. "He— uh—he made a few passes at me when I first started to work for him last year. I turned him down, of course, and he finally accepted that my answer was final. I guess he's still holding a grudge, though."

Beau glared after her supervisor, his fist clenching, knuckles itching to connect with a certain loose-skinned chin. "And you still work for the jerk?"

She shrugged delicately. "He knows the job, though he's only adequate at it. By this time next year, I plan to have his office."

He eyed her warily, not quite certain how to take the brittle ambition in her eyes. "Do you?"

She smiled. "That's the business world. Oh, look. There's Julia. She's a friend of mine. You'll like her."

He did, as a matter of fact, though he wasn't sure at first that he would. Julia was tall, slim, dramatically dressed and spoke in a biting, sharp-edged Southern drawl that hinted at a formidable temper. She was also the most natural, up-front person Beau had encountered that evening. He liked the way her dark eyes gleamed with wry humor, and he particularly liked her acerbic remarks about the others in attendance. "God, I hate these things," she complained. "But Lakeland's one of my firm's biggest clients. It's all part of the game."

"If you choose to play it," Beau commented, watching Alison chatting breezily with two women across the room.

"Yes, and I have. I've a fondness for money and power. What about you, sweetie? How come you spend your days climbing poles and playing with wires?"

He grinned at her tone. "I like being at the top, myself. I'd just prefer to climb up on spikes rather than over other people's backs."

Julia laughed huskily and patted his arm. "You're quite a guy. Any more like you at home?"

Beau wondered how she'd like Tommy—and vice versa. Maybe he'd suggest a double date to Alison. Might be fun.

Alison rejoined them then with a murmured apology for being gone so long. "Have you two been slashing everyone here?" she asked, smiling at her friend.

Julia returned the smile. "Of course. I like this one, Alison. Hold on to him."

Alison looked up at Beau with an expression that made his loins tighten, tempting him to toss her over his shoulder and get the hell out of here to someplace private. "I just might do that," she murmured teasingly.

Neither Beau nor Alison noticed when Julia sighed enviously and moved away.

"THOSE PEOPLE weren't my real friends," Alison assured Beau much later that evening, sounding a bit worried as she nestled into his shoulder. "Except Julia, of course. And you liked her, didn't you?"

Lying on his back beside her, he stroked her bare hip and stared at the darkened ceiling. "Yeah, I liked her. But those others..." And then he grimaced. "But I guess they were no worse than the ones we were with last night. Believe me, you'd like my real friends much better than those guys."

"I'm sure I would." She didn't sound convinced.

Beau scowled. "So, how are the doctor and the English professor going to feel about their daughter dating a blue-collar worker?"

She lifted her head abruptly, her expression indignant. "My parents are very nice people! They would like you for who you are, not for what you do."

"Well," he murmured soothingly, tugging her back down into his arms. "That's a relief. My folks are going to love you, too."

"I hope so," she whispered.

"We'll have to do that soon, won't we? Meet the families, I mean." He held his breath as he waited for her answer, knowing how important the moment was.

She lifted her head again, looking at him searchingly. "Will we?"

"I think it's about time." He hesitated. "Don't you?"

Her smile went straight to his stomach. "Yes," she answered. "I think it's about time."

He released his breath and rolled to crush her bare body beneath his, kissing her deeply to express his whole-hearted approval.

Chapter Eight

AS THE OLD SAYING WENT, March came in like a lion, and brought with it more trouble than nasty weather. Alison had known, of course, that she and Beau had a lot of work to do in establishing a relationship. After all, they were very different people, despite the attraction that drew them together. She just wished she'd had a little more time to enjoy him before the adjustment period began.

First it was her work that interfered with their time. A company-wide restructuring began, which kept Alison and other members of upper management at the office for long hours at a time, weekends included. Beau tried to be understanding, assuring her that if the spring ice-storm that had been predicted came through, he'd be working double shifts, himself. He didn't like it, though, that she was spending so much time with her boss, a man he detested and whom Alison had admitted had tried more than once to talk her into bed. Twice he made evening plans, only to have them canceled at the last moment by apologetic telephone calls from Alison, unable to get away from the office.

Finding that they both had the first Friday night in March free, they arranged a double date with Julia and Tommy. Alison had agreed that Julia might like Beau's unpretentious friend, and Julia and Tommy—each approving of their friends' new companions—were interested.

Everyone agreed it would be great fun.

BEAU FOLLOWED ALISON into her apartment at nearly midnight Friday night and tossed his coat over a chair. "Well," he said, shoving his hand through his hair with a sigh, "*that* was a mistake."

Alison nodded, rather depressed by the outcome of the evening she'd looked forward to for days. "Yes, it was, wasn't it?"

Julia and Tommy hadn't taken to each other at all. Tommy told Beau that Julia was too hard-nosed and career-obsessed; Julia had implied that Tommy's lazy manner indicated a lamentable lack of ambition and intelligence.

They had chosen to meet at J.T.'s Place. To Alison's disappointment, the band wasn't nearly as good as the one that had played on Valentine's Day. This group geared their selections toward strictly country-and-western fare, without the crossover country-pop numbers Alison liked. Julia, a classical and show-tunes fan, abhorred the music and couldn't resist a few comments about the overabundance of Western shirts, denim miniskirts and fancy tooled boots surrounding her.

"Tommy's nice enough, I suppose," Julia had told Alison when they'd found themselves alone for a few minutes during the evening. "It's just that he and I have absolutely nothing in common." Something in her eyes when she'd said it had made Alison aware that Julia was beginning to doubt whether Alison and Beau had any more in common than their badly mismatched friends.

"Remind me not to ever set up another blind date, will you?" Beau asked, walking up behind Alison to loop his arms around her waist. "This Cupid stuff is just too risky."

She crossed her hands over his, leaning back into him with her eyes closing wearily. "I agree. Maybe we'll try going out with an already established couple next time. Like Carole and Ted.''

"You mean the guy who makes King Kong look like an organ-grinder's monkey?''

Alison chuckled. "That's the one. He's really a sweetheart, though. He's a high-school football coach.''

"I'll have to meet him sometime. I know you and Carole are close. Or,'' he drawled, turning her in his arms, "I could just keep you all to myself so I don't have to share your time with anyone else. I kinda like that idea.''

"So do I,'' she assured him with a smile, rising on tiptoe for his kiss. But even as she allowed herself to drift into the mindless pleasure of Beau's sensual skills, she was plagued by a lingering concern that they couldn't simply stop having friends because their interests to this point in their lives had been so different. They were both social people and, as much as she adored being with Beau, she knew she'd want to spend time with others, as well. Not that she had any interest in dating other men. She just wanted friends. And she wanted Beau to like them and fit in with them, just as she wanted to be accepted by the people who were important to him.

Dammit, why did love have to be so difficult?

She threw her arms around his neck in a sudden surge of what felt suspiciously like desperation. "Make love to me, Beau. Now,'' she whispered, crowding closer to him.

He seemed a little surprised by her fervor, but didn't question her. Instead, he swung her into his arms and carried her into the bedroom in truly romantic style, one of the things she loved so much about him. He satisfied all her old, unfulfilled longings for romance and passion. Now, if only they could overcome the other obstacles looming ahead of them.

THE PREDICTED ICE STORM hit with a vengeance a week later. Though March was late in the season for winter storms in Arkansas, longtime residents were rarely surprised by any unusual developments in the weather. The sleet and freezing rain fell all through the night, leaving a deadly, three-inch layer of ice on the roadways by dawn. A light freezing rain fell sporadically, making the roads wet and treacherous. Road crews worked frantically, but there was little they could do other than scatter salt on the bridges. Snowplows weren't exactly common this far south, and wouldn't have been of much use if they had been.

Alison and Beau had been awakened before daylight when Tommy had phoned, looking for Beau, telling him that all line crews were being called in to restore power lines downed by heavy layers of ice and fallen tree branches.

"You are *not* going on the roads today," Beau proclaimed, shoving his legs into the long underwear and clean jeans he'd brought with him to Alison's the night before. Though they'd been dating only five weeks, he'd already fallen into the habit of sleeping in her bed almost as often as his own.

Brushing her sleep-tangled hair out of her eyes, Alison climbed out of bed and reached for a robe. "But I have to go to work. I have a ton of things to do."

"Weren't you listening to the radio report? Half the streets in town are closed, the others nearly impassable. The police are begging people to stay indoors except for emergencies, and the wreckers and ambulances can't keep up with the calls. They're working over a hundred accidents an hour out there! You are *not* going to the office. Got that? You couldn't get that little car of yours out of the parking lot, anyway."

She lifted her chin defiantly, her hands on her hips. "Then, why are you going?"

He pulled a heavy, quilted flannel shirt over the long underwear top he'd already donned. "I've got to go. Power's out all over the place. We're lucky we still have ours. God knows how many lines this ice has brought down. I'll be lucky to be home by midnight."

"Isn't it just as dangerous for you to be out as it would be for me?"

He glared at her in exasperation. "No. I have to go or a lot of families are going to be without heat during this mess. The whole southwest part of the city's without electricity, according to the radio—in addition to several outlying areas. The crew needs me. Besides, I have the four-wheel-drive, remember? Even that's not foolproof on ice, but it helps. Believe me, you won't be the only one to show common sense and stay home. I've gotta go. Tommy's waiting for me to pick him up."

She clung to his shirt when he kissed her on his way out. "It's so cold and wet out. Are you sure you'll be all right?"

He smiled at her concern. "Thanks, babe, but I'll be fine. I'm used to this, remember? I'll bundle up. You stay in where it's warm. I'm warning you, if your car has been moved half an inch when I get back, there's going to be hell to pay."

She sighed. "I don't like being told what to do, Harmon." Her tone was only half teasing. She wasn't at all accustomed to taking orders from anyone who didn't authorize her paycheck. She didn't want Beau to make a habit of it.

"Then take care of yourself just because I've asked you to, okay?" he suggested more gently. "Because I care too damn much about you to want you to risk your life for a few hours at the office."

There wasn't much she could say in answer to that. She kissed him again, lingeringly. "Be careful, Beau."

"I always am, honey," he reassured her with his trademark grin. And then he was gone, leaving her to pace restlessly around the apartment until she finally pulled out her portable computer and tried to assuage her guilty conscience about missing work by tackling a stack of paperwork she'd brought home in her briefcase.

She didn't see Beau again that day. She assumed he'd been home to grab a few hours' sleep and change into fresh clothes, but he'd evidently gotten in so late he hadn't wanted to disturb her. She found a note taped to the inside of her door Wednesday morning—she'd given Beau a key only the week before. Smiling, she pulled the note down, wishing he'd awakened her—if only for a quick kiss on the way out again.

The note made her smile fade. "The roads are better, but there are still lots of icy places," it read. "If you insist on going to work, watch the bridges and give yourself an extra hour or so to get there. I wish you'd stay home, but if you must leave, be careful." The latter two words were underlined twice.

She turned on the radio for a report on street conditions, knowing there were several roads that remained closed due to steep hills and sharp curves made impassable by ice. She thought of following Beau's advice and staying home again, but restlessness was already setting in. She couldn't bear the thought of another day at home alone. She was pleased when a coworker called a few minutes later with an offer to give her a lift in his four-wheel-drive truck, telling her he was already picking up his secretary, who lived close to Alison. She accepted gratefully, thinking that Beau would approve.

Funny how her life had changed in the past five weeks. For so long she'd answered only to herself. She wasn't accustomed to having anyone worry about her safety, trying to protect her. Though her independent spirit might chafe at Beau's rather macho protectiveness, she was aware of a warm glow deep inside her. He cared about her, she thought with a secret smile. He really cared about her.

Maybe this thing was going to work out, after all.

She was almost surprised to discover that she'd crossed her fingers, as though still not entirely confident of a happy ending to their tumultuous love affair.

Chapter Nine

ALISON GOT HOME an hour later than usual that night, since the flow of traffic had been badly hampered by patches of ice. Shivering in her heaviest coat, she thanked her associate for the ride and hurried toward her apartment, cursing bitterly when her foot skidded on an icy spot on the sidewalk. It took a great deal of awkward flailing to keep herself from sprawling flat on her face. As it was, she dropped her purse and briefcase, scattering the contents on the damp, frosty, mud-patched ground.

It had been a long, tiring day at the office. She'd fallen two days behind during her one day away, as it so often seemed to happen, and the office was pitifully short-staffed because so many employees lived in rural areas isolated by road conditions. Alison had rather hoped Beau would be home by now, but his apartment was dark and obviously empty, as was hers. She'd skipped lunch and was hungry, but had nothing particularly enticing in the kitchen, since she'd been planning to stop by the grocery this week.

She changed into a red-and-purple velour lounging set, then noticed that she'd splattered mud all over the back of the new wool slacks she'd worn to the office in deference to the frigid weather. She must have done it with her fancy footwork during her near fall. "Damn," she griped, tossing the filthy slacks into the hamper of clothing for the dry cleaner. "What else can go wrong?"

Only then did she notice that her answering machine was flashing a signal that she had messages waiting. The first voice was Beau's. He sounded tired and cross and not at all pleased that she wasn't home. "I'm going to be late again," he warned. "We've got a real mess out here. I hope you're not taking any foolish chances."

Alison frowned. Okay, so he was tired and overworked. That didn't give him an excuse to talk to her as though she were dim-witted. She'd been taking care of herself quite well without him, thank you very much.

The next message was from her college roommate, now a stock analyst who lived in St. Louis. "Ali—hi, it's Barb. Listen, I'm home for my mother's birthday and I have my new guy with me. We're kind of stranded here by this nasty weather for a few days, and I'd love to see you and have you meet Walter. If it's okay, we'll be at your place at six-thirty. If you have other plans, call me at Mom's, okay?" She gave the number, but it didn't matter. It was already six thirty-five.

Alison groaned and ran a brush through her hair. Then she ran to the kitchen to start a pot of coffee. She had nothing to offer in the way of refreshments except a half-eaten bag of Beau's favorite chocolate-chip cookies. She dumped them onto a plate and covered it, deciding that would have to do. The coffee had just finished brewing when the doorbell rang.

"Ali!" Barbara barely allowed Alison to open the door before attack-hugging her, almost smothering her in a soft cloud of fur. "You look *wonderful*. Must be a new man. Tell me all about him."

Laughing at her old friend's absurdity, Alison pulled her inside. "Didn't you have trouble driving over?" she asked.

Barbara shook her artfully-styled blond head. "Walter's from Michigan. He's used to ugly weather, aren't you, darling?"

Barbara's friend was tall, lean, elegant. He reminded Alison of a young David Niven. Barbara had always liked the debonair, urbane type, Alison reflected in private amusement as she shook his hand. She couldn't help noticing the contrast between Walter's smooth, soft palm and Beau's rough, callused hands. Naturally, she preferred Beau's decidedly masculine touch.

"Could I get you some coffee and cookies?" she offered. She wasn't displeased by the impromptu visit. At least visiting with Barbara and Walter would give her something to do other than sit around missing Beau.

IT WAS NEARLY NINE o'clock when Beau climbed out of his Jeep at his parking space. He'd been working almost forty-eight hours straight in below-freezing weather. He hadn't taken time to shave that morning after getting less than six hours sleep, so he was grubby and itchy and bone-tired. He was also irritable and on the verge of snapping at anyone who looked at him funny, so he told himself the sensible thing to do would be to head straight to his own apartment for a shower and a good night's sleep. Alison didn't deserve to have him descend on her in this lousy shape.

Yet, he found himself walking toward her door rather than his own. Since he was reasonably certain she'd ignored his advice and gone to work that day, he wanted to make sure she'd gotten home safely. Besides, he was weary and down, and he couldn't resist the longing to be pampered by Alison and then fall straight into bed—with her. The lights from her windows looked warm and welcoming in the cold, dark night.

He fumbled in his pocket for the key she'd given him, but his hands were cold and awkward and he finally gave up and just rang the bell. The door opened.

Alison looked him over and quickly drew him inside. "Beau, you look terrible," she murmured compassionately.

His smile felt strained. "Hey, thanks a lot," he replied, trying to tease. And then he stiffened when he realized they weren't alone. A man and a woman had risen when he'd walked in. The woman was pretty in a carefully wind-blown, Marilyn Monroe sort of way. The guy looked like he'd just stepped out of *GQ*. Beau winced, vividly aware of his two-day-old beard and the dirt on his face and hands and ground into his clothing.

"Sorry, Alison. I didn't know you had company. I'll just head on home, now that I know you're okay."

"Don't be silly," she scolded, taking his hand, dirt and all. "You're so tired you can hardly stand and I'll bet you haven't eaten. I don't have much to choose from, but I'm sure I can find a can of soup or something. By the way, this is my friend, Barbara Harris, and her friend Walter Sturdivant. Barb, Walter, this is Beau Harmon."

Walter hesitated visibly before offering a rather limp hand. Beau glanced at it and held his own palm outward. "Sorry. I've just gotten off work."

"You're in—uh—construction?" Walter hazarded.

"Lineman," Beau replied shortly. He was getting damned tired of feeling as though he should apologize for what he did. His work was honest, necessary and paid damned well—particularly when he put in the overtime hours required by power outages. And why the hell hadn't Alison told him she was expecting company tonight?

"Beau's been working very long hours because of the ice storm," Alison explained quickly when Barbara and Walter continued to look at him while obviously trying to think of something to say.

Beau wasn't in the mood for social niceties. And he damned well didn't intend to stand here and let Alison apologize for his appearance to this elegant couple. "Look, I really need a shower," he said abruptly. "Alison, you go ahead and visit with your friends. I'll see you tomorrow."

He didn't give her a chance to argue, but left with only a curt nod to her friends. He headed toward his own apartment in a seething temper, entering with a frustratingly unsatisfying slam of the door behind him.

BARBARA AND WALTER didn't stay long after Beau's brusque departure. Alison saw them off with a forced smile, knowing they'd gotten a less-than-favorable first impression of her lover. She didn't really blame them. He'd entered in a lousy mood, his eyes hard and an almost-visible chip on his shoulder. He'd also looked so tired her heart had twisted; but that was no excuse for him to be so rude to her friends. Or to her, for that matter. What had *she* done to set him off?

She fumed for half an hour before abruptly deciding not to let him get away with such behavior. Hesitating only long enough to grab her coat, she stormed out of her apartment and across the compound to his, retaining just enough good sense to pick her way carefully around the ice patches. It annoyed her even further when she realized that she had no key to his apartment. For some reason, it had never come up before, since they usually went to hers.

She pressed the bell, then impatiently pounded on the door with her fist.

"*What?*" Beau looked half asleep when he jerked the door open, his hair still damp from his shower, his face freshly shaven, though he'd cut his jaw in two places.

Served him right, Alison thought before launching into the attack. "What the hell is wrong with you tonight?" she demanded, pushing past him into the minimally furnished living room. "You were very rude to my friends, and you weren't all that pleasant to me."

"Well, excuse me, but I'm tired," Beau snapped in reply. He was wearing only a pair of unbuttoned jeans and Alison refused to allow herself to be distracted by his sexual appeal. "I really wasn't in the mood to be sneered at by your snobby, tight-assed friends," he added caustically.

She gasped in renewed outrage. "Why, you— I'll have you know that Barbara is a very nice person, and Walter seemed nice, as well. You didn't even give them a chance to like you. You just assumed they were going to put you down."

"Oh, come off it, Alison. They just stood there and stared at me as if I were some sort of alien. They couldn't even think of anything to say when you introduced me. You don't really think they'd lower themselves to actually like me, do you?"

Furious now, she barely resisted the urge to stamp her foot. "Dammit, Beau, you came in with a chip on your shoulder the size of Rhode Island. You looked like you wanted to chew raw meat or something. Of course, they didn't know what to say to you."

"That seems to be a common problem for your friends, doesn't it, Alison?"

She lifted her chin. "I suppose you'd rather spend your time with a group of foul-mouthed drunks?"

His eyes narrowed. His voice dropped an octave, coming out silky and dangerous. "Maybe I would," he agreed. "At least they don't judge a person by what color collar he wears to work."

Suddenly near tears, Alison threw out her hands in frustration. "I can't believe we're doing this to each other. Dammit, I knew all along—" She stopped abruptly.

"What did you know all along?" he demanded, taking a step closer, his tone taking on a cutting edge. "Did you know I was all wrong for you, Alison? That I wouldn't fit in with your upwardly-mobile crowd? That you were making a mistake by going out with me? Just what did you see in me, anyway? Am I so good in bed that you forgot all the sensible reasons you'd had for turning me down for three months?''

"If that's what you think of me, then maybe we *have* made a mistake," she agreed tensely. "I've given you more in five and a half weeks than I've given anyone in my entire life, dammit, and it wasn't enough for you, was it? You want me to turn my back on everything I had before you came into my life. My career, my friends. Well, forget it, Beau!"

"I've never asked you to give up a blasted thing!" Beau shouted in return, goaded into raising his voice. "I'm just fed up with being treated like an outcast. And I'm damned tired of waiting for you to dump me in favor of some guy like Walter, who fits so nicely into your Yuppie life-style!"

"Maybe we should just let it go," Alison said proudly, forcing back her tears with a massive effort. "Maybe we should just admit our mistake and go back to our own lives."

"Yeah. Maybe we should." She couldn't read his expression. For the first time, his thoughts were completely closed to her.

She turned blindly and ran for the door. Throwing it open, she stepped outside and slammed it behind her. The slam echoed with a depressing air of finality through the eerily empty compound. She managed not to cry until she was safely inside her own apartment. And then she curled into her lonely bed and wept bitterly, telling herself she should have known better than to trust a relationship begun in the romantic hysteria of Valentine's Day.

Chapter Ten

ALISON HAD NEVER BEEN so miserable in her entire life. She prided herself that no one could possibly have known by observing her that her life had been shattered, her heart broken. She performed her job with her usual competence, bought two new suits and three very becoming blouses—even accepted an invitation to dinner with Dane. And then was appalled when she found it necessary to excuse herself in the middle of the meal and escape to the rest room to prevent herself from bursting into tears in front of Dane and everyone else in the restaurant.

Would her life ever be the same without Beau?

BEAU WATCHED from his window when the man in the tweed jacket brought Alison home. His fist clenched around a beer can when the jerk kissed her at the doorstep, though the kiss was only a brief one and the man left soon afterward. Beau hated the thought of anyone else kissing Alison.

He'd been out the night before with a waitress he'd dated a few times before Alison. He'd had a lousy time. And he'd discovered he didn't want to kiss anyone but Alison.

He glared at the partially-crushed beer can, then tossed it into a wastebasket, though it was only half emptied. He'd bought a six-pack on the way home from work, figuring it couldn't hurt—might even help dull the ache that had centered in his chest for the past few weeks. It hadn't helped at all. He didn't even care for the taste anymore. He preferred ginger ale.

IT WAS A QUIET Saturday afternoon—a much *too* quiet, depressingly lonely Saturday afternoon—when Alison pushed the Play button on her CD player, hoping music would cheer her up as she worked at her portable computer. She hadn't checked the label on the CD in the player. She wished she had when she realized it was one Beau had left. Restless Heart. "A Tender Lie." "Say you'll come back to me," the singer moaned, "and I'll believe it's true."

Alison promptly burst into tears.

ON THAT SAME SATURDAY afternoon, Beau prowled his apartment like a caged animal, slamming doors, kicking scattered newspapers out from under his feet. He really should call Tommy and get up a game of basketball or something. There was certainly nothing more interesting to do here. But basketball required too much energy, and being social would call for even more effort on his part. He decided to spare his friends his company.

Needing to fill the haunting silence in his apartment, he snapped on the radio. George Strait was singing about how "nobody in his right mind would have left her." Even his heart, the singer complained, had been smart enough to stay behind.

Beau rubbed his own empty, aching chest. "Damn," he groaned, closing his eyes wearily, his head falling back against the couch. "How long can it hurt like this?"

IT WAS INEVITABLE, of course, that they'd cross paths during those weeks. Several times Beau had almost reached out to her, but Alison, usually accompanied by her friend Carole, always turned her head and hurried away. Beau noticed that Carole was the one who looked back at him, her expression an odd mixture of sympathy and belligerence.

He'd put off doing laundry until he was down to his last ratty pair of underwear. Finally he threw a wildly mixed load of jeans, towels, underwear and sweaters into "his" washer and slumped into his usual position in the back corner of the room. He'd brought a book, but the story seemed unusually lifeless when he tried to read. It was science fiction by Orson Scott Card, an author he usually enjoyed, but today it couldn't hold his interest. He heard the door open and close behind him and huddled—definitely not in the mood for small talk.

He smelled her cologne before he saw her. His entire body tightened in response. *Alison. Damn!*

She walked to the dryer directly beside him, which had stopped spinning only a few minutes earlier. She'd opened the door and removed the first item before she spotted him from the corner of her eye. She jumped, her hand going to her heart. "Oh! You startled me. What are you doing there?"

He shrugged. "This is where I always sit when I'm doing laundry."

It took her only a moment. She glanced from him to the row of washers she and Carole had used that day in early February. "So that's how—" she murmured, then stopped herself and turned away. She loaded her clean towels into the small hamper she'd brought with her without saying anything else, keeping her face averted.

She'd turned to leave when her name left Beau's lips, almost before he'd known he was going to say it. "Alison."

She hesitated, still not looking at him. "Yes?"

She looked as approachable as a marble statue. He sighed and lowered his gaze to his book. "Never mind," he muttered.

She all but ran from the room.

IT HAD BEEN NEARLY a month since the breakup when Alison was awakened early Sunday morning by the doorbell. She'd been dreaming of Beau, imagining herself naked in his arms, his husky voice telling her how much he loved her. She woke disoriented and depressed, blinking at the clock. Nine o'clock. Who—?

Tugging on a robe, she ran her fingers through her hair as she hurried into the living room in response to another impatient summons. "Who is it?"

"It's Beau. Open up, okay?"

Beau! Her hands suddenly trembling, she opened the door.

He looked wonderful. Freshly showered and shaven, dressed in a soft blue sweater that matched his eyes, and tan poplin slacks that molded his muscular thighs. He'd had a haircut since she'd last seen him. The heavy golden waves lay closely against his head, except for that one boyish lock that insisted on falling over his forehead—the one she'd taken such pleasure in brushing back with her fingertips.

"What is it?" she asked blankly.

Somewhat sheepishly, he pulled a huge bouquet of flowers from behind his back. "Just hear me out, okay?" he asked when she automatically took them from him, stepping back to let him enter the apartment.

She looked at him with her heart in her throat, unable to do anything more than nod. The flowers trembled in her hands. She clutched them so tightly, it was a wonder the stems didn't disintegrate in her grasp.

"I miss you," he said quietly, standing just close enough to touch her if he tried. He kept his hands at his sides. "I miss you so much I'm half crazy with it. I can't believe you're any happier than I am. Are you?"

Hope flooding through her, she shook her head, not quite capable of intelligible speech.

His eyes flared hotly, though he didn't move. "I'm sorry, Alison. You were right. I came in here that night in a lousy mood and when I saw your friends, I automatically got a chip on my shoulder. I didn't give them a chance."

"No," she whispered, tears prickling at the backs of her eyes.

"You should've hit me over the head with something," he told her ruefully, lifting a hand to push back that untamed forelock. It tumbled right back onto his forehead when his hand fell to his side. "I know we said some rotten things. Some of them may have even been true. We *don't* have everything in common. We both know that. But I've been thinking of some of the things we do have in common. Like a preference for Chinese food. And pizza."

"And public-television programs," she suggested.

"We both like kids and animals."

"We're both dedicated to our jobs, even if they do require different skills," Alison said, her mouth tilting into a helpless smile, the flowers clutched close to her breasts.

"So what if I like country and western and you like rock and roll?" Beau asked, beginning to relax, his endearing grin tugging at the corners of his sexy mouth. "We'll use headphones."

"And so what if your favorite movies involve action and violence and mine are romantic comedies?" she added, her heart singing with happiness. "We could always take turns choosing. Maybe see an occasional movie with our friends."

"And speaking of friends," he said with a wince. "I like Julia. And Carole seems nice. I'm sorry I was rude to Barbara and Walter."

"Tommy's a really great guy. So what if he and Julia didn't get along? And Barbara will forgive you. She understood that you were tired and cross."

"And scared?" he asked unexpectantly, watching her closely. "Do *you* understand how scared I was?"

"Why?" she asked in little more than a whisper, though she thought maybe she knew. Thought she'd probably been just as scared, and for exactly the same reasons.

"Because I love you so damned much and I didn't want to lose you. I didn't want you to change your mind about wanting me."

"How could I?" she asked, the tears finally escaping to trickle down her cheeks. "I love you, too."

His eyes closed briefly, then reopened, looking brighter than usual. "I guess that's the most important thing of all that we have in common, isn't it?" he asked hoarsely.

"Yes," she whispered. "I guess it is."

Beau moved so suddenly that he caught her completely unprepared when he lifted her off her feet to spin her around before covering her mouth with his in a long, passionate kiss. The flowers scattered on the carpet around them, unnoticed. Alison locked her arms around Beau's neck and returned the kiss with all the pent-up longing of the past unhappy weeks.

"I love you," he murmured again and again, between kisses.

"I love you, too," she replied when he gave her a chance to speak.

"We can make it work, Alison. We both thrive on challenges. We can make this last a lifetime." He sounded utterly confident as he lifted her high against his chest, one arm beneath her thighs.

Snuggling into his shoulder, she nodded happily, aware that he was already walking toward the bedroom. "Yes, Beau. I think we can."

Maybe there was some magic to Valentine's Day, after all, she thought as she and Beau tumbled together to the unmade bed, his hand already seeking the belt to her robe.

Or maybe the magic was love, and every day was Valentine's Day.

THE VALENTINE RAFFLE

Kristine Rolofson

A Note from Kristine Rolofson

I have always loved Valentine's Day. Not only because I'm a romantic person, but because I love theme parties. February 14 means heart-shaped pizza (I make it myself), pink-frosted cookies, doilies, candy, flowers and little gifts at everyone's place at the dinner table. We make elaborate cards and I mail anonymous valentines to those friends who live too far away to join us for dinner.

Celebrating holidays is my specialty. Halloween? I've baked (and frosted) pumpkin cakes, and driven around town dressed as a witch. Meanwhile, back at home, rubber spiders and bats dangle from the chandelier and pumpkins glow in the windows. Christmas means cutting thousands of sugar cookies into appropriate shapes, and having a neighborhood party to decorate them. The Super Bowl is a personal creative triumph, giving me a chance to make Jell-O salad in the teams' colors. There's Easter, Memorial Day, Fourth of July, Labor Day and—my personal favorite—the first day of school. A box in the closet holds the decorations for each one.

The other days of the year, I spend dreaming up ideas for books. Writing a valentine story set in Valentine, Nebraska, seemed a natural choice. After all, twenty-one years ago I married a Nebraska man, and *I* had a happy ending! Why wouldn't my heroine Stella have the same good fortune? Like the hero Matt, my husband is a man of few romantic words. Like Matt, he believes that actions speak louder than sweet talk *any* day of the year.

I wish you all—especially those of you who are in love with Nebraska men—a Valentine's Day filled with love, laughter and romantic gestures. Excuse me, will you? I think my pizza is ready....

Chapter One

"I CAN SEE I'M GOING to have to do some matchmaking."

"Please," Stella begged. "No blind dates." She studied Edith's reflection in the mirror, then tugged the roller cart closer to the chair.

"Well, I'll do what I can. But this is a romantic town, and we're two weeks away from one of the most important days of the year."

"I didn't know a town could celebrate Valentine's Day so much. I'm not complaining," Stella added, "but you have to admit, it *is* unusual."

Her favorite customer simply shrugged. "Not for a town named Valentine. That's the reason a pretty girl like you isn't married."

"What do you mean?" Stella unrolled the curlers from her friend's head. Edith Runke was one of her steady customers, with a standing three o'clock appointment every Friday. She was fifty-five, an attractive woman with strong features and wavy silver hair.

"You don't know how to celebrate Valentine's Day."

"That's my trouble, is it?" She tossed the curlers into the pink plastic bin and smiled at Edith's reflection in the large mirror.

"That's right, sweetie. Valentine, Nebraska, knows how to celebrate Valentine's Day." She winked at Stella's reflection in the mirror. "Just stick with us old Nebraska biddies. We'll see what we can do to teach you about romance."

"Okay," Stella agreed. "I'm willing to learn, Edith. But you have to find me the right man." Stella didn't attempt to argue. Beauty was her specialty, not the hearts-and-flowers kind of love. Still, she wouldn't refuse a romantic holiday. Especially if the right man came along. Unfortunately, right men didn't wander into Stella's Salon to have their hair done, and she didn't like going to the local bars alone. It looked . . . cheap.

"Give me credit, Edith. I'm trying to get in the swing of things around here. The raffle box is almost stuffed full already, and there's two weeks left to go."

"The windows look real nice, too."

"Thanks. I had fun." She'd decorated the shop in red and white, with shiny cutout hearts, in honor of the festivities.

"That's only the beginning. You're going to the coronation, aren't you?"

"Sure. I've heard your youngest could be a candidate for queen."

"Well, she'd like to be. Sure would be fun for her. You'll have to give her a new hairdo."

"Maybe she'll win my beauty make-over, even though she doesn't need it." Edith's three teenage daughters were all auburn-haired beauties.

"I'm not worried about her. It's you who needs a Valentine date."

The door swung open, tinkling the bells. Stella looked up as Ruth MacArlys, a short woman with naturally curly auburn hair, entered the salon with two little boys. Ruth unwound a bright red scarf from around her neck. "You boys hang up your coats and try to sit still," she said. "I won't be too long." She hung her coat on the rack and turned to Stella. "You runnin' late, honey? Hi, Edith."

"Nope. We're almost through."

"Doesn't take much to make me look beautiful," Edith said. "Just four or five hours of intense pampering."

The women laughed, and another woman waved from her position near the hair dryers. Her hair was stuck up in wet spikes. "Hi, Ruth."

Ruth waved. "What color you want to be this time, Sandy?"

"I'm always a blonde in February," Sandy hollered. "Don't you remember?"

"Who are your friends?" Stella asked, watching the boys' eyes widen as they looked around the shop. One of them sniffed and then made a face. The smaller one looked at Stella and shot her a shy smile.

Ruth poured herself a cup of coffee from the pot Stella always kept on the counter. "Matt McNeil's boys. He had to come into town for a meeting and asked if I'd watch them for a while. So I brought them along while I ran my errands."

Matt McNeil's sons. Now that they'd taken off their coats she recognized them. Handsome, like their father. Quiet, too. Also like their father.

"You know Matt, don't you Stella?"

She nodded. "He's the man who helped me when my car broke down last summer. He was very... kind."

Edith and Ruth exchanged glances, but Stella ignored their speculative expressions. She'd forced herself to quit daydreaming about Matt McNeil. She glanced over at his sons. They were busy filling out the entry blanks for the Cupid's Bag Raffle.

"You're wasting your time with that one," Edith said in a low voice so the children wouldn't hear. "He's hopeless. He's been hurt real bad, ever since his wife left him and those two little ones. Can you believe such a thing?"

Stella shook her head. She couldn't believe a woman leaving a man like Matt or little boys like the ones in the waiting area scribbling their names on raffle tickets. "No, I can't. You want spray today, don't you?"

"Just a little."

"Close your eyes." She waved the spray around Edith's head, then retouched the front wave. How could she forget Matt McNeil? He'd brought her into town and arranged for help. He'd tipped his hat, then strode away. That's all she'd ever gotten out of him—that respectful tilt of his cowboy hat and a mysterious appraisal from his dark green eyes. And maybe, if she was real lucky, he'd actually open his mouth and call her "ma'am." She was twenty-nine, and nobody's ma'am, thank you very much.

"I always wondered why you decided to stay in town," Ruth teased.

"Fate," Stella answered. "I saw that For Sale sign on Ida May's shop and figured somebody was trying to tell me something."

She handed Edith a hand mirror and then turned the chair around so she could see the back. "What do you think?"

"Wonderful. Thanks a lot, hon. I'll see you tonight at the meeting. Don't forget to bring this week's ballots. We're going to draw a few names early, just to get the spirit rolling."

Stella stepped over to the counter near the boys and put Edith's check into the cashbox. She watched the boys for a minute, and they looked up at her with strange expressions. She offered them a soda, and when they nodded, she put change in the pop machine and let them punch whatever flavor they desired. Then, because they were having such fun, she reached underneath the counter and put out a new pad of ballots. The hardware store donated bikes every year.

"What's your name?"

"Matthew McNeil," the larger one said. "I'm nine."

The one with the shy smile looked up, peeking at Stella through long straight bangs. "I'm Jason. I'm eight."

"What are you trying to win?"

"Bikes," they answered in unison.

Stella slid the pad closer. "Well, good luck. It was nice to meet you. If you need anything, just let me know."

They looked surprised. How could anybody need anything more than their own can of soda and a hundred chances to win a Valentine prize?

STELLA MANAGED to finish up before the chamber-of-commerce meeting at seven o'clock. The Home Café was the traditional site of the chamber meetings, and Stella wondered if Matt would be there. Sometimes he showed up, and although he didn't have much to say, his well-chosen comments were full of common sense. She looked forward to chamber meetings—not because it was a chance to see Matt, but because she'd worked hard to become a member of the community. It was important to her. She'd given makeup tips at the high-school home-ec classes, donated time to the residents at Pine View Manor, and cheered at high-school football games. She'd even bought a red-and-white sweater—the school colors.

Stella decided against one more cup of coffee, thinking she'd fix a sandwich when she returned home. Her feet ached, and she had to be up early tomorrow for another full day of work. She looked at her watch. Almost seven. With luck, this would be wrapped up by eight. She handed Edith her bag of ballots and found an empty metal chair near the aisle.

After the business meeting, Harve Runke hauled a large black plastic garbage can before the podium. "I'm going to get the ball rolling this year. Any volunteers for drawing?'' There weren't any. ''All right, Edith. I know how you love this job.''

Edith stuck her arm into the can and swished the paper around. Someone from the audience yelled, ''What are you drawing for?''

Harvey looked at his list. ''Well, how about starting with me? I'm donating a month of sundaes right here from the café, and we're not going to talk about cholesterol.''

A few people cheered. Edith pulled out a paper and read the name. ''Bobby Jenkins, of Cody.''

''There a phone number there?''

''Yep.'' Edith handed him the paper and he handed it to the secretary. Edith whispered something to him.

''It's been brought to my attention that we should draw for the day of beauty at Stella's Salon, so the ladies in town have plenty of time to make themselves beautiful before the coronation festivities begin. Stella's new in town, you know, but she's working hard.'' He winked at the crowd as Edith, closing her eyes, once again rummaged through the papers, and pulled out a piece of paper.

''The winner is . . . Matt McNeil.''

The audience tittered, then they applauded. Stella looked for Matt, and followed people's gazes to where Matt stood leaning against the wall near the refreshment table. He straightened, and looked as if he didn't quite understand.

Harve chuckled. ''Stella, look what you get to work with!''

Matt McNeil strode to the microphone and flashed a quick smile at the crowd. ''Thanks, but I'm sure the ladies in Valentine won't mind if we draw another name for this prize.''

It was the longest sentence she'd ever heard him say—absolutely the most words per second. Stella felt the heat rise to her face, which was her usual reaction to the sight of the handsome rancher.

Harve shook his head. "No way you can get out of this one, Matt. This is good publicity."

The Valentine newspaper photographer held up his camera. "I'll put it on the front page. How about before-and-after shots, Matt, like they do in the magazines?"

Stella was urged to come forward to stand beside Matt while the photographer moved into place before them.

"Smile!"

Stella smiled, although standing pressed against the warmth of Matt's cotton-flannel shirt and feeling Matt's muscled arm against hers made her knees weak. How could she not smile? This was the closest she'd ever come to Matt. And the closest she would. The man would never submit to Beauty Day at her salon.

Lights flashed in their eyes.

Matt knew he was never going to go through with this. The little blond piece of fluff stationed next to him was never going to get him to set foot in her beauty shop. Not if he was dragged by his Angus bull and tied up to a post inside. When the flash went off one more time and the photographer moved away, Matt breathed a sigh of relief. This whole thing might fade out of people's minds if he didn't fight it.

Matt looked down as Stella looked up. He met those beautiful blue eyes of hers and he couldn't take his gaze away from her face.

Big mistake. He'd like to touch that perfect skin, the flawless kind that looked like rose petals. And her hair was a particular shade of gold, like the morning sun on buttercups. Soft and fluffy, it waved to her shoulders. Those curls couldn't be real, but what did he know about women's hair? Her smile seemed real, though, and she looked almost shy. How could a woman who looked like a movie star be shy?

Well, no one said he ever knew much about women, either. Matt cleared his throat and attempted to look away, but the damned woman began to speak to him. Softly. He had to lean over to hear her and inhaled the scent of rose petals.

"Thank you," she said. "Thanks for being such a good sport."

"Well, I—" He wanted to say something but it flew right out of his mind.

"Front-page publicity should help business," she explained.

Matt took her elbow and guided her away from the limelight. Harve went on to announce one more raffle draw, but Matt didn't pay attention.

"Front page on the Valentine newspaper isn't exactly like the *Omaha World-Herald*."

"It's close enough for me." She stopped and looked up at him. "When do you want to do it?"

Do it? "What?"

"When do you want to come in? I do give men's haircuts, you know. Although no one around here does, in Chicago almost half my clients were men."

He knew why, all right. Imagine sitting in a barber chair looking at that face in the mirror. Why, it was almost indecent. "I think I'll just give the gift certificate to Ruth MacArlys, if you don't mind."

"You had your picture taken. You agreed already."

"Well—" Matt wanted to resist her plea. He knew she was the kind of woman who spelled trouble, especially for a hardworking rancher who didn't have time to spend on women. He didn't have the time to dress up, go out to fancy restaurants and make small talk with a woman whose biggest decision in life was probably what color lipstick to wear in the morning.

"It won't take long. And you get a free haircut and I get some badly needed publicity."

Matt reminded himself he was through with women. Since Page left—sick of ranch life, sick of being married and tired of being a mother—Matt had resolved to stay by himself. The boys kept him busy, and so did the ranch. When he wanted a woman, there were plenty available during business trips. With no strings attached. But still, he couldn't blame Stella for wanting the publicity. It must have taken a lot of courage to walk into a new town and start up her own shop. He couldn't figure it out. Just why had she picked Valentine? "Well, all right." He swept his long roughened fingers through his hair in agitation. "Guess I could use a trim."

"Are Saturdays good for you? I'm done with my last customer around four-thirty. Why don't you come in tomorrow at five o'clock and that way there won't be any women around making you feel silly."

He winced. "I already feel silly."

"Well, what time do you want to come over?"

Matt gave up. He was caught between a rock and a hard place, and he was smart enough to know when to quit. "Five o'clock is fine."

SATURDAYS WERE ALWAYS busy, but the next few weeks promised to be insane. Stella had been booking so many appointments she'd soon have to think about taking on an assistant. Her one-chair business was growing quickly, despite the number of beauty shops in town. Valentine was a small town, with a population under three thousand, but it served a large number of people who lived at the north-central part of Nebraska and drove into town—for some a very long trip—for everything they needed.

Small-town life was everything a city girl from Chicago could dream of. Her family had moved away, her job in the suburbs frustrating, and her longtime boyfriend said he had no intentions of getting married—probably not ever; but if she wanted to live together, that would be fine.

Well, that would be fine for him but not for her.

So she'd decided a vacation was in order, and she'd chosen the Black Hills and Mount Rushmore and set off to see them. Until the afternoon when her car broke down on Highway 83.

That's when the handsome owner of the Double Bar M—it was printed neatly on the door of the blue pickup truck—stopped to rescue her. And she believed in love at first sight for the first time in her life. She'd told herself it must have been the heat—105 that afternoon—but she'd remained starry-eyed throughout the fall and winter. Silly Stella. Deep down she was a romantic, but being a romantic woman could get pretty lonely.

Stella looked at the large clock stationed above the row of chairs. Five-fifteen. Her cowboy was late. She wondered if he'd chickened out. Well, maybe it wouldn't be the end of the world if he had. She'd gotten through in record time today, and the talk in the shop had been of Matt winning the prize. No one thought it was odd; just funny. And there were some comments made about matchmaking. But even the local ladies with romantic souls couldn't picture Matt McNeil getting involved with another woman—not after that snippy Page got too big for her britches and decided that Nebraska wasn't good enough for her anymore.

Stella had heard several versions of the story since she'd moved to town. She hadn't really asked specifically, but the mention of the rancher who had rescued her had gotten her an earful in return.

Her feet hurt, but she'd brushed her hair and applied fresh makeup. The shop was quiet; she'd finished sweeping. It was dark out, but the snow had stopped sometime last night. Still, she could hear the wind howl and knew it would be another bitter January night in the Nebraska sand hills.

She heard the bells jingle and felt the blast of cold air before she turned around to see Matt walk inside. He shut the door with a firm bang and attempted to wipe his boots on the mat. He looked up and their eyes met before he removed his cowboy hat. "Evenin'," he said, his voice a low drawl.

"Hello, Matt. I'd almost given up on you," she said, stepping closer. "You can hang your coat over there." She pointed to the rack near the door.

"There's always something that comes up on a ranch," he said. "I had to drop the boys off at Ruth's." He looked around the salon, then back at her as if to say "Now what?"

She swiveled the chair towards him. "Have a seat." As he reluctantly did what he was told, Stella selected a blue shampoo cape and fastened it around his neck. "I met your boys yesterday. They were here with Ruth while she had her hair done."

"I hope they behaved themselves. I can't picture them sitting still in a place like this."

"Oh, they stayed busy. They stuffed the raffle box."

Her fingers touched the nape of his neck while she fastened the Velcro tabs in place. His skin was warm, and she pulled her hand away quickly. She had to treat Matt McNeil like any other customer.

It just might be harder than she thought it would be.

"Maybe that explains it," he muttered.

She looked into the mirror and met his gaze. "Explains what?"

"My name being drawn."

"How?" She touched his hair. It was thick, dark, with a natural wave. No silver at all.

"My oldest is Matthew, Jr."

Stella tried to hide her smile. "You think it was really your son who won the make-over? You didn't enter anywhere else?"

"Only at the feed store."

"What about Matthew? Where else was he yesterday?"

Matt frowned. He wasn't looking at himself in the mirror, just absently watching Stella lift sections of his hair and drop them back into place. "Everywhere Ruth went."

"Which could have been a lot of places."

Matt sighed. "What are you going to do to me?"

"The works."

"Just a haircut," he countered.

"The works," she repeated. "You won it fair and square, so sit there and be quiet." Telling Matt McNeil to be quiet was like telling a cow to eat hay. It just came naturally.

"Come on," she said, stepping back from the chair.

He slowly stood, but didn't take a step forward. "Where are we going?"

"To the sink."

He started to protest. "I washed my hair this morning."

"I have to cut hair when it's wet." She walked over to the sink, forcing him to follow her. He sat down in the chair with a great show of reluctance. Stella made certain the towel around his neck was secure. "Okay, lean back."

He did as he was told, but she could tell he wasn't pleased. Stella adjusted the water temperature and used the spray on his hair. Then she squirted her favorite papaya shampoo into her palm and began to lather Matt's hair, using the pads of her fingers to massage his scalp. Okay, so maybe she took longer than usual, but no one was waiting for her to finish. She could take her time, couldn't she? He groaned. "Water too hot?"

"No. That feels good."

"See? I told you this wouldn't be too bad."

Matt bit back an answer. It felt good, all right, but not the way the little hairdresser thought it did. He was glad the plastic thing covered his lap. Her fingers on his scalp were causing riots through the rest of his body and he preferred to keep the reaction private. Next, the warm water washed over his head and he closed his eyes once again. He wondered if other men had their hair cut this way, and if Stella's hands on them caused the same reaction. A sharp stab of jealousy distracted him.

"Do you have any other men, uh, clients?"

"Not in Valentine."

"Oh." Her fingers were on his scalp again, rubbing something else into his hair. It smelled minty.

"This is conditioner," she said. "But don't worry, you won't smell like perfume when you leave."

"Fine." *Leave?* He'd be lucky if he could walk out of here. He kept his eyes closed. His hands gripped the vinyl-coated arms of the chair to keep from grabbing Stella. He didn't think she'd appreciate the interruption of her work. She certainly seemed serious about it.

"One more rinse," she said, and Matt felt the soothing stream of warm water once again. He almost groaned out loud as she wrapped a white towel around his head. "There. You can sit up now."

He did as he was told, including following her back to the chair in front of the mirror. She rearranged the plastic cape to make sure it covered his jeans and then pumped up his chair to the right height as she looked in the mirror at him. "Now the good part."

The good part? He'd just had the good part, which was difficult enough. Maybe he could stagger out of here now. "There's more?"

"Well, sure." She toweled his hair, gently squeezing the ends before removing the towel. "Do you want to keep it long at the back?"

"Yes."

"Do you want the sides trimmed? We might shape them a little more, all right?"

"Fine."

She ran her fingers through his hair and fluffed the top. It gave him goose bumps. "I like the extra length on top, but it could use some shaping."

"Fine." *Just let me get out of here. Preferably without embarrassing myself in the process.*

"You part your hair on the right?"

"Yes."

"Okay." Stella pulled a pair of scissors out of the drawer underneath the mirror and took a narrow black comb from a container on the shelf. He had gorgeous hair—hair that matched the rest of him. She hoped he didn't suspect what kind of effect he had on her. Her knees were practically banging together. If he looked at the mirror he might see her hand shake.

She trimmed. She snipped. She shaped. She combed. And she attempted a conversation. "How old are your boys?"

"Eight and nine."

She waited for him to offer more information but he didn't, so she tried again. "Your ranch is outside of town?"

"Thirty miles east of here."

Silence again. Stella searched her memory for something else that might interest him, but the college football season had ended on New Year's Day and the Super Bowl was over three weeks ago. The Cornhuskers had blown their shot at the Rose Bowl this year, which still remained a sore subject for all the University of Nebraska fans. The town held a lot of them, too—at home-game times, Valentine was deserted, because everyone had gone to Lincoln to cheer "Go, Big Red" at the stadium. Stella hoped to go to a game next year. She'd buy a red sweatshirt and fit right in.

"What do you raise out there on the Double Bar M?"

"Feeder cattle." He cleared his throat.

Stella made a mental note to find out exactly what feeder cattle were. "Oh. Is your ranch a big place?"

"I have a few acres."

A few acres probably meant a few thousand, Stella knew. So much for agriculture. Matt had a strong jawline, a firm chin, a handsome profile. No wonder she'd been struck dumb when she'd first seen him on Highway 83. He'd hopped out of that silver-blue pickup like a knight in shining armor. The road had even shimmered in the brutal afternoon heat. Like a mirage, almost.

Her romantic notions haunted her. And here he was, practically captive, and she wasn't sure what to do with him. He was single, well-liked and respected in town. He'd been kind to her twice now—once with her car and now with this—but what could she do? Only pray that this would be over before she embarrassed herself.

But still, when it was over, Matt would leave and she would see him walk by on the sidewalk every once in a while, and that would be all. It was tempting to try to make this last. To make touching him last for as long as she could. Even if it was torture at the same time.

Torture, Matt decided, had to be sitting in a chair watching the most beautiful woman he'd ever seen. He tried not to stare in the mirror, but since mirrors took up all of the wall space above the counters, it was pretty hopeless. Stella was certainly a beautiful woman—with that blond hair shining under the lights and the pearly skin with its pink blush.

She'd blushed when she'd looked up at him at the chamber-of-commerce meeting. He'd been surprised. He didn't know beautiful city women blushed. He'd thought it was the heated room, or maybe she didn't like to have her picture taken, but she'd blushed again when he walked into this damn place. He sat silently, wondering how on earth anyone could take so long to trim his hair.

But he wasn't complaining anymore. He relaxed his shoulders and readjusted his booted heels on the footrest.

"I'm almost finished," she said, misinterpreting his restlessness.

"Take your time," Matt answered, surprising himself by meaning the words.

She stepped away and grabbed the blow dryer. She held it up. "Do you mind?"

Mind what? Then he noticed the machine in her hand. "No."

The whine of the dryer filled the air, and the warm air flicked across his neck and around his ears. She wielded the brush like a magic wand and stroked it against his scalp as she waved the nozzle of the dryer around.

When her breasts came perilously close to his face, Matt almost jumped out of the chair. He wondered for an instant if she'd done it on purpose, but when he glanced at her he saw she was completely absorbed with his hair. He didn't know why. His thick hair had an unruly wave that he'd given up trying to tame. It wasn't as if it was that important—most of the time his hat mashed it down. And he wasn't trying to impress anyone. He grit his teeth until he felt a muscle in his jaw begin to ache.

He heard a click and the sound stopped. She dipped a large brush in powder and whisked the nape of his neck before unfastening the apron from around his neck. "There. You're all finished." She smiled at him. "It wasn't that bad, was it?"

He leaned forward and grasped one of her hands as she stepped beside him to take the apron. "Yes, it was."

Stella stared at her hand enfolded in his. Then she looked up into his face. She looked surprised, but there was no fear in those big blue eyes. "Matt?"

He tugged her one step closer, until he rose out of the chair. He couldn't take it anymore, he told himself as his other hand slipped beneath the soft yellow curls and entwined around the nape of Stella's neck. He would kiss her—out of frustration or "nerves" or whatever—but it would only be this one time, because he was a man and a man couldn't be expected to resist this kind of woman. Even if she was the wrong kind of woman for a hard-working rancher.

He drew her closer to him, and felt little resistance on her part. Before he knew it, his lips were on hers.

He'd meant it to be a quick, hard kiss—just a release of tension or a way to assuage his curiosity. But when he brought her body near his, felt the tips of her breasts graze his chest, shock waves of awareness careened throughout his taut body.

She was a tiny little thing, but her lips packed one hell of a wallop. He deepened the kiss, and when her lips parted almost hesitantly, he tasted the sweetness of her mouth on his tongue. Her fingertips caressed the nape of his neck, and he felt her soft touch caress his back through the cotton shirt.

Stella liked touching him. The kiss surprised her—the fierce look on his face did not. He'd given her that look shortly after realizing he'd have to give her a ride to town. She figured he had something against women—and she'd been right.

But he didn't seem to have any problem right now.

It was over quickly—sooner than she expected. He broke it off, and she took a step backward. He moved away from the chair sideways so it wouldn't look like he was charging after her.

They never heard the knock on the door.

Chapter Two

"MATT MCNEILL, this must be your lucky day!"

A tall young man in jeans and a black parka closed the door behind him, jangling the bell. He lifted his snow-dusted cowboy hat toward Stella. "Excuse me, Miss Hathaway. I sure didn't want to interrupt Matt's, uh, beauty time."

"He's finished," Stella assured him.

Matt stepped closer to Bud. "My lucky day?" After that kiss, Matt had another definition of "lucky day" in mind. Had Bud seen that embrace? He hoped not.

Bud grinned and pulled an envelope out of his jacket pocket. "Harve drew a few more prizes tonight, and you won yourself a pair of dinners. Thought since you're all fixed up and all, you might want to go out and eat."

"Thanks," he muttered, taking the envelope. Food was the last thing on Matt's mind. He could still taste Stella, could still feel the softness of those sweet lips on his. *Damn.*

"It's for The Pepper Mill. You ever been to The Pepper Mill, Miss Hathaway?"

"Call me Stella, and no, I haven't." Mortified, Stella clutched the back of the chair. The young man was practically insisting that Matt use his dinner prize to take her as his date. She attempted to change the subject. "How's Maddie doing?" Bud's wife was expecting their first child any day now, and had just begun getting her hair done at Stella's in order to boost her spirits.

"Pretty good," he said, but wasn't easily led from the subject. "Be sure to try the chicken-fried steak."

Matt glared at Bud. "Thanks for bringing these by."

"Well, I—"

"Say hello to her for me," Stella said. "Any sign of that baby?"

"Not yet, but she's not due until Valentine's Day, and a baby born on February 14th gets a lot of free gifts, so I keep telling her she'd better hang on for two more weeks."

Stella didn't think any woman in her ninth month would appreciate that attitude, but she kept her amusement to herself while Matt guided Bud to the door. "See you later, Bud."

"Yeah." He grinned, understanding finally flickering across his face. "Yeah, right."

The door clanged shut and Matt turned to Stella. "I hope Bud didn't embarrass you. Would you have dinner with me tonight?"

She figured it was a pity offer. After all, he'd been forced into it. "Thank you, but no."

The lines around his mouth deepened into an attractive frown. Stella stared at that mouth. He'd practically knocked her over with that kiss. Since last summer she'd wondered what it would be like to kiss him, and now she knew. Only she wondered if she'd be better off not knowing, especially since the chances of it happening again were practically zero.

"Why not?" he asked.

"It was Bud's idea, not yours."

"Why not? I'll come back in—" he looked at his watch "—two hours, at eight o'clock, and pick you up."

"I really don't think—"

He was still frowning. "Look, about what just happened—"

She held up one hand. "Let's just forget it, okay?" Of course, she knew she'd never forget it, but what was one little lie? "You don't have to be polite."

"Polite? Damn it." He strode over to the coat tree and grabbed his jacket and his hat. He slammed the hat on his head and shot her a furious look. He was still muttering when he walked out the door.

Stella waited until he'd passed the windows, then went over to lock the door and flip the Open sign to the Closed side. Of course, he was being polite—Matt McNeil was the polite sort of knight. His unwillingness to embarrass her was what had forced him into the salon for a haircut.

She didn't need anyone fixing her up with him, that was for sure. Stella grabbed the broom and started sweeping Matt's hair into the dustpan. She had her pride.

She washed out the sink, disinfected the counters and emptied the cash drawer into the vinyl bank pouch before going upstairs to her apartment. She needed a hot bath and a cold drink. And some time alone to think why Matt had kissed her. That kiss had surprised her, and she'd bet money that it had surprised him, too.

Where had all that passion come from? Maybe he wasn't the remote person the entire town thought he was. Intriguing idea, she decided, but not anything she could pursue. Her customers had been right: It was dangerous to spend time thinking about the handsome rancher.

Stella put a frozen turkey dinner in the oven and set the timer. She'd been lucky to find the beauty shop with the little one-bedroom apartment behind it. Ida May, the previous owner, had rented it out to one of her operators, but Stella had been pleased to use it herself.

She spent an hour and a half in the bathtub, soaking and reading the latest women's magazines. February issues, they'd promised romance with the man of her dreams. She hadn't read anything that would help deal with a quiet cowboy. She'd promised herself that all her romantic notions about Matt McNeil would have to stop. She shouldn't believe in love at first sight anymore. He'd kissed her. She'd kissed him back. That was the end of it.

The end of it until she heard the knock and turned to see Matt standing at the back door. She pulled her long pastel blue bathrobe tightly around her and opened the door.

Matt stepped inside as if he arrived every Saturday night. "You look like you're ready for bed."

Stella backed up a step and blushed. She'd taken off her makeup and piled her hair into a knot at the top of her head. "I said no to your invitation, remember?"

Matt winced. "I remember, but I hoped you'd have changed your mind by now and decided to have dinner with me."

Stella stared up at him. That was possibly the longest sentence she'd heard him speak. "You didn't have to ask me to share the prize."

"I wanted to."

"It wasn't your idea."

"Does that matter?" He flashed her his charming smile. "I thought it was a pretty good idea."

She clutched the folds of her terry-cloth robe around her tightly. "I'm not dressed."

"I'm not in a hurry."

No surprise there. The man always looked as if he had all the time in the world. In fact, most of the men she'd met in Nebraska acted the same way. "I'm sure you're not."

"What's that supposed to mean?"

Stella didn't bother to answer. "Why did you come back here?"

"I told you, Stella. To take you to dinner." He smiled once again, an alarming white flash of teeth. "Are you hungry?"

"I just put dinner in the oven."

"I'll take it out while you get ready. Do you like steak?"

"Yes, but—"

"Then you'll like The Pepper Mill."

She watched as he picked up the red calico hot-pads on the counter and opened the oven door. He slid the aluminum tray out and set it on top of the stove.

"There." He looked over his shoulder at her. "Do we have a date?"

Stella was torn. Matt looked gorgeous in a dark suit, ivory shirt and maroon-print tie. Fancy boots peeked out from under the hems of his slacks. But what did he want? Did he think she was going to fall into his arms again?

Still, she couldn't resist a chance to get dressed up and go out to dinner. She'd wanted a date with him for six months, so she'd be a fool to send him out into the cold January night alone.

Stella was nobody's fool. "Okay," she agreed. "But it's going to take a little while."

"I'll wait."

He'd wait, all right. She went into her bedroom and shut the door behind her. She'd wear her favorite outfit—the dark rose knit. Thank goodness she'd taken a bath already. She tugged on panty hose and slipped the dress over her head and adjusted it over her hips, letting it fall to her knees.

This was turning out to be quite a day. First, she had Matt in her chair. Now he was in her kitchen. All dressed up and waiting. For her, Stella Hathaway.

She looked at herself in the mirror and grinned. She grabbed a brush and fixed her hair, then put on a pair of gold-hoop earrings. Before she left the room she dabbed on her most expensive perfume.

Matt McNeil just better watch out.

FROM WHAT MATT could see, Stella was easily the most beautiful woman in the room. He wanted to keep on looking at her, but couldn't be rude. Especially since he'd practically ordered her to go out with him tonight.

"What would you like to drink?" he asked instead.

"Just a glass of white wine, please."

Matt signaled the waitress and ordered the wine for Stella and a beer for himself while Stella examined the menu.

"I've never won anything before this weekend," Matt said. "Do you think this might be the beginning of a streak?"

"It's possible," she said, her blue eyes smiling into his. "Are you thinking of going down to Reno to try your luck?"

He shrugged. "Anything's possible, but I don't think I should leave the ranch right now."

"What do you do out there in the winter?"

He rested his arms on the table, grateful for the excuse to keep looking at her. "Catch up on paperwork, take care of the livestock, get ready for spring. There are always a few auctions to go to. I'm always trying to improve the stock."

She didn't know what "improve the stock" meant. "And the boys keep you busy."

"Yes."

"You're divorced, I hear."

Matt frowned. "Three years ago. My wife—ex-wife—didn't want this kind of life anymore."

Stella knew she was treading on dangerous ground, but she couldn't help asking, "What do you mean?"

He hesitated as the waitress delivered their drinks, then took a swallow of beer before answering her question. "She wasn't happy on the ranch. In fact, she'd lived near here all her life and finally said she couldn't stand knowing she was going to die here, too. Without knowing anything else."

"Where did she go?"

"Dallas. With another man."

"I'm sorry."

Matt shrugged. "It happens."

"What about the boys?"

"What about them?"

"Does she ever see them?"

His fingers tightened around the thick glass. "Page said she wanted a clean break. She didn't want to drag the past behind her."

Stella sensed that that was a direct quote and decided she didn't like Page McNeil very much. The waitress appeared to take their order, saving Stella from having to continue the conversation. Then several members of the chamber of commerce came over to the table to say hello and comment on what a handsome couple they made. A cousin of Matt's and three of Stella's customers strolled over to say the same thing.

"Are you counting?" Matt asked her.

Stella sipped the last of her wine. "Counting what?"

"How many times someone says what a handsome couple we make."

"Nine." She already knew they made a good-looking couple. Stella figured that out right away. They were both single, not teenagers, and old enough to know what they were doing. But what *were* they doing?

"Right." His smile threatened to dissolve her. "I think we're giving people something to talk about."

"Do you mind?"

"No. But I wouldn't want you to be embarrassed by gossip."

She laughed. "That's all I hear all day long. Nothing harmful. Just what's going on in town."

"And what's going on in town?"

"If I told you, I'd be guilty of spreading gossip. And I don't do that."

"Is that some sort of hairdressers' code?"

"Yep." She smiled at him. "But I do find out the nicest things, such as who is going to have a baby and whose children are getting married. Happy things."

"You like your job."

"Yes, very much."

Their dinner arrived: big thick steaks—hers medium, his rare. She had a baked potato, he had fries. A three-piece band set up in the corner near the small platform that passed as a dance floor and began to play a country-western ballad.

Matt figured he'd lost his mind. He had no business dating. But Stella Hathaway was pretty hard to resist. He'd be crazy to miss out on an opportunity to spend Saturday night with her. Yet there was something about her that scared him to death. A woman like this wouldn't be content in Valentine for long. She'd grow bored and restless and want the city life again. When she left Valentine, he'd be sitting out on his ranch like three kinds of fool.

"Where are you from?" Matt ventured.

"Chicago," she said. "Actually, Oak Park, a suburb."

"You were on your way to the Black Hills last summer. Did you ever get there?"

"No." And her blue eyes twinkled at him. "After you took me to the gas station, they towed my car back to town. In the meantime I walked around and saw the For Sale sign on the beauty shop. It seemed like . . . fate to me, I guess. Sound silly?"

"Yep."

"I know. At first I couldn't believe it, either. But everyone was so nice, and I'd always dreamed of living in a small town—the kind of place where everyone knows everybody else—and all of a sudden, I was here. With enough money in my savings account to open my own shop. So I took a chance."

"You're a brave lady."

"I guess that depends on how you look at it. My friends thought I was crazy."

"What about your family?"

"My parents retired to Florida a few years ago. I'm pretty much on my own."

Not for long, he thought. Especially in a Western town with cowboys and ranchers. The farther west, the harder it was to find single women. And this particular woman was something special. "Do you like it here?"

There was more to his question, she knew. "Yes, very much. My business is picking up and the cost of living is so much lower here. I think I can make it, if I'm careful."

Stella began to relax and enjoy herself. Dinner was as delicious as she'd been promised, and the cozy corner table afforded a small measure of privacy, even though it seemed as if everyone in town was eating dinner at The Pepper Mill tonight—and watching the little table for two in the corner.

"Tell me about your boys," Stella said. "Do they go to school in Valentine?"

"They're in the second and third grade." He pushed his empty plate away slightly and leaned on the table. "I had a talk with them about the raffle box in your shop. It seems they were trying to win a bike."

Stella tried not to laugh. "They said something about that."

"Have you ever been married?"

"No."

He looked surprised. "Why—" Then he stopped.

She sensed his embarrassment. "Why not? I've been asked that before, especially by my parents. I guess the right man hasn't come along yet."

"Not even in Chicago?"

"I had a boyfriend for many years. I always assumed we'd get married, but one day I asked and he said he had no intention of tying himself down." She winced. "I really hadn't expected that answer—not after four years together."

"Is that why you came here?"

"Oh, no. I was really looking forward to a vacation—just me, by myself, on an adventure to the Black Hills. My parents had taken me there once when I was a child and I'd always wanted to return and see the donkeys again—remember how they come up to your car and beg for food? I had it all planned—except for the alternator going out on my car."

"Which is where I came in."

Like a knight in shining armor. "Yes. Lucky for me."

"Not luck. People around here always help each other."

"I've noticed."

"We've attracted a lot of attention," Matt said, looking around the dark room and nodding at people who lifted a friendly hand in greeting.

Stella took a second to admire his profile before he turned back to her. "Makes you wonder what you'll win tomorrow, doesn't it?"

"It's Sunday. Harve won't bother with the raffle then."

"And you've never won anything before this?"

He shook his head. "Not a thing."

Stella wondered who supervised the name drawing. She had the uneasy feeling that Edith Runke had had more to do with this than she would ever let on. Matt had been forced to come to Stella's, and now he'd won a dinner— convenient that he should win at the same time he and Stella were together. Stella made a mental note to check her appointments for next week and see when Ruth was coming in for her weekly hairdo. She'd have to try to wheedle the information out of her.

They ordered coffee and, although Stella refused dessert, Matt made a huge piece of apple pie disappear in minutes. The silence grew awkward, and Stella wondered if Matt was having second thoughts about the date. The band began a countrified rendition of "The Tennessee Waltz"; the couple seated at the table next to them stood and moved toward the dance floor.

"Would you like to dance?" Matt asked. She stared at him, not believing what she'd heard. "We may as well give them something to talk about at the shop on Monday morning," he urged, his voice low. He stood and held out his hand to Stella.

She put her hand inside his big calloused one and allowed him to lift her to her feet. Stella found herself in Matt's arms, waltzing to the music. His big palm was spread across her back to hold her securely against him. Her knees trembled a little. He had that effect on her, which she'd decided he shouldn't. She tried to ignore the fluttering in the pit of her stomach as her fingers touched his collar. A few short hours ago she'd been in his arms, and he'd been kissing her, which she had enjoyed. Very much.

Dancing together was almost as exciting.

The song ended too soon, but Matt released her slowly. The band quickly moved into a rendition of "Tequila Sunrise," and Matt pulled Stella into his arms once again.

"Do you go out dancing every Saturday night?" she teased.

"Not on your life. I'm a hardworking cowboy."

Stella laughed. "This town is filled with hardworking cowboys on Saturday nights."

"And how do you know that?"

"I hear all about it on Monday morning, remember?"

"Do you like country-western music?"

"I'm beginning to."

His arms tightened around her as he swung her gently to the music. "That's good, because I'm beginning to like dancing."

THE RIDE HOME LASTED only minutes. *Much too short,* Stella decided, wishing the restaurant had been at the other end of the state. Matt was the perfect gentleman, the perfect companion, and they had danced and laughed and visited with people they knew. In other words, they had made an evening of it. Now it was after eleven, and it was over.

She shivered when he helped her out of the truck. The black sky held no trace of snow, the stars shone brightly in the clear night air. Matt helped her over the slippery part of the sidewalk, but remained silent as he walked her to the door.

Stella spoke into the suddenly awkward silence. "Would you like to come in for coffee?"

He hesitated, then took the keys from her gloved hand. "All right."

Now what? She switched on the lights and unbuttoned her coat, then turned up the thermostat. Matt shrugged his heavy jacket off and laid it over the back of the little couch. Stella hung her own in the closet before returning to the middle of the room. She looked at him, big and sturdy, standing there in the bright light. Her room looked small and slightly shabby and very feminine. It practically screamed "Single Woman" from the very walls.

Matt looked down at the pile of magazines on the kitchen table. "You read all these?"

"I subscribe to them. The customers love to have something to read while they're waiting for their hair to be done." She went over to the coffee maker and filled the carafe with water. "Is decaf okay?"

"Either. It doesn't matter."

Stella selected the can of decaffeinated coffee from the refrigerator and put two scoops into the basket. "Decaf it is."

Matt paced around the room, almost as if he couldn't wait to leave. Stella cleared the table, putting the magazines on the floor beside the love seat, and set out two cups, saucers and spoons. "It's a small place," she said, "but it's perfect for me so far."

"Convenient," he said.

"It came with the shop," she explained, moving to the coffeepot. "I was lucky."

Lucky. That word again. Only Matt didn't feel lucky anymore. This whole thing had gone too far. He'd actually enjoyed himself tonight, which was the biggest surprise of all. And luck didn't have anything to do with it. Or did it? Maybe he should cut his losses and get out while he could.

But he made the mistake of looking at her, all soft and luscious in that pink color. Her hair was golden in the light, and her eyes smiled at him after she poured the coffee into the cups.

He ignored it, instead stepping closer to finger a lock of those gold curls. She waited, looking up at him as if she was holding her breath. That just about did him in. His hand snaked up to the nape of her neck and pulled her close to him. Her neck tilted and he brought his lips down to hers—gently at first, to see if she was willing.

She didn't protest, just gave a smothered gasp that was no clue. But those little hands of hers twined around his neck and she stood on tiptoe to meet his mouth with her own.

She was so sweet, Matt thought he'd die from wanting her.

He kissed her for long moments, exploring with his tongue, letting it mate and twine with hers as he pressed her body against his, needing to feel her soft warmth. Her breasts grazed his chest, and his body responded.

Matt lifted his head and released her mouth, but trailed kisses down her cheek and along her neck to where the pink material bordered all that soft skin. His hand swept along her shoulder and lower, to caress the soft fullness of her breast before sliding back up to her neck.

He found her mouth again and took it willingly, harder now, with every intention of making love to this woman right here on the floor if he had to.

But he came to his senses and lifted his head.

This was no ordinary woman. And no cheap roll in the hay.

This was the stupidest thing he'd ever done. "Sorry, Stella." He moved away and grabbed his hat and coat from the sofa, then clamped his hat on his head and moved toward the door. "I'll have to take a rain check on the coffee."

Matt strode out quickly, shutting the door harder than he intended, and got into the truck. It still had a bit of warmth to it, from the trip from the restaurant. Damn the Cupid's Bag Raffle anyway! Foolish thing got him into all of this in the first place. He knew better than to get involved. It had been one hell of a long time since he'd had a woman. The ones since Page had been impersonal, one-night stands with little involvement.

This wasn't the same thing at all.

He put the truck into gear and headed down the silent street into the darkness of the prairie. No, he'd gotten himself into it when he'd played rescuer and stopped for the stranded tourist with the Illinois plates. He'd looked into that face and taken three steps back.

Well, he'd avoided her since then. He ought to be able to keep doing it. He stepped harder on the gas pedal. The boys were spending the night with Ruth; there was nothing to rush home for. He could have a drink and listen to a little music in the new place right outside of town.

No. Matt simply wanted to go home to the safety of the Double Bar M. And as soon as possible. His bachelor quarters would never look so good—or so safe.

Chapter Three

"HONEY, PUT A LITTLE more curl on the top this time," Mary Lou Crawford insisted.

"Are you sure, Mary? Last time you were nervous about the extra height."

"I'm sure. I'm getting braver in my old age."

"Well, I guess you are." Stella smiled and reached for the proper-size roller. Mary was almost one hundred years old, and Pine View Manor's most revered resident. She also insisted on coming to the shop every Monday morning to have her hair done. Nothing fancy, just the "basic set" many of the nursing home's residents preferred.

"Heard you had a date Saturday night, honey." The old woman chuckled at Stella's surprised expression and met her gaze in the mirror with wide-eyed innocence. "You can't keep anything a secret in Valentine, you know. Not like in that Chicago you're used to."

"Stella, that right? You had a date?" another woman called from her perch near the hair dryers. Jassy was in the middle of a tint.

"Well, that's right. Sort of." *Only because the man won a free pair of dinners right in front of my eyes.*

"Sort of? What does that mean—you paid your own way?"

"No, he won the dinners in the Valentine raffle."

"Just like he won the make-over," Mary Lou teased. "Tell Jassy who you went out with, honey, or she'll never let you hear the end of it."

Stella just chuckled and kept rolling the thin gray hair onto the rollers. "Nobody special."

"Hah!" Mary Lou snorted. "Just that handsome cowboy you moon over whenever he walks by the window here."

"I do not 'moon' over anyone. Put your head down so I can get the back."

"You think that's gonna keep me quiet? No, no. Sometimes he comes into town on Monday mornings to do his errands, and don't you think I haven't noticed you watch him walk past this here window."

Jassy, another energetic resident of Pine View, stepped over to Stella to stand near Mary. "Don't pay any attention to this old woman's teasing, now." Then, unable to stand the suspense, she whispered, "*What* cowboy, Stella?"

But Mary supplied the answer, in a somewhat muffled voice. "Matthew McNeil, that's who."

"The one whose wife ran off a few years back?"

"That's the one, all right."

"She was a spoiled thing, that's for sure. Who would have thought a nice ranch girl like that would get such ideas? And to leave those little ones—"

Mary's muffled protest was indignant. "They haven't suffered any, not that I can see—"

"What can you see from Pine View—"

Stella tried to head them off. They loved to argue, and had known each other for years, but hearing them discussing Matt was more than she could take. "Did I hear your timer go off, Jassy?"

"No."

Stella sighed. Loudly.

"Matt's grandmother lived at Pine View till she died three months ago. Wasn't right in her head, poor thing, but he came with those kids to visit anyway, until it just seemed pointless and the doctor told him not to put himself through it anymore. Nice little boys. Always said hello. Seemed happy enough.''

"Well," Jassy said, needing to interject some pearl of wisdom. "You just never know what's going on under the surface, do you?"

A brief moment of silence answered her, as Mary contemplated such a statement.

"All right, Mary. You come with me." Stella helped her over to the row of hair dryers, settled her in the middle seat, and adjusted the dryer above her head. "Ten minutes," she told her. The timer rang for Jassy, and she obediently went to the chair and let Stella comb the gooey dye through her hair. "Sit there for five minutes, then we'll rinse."

"Matt McNeil. Now, there's a handsome man."

"Want some coffee while you wait?"

"No, thank you, dear. I'll float away if I have another cup."

Stella poured herself a cup of coffee she really didn't want and walked over to the window to see what was going on in Valentine at ten-thirty Monday morning.

Not much.

If anyone else asked her about Saturday night, she'd either scream or lie. Screaming would not be good for business. Besides, she didn't think anyone in Nebraska screamed about anything. They didn't lie much, either.

Saturday night was in the past. What was the phrase? Better to have loved and lost than never to have loved at all. Well, she hadn't even approached the "loved" part— not that she was the kind of woman who loved on the first date, mind you—but she'd been royally abandoned, just the same. One kiss and the guy ran to his truck and hot-footed it out of town in record time. She wondered if he'd gotten a speeding ticket on the way out.

So much for romance.

The whole thing had been a mistake. Her romantic fantasy revolving around Matt McNeil was foolish. She had to give it up.

She returned to the chair and told Jassy to come to the sink. Once the woman was settled, Stella completed the automatic process of washing the dye from Jassy's chin-length hair and hoped the subject of Matt McNeil was closed forever.

She was wrong. Several customers mentioned seeing Stella and the handsome rancher dancing together Saturday night.

Stella tried to remain patient, and didn't have much to say on the subject if she could avoid it. But the talk of Valentine's Day in Valentine continued to fill the beauty shop.

"The candidates for king and queen will be in Wednesday's paper," Ethel Johnson informed Stella. "My twins are hoping one of them will be picked."

"I'll keep my fingers crossed for them," Stella promised.

"They'll both want new perms before the coronation, I suppose."

Martha Selle moved over to the coffee table to pick out another magazine. The pink plastic cape billowed around her tiny body as she searched for something else to read while she waited for her permanent to take effect. "Too bad some silly man won the make-over, isn't it?"

Some silly man. Stella smiled at the description. She liked it.

Ethel sniffed. "The same *silly man* took Stella out to dinner Saturday night."

Martha's gaze darted to Stella. "He looked good, I suppose?"

Oh, he looked good all right. Felt good, too. Damn him. "I just gave him a haircut, that's all."

Another elderly woman, waiting in a chair by the door, joined in the conversation. "I wouldn't mind giving McNeil a haircut—or anything else, for that matter."

Martha sniffed. "You're eighty-one years old, Auntie Beth. You shouldn't be giving anybody anything."

The women all laughed and Stella attempted to change the topic of conversation again. "Did anybody I know win anything in the raffle today?"

It didn't work. "How about one of these handsome young cowboys doin' something for me?"

"Go read your magazines, Mary Beth."

"There's a lot in here," she sniffed, pointing to the cover of *Glamour.* "Like how to heat up your romance on Valentine's Day. Here's another one—'Add Sex and Sizzle to Your Boring Love Life.'"

"Sex and sizzle! Lord help us!"

Stella agreed with that. She'd take some help from wherever she could, right now. These ladies weren't shy about discussing anything, and she didn't want to be the topic—no matter how much she liked them.

"Well, I agree with Edith Runke."

Stella reached for a small curler, then looked at it and tossed it back into the bin before selecting a larger size. "About what?"

"It's a shame a sweet thing like you isn't married, that's what I say." She leaned forward and called to Mary Beth, "Anything in those magazines on how to get married by Valentine's Day?"

"I'll look," she hollered back. "Give me a minute."

Stella sighed. They were hopeless romantics, and she herself was the worst of all. Past tense, though. She'd learned her lesson Saturday night, when the man of her dreams—the shining hero of Route 83—kissed her and ran out the door without saying a word.

Some hero.

Some romance.

Stella glanced over to the window and wondered what she'd do if Matt walked in right now. Although a big blue pickup truck lumbered past the shop, Stella couldn't tell if Matt was behind the wheel. There was a bunch of blue pickups around town, and she didn't know a Ford from a Chevy.

ON TUESDAY, Myrna Bennett announced she'd won a gift certificate to Flower Land. Stella heard Myrna planned to order herself a nice centerpiece for Valentine's Day. Maybe live it up a little and have the thing delivered right to her door.

Wednesday, the weekly edition of the Valentine newspaper came out, with the pictures of the high-school seniors who were nominated for king and queen on the front page. The mothers were understandably proud of their sons and daughters, as the coronation at the high school was one of the town's most popular events. Coronations at Pine View Manor and the Senior Center also provided much of the conversation at the shop.

The phone rang almost all the time. And the Cupid's Bag Raffle continued as the most popular topic of conversation. Jan Kozwolski and Betty Durwin each were the lucky winners of a salad spinner from the hardware store. Both already owned salad spinners, but decided they'd make good shower gifts for any upcoming weddings. There were always upcoming weddings.

Betty eyed Stella when she said that.

"Don't look at me," Stella warned. "I can see that gleam in your eyes."

"Haven't you read that article yet?"

"Which one?"

"'Fourteen Ways to Get Your Man.'"

"I think I must have missed that one, Betty." She reached for the stand of curlers. "I'll bet the man winning a beauty make-over wasn't mentioned, was it?"

Betty chuckled. "'First rule: You have to be interested in what he's interested in.'"

Stella sighed. "That's out. I don't know anything about cows. Or ranching."

"You can learn. There are library books, and I have three years of back issues of *Farm Wife*."

Intrigued, Stella grabbed the misting bottle and dampened Betty's hair. All this talk about Valentine's Day slowed her down. "I could borrow them?"

"Sure, honey. I'll have Sam drop 'em by this afternoon." Betty opened the magazine back to the proper page. "And you have to show him you're interested. Be aggressive."

"I'm just not the aggressive type." Which was really a shame, because it might help.

"Well, let's skip it then." Betty read silently for a moment. "How about this one—'Pamper him with a home-cooked meal.'"

"I'm below average at cooking, and inviting someone to dinner goes right into that 'aggressive' category, doesn't it?"

"Well, I suppose.... Here, number nine. 'Establish eye contact.' That's a good one."

"If I ever see him again."

"Oh, you'll see him, all right. It's a small town, you know. You'll have lots of time to establish eye contact."

Stella remembered Matt didn't have any trouble with eye contact—it was the body contact that terrified him. Or maybe it was simply that Stella Hathaway didn't turn him on. Stella sighed. Just her rotten luck—to believe in love at first sight and happy endings.

"Surely you must have had a boyfriend in Chicago?"

Stella tried not to wince. "Yes."

"And he let you get away?"

"Well, he didn't want to get married. So I kind of let myself get away. I think he was relieved."

"Oh, I can't believe that, honey. He's gonna regret it someday, especially when you're happily married to some fine Nebraska man."

"You all want to see me married, don't you?"

"Sure—then I can get rid of one of my salad spinners."

THURSDAY CAME AND WENT, leaving Stella exhausted from the constant Valentine-celebration conversation. Each customer had to ask how Matt's make-over went, having seen the picture of the two of them on the front page of the Valentine newspaper the day before.

Stella already knew they made a good-looking couple. "But," she told her customers, "I think that man has too much ranching to do to think about going out with the new girl in town."

Disappointingly, the women agreed.

Judie, one of the county clerks, waved a magazine. "There's an article here about how to talk to a quiet man. Have you read it?"

Stella thought she had. "'Understanding the Strong, Silent Type'?"

"That's the one."

Cherry, one of Ethel Johnson's twins, preened in front of the mirror at her new curly image. "I don't know what you see in the silent type," she drawled. "I like a guy who talks."

"You have a point."

Judie ignored the teenager's comment. "You shouldn't be alone on Valentine's Day, Stella."

"I don't mind being alone," she fibbed. "I'm going to the coronation next Friday, and I may even go over to Edith and Harve's afterward. Their daughter might be queen, you know."

"That's not very romantic—hanging out with the married people," Judie sniffed. "You ought to be living it up. You're only young once."

"And you're only married once," Stella countered, grabbing the curling iron from its holder. "I'm fussy, I guess. I'll find the right man one of these days, and when I do you'll all be the first to know."

FRIDAY AFTERNOON, Edith Runke arrived for her standard wash and comb-out. By this time Stella was bordering on exhaustion. Her feet ached. Her hands ached. Her head ached.

Edith looked as if she knew a delicious secret. "Want to hear the latest on the raffle?"

"Did you win a salad spinner, too?"

"No, but—"

"Edith, I don't know if I can hear another word about Valentine's Day. I think I've overdosed on the whole holiday."

With that, she put the shampoo cape around her favorite client and corralled her into the chair in front of the sink. Stella lathered and rinsed and conditioned and rinsed until she was satisfied. "There, Edith. You can sit up and come with me, but not one more word about you-know-what."

"You're a stubborn little thing," her friend grumbled. "Here I came over here to tell you—"

"You came over to look beautiful," Stella interjected. She squeezed the ends of Edith's hair with a towel, then picked up a comb and started to work out the tangles.

"I came to warn you—"

The bell jangled, and Stella turned around to see who it was. She didn't have an appointment scheduled for another forty-five minutes and intended to use that time to grab a sandwich and a diet cola.

Matt McNeil stood inside the door, his two boys close behind him. He removed his hat and nodded, his eyes dark and unreadable. "Stella," was his greeting.

"Hello, Matt."

She waited, her comb still in her hand, wondering what on earth he wanted. Surely he would tell her.

"Hello, Edith," he said. "We keep running into each other."

"Hello again, Matt. You're a busy man these days."

He nodded, then looked at Stella again, as if waiting for her to say something.

And she looked back. "Do the boys need haircuts?"

"Uh, no."

Obviously this called for the direct approach. "Excuse me for a minute, will you, Edith?"

"Oh, sure. But I get to sit here and watch."

Stella walked over to the children. "Hi—you guys want a soda pop?"

They nodded shyly and she put down her comb and pulled some change out of her pocket before looking over to Matt. "It's okay, isn't it?"

"Sure."

She barely heard the children's shy thanks as they hurried over to the soda-pop machine. She could smell the fresh air from Matt's jacket and wished she could unbutton the jacket and slip her face inside and inhale the scent of him. *Ridiculous,* she decided. Too many fumes in this place have made me crazy.

Stella tried again. "Nice picture in the paper. I hope you weren't teased too much."

"Not really. It's a good haircut."

She waited. Was he going to ask her out again? She'd be damned if she was going to mention Saturday night first.

"What do you want me to do with the calf?"

"The calf?"

"Yeah. What do you want me to do with it?" His voice was patient, as if he were speaking to one of the boys.

She had no idea what he was talking about. "Well, you're the rancher. What do you want to do with it?"

Edith's chuckles didn't help the situation. Hattie turned off her hair dryer in order to listen.

"It's your calf, Stella. You tell me."

"*My* calf?"

He frowned. "I thought you'd have heard by now. You won a calf in the raffle." At her blank expression, he prompted, "A calf from the Double Bar M."

"Your calf?"

He nodded. "I'll take it to a butcher for you, if you'd like."

"No, not yet." She tried to think quickly, but taking a step backward didn't help. She still stood in the same space as Matt, still looked up into those dark eyes.

"Well, you just let me know what you want me to do with it, and I'll...do it."

Stella was suddenly aware that everyone was listening. Except the boys, who were back at the counter stuffing the box with ballots again. "Okay. Could I see it?"

"It's out at the ranch, Stella."

"Well, that's not impossible." He made it sound like the calf was on Mars, for heaven's sake. "If you don't mind, I'll come out sometime this weekend and see it."

Matt looked like he minded very much. "Not in that car of yours, you won't." He slapped his hat on his head and glared down at her. "I'll come in to pick you up tomorrow afternoon."

"When?"

He paused, then said, "One o'clock."

"Okay." She'd have to shuffle some appointments, but she wouldn't miss a trip to the Double Bar M for anything in the world. Matt left, signaling to the boys. They obeyed quickly but still held their cans of soda pop. The little one waved to Stella and she waved back before picking up the comb and returning to Edith.

"Interesting," her friend commented.

The dryer was turned back on.

Stella misted Edith's drying hair with water. "What am I supposed to do with a calf?"

"Feed it. Sell it."

"You mean, just let Matt deal with it."

"Why not? Or— Never mind."

"Or what?"

"You can keep it."

Hattie struggled up from the chair. "I'm dry."

"Have some coffee, and I'll be with you as soon as I finish Edith, okay?"

"No problem." She poured coffee and wandered over to sit in the empty chair beside Edith. "If you keep it, you can visit it."

Edith and Stella turned toward Hattie and assessed her statement. "True," Edith said.

"I don't want him to think I'm chasing him," Stella said. "And if I keep the calf, that's exactly what he's going to think."

"You read up on calves," Hattie suggested. "You have enough issues of *Farm Wife* around here."

"Impress him with your knowledge," Edith added. "Go out to the ranch, name the calf, pay its feed bill until spring."

"Well, I would like the calf. I've never owned any...livestock before."

"Maybe this is your lucky day."

"Maybe you're right." Stella turned on the blow dryer and worked Edith's hair into a sleek pageboy. She might not have a social life, but at least she owned the beginnings of her own herd.

MATT NEVER FIGURED she'd want to see the damn animal for herself. He should have known, of course. *City women!* He should have backed out of that beauty shop, but she'd looked up at him with those big blue eyes and he'd been unable to speak a word to keep her from coming out to the ranch today.

Hell, he'd even offered to pick her up. He turned the truck onto her street and pulled alongside the curb behind the shop. He hoped she'd wear something practical, but he really didn't hope for anything much. His ranch was off-limits as far as females were concerned; he'd been up since five doing chores and trying to clean up the place.

He and the boys usually managed just fine by themselves. But what could happen? He could certainly resist one little female, no matter how beautiful. Put Stella in an old pair of jeans, take off her makeup, and she'd look just like anyone else.

Stella must have been watching for him, because she opened the door before he could turn off the truck engine. She wore jeans. Snug jeans, with a few years' wear in them already. A sky-blue parka covered the top half of her, and a pink-and-yellow striped scarf hung from her neck and draped over that beautiful chest. Which, for his own physical and mental well-being, he should be glad he couldn't see the shape of.

Matt leaned over and yanked the door handle, then gave the door a shove. She could get into the truck by herself, he figured. After all, this was a workday, not a date to the prom.

"Hi." Stella climbed into the truck, bringing a blast of frigid air with her. She shot Matt a dazzling smile, dumped a large yellow tote bag on the seat, then struggled to close the door.

He'd been wrong. She'd never look just like everyone else.

"Here," he growled, feeling a little guilty as he started to reach in front of her for the handle of the door.

The solid *thunk* of the door stopped him. Matt pulled back, but not before his arm grazed the ends of the fuzzy scarf. Stella pulled off her blue mittens, settled back against the seat and reached for the seat belt. Then she flashed Matt another disarming smile and said, "I know this is a lot of trouble, Matt, but I really appreciate it."

He grunted something appropriate and put the car in gear.

"I never dreamed I'd win a little calf," she continued. "What color is it?"

"Black. And it's not exactly a baby." He negotiated a U-turn in the middle of the street, then headed out of town.

"How big is it?"

"A few hundred pounds."

"I'm not sure what I should do with it. Is a little calf worth a lot of money?"

"In some places, I guess. You can sell it back to me, if you'd like. We can figure something out." *If I survive this afternoon.* Matt glanced over to her feet tucked neatly under the heating vent. "New boots?"

Stella looked down and then smiled. "They told me they were work boots."

"You planning to work?"

She shrugged. "I didn't know what you'd expect me to do."

"You mean you bought boots just for today?"

"Sure. I've never been on a ranch before and I wanted to wear exactly the right shoes."

"Those should do it."

"Great." She patted the tote bag. "I brought some of Hattie Gambel's homemade bread for you, and Ruth sent some currant jelly to go with it."

Very domestic. Matt worried. *New boots and homemade food, gifts from a blond bombshell with big blue eyes.* Was there any place in Nebraska where a cowboy could be safe? His gloved hands gripped the steering wheel tighter as he guided the truck onto the highway and headed for the Double Bar M. He'd introduce Stella to the calf, explain the facts of life—cattle-style—and take her home again.

She'd never have time to unwrap the bread.

HE DIDN'T BARGAIN ON the boys. Two small faces peeked through the front windows, and Matt hoped they'd finished their share of Saturday-morning chores. He'd have to offer his guest a cup of coffee, he supposed. He'd have to be polite and show her around.

He wasn't fighting that much, actually. Stella Hathaway was beautiful and sweet and genuinely interested, but Matt knew he wasn't ready for another woman to move out here. He'd risked that once—and he'd been left with more sleepless nights than any man deserved, and two heartbroken little boys who only slept after they'd cried themselves to sleep, calling "Mommy!" into the darkness.

The boys who opened the front door of the white clapboard farmhouse didn't look heartbroken. Their dark eyes shone with excitement as Stella opened the door of the truck and put her mittens on. She looked around at the array of outbuildings behind the old barn, then back toward the house. "I didn't know you had such a big place."

Jason peeked out from behind his brother and struggled to see. His voice carried in the clear air. "Dad, you brought the pretty lady?"

Matt hurried to explain. "They've called you 'the pretty lady' ever since the afternoon they stuffed the Valentine box."

Stella laughed, and the sound lightened Matt's mood. She grabbed her bag and jumped down onto the packed snow of the driveway.

"Careful," he warned.

"I'm okay." She slammed the door shut and Matt quickly strode toward her.

"Hold on to me. It's slippery."

"I have my new boots, remember?" Her laughing eyes smiled up into his face, and Matt wished he could take her into his arms and kiss those soft lips. He knew they'd be warm in the cold air. He remembered all too well how sweet she'd tasted.

Matt blinked, and Stella turned away from him to wave to the boys. Then Matt ushered her up the steps and through the front door. Matt wiped his boots on the thick rug protecting the beige carpet, and Stella imitated him. "Thank you for inviting me today," she told the boys as she shrugged off her jacket. "I've really been looking forward to it."

Matt took her scarf and jacket. "Go stand by the stove and warm up."

The boys tugged Stella across the room to where a woodburning stove blasted heat. Careful not to get too close, Stella warmed her hands above its surface. Jason sidled up against her. "I think it's really neat you won a calf."

"Me, too. I've never owned a calf before, but I had a cat once." She looked around the room at cream-colored walls covered with family pictures. Three windows faced south, toward the driveway. Behind her was an oak banister and carpeted staircase.

"We have lots of cats," Matthew offered, standing close to Stella's left side. "Out in the barn."

"In the winter?"

"They stay warm in the hay," his father explained. He tossed the coats over the back of a chair, but didn't cross the room to stand with them.

"You can have a kitten if you want. We should get some new ones in the spring, huh, Dad?"

"Yeah." Matt ran a hand through his hair. "There's never any shortage of kittens around here."

Stella backed away from the stove and smiled at the handsome rancher. He wore one of those blue-checked flannel shirts that looked so good on him, and slim jeans. "I think I'd better get used to having a calf."

Jason reluctantly agreed. "But if you ever want a kitten, you know who to call."

Stella promised.

"Go get some work clothes on," Matt told his sons. They scurried up the stairs to change, and Matt shoved his hands in his pockets and turned to Stella. "I can take you out to the barn now, or we can have some coffee first."

"Coffee sounds good." She retrieved her tote bag from the floor and followed Matt through a wide hallway where a large kitchen stretched along the back of the house. "I like your home."

"It wasn't very big when we—I bought it. I added on the kitchen and a back porch," Matt said. He pointed to another hallway. "There's a bathroom, a bedroom, and my office through there, and the boys' bedrooms and bathroom upstairs."

The kitchen was blue and white, with light-oak cupboards. Utensils hung neatly from hooks on white peg board, and the wood-grained Formica countertop gleamed. Strictly utilitarian and very practical, there were no frills—like the man who owned the house.

Matt gestured toward the round oak table. "Have a seat."

Stella sat down in a press-back chair she guessed was a hundred years old. She would have liked to sit in that kitchen for a long, long time, just looking at Matt's strong hands pour coffee into white mugs.

"You take it black, don't you?"

"Please, but you don't have to wait on me."

He set the mug in front of her. "Sure, I do. You're a guest."

She rummaged through the bag and handed the bread and the jar of jelly to Matt. "You don't have to use them now. You can save them for another time."

"Now's fine." Within minutes he set the table with plates, flatware, napkins and butter, and pried the lid off the jelly jar. By the time the boys ran into the kitchen, Matt had sliced the bread and poured two glasses of milk.

"Don't you want to see your calf?" Jason asked. "We picked out the best one for you."

"Let Miss Hathaway warm up first," his father warned.

"Tell me about him while I drink my coffee. Why is he the best one?"

The children sat down beside her and rested their elbows on the table. Jason answered, "Dad said so."

Stella liked the sound of that. She looked at Matt, who shrugged. "There were several candidates. These are yearlings who'll be heading for auction."

Stella nodded as if she knew what he was talking about.

Matthew spread a thick layer of red jelly on a slice of bread. "I like your yellow hair."

"Thank you."

"It's curlier than mine," he said with a sigh, then took a mouthful of bread. "Why do you have such long fingernails?"

Stella looked at her hands. Her pink manicured nails must look like fangs to a child. She held them out for his inspection. "I guess I just like them that way."

"Cool," Jason said. The elder Matt just leaned back against the counter as if he had all the time in the world.

"Where'd you live before you moved here?"

Stella helped herself to a piece of bread. "Oak Park. It's near Chicago."

"Dad's been to Chicago, haven't you, Dad?"

Matt nodded. "Yep." He joined them at the table. The boys chattered on about the ranch, the cats, the hog they'd butchered last October, and how they hoped they'd win one of the bikes from the raffle. Stella listened to every word. She hadn't been around little boys since she'd moved to Valentine. She resisted the urge to smooth back a lock of Jason's hair from his forehead, for fear of embarrassing the boy.

Then Stella looked at Matt. He always looked so calm, so in control of himself and his world. And it was his world, all right. This ranch was obviously his refuge, his pride, and the center of his life. Stella envied his solid connection to the work he did and where he lived. It was all part of him, and she felt a stab of pity for the woman—his former wife—who had given all this up for a man in Dallas.

Chapter Four

"ALL SET FOR the grand tour?"

"I think so." Wrapped from head to toe in Matt's jacket, Jason's thick brown scarf, and Matthew's leather work gloves, Stella decided she was ready for anything the Nebraska winter could blow her way. They'd insisted on loaning her clothes that wouldn't mind the sharp cold or the dusty barn. Jason handed her an extra scarf to wrap around her neck and pull over her face in case the bitter February wind was too much for her. "I could probably walk to South Dakota and never feel cold."

"Can we show her Midnight first?"

Midnight was obviously the calf. Stella looked hopefully toward Matt. "Not yet," he answered. "We'll save the best for last. And we're not going to be outdoors for long."

Stella felt quite overwhelmed. "You don't have to pamper me," she protested. "I'm from Chicago, 'the windy city.' It's not exactly Miami Beach, you know."

Matthew disagreed. "But you're a gir—"

"Guest," his father corrected. "We try not to let our guests get frostbite."

"So they'll come back," Jason added. "You'll come back and take care of your calf, right?"

She looked down at the little face and the hopeful expression in those brown eyes and knew she had no answer to that question. Nothing truthful, that is. "Well, sure."

They spent the next hour touring the buildings within walking distance. Matt showed her the feedlots; in one lot his first calf heifers had begun calving. Stella could have stood and watched the animals all afternoon, but all three McNeil men were anxious to keep moving. She asked many questions and Matt patiently answered every one. He explained how computerized methods helped him feed his cattle, although most of his cow herd and herd bulls were in pastures on the north side of the valley. He proudly told Stella how he'd bought a neighboring ranch as an investment for the boys; hired help ran it for him, and he planned to combine cattle operations in the coming year.

She'd never heard him talk so much. He sent the boys to finish their chores and took Stella to the building he called the West Barn, an old-fashioned barn that looked as if it had stood in the same place since the pioneers built it. Stella sneezed.

"We don't have to stay in here long," Matt said, guiding her down the wide aisle that ran between the stalls. "Here he is." He ushered Stella toward a stall on the left side. Stella looked through the worn wooden bars at a black calf.

"Why did you donate him to the raffle?"

"This guy was an orphan. I put him in the barn when we had that freak snowstorm in October."

"But why don't you keep him?"

"He's become something of a pet around here, but he's expensive to feed. Most of the cattle I raise have gone to the auction barn—to the cattle feeders in Omaha or Des Moines—by now. The practical solution was to donate him to the raffle and let someone else take care of him for the winter."

Stella hadn't figured out how she was going to do that. "I could pay his feed bill."

He looked surprised as he gazed down at her. "You don't look like much of a rancher."

Stella spread out her arms and twirled around, showing off Matt's old jacket, which, despite being much too big for her, somehow felt perfect enfolding her body. "I thought I looked pretty good."

"Oh, you always look good," he growled.

"I get the feeling that's a problem for you."

He grimaced. "Let's just say beautiful women don't belong on ranches."

"Why would you say something like that?"

"Personal experience."

"Which is why you raced out of my apartment last week."

Matt reached over and touched her shoulder, urging her to take a step forward. He then tipped Jason's knit ski-cap off her head and let the gold curls spill down to her shoulders. "I ran because I'm a coward."

"I didn't know I was that scary."

"Oh, you are, lady." He stepped closer and lifted her chin with one gloved finger. "And you damn well know it, too."

His lips touched hers in an undemanding whisper of a kiss, a brief second of warmth. Stella didn't close her eyes. She watched his mouth as he moved away from her and then she reached up to his lapel. "Not so fast, cowboy," she murmured, tugging him toward her. "You owe me one for Saturday night."

His chuckle lasted only a brief second before his lips claimed hers once more. She stood on tiptoe to reach him and wondered if the smell of the hay had turned her into a shameless hussy of a woman—a woman who grabbed cowboys in barns and insisted on a decent kiss. Or an indecent kiss, depending on one's point of view.

Matt dropped his gloves at Stella's feet. Then his roughened hand caressed her face and combed through her curls to the sensitive nape of her neck. His tongue eased her lips apart and delved inside. She met him with a need of her own, pressing her body against the bulky warmth of his. Surprising, she mused briefly, how they fit together. Surprising how the passion boiled to the surface whenever they touched.

Stella knew he was the man for her. She'd known since he'd rescued her last summer. But she hadn't expected the spontaneous physical attraction whenever they touched, and she wondered if Matt also felt that shock of connection, the feeling of having found the person you didn't know you'd been looking for.

When the kiss ended, she stayed in his arms and rested her cheek against the wool lapel of his jacket, until the boys' voices intruded.

Stella stepped quickly away from Matt's warmth and she looked up at him, hoping he'd smile down at her. But he turned quickly and bent to pick up the gloves he'd dropped.

Jason raced up to Stella and tugged on her coat. "Do you like him?"

Stella looked at Matt, whose gaze was steady and unreadable. "Oh, yes," she said, turning back to the calf. "Very much."

Matthew stood on the boards and hung over the gate to look at the large calf. "What are you gonna do with him?"

"I don't know. Maybe you guys can give me some suggestions."

"I think you should keep him," the child said. "You can visit him anytime you want to."

"Why, thank you, Jason."

Matthew nodded. "Yeah, that's a good idea."

"And you can visit me in town anytime you want to." She couldn't help liking the boys. They were straightforward and handsome, and full of energy. And they looked so much like Matt.

"I don't think I'd better get my hair cut there, do you?"

She looked into Matthew's worried expression. "You don't have to—I mean, you won't hurt my feelings if you just stop in and say hi."

Matt put a hand on each boy's shoulder. "Okay, you guys. Time to go back to the house and clean up." They started to protest and he cut them off. "You can set the table for four, if Stella will agree to join us for dinner tonight." He smiled at her. "It's nothing fancy. Just hamburgers and French fries."

"I'd love to."

"Good, it's settled. You two need showers. We'll be in later—we have some cattle business to discuss."

The boys reluctantly left the barn, closing the large door behind them and leaving only a dust-covered light bulb for light.

Matt stepped close to Stella and wrapped his arms around her. "Now, what were you saying I owed you from last Saturday night?"

She hooked her hands around his neck, but the thick collar prevented her from touching his skin. It was a rather bulky caress. "Conversation?"

"Uh-uh."

"Coffee?"

"Nope." His lips came closer and brushed against hers in a feathery touch that sent chills down her spine.

"I give up," she whispered against his mouth.

"That's my line." He took her mouth again, and Stella loved the feel of his lips against hers. She'd never known such a kiss, and for a few seconds she forgot everything around her—the animals, the barn, the dim light. It was different from that afternoon in the beauty shop—that was a kiss of sudden ardor, and angry surprise. And the night after dinner had held frustration and promise. Now there was only the stuffy intimacy of a quiet barn and the exciting passion that didn't have to be reined in or run away from.

Stella leaned against the boards and Matt surrounded her with his arms and his large, rangy body. She felt a strand of hair catch on the rough wood and groaned, and Matt stopped kissing her. He didn't move away from her, though. "What?" he asked.

She reached up to pull her hair away from the splinter.

"Let me." His fingers quickly released the curl, and Stella shifted away from the board.

"Thanks."

"This isn't going to work."

"Kissing in the barn or being with me?"

"Neither one, I guess." In one easy motion he swept her into his arms as she clung to his neck. He kicked open a door and entered a room filled with an assortment of riding gear and medicine bottles. "Are you afraid of heights?"

"No."

"Want to see the haymow?"

"Is that a standard line in Nebraska?"

"Sure is." His grin was wicked.

"I've never been in a haymow before," she teased.

"Even better." He put her down in front of a ladder. "This way to my private office."

She made the easy climb up the ladder and sneezed once again when she inhaled the fresh smell of alfalfa hay as she tumbled onto the wooden floor of the hayloft. Light filtered through the narrow cracks in the roof, but the air was warmer than she expected it to be. She scrambled to her feet and brushed the bits of straw from her pants. "Nice office you have here, Mr. McNeil."

He joined her. "Glad you could make it." He touched her face, the palm of his hand warm against her cheek.

"Me, too."

She hoped he'd kiss her but he didn't, instead looking at her as if he expected her to disappear. "You don't belong here."

"Then where *do* I belong?" she whispered.

"In Chicago," he muttered.

"No. In Valentine."

"Why Valentine?"

Could she admit she'd fallen in love with a stranger last summer? The same stranger who was kissing her in his barn? "It felt right."

"That's not much of a reason." He reached for her jacket and began to slip the thick barrel-shaped buttons out of their leather loops, his long fingers sending frissons of sensation into Stella's skin.

She struggled to ignore the feelings he aroused. "Haven't you ever done anything just because it felt right?"

"No, but I think I'm about to." He opened her jacket, his hands revealing the pink angora sweater she wore underneath.

Stella knew she should protest, but a languorous heat swept over her as his hands gently cupped her breasts. His lips claimed hers and they clung to each other in the murky afternoon light. Her jacket dropped to the floor, but Stella didn't feel the least bit cold. She helped him shrug off his thick jacket and reached for him, silently cursing the heavy sweatshirt that covered his chest.

"We're wearing too many clothes to make out in the hay," Matt said, a chuckle in his voice.

"You're pretty experienced at this, aren't you?" she teased, watching him as he pulled the red sweatshirt over his head and tossed it aside.

"You expect me to answer a question like that?"

She caressed the soft flannel that covered his chest. "Yes."

"Spending an afternoon in the haymow in February is a first for me. I usually have more sense."

"It must get hot up here in the summertime."

"I can't remember. It's been too many years." His fingers tripped lightly over her shoulder. "I don't bring women out to the ranch."

"You brought me," she whispered. "Why?"

His hand slid under her sweater and his fingers found her breast and encircled one nipple, stroking the soft nub. "To do this."

Stella closed her eyes for a brief moment. His touch sent heated tremors through her skin; she couldn't remember the last time a man had touched her like this. She wanted to melt into him; she also wanted to run like hell before it was too late, to escape before he said something about a "quick roll in the hay." She pulled away from him—just a fraction of an inch, but enough to let him know she couldn't bear the intimacy any longer. "I guess I deserved that, getting myself invited out here, coming up to the hayloft. And everything . . . else."

"That's not what I meant." He frowned as his hand left her skin. "You're a very hard lady to resist," he began. "Every time we're together, all I want to do is strip off your clothes and make love to you. It doesn't matter where or when, either, damn it."

Stella hid her surprise. "You don't have to look so *angry* about it."

He grimaced. "You don't have to look so pleased."

"It shows you're human, after all, Matt McNeil." *It shows I haven't been wrong to believe in love at first sight. Or heroes in pickup trucks.*

"Oh, I'm human, all right," he growled. "So human that if you don't step away *right now* and put on your jacket, I'm going to do what I've been wanting to do since you gave me that goddamn shampoo."

Stella hesitated, then reached down for her coat and grabbed its collar. But Matt put his boot down and stopped its progress across the hay-strewn floor. "No way, lady," he growled.

Stella straightened, dropping her grip on the coat's rough fabric. She didn't touch him, although she was certainly close enough to. Stella only looked up into his dark eyes and held his gaze. "I thought I'd use it as a pillow." Her voice only shook a little bit.

He lifted his boot.

Stella felt the bottom drop out of her stomach and her knees trembled as if she were fourteen, not twenty-nine. The man meant business, even if he didn't say it in so many words.

This time when he kissed her, there was no holding back. Stella went unresisting into his embrace, and when he wrapped those strong arms around her, she knew she was sheltered from the rest of the world. She heard the wind, fresh from the plains of the Dakotas, whip around the barn, but she only felt Matt's lips, tasted his mouth, felt the heat of his hands as her skin reacted instantly to his exploring fingers. He slid his hands underneath her sweater and caressed her back.

Matt seemed to sense when she couldn't stand up anymore. His mouth left hers and he lifted her easily into his arms and carried her over to a bed of hay made of broken bales. He followed her down into the soft nest, and their bodies tangled together.

He lifted himself off her and gently drew her sweater over her head. He touched the soft skin exposed above the lacy bra. "You're beautiful," he whispered. "You deserve more than this."

Did *this* mean making love in the haymow or living in Valentine? Stella wasn't sure what he meant, but she knew this man was out of his mind to think she didn't belong here. Today was Christmas, her birthday and Valentine's Day, all wrapped up together—and she was still unwrapping presents.

"Matt," she began, but his mouth on hers stopped her words. His lips roamed over her mouth, then against her neck to her collarbone, and lower, until his tongue worried the lace that framed her breasts. He lifted his head to unzip her jeans, which he did in one swift motion.

"When I let myself think of you," he continued, "we were in a very soft, very large bed." Then his mouth trailed lower, to the tender skin above the bikini panties that bisected the soft swell of her abdomen before he tugged her jeans off her hips. "But I tried not to think about you because it drove me crazy."

"I thought about you all the time." Stella tried to catch her breath, but his hands on her thighs made it difficult to think, much less talk. "Wait, my boots—"

"I'll take care of it." And he did, with the same economy of motion with which he removed the rest of her clothing and all of his. "You have a gorgeous body," he whispered, smoothly tugging her underpants over her hips. Stella kicked the scrap of nylon off her ankles, then Matt tucked his sweatshirt under her head, his jacket under her back, and slid his very large, warm, naked body on top of hers.

"So do you," she murmured. She caught her breath as the hard length of him swept over her thigh. "Matt, I'm not protected against—"

"It's taken care of." He nuzzled her neck, his lips trailing kisses along her neck to her earlobe. His voice became a soft murmur in her ear. "Even in the Midwest we believe in safe sex, you know."

His lips swept lower, skimming a trail of heat between her breasts, until at last his tongue teased the pebble tips of her breasts. Shocks of desire swept through Stella's body, and she decided she never wanted to leave the barn.

Matt eased himself lower, and his long fingers moved across Stella's abdomen to tangle in the nest of blond curls. "I've wanted to touch you like this since the first time I saw you," he whispered. He explored lower, his hand urging her thighs apart, until his fingers brushed slowly, erotically, between the moist folds in an intimate caress. "You're so soft," he groaned, carefully easing his fingers inside of her. "And so tight. I don't want to hurt you."

"You're not," she gasped, melting around him. His probing touch was an exquisite torture, teasing her with the promise of his body. She closed her eyes and let the heat sweep over her.

"I wish we had hours."

"I don't want to wait."

He left her for a moment, then slid above her. Stella opened her eyes and reached for him. His back was smooth to her stroking fingers. Chest hair tickled her breasts as he eased himself between her legs.

"You deserve more than a quick roll in the hay," he groaned, but he probed the moist softness between her thighs and eased her open. Stella gasped at the pleasure he gave her, simply by holding himself against her. "But I can't go slow," he said. "Not this time."

He moved his hips, and her fingers gripped the hard muscles of his buttocks as he eased into her. She was ready, hot and melting around him as he filled her. He paused, slowly urging more of his hard length into her—more than she had ever thought possible. Stella didn't know she'd been holding her breath until she released it in a long sigh, and then gasped quickly as he began to move.

"Are you all right?" He stopped to look down at her. "I don't want to hurt you."

"Yes— " His lips caught hers, and their tongues tangled together as he thrust deeply into her.

"I'll slow down," he promised, lifting his mouth away from hers. "I needed to be inside you. Ever since you stepped foot on this ranch."

"I never would have known."

"I fought it."

"Why?"

He began to stroke her with deep movements. "I'm a little too old for seduction scenes."

"It doesn't feel that way to me." She smiled, and he moved into her in the familiar, timeless rhythm of lovers. He reached underneath her and his rough hands swept along her buttocks to hold her tightly against him. He claimed her mouth with his tongue, filling her, stroking her, until the passion built so high that Stella felt as if she were exploding into a thousand pieces. She tightened around him, felt him shudder deep inside of her, heard him groan into her mouth. Matt lifted his head and kissed her neck before sliding his hands away from her buttocks and easing onto his side. He lay beside her and touched the tip of her breast. When she shivered, he reached behind him for her jacket and spread it across her chest. "Better?"

"Yes. Thanks." She snuggled under it as best she could, although she missed the feel of his skin on hers. She rubbed his hair-roughened leg with her foot.

"I don't know what to say."

"I'll bet this is easier in the summer," Stella said.

He tucked a kiss into her neck. "You come back in July and we'll find out."

"We could practice before then."

"Yes." He grinned. "We sure as hell could."

"How long does it take two kids to set the table and take baths?"

"Not long enough to do this again."

Stella sighed, and touched Matt's arm. "Too bad."

"We're lucky we had fifteen minutes alone together."

"You made the most of the time," she teased. She'd thought she'd feel awkward, but she'd relaxed, feeling as if they'd settled something important.

"You should have had a bed, clean sheets, pillows." He picked up their discarded clothing and rearranged the cushioning hay.

"I'm not complaining. You've very good at this," she observed as she snuggled into the cozy nest.

"I told you, I don't take women—"

"I know that," she interrupted. "I meant you're good at making beds in the hay."

Matt tugged on his jeans and sat down beside her. "I've spent half my life sleeping in this barn for one reason or another." He caressed her cheek, and touched his lips against hers for one brief, reluctant moment before moving away. "And it's never been like this."

"WHADDAYA THINK of Midnight?" Jason rushed over to her and stopped short of giving her a hug. Stella wished he would. She had the uncontrollable desire to be wrapped up in the arms of McNeil men, no matter how small.

"I liked him a lot," she answered, sweeping the hair from Jason's brow. "He's very handsome."

"You're lucky," he said. "I'll bet lots of people wish they had a calf like him."

"I'll bet they do, too."

Matt ushered Stella farther into the warmth of the kitchen. "Let Miss Hathaway warm up, now." He glanced over at the large table. "I see you boys did your chores."

"And took a shower, too. I'm through with the plates."

Stella had never been so content. Warmth encircled her, warming her face, and the clattering of the cutlery and a cheerful child filled the kitchen. From the other room she heard the sound of gunfire and helicopters from the television set.

Matt helped her off with her jacket—not as sensually as the time before. Just as she was missing the intimacy between them, Matt's lips brushed her ear after she unwound the scarf from her neck, and she smiled at him. Their eyes met, and the briefest secret feeling passed between them.

Falling in love, Stella mused, was as simple as she thought it would be. As simple as a cozy house and a man to keep her warm at night—and any other time she needed it. Maybe life was as simple as that, too. Staying together, raising a family, putting food on the table and feed in the barn.

"You guys were gone a long time," Matthew called as he entered the kitchen. "You like the calf?"

"I sure do. I'm still not sure what to do with him, though."

Matt went over to the sink and washed his hands. "Guess we can decide over dinner."

"You don't mind bringing me home tonight? I hadn't planned to stay after dark."

"No problem," he said, but one part of his mouth turned up. "Didn't mean to keep you in the barn so long."

"That's okay," she said, trying to look casual. "I enjoyed learning about... Nebraska."

"Dad tell you about the sand hills?"

"Uh-huh," she fibbed, hoping he wouldn't ask any more geographical questions.

But Matt came to her rescue. "Matthew, go down to the freezer and get the bag of French fries. What's your favorite vegetable?"

It took a second for Stella to realize he was talking to her. "Corn."

He turned to the child. "Okay. Get a bag of corn, too."

Jason joined Stella at the table and rested his elbows on the blue plastic tablecloth. "I like the Chicago Bears."

"Me, too."

"Think they could beat the Cornhuskers?"

Stella pretended to give a great deal of thought to the question. The Nebraska college football team was greatly admired, and fans from the entire state were loyal to the "Big Red." "No way."

He grinned. "Maybe you could cut my hair. Just like Dad's."

"Okay." She offered to help make dinner, but Matt was firm in his refusal. She washed up in the bathroom, looking longingly at the bathtub and wishing she could rinse off the itchy hay she was certain still clung to her skin. Still, it would look weird if she jumped into the tub on her first visit to the ranch. The boys were certain to think that was very strange.

Stella did what she could by removing her sweater and using a soapy washcloth on her back, or at least what she could reach of her back. Feeling better, she let herself out of the bathroom to join the McNeil men in the kitchen.

The boys had disappeared, and she could hear the television from the other room. Matt was pure male, with the dish towel wrapped around his hips and slapping hamburger between his large palms. Stella sighed. She remembered the feel of those hands against her skin. She remembered the feel of those hips under her hands as she urged him deeper.

"How about a glass of wine?"

Stella blinked. "I'd like that."

He started to wipe his hands, but Stella went over to the counter. "I can pour myself one."

"The bottle is in the fridge. I just opened it."

He pointed to the cupboard where the glasses were, and Stella felt momentarily strange, as if she was in another woman's kitchen, using her wedding presents. Matt seemed to sense her sudden hesitation. "Ruth gave me those for Christmas last year. I think it was a hint that I should start entertaining."

She took one of the nonthreatening glasses. "Have you?"

"Not unless you count today."

"I forced you into the invitation."

"Nobody forces me into anything."

She believed it. "Do you want a glass?"

"No." He waved toward a can on the counter. "I'm having a beer."

She looked at the mound of hamburgers on the broiler. "That's an awful lot of food."

"It'll disappear," he assured her. "And the bread and jam, too."

She stepped closer and he swooped down to give her a quick kiss. Or at least it started out that way. By the time he lifted his mouth from hers, they had identical silly grins on their faces. Stella loved seeing him smile. "This is fun."

"I can think of more ways to have fun."

"You already did," she teased. "Now we're graduating to food."

"I want to be a good host." He returned to his relentless task of shaping hamburgers.

"I'm glad you won the make-over."

Matt stopped, wiped his hands on several yards of paper towels, and then turned to the tiny woman with the big blue eyes. Dragging her into the barn, caveman-style, had a certain appeal. Too bad he had sons to feed. Too bad it was February. Too bad it was Saturday night instead of a weekday when the boys were in school.

Being alone with Stella sounded much better than anything else he could think of. "I didn't need a haircut."

"Oh, yes, you did."

"I needed a woman."

"There are a lot of them in town."

"True." She didn't look as if she knew he was teasing, so he added, "I'm teasing."

"All right, you're teasing. You've been divorced about three years. You're a good-looking man, an independent businessman with a great home and a sexy body. There must have been a lot of women who would have . . . baked you a pie."

"Maybe I'm particular."

She smiled, and the dimples winked at him. He wanted to wrap her in his arms and make her stop asking questions, but he didn't know how to shut her up. "You talk too much."

With that, he wrapped her in his arms and kissed her until he heard the boys turn off the television set.

DURING DINNER Matt started to withdraw. The half hour spent around the oak table was fun, noisy and, Stella guessed, typical. The children ate an enormous amount of food and managed to talk almost constantly. Their father managed not to say much of anything. She tried to catch his eye a few times, especially when Matthew shared a story about Aunt Ruth, but Matt looked preoccupied.

It was as if they'd never shared the lovemaking in the barn, as if their bodies hadn't blended together in such a special and intimate way. Maybe, Stella told herself, he didn't want the boys to get the idea that someone was going to take their mother's place.

So she backed off. She attempted to be quiet, despite the boys' enthusiasm for practically every subject, especially what kind of ice cream to have for dessert. There were seven different flavors in the basement freezer, and Matthew listed each one for his new friend. Stella chose chocolate chip. Matt picked fudge ripple, and the children wanted one scoop of each. Matt limited them to two flavors, but he didn't smile.

"I'll scoop," Stella offered.

"No," Matt replied.

Stella stayed where she was, with a boy on each side of her. Matt made coffee, she drank it. He fixed bowls of ice cream, she ate it. Finally, when dinner was over, she offered to help wash the dishes.

Jason started to accept, but Matt shot him a warning glance. "The boys clean up every night, Stella. I'll take you home."

"All right." What on earth was the matter with Matt? Perhaps she'd overstayed her welcome, after all; but the groans of disappointment from the children made her feel a little bit better.

"But she hasn't seen my room," Jason wailed.

Stella turned to Matt. "I did promise."

Matt didn't smile back, but he stood up with two empty bowls in his hand. "Go with Jason, then, and we'll leave when you're done."

The child proudly showed her his room, complete with posters of Nebraska football and a legion of football cards. There was a picture of a dark-haired woman on the dresser, and Stella assumed it was the missing Mrs. McNeil. Jason showed her where the upstairs bathroom was, and Stella decided to use it before the long ride home. She needed a few minutes alone to pull herself together. She ran her fingers through her hair, wondering if she looked different. Wondering what Matt was thinking.

When Stella went downstairs, she was halfway through the hall when she heard Matthew and Jason talking to their father in the kitchen. She hesitated when she heard her name.

"Is Stella gonna come back?"

"Yeah, is she? Tomorrow? Or can we see her in town?"

"She could see Midnight again, can't she?"

Matt's voice intruded on their excitement. "I don't think that's going to happen."

Jason yelped. "Why not?"

Why not? Stella's heart called silently.

Their father didn't answer. Stella heard water running into the sink and the faint click of dishes.

The boys weren't about to give up. "C'mon, Dad," Matthew urged. "Bring her back. Please?"

"No." A long pause followed. Matt sounded exhausted when he finally spoke again. "Clear the table. We need to get this place cleaned up."

He'd told her a lot more than she wanted to hear. He had no intention of letting her into his life any more than he had already. For twenty minutes of passion in the barn—and nothing more. A painful ache spread through her heart and up to her throat, turning into a choking tightness. So much for love at first sight, for feeling she'd found the place where she belonged and the man she belonged with. He didn't feel the same way at all.

And he never had.

Stella counted to ten, then stepped into the kitchen. "I'm ready," she said, forcing a cheerful smile. *Ready to go home and cry for about a hundred hours and try to forget this afternoon ever happened.*

Matt turned away from the sink and wiped his hands on a blue-checked dish towel. "I'll get your coat."

Chapter Five

STELLA STARED OUT the window of the truck as if it were broad daylight and she could see halfway across Nebraska.

"You're quiet," he said.

"That's a change, isn't it?"

She shivered, and he pushed a couple of buttons on the dashboard. "We'll have some heat in here in a minute."

"It doesn't matter. I'm fine," she said. But she really wasn't. There wasn't any way to say it, either, though she would have liked to have said a whole lot. She rubbed her gloved hands together, leaned back on the seat and tried to look relaxed. She waited for him to say something like "I had a great time" or "When can I see you again?" or even "What a great roll in the hay, we'll have to do it again sometime"; but Matt remained silent, gripping the steering wheel, staring straight ahead into the darkness.

For the first time since she'd met him, Stella found his silence a blessing. It kept her from talking when she didn't have the heart. The lovely day full of dreams and love and laughter was over. The special man who made her feel beautiful didn't exist anymore. So much for romance, and Valentine's Day in Valentine, and all the suggestions in the magazines on how to romance the man of your dreams. Where were the articles about what to do when the man of your dreams kicked you out of his?

Valentine's lights appeared in the distance, and after endless minutes Matt parked the truck in front of Stella's building.

"When—" he began, then stopped and closed his mouth into a hard line. Stella waited for him to finish, but he said nothing further.

"When what, Matt?" she urged, anger building inside her.

"When do you want the calf butchered?"

"I don't."

"You have to do something with him, Stella. You just can't—"

"Can't keep coming out to the ranch and bothering you?"

He turned away to jerk open the door handle. "Forget it, Stella. Please."

"Wait," she ordered, and Matt turned back to face her. Stella leaned forward, her voice low and angry. "That's what you meant, isn't it? *Don't come back to the ranch, Stella.* You don't have to worry about my intruding on your life anymore. I'll give Midnight to the boys—maybe they can use him for a 4-H project or something. I'll send you a check for the feed." She looked away and opened the door before looking back at him one last time. "You're a real jackass, Matt McNeil."

"That's not news," he drawled, his eyes cold and dark. "I've had women call me worse."

"Well, I'll just bet you have." She opened the door and hopped out onto the slick road surface, then regretted her decision as her feet skidded on black ice. Matt jumped out of his side of the truck as soon as she slammed the door. She used the truck to lean on so she wouldn't slip and made her way to the sidewalk before Matt could grab her elbow. "You don't have to walk me to the door."

"I don't want you to get hurt."

"Too late." She shook her elbow away from his grip and looked up at him. "Was it just for the sex, Matt?"

His face looked drawn and tired. "No."

"Curiosity, then."

He reached up to finger one of the curls on her shoulder. "No," he rasped. "Not that."

Stella jerked her hair away from his touch. "You don't think I'd fit into your life—some fluffy city woman couldn't possibly be good enough for you. Is that it?"

Matt didn't answer.

"I may not know anything about ranch life, Matt, but I do know about love."

"And I don't?"

She shook her head. "If you did, we'd be back in the hayloft loving each other and being happy about it." She waited for him to say something, but he glared at her and then turned away. Stella wasn't finished. "Your wife left you. I'm sorry. Or maybe I'm not," she called to his back. "Because she didn't deserve you or those kids. But you don't have to go through the rest of your life thinking you don't deserve anybody else."

She watched him get in the truck and drive away. He'd never bothered to turn off the ignition.

"Big, stupid ox," she muttered, her breath forming clouds in the crisp air.

Later, when she was safely ensconced in a hot bath, bits of hay floated to the surface of the scented water, reminding her of Double Bar M's barn. And of the Double Bar M's owner's body.

She closed her eyes and remembered how they'd fit together. He'd been strong and hard and passionate, and she'd wanted to stay up there with him for the rest of her life.

So much for that idea.

Stella opened her eyes and started scrubbing. She refused to sit in the bathtub weeping into a washcloth.

"I FORGOT TO WISH YOU a Happy Valentine's Day, Stella!"

"Same to you, too, Jassy." Stella combed through another section of hair and reached for a curler. "How was the party at the manor Wednesday?"

"It was a real nice time," Jassy said. "The Kitchen Band's always so peppy—they played for Pine View last year, too—and George and Ida crowned the new king and queen."

"It sounds lovely," Stella murmured. "Hold still while I get this last curler in, okay?"

"I'll bet Chicago never had Valentine celebrations like this, did they, hon?"

"They sure didn't." Thank God. She never wanted to see another red heart or hear the word *Valentine* again.

"Valentine's Day in Valentine is more romantic than you thought it would be, isn't it?"

Oops. Stella didn't know how to answer that particular question, but she finally said, "This sure is a romantic town, Jassy. That's obvious."

The elderly woman smiled, pleased to have forced the answer she wanted to hear. "Any special Valentines in your mailbox today?"

"Not a one," Stella said.

"Well, what's the matter with the men around here, anyway?"

I ask myself that every day. "Guess I spend too much time working." She lowered the chair. "You go sit under the dryer for fifteen minutes and then I'll do the comb out."

Jassy did as she was told, and Stella waved Edith over.

"You look busy today. I'm glad I had my regular appointment."

"I have you down for every Friday, Edith." Stella picked up a comb. "I'm running a little behind. It's been crazy, but I only have one more customer after you."

"Take your time. I don't have any plans until the coronation. And I put a pot roast in the oven before I left."

"Anything special today? Or just the usual shampoo and blow-dry?"

"Just the usual, I guess. Maybe a trim on the bangs." She lifted the front of her silver hair. "What do you think?"

Stella nodded. "I'll take a little bit off the back, too. Just half an inch. I have a new peach-blossom shampoo you're going to love. Come on."

The shampoo didn't stop Edith from talking. "I haven't talked to you since you went out to Matt's ranch last week. How'd it go?"

She hesitated. "Not exactly like the magazines said it would."

"He's a tough one, honey. That wife of his hurt him real bad, but I would have thought he'd be over it by now."

"He's not."

"Funny, I thought you were just exactly what he needed." Edith sat up, and Stella wrapped a towel around her hair.

Stella tried to smile. "That's what I thought, too, Edith. But Matt didn't think so—at least, not for long."

"I'm sorry, honey," she said in a low voice. "What are you going to do about—"

The phone rang, and Stella excused herself. "I've been so busy this week I hardly know which direction to go." She booked a haircut for next week, apologized for being too busy today to fit the woman into the schedule, and turned back to Edith. "Don't worry about me, Edith. I'm okay—"

"I hate to see you hurt."

"I'm not hurt," she countered brightly. "But I have a pair of sore feet. I swear, half the time I feel like I'm walking on turkey platters."

Edith frowned. "I'll bet you've been going a hundred miles an hour all week. I'm so glad the coronation is tonight, because you can't keep up this pace much longer."

"Except for these feet, I'm fine." *Except for missing Matt every single day, I'm fine.*

"You need a vacation."

"There's no place I want to go."

"Then just hang out the Closed sign and take a few days off."

"I've already planned to close up shop for the weekend. I don't think anyone will miss me."

The tinkle of the doorbell made Stella turn to see which customer had arrived. She paused, her scissors in midsnip as Bud Newman stepped through the open door. "What on earth are you doing?"

Edith swiveled to look as Bud finished backing through the door while hauling a bale of hay with him. He set it down near the door and then tipped his hat to the ladies. "Afternoon, ma'am. Where do you want this?"

"I don't want a bale of hay," Stella said. "You've made a mistake."

"No mistake, ma'am."

"Why would a hairdresser order a bale of hay?"

"You didn't, ma'am. It's a Valentine present."

Stella didn't know whether to laugh or scream. "From who?"

"I'm not supposed to tell." He grinned, tipped his hat and left.

"Who'd send you hay as a Valentine present?" Edith wondered out loud. "Some crazy cowboy, I suppose."

Or one crazy rancher.

"Just a second, Edith." Stella put the scissors in her pocket and strode over to the door. She opened it, bent over and dragged the hay through the door to the sidewalk, carefully pushing it out of the way of any passersby. She looked around to see if Matt's pickup truck was parked along the street, but it had started to snow and she couldn't see much of anything.

When she returned to the shop, goose bumps still on her arms, the shop was quiet, with only the faint background sound of country music on the radio. Three pairs of eyes watched her. "Well? What's everyone looking at?"

"Never seen a Valentine present like that." Jassy chuckled.

Hattie Gambel, seated under the hair dryer beside her, agreed, then returned to reading *Good Housekeeping*.

"Perhaps it has a hidden meaning," Edith said shrewdly. "And Stella doesn't want to tell us."

"That's right," Stella agreed. "I don't want to tell you."

Hattie agreed. "Must be some new fad, Jassy."

The hay must have come from Matt. But what did it mean? Did he want to make love to her in the barn again? Fat chance, if he thought she'd be nothing more than a sexual release, and an outdoor one at that. "I'm going back to work," she announced. The dryers started up again, their comforting hum filling the room and muffling the conversation.

"This is darn interesting," Ruth MacArlys said, entering the shop to the familiar tinkle of the bell. "There's a bale of hay out there."

Edith answered. "It's Stella's Valentine present. From a secret admirer."

"Who is he?"

"She won't tell."

"My goodness." Ruth hung up her coat. "There's all sorts of excitement around here today. And it's starting to snow again."

The bell tinkled again, and Bud brought another bale of hay inside. "Here, Miss Stella."

This time Stella was ready for him. "Take it out," she demanded, hoping she sounded intimidating.

"Sorry, I can't do that. I have my orders." He dropped it on the floor, tipped his hat, and left the salon.

Stella eyed the "gift" with disgust. *So much for intimidation.*

Ruth stepped over the hay and poured herself a cup of coffee. "Guess you've got yourself a Valentine present, whether you want it or not. Looks like somebody's trying to tell you something, Stella."

Edith couldn't restrain herself. "My guess is that hay has some deep romantic significance."

"I saw my nephew's truck parked out in front of the café," Ruth drawled. "Think there's any deep romantic significance in that?"

Stella's heart climbed to her throat. So Matt was in town. *Surprise, surprise.*

Jassy couldn't resist calling from the other side of the room, "You moving that one out, too?"

"I'm going to finish Edith's hair before I dump that block of Nebraska outside," Stella declared. She misted Edith's hair, then combed the moisture through before picking up her scissors. The shop was blissfully quiet for a full five minutes.

Ruth sipped her coffee and leafed through the magazines on the table. "I wish you'd tell us who's sending these...gifts. I'm sick and tired of reading about Madonna."

"There's an article on Kevin Costner in the new issue of *People*."

"I'm dry," Hattie called.

"Okay. Turn off the dryer and give me a few minutes, okay?"

"No problem."

Stella quickly used the curling iron to add the finishing touches to Edith's hair, then combed out Hattie, who insisted on half a can of hair spray to preserve her new waves.

Edith wrote out a check and then took a seat near the coffee. "I think I'll make a fresh pot. I'm not going out in that storm right away," she explained. "Maybe it will ease up."

"Good idea," Hattie said, joining her. "This is better than watching *The People's Court* on TV. Besides, I got all the time in the world."

Every few minutes the tinkling of the bell introduced Bud with another bale of hay. A bale of hay that Stella promptly dragged outside after Bud left. She didn't know what Matt was up to, but she wasn't going to fall into his arms again. She'd learned her lesson: Every time she got close to the man, he clammed up and took off. She didn't know what he was trying to say, but if he thought she would listen, he had another thing coming.

"How's she taking it?" Matt stood in the pickup's bed and shoved another bale of hay toward Bud.

Bud shook the snow off his hat. "Not too well. She's stopped glarin' at me and now she's ignorin' me, but you can sure see how mad she is. All those women in there are pretty interested, I'll tell you that."

"Good. That means Stella won't leave—not while she has customers."

"That little gal is sure strong. She drags those bales around like she's been doin' it all her life." He grinned up at Matt. "You sure she's from Chicago?"

"Yeah." He'd seen the stack of hay outside Stella's Salon. Pretty soon she'd have to start forgiving him for last Saturday. Bud picked up another bale and started to leave. "Wait," Matt called. "It's time for Plan B."

"THERE'S A ROSE on this one," Edith said. "He's starting to get romantic."

Hattie peeked down to look. "What do you think he's trying to say?"

Stella swiveled Jassy's chair around and gave her a hand mirror so she could see the back of her hair. "If he has anything to say, he can do it in person."

Jassy shook her head. "You're a tough woman, Stella."

"No, I'm not. I just prefer a man who speaks his mind." The phone rang, and Stella jumped.

"Maybe that's him," Edith suggested.

Stella glanced at the clock. "My four o'clock is late—I'll bet she's calling to say she can't come because of the storm." Despite her casual words, Stella's heart beat faster as she lifted the receiver. "Hello?" She listened. "That's no problem, you just take good care of yourself and— Wait, I know where he is. I'll tell him. Okay."

Stella hung up the phone and turned to the curious women. "That was Maddie Newman. She's about to give birth to the Valentine baby."

The next time Bud arrived they were ready for him. Stella barely glanced at the hay bale decorated with roses and Valentine cards as he deposited it at her feet. "Bud," she began.

"Sorry, Stella, but I have a job to do."

"I know, but I think you'd better—"

"Can't, ma'am." He started backing toward the door, leaving a trail of melting snow on the blue vinyl floor.

"Bud, Maddie just called. She's having that baby now. You need to go home and take her to the hospital."

The young man's face drained of color, and Edith quickly grabbed his arm as he swayed toward the wall. "Everything's going to be fine," she reassured him. "You take good care of that wife of yours—and make sure to tell us tomorrow whether you have a son or a daughter."

Bud blinked a couple of times and attempted to pull himself together. "Yes, ma'am."

Stella opened the door for the stunned expectant father. "She said that the contractions were eight minutes apart, so there's plenty of time. You don't have to drive fast."

"Yes, ma'am." He stumbled outside into the storm and Stella quickly shut the door behind him.

"I'll call Maddie back and tell her he's on his way." After Stella made the phone call, she told Ruth to hop in the chair.

Jassy admired herself in the mirror, tucked fifteen dollars into the pocket of Stella's shift, then sat down beside Edith. "You can't expect me to leave now—not with all this excitement going on, can you?"

"I don't think Ruth's shampoo and set is going to be all that exciting."

"We'll stick around and see."

That was what Stella was afraid of. Once Matt learned that Bud had gone home, Matt would either have to give up his hay deliveries or enter the salon himself. And what he would say if he crossed the threshold, Stella had no idea. She sure didn't expect him to make any passionate speeches in front of an audience of freshly-coiffed women. Still, she whipped Ruth through a shampoo and set in record time before popping her under the hair dryer for ten minutes.

Five pairs of eyes continued to flicker toward the window where snowflakes blocked their view of downtown Valentine. Five coffee cups required refills. Four pairs of hands exchanged magazines, while Stella picked up a broom and started sweeping up.

No one was disappointed when Matt McNeil strode through the door. The tinkle of the bell was almost anticlimactic. His wide cowboy hat and heavy coat were coated with snow. He stomped his feet on the mat, leaving tiny mounds of white behind, before stepping over two bales of hay. The cards and roses were still attached.

Stella leaned on her broom handle and watched him approach. He didn't look too pleased, she was happy to see. Those gorgeous eyes of his flashed as he looked at her, and his lips thinned. She waited for him to say something—which was the story of her life. Finally Stella couldn't stand it any longer.

"Hello, Matt," was all she could think of.

"Hello, Stella," he answered. He turned back to the three women by the window. "Afternoon, ladies."

"Did you need a haircut?"

He frowned. "No. I came to talk to you."

"I'm working right now." To prove her point, she walked over to Ruth and lifted the hood of the dryer. She unrolled a curler and felt the strand of hair. "You're dry," she pronounced. "Come on over to the chair and I'll comb you out."

Matt stood like a tree trunk in the middle of the salon. "I need to talk to you."

That's a first. "Well, I can't—"

"Well, hello, Matt!" Ruth struggled to her feet and left the magazine on the chair. "Thought I saw your truck in town. Where are those boys?"

"At your house. With their uncle."

Ruth settled herself in the chair and rearranged the cape around her while Stella unfastened the curlers. "Are you taking them to the coronation tonight?"

"After I talk to Stella."

Stella looked in the mirror and caught Matt's intense gaze. "Go ahead, talk."

A muscle worked in his clenched jaw. "Privately."

Stella picked up a brush and ran it through Ruth's hair. She wanted to drag Matt into her apartment and hear every single word he had to say, but no one ever said she wasn't stubborn. He'd have to do a lot more than dump hay in her shop and demand a conversation. "I'm sorry, but you'll have to wait until I'm done here."

"No, I don't," he growled, then turned to the three women in the waiting area. "Would you ladies mind leaving us alone?"

"We certainly *would* mind," Jassy sniffed. "We've been waiting for this part."

Edith shrugged. "I don't know, Matt. I really hate to leave now, when I feel sort of responsible...."

"How?" he demanded.

"If it wasn't for me fixing it so you'd win the beauty make-over, none of this would have happened."

Stella and Ruth turned wide eyes in her direction. "You *rigged* the Valentine raffle so Matt would win?"

"Damn it," Matt muttered, striding toward the door. "I don't understand women."

"Yes, Stella, I did. And I'd do it again," Edith declared, ignoring Matt's exit from the salon. "It was perfect—and no one questioned the winner, especially since

Matthew and Jason stuffed the raffle box here. You two needed help getting together.''

"I helped, too. I baked the bread," Hattie added.

Jassy cackled and slapped her knee. "Why, Hattie, you sound like the little red hen!"

Matt backed through the open door with a bale of hay and dumped it at Edith's feet.

Stella stood amazed. "Matt, what are you doing?"

"I came to town to give you a Valentine's present and you're damn well going to get it." He pulled his hat lower on his forehead and marched out the door.

"How did I win the calf? Was that fixed, too?" Stella watched as Matt dumped another bale of hay, this time in front of Jassy, before going back outside. Stella looked at the blank expressions in front of her until Ruth cleared her throat.

"I have to confess, honey. I did that one myself." She climbed down from the chair and took off the cape. "I'm not going to tell you how, so don't ask."

"Where are you going, Ruth? I'm not finished."

Ruth patted her on the cheek. "Yes, you are. I know my nephew—he won't stop until he's brought every single bale of hay back inside this room." She stepped over the hay bales and lifted her coat from the hook. "Come on, ladies. We should be real proud of ourselves, but let's let these two get together by themselves now."

"Smart move," Matt mumbled, shoving another bale through the door. The women picked up their coats and purses and reluctantly prepared to go out into the storm.

Edith bent over and pushed a bale out of the way. "You bring any more of that stuff in here, we'll never be able to get out."

Matt held the door open and tipped his hat as the four women filed out. "Happy Valentine's Day," he said. Once they'd left, Matt shut the door and turned the lock. He hung up his coat and hat on the empty pegs, and then turned to Stella. "All the hay is in."

She hadn't said a word since Ruth stepped out of the chair, and she didn't know if she could. Matt looked so handsome—and so fierce. She'd pushed him too far, of course, but he looked determined to stay this time. She shoved her hands into the pockets of her tunic and waited.

"You were right," he admitted.

"Right about what?"

"About . . . love. About me. I was stupid to let you go." He took a step toward her, then another. "I had to walk away from you—not because you *didn't* fit into my life, but because you fit in too well. The boys and I needed you—too much, and too fast." When Stella didn't respond, he walked closer to her until they were inches apart. "Needing you—*wanting* you—just scared me to death. I couldn't believe a beautiful woman like you would be happy in Valentine, and with me."

Stella's throat tightened with unshed tears. "I'm happy," she insisted, but two fat tears overflowed past her eyelashes and down her cheeks.

"You sure?" Matt opened his arms. Stella went into them, rested her cheek against the soft flannel of his shirt and burst into tears. His large hands stroked her hair as he held her. "Then, why are you crying?"

Stella took a deep breath and lifted her head. Matt dropped his arms and reached into his back pocket for a handkerchief. "Here," he said. "It's clean."

"Thanks." She wiped her face and daintily blew her nose. "I didn't want to fall in love with you. It just happened—all at once."

"I think the Valentine raffle had something to do with it."

"You were tricked," she sniffed, her eyes starting to fill up again. She wanted to put her head against his strong, solid chest and cry for about a week.

Matt pulled her to him. His voice was a low rumble in her ear. "For which I'll be eternally grateful."

She looked up at him. "Really?"

He nodded. "Really. If you marry me I'll spend every Valentine's Day for the rest of our lives making love to you." His arms tightened around her. "And the other three hundred and sixty-four days of the year, too."

"But, Matt, do you *love* me?"

Surprise flickered in his eyes, and he frowned. He waved one arm at the bales of hay. "Of course, I do. What do you think all this is?"

Stella realized that no more words were necessary. "I think it means you're about to make love to me."

"That's for damn sure. Why do you think I dragged all that stuff in here?" He held her face between the palms of his hands and kissed her until she thought her knees would buckle and topple both of them to the floor. He released her and held her gaze with his own. "But you haven't said you'll marry me."

She couldn't help teasing him. "You need the words?"

"Just one."

Stella reached for him and touched his lips with gentle fingertips. "Then . . . *yes*."

"Good." He swept her into his arms and carried her over to the pile of hay. "That's all I wanted to hear."

A VERY SPECIAL DELIVERY

JoAnn Ross

A Note from JoAnn Ross

When I met my valentine, a lean and sexy Elvis had been discharged from the army, Chubby Checker was teaching a nation of kids how to do The Twist and Hollywood had begun making movies especially for us. While Frankie and Annette frolicked on the beach, Natalie Wood and Warren Beatty showed us a darker side of teenage love. Saturday nights we sat in the balconies of darkened theaters, believed everything we saw on that huge silver screen and longed for a larger-than-life, Technicolor romance of our own.

My grand romance started in a television appliance store, of all places, where I was working part-time. One Saturday, the most handsome boy I'd ever seen came into the store to get his stereo repaired.

Although I'll be the first to admit the situation doesn't lend itself to romance, when I handed him the repair tag, our fingers brushed, and an amazing jolt of lightning shot through us. Jumping back, we stared at each other, both aware that our lives had inexorably changed.

I've told this story to other romance writers who have written similar instantaneous physical reactions while secretly admitting they don't believe it happens. Trust me, it does.

In that blinding moment, I knew I'd met the man I was going to marry. Unfortunately our parents considered our ages—fifteen and eighteen—too young to know what real love was all about. As our romance blossomed, their disapproval grew, until finally, they forbade us to see each other again.

With Jay away at college, our relationship became one of clandestine letters. We saw ourselves as a truly tragic couple—Romeo and Juliet, or better yet, Tony and Maria, from that year's Academy Award-winning movie, *West Side Story*. Unable to remain apart on the most romantic day of the year, Jay returned to town for Valentine's Day, and with the help of friends and a borrowed high school ID card, sneaked into the Sweetheart's Ball (A daring feat, considering his father was one of the chaperons.)

That long-ago night was one of the most romantic of my life. It was also our last night together for a long time. Distance did our romance in, leaving us with bittersweet memories.

Years later, Jay stormed back into my life, determined to make up for lost time. Although I was engaged to marry another man, five whirlwind days later, I agreed to be Jay's wife.

That was nearly twenty-seven years ago and by the time you read this, our son Patrick (who, last Valentine's Day proposed on bended knee, to the delight of the other patrons in the restaurant) will have been married.

And I know from past experience that when we walk out onto the dance floor at Patrick and Lisa's wedding reception, and Jay takes me in his arms, time will spin backward to that long-ago Sweetheart's Ball, and we will be in the Klamath Union High School gymnasium, swaying to the sweet sounds of The Shirelles singing "Will You Love Me Tomorrow."

They say you never truly forget your first love…which is why I'm so very happy I married mine.

So, I hope you enjoy my story of teenage love the second time around, and here's wishing you all a happy and blissfully romantic Valentine's Day.

Chapter One

New Year's Eve

THE FIRST TWINGE came twenty minutes before airtime. Assuring herself that she couldn't possibly be in labor, Valentine Alexander tried to ignore it. But as she applied her lipstick—a bright scarlet that matched her beaded holiday sweater and would not disappear under the strong television lights—the twinge escalated into a genuine pain.

"Damn."

"What's the matter?" Dixie Fairchild, meteorologist for Washington, D.C.'s WABC, was engrossed in her nightly attempt to tuck her hair into some reasonable semblance of order. As usual, her wild auburn mane was winning. Her idle curiosity turned into alarm at the sight of Valentine's pallor. "Val? Are you all right?"

"I'm fine." Valentine took a tissue and wiped at the bright scarlet swatch that ran from her top lip to her nose. "Really."

When Dixie looked inclined to argue, Valentine said, "I've got to practice my lead-in. John's changed it three times in the last hour." Without giving the meteorologist a chance to respond, Valentine escaped from the makeup room to the sanctuary of the cavernous Studio A.

Fifteen minutes before airtime. Ten. Five. When the stabbing pain didn't reoccur, a relieved Valentine decided that was what she got for giving in to that overwhelming craving for a chili dog.

She made it without incident through the top of the news, reporting on the latest Middle East developments before turning to her co-anchor, Quinn Bannerman, for his report on the city's efforts to house the homeless on this coldest night of the year.

Then it was Valentine's turn for an update on tomorrow's New Year's Day economic summit.

The second twinge came just as she turned the newscast over to Dixie, who informed viewers that the snowstorm battering away at the nation's capital would probably be officially upscaled to a blizzard before the night was over.

Sports were next. Since the entire East Coast was under attack by a cold front, there were few scores to report. The top sports story of the night was a report on the grounds crew's efforts to protect the R.F.K. Stadium playing field for the upcoming Super Bowl.

"Are you all right?" Quinn asked during the commercial break.

"Of course." Valentine resisted the urge to rub her back.

"You went pale during that last story."

"It's nothing," she insisted. "The Super Bowl footage must have motivated the kids. I swear one of them's going to grow up to be a field-goal kicker for the Redskins." She rubbed her hard belly, grimacing as the twins pounded away in unison.

"It's more than that." Having been in the delivery room for all four of his children's births, Quinn considered himself the station expert on maternity matters.

But there was no more time to argue. The producer was talking in her ear and the jeans-clad floor director was counting down the time. Five. Four. Three. Two. One. Showtime.

"The storm has done little to dampen holiday spirits," Valentine continued. "Ignoring advice from police to stay at home, revelers have crowded into district hotels and restaurants to ring in the New Year. Brandon MacGregor is at the Shoreham Hotel, where the annual black-tie gala is in full swing." Another twinge made her blink. "Brandon, what's the mood where you are?"

When the coverage cut to her colleague at the hotel, Valentine slumped in her seat and exhaled a deep breath.

"I knew it," the anchorman crowed. "You're in labor."

Although Valentine enjoyed working with Quinn Bannerman, there were times when she grew extremely tired of his know-it-all attitude. "Sorry to disappoint you, Quinn, but you're wrong. For your information, I went into the hospital this morning and was sent home."

His brown eyes widened. "You were in the hospital? Today?"

"I thought the babies were coming," she admitted. "But my obstetrician assured me that it was only false labor."

"Braxton-Hicks contractions," he said knowingly. "Named for the guy who first described them in medical literature."

"That's what Dr. Osborne called them—" Valentine decided never to play a Trivial Pursuit game with this man "—right before she sent me home."

"*Home* is the operative word there, Val," Quinn began to argue. "What the hell are you doing here at the studio, in your condition, in the middle of a damn blizzard?"

"Would you two mind saving your tête-à-tête for after the newscast?" The producer, his voice dripping with sarcasm, was talking in her ear again; swiveling on her stool, Valentine was grateful to escape Quinn's probing eye and return her attention to the screen behind the anchor booth.

Brandon was closing his report. "So, with champagne flowing like Niagara, everyone seems prepared to spend the rest of the night and tomorrow, if necessary, right here. Back to you, Val."

Turning to camera three, Valentine smiled and began her wrap-up. "Thank you, Brandon. And that's our news for tonight. We'd like to end our last broadcast of the year with greetings from members of the news team you don't get to see. These people usually stand behind the cameras, but without their dedication and talent, we'd never make it on the air.

"Thanks for tuning in and from all of us at WABC, Happy New Year."

DAMN IF SHE WASN'T still gorgeous. Even pregnant with twins. Her blond hair had been styled in a chin-length bob that attractively framed a face dominated by wide-set blue eyes. Bewitched by Valentine's dazzling smile, Virginia State Police trooper Patrick Sullivan sat on the barstool in the Sign of the Dove pub. He wrapped his fingers around the white coffee mug and shut out the world.

As the daughter of a former U.S. vice president whose ancestors included Virginians John Rolfe, husband of Pocahontas, Thomas Jefferson, General Robert E. Lee and John Alexander, founder of Alexandria, Valentine Alexander had grown up in the Washington spotlight.

For her fifth birthday, her father—then a U.S. senator from Virginia—had hired the Ringling Brothers/Barnum and Bailey Circus to perform for her fellow students at the Mount Vernon Preschool. Photos of a giggling Valentine being lifted aloft in the elephant's trunk had appeared in newspapers from Seattle to Sri Lanka.

The society columnist for the *Washington Post* had gushed that Valentine's debut, held at the Mayflower Hotel two weeks after her father had been elected vice president, set the standard for future debs. Her elaborate formal wedding four years ago at the National Cathedral had been covered by CNN and, displaying a masochism he'd never known he possessed, Patrick had tuned in to watch his former wife marry the ridiculously handsome undersecretary of the Interior.

After Valentine Alexander and Hamilton Somers exchanged vows to the delight of an entire nation, Patrick got drunk for the second—and, he swore the next morning, the last—time in his life.

News of her separation—which rumors attributed to her husband's infidelity with a certain twenty-four-year-old congressional aide—had broken on the *Post*'s "Personalities" page. With the public's tendency to separate everything into black and white, the abandoned and pregnant Valentine was elevated to near-Madonna status.

Letters of encouragement poured in to the station; Patrick remembered reading that in the first week after the news broke, she received twenty-five proposals of marriage. So many baby presents—ranging from silver toothbrushes to handmade booties—began arriving at WABC that she was forced to go on the air and suggest viewers donate their gifts to the Salvation Army for distribution to the needy.

The *Post*, recognizing a subscription builder when it saw one, began running a name-the-babies contest. Pools predicting the date of the twins' birth circulated around congressional offices. In a recent poll, Washington's television viewers voted Valentine their most trusted newscaster.

"I still can't figure it out." Patrick's partner's deep voice broke into his reverie. "With that luscious lady at home, what man in his right mind would want to fool around?"

What man, indeed? Experiencing a painful, sensual tug, Patrick didn't answer. The news was coming to a close and Valentine was wishing everyone a Happy New Year. Patrick remembered a time when she had smiled at him like that. But that had been long ago, and he'd learned the hard way that the earth didn't stop spinning just because he might want it to.

She faded from the screen like a particularly wonderful dream, to be replaced by a used-car dealer dressed in a powder-blue tuxedo and ruffled dress-shirt. The car salesman was loudly proclaiming the best deal of the year, so long as buyers made it into his Falls Church dealership before midnight.

"We should arrest that guy for encouraging people to drive tonight," Patrick muttered.

"No law against bein' an idiot," Jeb Stuart Longstreet pointed out on a soft drawl attesting to a family tree that went back to the Confederacy. "If there was, a lot of those jokers up on Capitol Hill would end up behind bars." He tugged on his leather gloves. "Well, as much as I'd like to stay in this warm place all night, I suppose we'd better hit the road."

Patrick cast one last glance at the television bolted above the bar, irrationally hoping to see Valentine on the screen. When the obnoxious car dealer gave way to a shot of the boisterous, albeit freezing crowd awaiting the New Year in Times Square, he tossed back the rest of his cooling coffee.

"I suppose so." His lack of enthusiasm equaled that of his partner.

"Soon as your book sells, you can kiss all this goodbye," Jeb said.

"If it sells, you mean." Patrick's novel had been making the rounds of New York publishers for eleven months. So far, it had garnered four rejections and although Patrick had never considered himself a pessimist, he'd begun to lose hope that the story he'd struggled over for two long years would ever find a home. Undaunted, he'd begun a second book last month.

"It will." His longtime and loyal partner apparently suffered no such doubts.

Patrick didn't answer. Tossing a few bills onto the bar, he rose reluctantly from the stool. There had to be better ways to spend New Year's Eve than patrolling the icy streets on the lookout for drunk drivers. He was struck with a sudden, irrational urge to be holding a beautiful blonde in his arms as they swayed slowly to a lush, romantic ballad. The image flashed before his eyes, too real to be imagined.

Memories—painful and evocative—flooded over him. The Alexandria Old Dominion High School's gymnasium decked out in red-and-white crepe paper and balloons for the Valentine's Day Sweethearts' Ball. It had been ten long years ago, but he could remember every intimate detail as if it were yesterday: the flowery scent of her shampoo, the warmth of her soft, feminine body against his as they danced to the sound of Eddie Rabbitt singing about how he loved a rainy night, the way her lips had trembled when he'd kissed her. Again and again.

And if that weren't enough to cause a bittersweet ache, most of all, Patrick remembered the way Valentine's blue eyes had shone with love later that night when the judge pronounced them man and wife. She'd been dressed in a white taffeta gown that had rustled seductively when she walked; her bridal bouquet had been the wristlet of red sweetheart rosebuds she'd worn to the dance. On her right wrist was the charm bracelet from which dangled the silver-heart charm he'd given her only hours earlier. More in love than he'd ever thought possible, Patrick had worn his own heart openly on the sleeve of his rented tux.

And now, years later, the pain, sharpened by nostalgia, hit him in the gut like the kick of a horse.

An icy gust of wind struck him in the face as he walked out of the bar. Jamming his hands deep into the pockets of his black leather jacket, Patrick vowed to finally put his disastrous, short-lived marriage behind him. The New Year provided the perfect opportunity to get on with his life. He was going to find himself some other woman. Someone who would love him for who—and what—he was. And he was going to forget he'd ever known Valentine Alexander.

The resolution was the same one he made every year. And now, as he threw himself into the driver's seat of the patrol car, Patrick knew that by the time Valentine's Day rolled around, he would have broken it. Again.

Chapter Two

THE PAINS HAD VANISHED. Vowing not to eat another chili dog for the remainder of her pregnancy, Valentine exchanged New Year's greetings and hugs with the crew. Then she took the elevator downstairs to the parking garage.

"Bad night to be drivin'," the attendant warned as he delivered her car and handed her the keys.

"Don't worry about me, Sam," Valentine said. "I've driven to Middleburg in worse weather than this."

Valentine was expected at her parents' home for New Year's Day brunch. Knowing that the roads could be impassable by morning, she'd opted to make the forty-mile drive tonight.

Sam's gaze dropped to her stomach, huge beneath her white wool coat. "Woman in your condition should be at home sittin' in front of a fire knittin' baby booties."

She'd heard that before. "It's a new world, Sam."

"Mebee." He took a long draw on the pipe he was never without. Although she was long past the morning-sickness stage of her pregnancy, the sweet cherry-tobacco smell made Valentine's stomach lurch. "You know, Miz Alexander, the way I figure it, you're lucky to be rid of that bum. A terrific lady like you deserves better than some guy who can't stop cattin' around."

Valentine, accustomed to having absolute strangers advise her on the most personal aspects of her life, merely murmured something vague that could have been agreement. She'd long ago realized that because people invited her into their living rooms each evening, they seemed to feel that they knew her personally.

"My wife's pregnant, too," Sam revealed. "With our fifth."

At this moment, Valentine couldn't imagine ever going through the experience again. "Gracious. That's a lot of children."

"My wife's the oldest of seven and I'm in the middle of eight," he revealed. "We wanted our kids to experience all the love you get in a large family."

Forgetting that only a moment earlier she'd found the idea of another pregnancy unappealing, Valentine recalled that there had once been a time when she'd dreamed of a house filled with children. Patrick's children.

Patrick. A pain lanced through her—a sharp, stabbing, all-too-familiar pain that had nothing to do with her pregnancy. Her gloved fingers, as they pressed against her temple where a headache threatened, trembled.

Taking a deep breath intended to clear her head of the suffocating loneliness, of unfulfilled dreams and thoughts of what might have been, Valentine wished Sam a Happy New Year then drove her car out of the garage and onto the nearly-deserted snow-covered street.

The blizzard was raging. Snow obscured the gleaming lights of the monuments. It pelted against the windshield, making the effort of the wipers increasingly futile. Fortunately the heater was blasting full force, keeping it warm inside the car as Valentine crossed the Potomac, and headed out of the city into the white Virginia countryside.

The already-scant traffic dwindled even more, the farther she got from the city. By the time she began making her way over the Bull Run Mountains, she could have been the only person in this snowy world. The wind was blowing stronger now; swirls of powdery snow kicked up by the

Intermittent gusts skittered across the curving roadway, and drifts piled up on the gravel shoulder.

Although Valentine knew that she should be directing all her attention to her driving, evocative, unbidden images of ten years ago began to flash in front of her eyes.

Her parents had been away, attending a party at the White House. Left to her own devices, as she so often had been, Valentine was having a New Year's Eve party at her Alexandria home when someone had got the idea to order pizza. It had been snowing, just as it was tonight....

When the delivery boy finally arrived, just before midnight, seventeen-year-old Valentine was struck dumb. He was, she decided as she invited him into the foyer, the most gorgeous boy she'd ever seen.

Despite the storm raging outside, he wasn't wearing a hat. Valentine was struck with a sudden urge to run her fingers through the wet, unruly black hair that flowed over his collar. He certainly wasn't conventionally handsome. His nose was crooked, as if it had been broken; his mouth was harshly cut; his lips, too full. Beneath shaggy black brows dusted with snow, his eyes were dark and wicked. They swept over her with a masculine appraisal that she knew she should find insulting. Instead, against all common sense, his intense gaze thrilled her.

All the boys Valentine dated could have come from the same mold: clean-cut, all-American types from successful old Virginia families like hers. And although they weren't above trying to grab a breast in a darkened movie theater, they were invariably safe. Unlike this one.

"That'll be fifteen dollars and seventy-five cents."

His deep voice rumbled in a way that stirred something unnamed inside Valentine. Entranced by the movement of his lips, she simply stared at him.

"I've got three other pizzas waiting to be delivered out in the truck, and if I don't get going, they're going to be pepperoni Popsicles."

"Oh." Flustered to be caught staring, Valentine could feel the color flooding into her cheeks. "I'm sorry." She took the pizza boxes from him and put them on the Sheraton table. Fumbling in her purse, she pulled out a twenty and a five.

"Here." She thrust the crisp bills at him. "Keep the change."

He pocketed the money without looking at it. Instead, his gaze remained on her face. Valentine's lips went dry; she resisted the urge to lick them.

At that moment her friends, who'd been watching the Times Square countdown on the library television, cheered. Outside, horns blared and people began shouting out greetings.

"Happy New Year," she whispered, as tumultuous feelings swirled inside her.

He didn't answer. Instead, he slipped one arm around her waist and drew her to him.

Valentine was stunned. Although her whirling mind told her to protest as his lips brushed against hers with a soft, but far-from-tentative exploratory pressure, she felt the rapidly-spinning world slowly slip out of focus.

Clouds covered her mind and there was only sensation. The glorious heat of this stranger's hand on her hip, the warmth of his breath, the rigid strength of his body as he pressed her against the wainscotted wall. Drawn into this seductive, misty, sensual world, she lifted her arms and curved them around his neck. Their bodies fit. Perfectly. Wonderfully.

His mouth was full and warm. His taste was dark and tempting. Succumbing to the flavor, she parted her lips and let him take more. The moist tip of his tongue traced a wet stroke across her mouth from one corner to the other. When it slipped between her lips to touch the tip of hers, Valentine went weak at the knees. How was it that her body was so thrillingly alive while her mind remained so clouded?

"I thought you needed to go," she murmured a long time later.

"In a hurry to get rid of me?"

"No. But I don't want to be responsible for you being fired, either."

"You're right." He cursed softly under his breath. "If I had my way, I'd never move from this spot again." His hand skimmed down her side, from her breast to her thigh, leaving sparks. "But I need this damn job."

She lifted her hand to his cheek, intrigued by the muscle she felt jerk under her palm. Valentine's social circle consisted of properly restrained Episcopalian WASPs. Never in her entire life had she ever met such an intensely passionate individual. Unreasonably nervous, she had to turn her eyes away to look out the windows, to where the snow continued to fall.

"You could come back after you finish your deliveries."

"Do you mean it?" He caught her chin in his fingers and held her gaze to his.

"Yes." Desire swirled in the depths of his passionate midnight-dark eyes. "I'd like you to come back. Very much."

His answering grin was warm enough to melt the snow. Bending his head, he pressed his lips against hers, giving her a quick, hard kiss that left her breathless. "Twenty minutes," he promised. "Then I'll be back."

Twenty minutes. It seemed like a lifetime. Through the mists still clouding her mind, Valentine was aware of the others calling her name. She ignored them.

He turned to leave, then stopped. "I don't know your name."

Valentine knew she should be embarrassed at having shared such an intimate kiss with a boy who didn't even know her name. But she wasn't. Because she was wrapped in the warm, velvety mists of love at first sight. "Valentine."

"Valentine." His deep, rough voice drew the syllables out slowly, as if he were tasting them on his tongue. "Perfect."

He opened the door. The wind blew in a scattering of snowflakes that looked like lace against the black marble floor.

"Wait!" Valentine called out after him. "I don't know *your* name, either."

He looked surprised. "That's right, you don't. It's Patrick," he said. "Patrick Sullivan." Flashing her one last grin, he left.

Valentine stood in the open doorway, mindless of the freezing wind that ruffled her hair and pressed her white angora skirt tight against her thighs as she watched him run down the icy walk with a masculine recklessness she admired, even as it made her heart stop.

He jumped into the cab of the pickup, sounded the horn in a brief farewell, then took off in a billowy cloud of exhaust. By the time the taillights disappeared around the corner, Valentine was missing him already....

The six weeks that had followed had been the most intense time of her life. And although she hadn't seen him in all these intervening years, she'd never completely stopped thinking about him. Especially on New Year's Eve. And, of course, on Valentine's Day.

It had been on her birthday—her name day—that she'd suffered the most personal debacle of her life. Even worse than having her husband, Hamilton, inform her that he wanted a divorce on the same day she presented him with the news of her pregnancy.

The babies stirred as another twinge jolted her from her reverie. Gritting her teeth, Valentine tightened her fingers around the steering wheel and peered out the windshield into what seemed like the unreal world of a snow-filled paperweight.

"Only a few more miles to go, babies," she managed through the escalating pain. "We'll be there before you know it."

As she turned off onto the country lane that led to her parents' farm—now a vineyard—Valentine decided that if that last pain actually was false labor, she definitely wasn't looking forward to the real thing.

PATRICK FELT AS IF he were driving into a monstrous snow-making machine. The white stuff was churning out of the heavens, making visibility next to impossible. And although such treacherous weather should have kept everyone home, six years on the force had taught him that New Year's Eve seemed to bring on a collective human insanity. He and Jeb had already pulled five cars out of snowbanks and arrested two drunk drivers. And there were still ten more minutes until midnight.

Midnight. New Year's Eve, ten years ago, his life had been inexorably altered when he'd met the most beautiful girl he'd ever seen. She'd been wearing a white dress that looked as if it had been spun from angel's hair, its top adorned with crystals that glittered like icy winter stars.

Her hair, illuminated by the enormous chandelier overhead, gleamed like hammered gold as it tumbled over her shoulders. Her eyes were wide and as clear and bright and blue as a summer sky. Her lips were shiny and pink and eminently kissable.

He couldn't remember a word they'd said—only that on the stroke of midnight, before he knew what he was doing, before his shell-shocked brain could send a warning to his vividly alive body, he pulled her into his arms and his lips were on hers, and he was kissing her; and instead of slapping his face the way she should have, the angel with the spun-gold hair had kissed him back!

Until that night, Valentine Alexander had been a stranger—a picture on the society pages, nothing more. Yet, from the moment his lips touched hers, Patrick had felt as if he'd known her for all of his eighteen years. Or perhaps he'd simply been waiting for her that long.

And ten years later, despite every ounce of common sense he possessed, Patrick knew he was still waiting.

"Something wrong?"

Patrick came out of the painful reverie with a start. "What?"

"I asked if anything was wrong," Jeb repeated. "You're gripping that steering wheel like you'd like to have your fingers around someone's neck."

Patrick flexed his clenched fingers. "I was just thinking."

"About your book?"

"Yeah." As guilty as Patrick felt about lying to this man who was as close as a brother, he wasn't prepared to share the most painful period of his life with him, either.

"It'll sell." Jeb repeated his earlier reassurance.

Patrick didn't answer. But as he steered the cruiser through the white-covered Bull Run Mountains, he found himself counting the hours until he finally went off duty.

ALTHOUGH THE BLINDING snow kept her from making out familiar landmarks, instinct told Valentine that she was almost there. A quick glance at the odometer corroborated her feeling.

"Only three more miles," she said into the darkness surrounding her. Even as she tried to reassure herself, at this ridiculously slow speed, three miles might as well be a million.

It was then that the nagging pain she'd been experiencing all day returned with a vengeance. It started slowly, like a gathering wave, then increased in intensity as it moved across her abdomen until it reached a crest. Just when she thought she was going to have to pull off the road, it blessedly subsided.

Valentine breathed a sigh of relief. "Three more miles, babies—" she spoke the words like a litany "—only three more miles to Grandpa and Grandma's."

She reached the crest of the hill and was suddenly blinded by the glare of headlights looming out of the snow. By the time she realized that the oncoming car was in her lane, it was too late. She swerved, sending the car over a slight incline, where it landed, hood first, in a snowbank.

Although she'd fastened her seat belt, Valentine was thrown forward hard enough to bang her forehead on the steering wheel. Although she didn't think she'd lost consciousness, the next thing she knew, she was slumped across the seat. Pulling herself upright, she rubbed her gloved hand against the fogged-up windows and saw the silent snow continuing to fall, covering the car like a muffling blanket.

Chapter Three

THE CALL CAME over the radio just after midnight. When the dispatcher related the name of the driver of the missing car, Patrick inadvertently jerked on the steering wheel, sending the patrol car into a treacherous spin.

"What the hell?" Jeb's foot pumped an imaginary brake.

Beads of sweat broke out on Patrick's brow as he struggled to regain control of the car. Time took on the slow-motion feeling of an instant replay; beside him he heard Jeb curse. The tires, which had been skidding across the ice like a penny across a newly waxed floor, gained purchase, the wheel became steady beneath his hands, and the patrol car finally came to a shuddering stop, its headlights cutting a wide swath in the opposite direction from which they'd been headed.

"Well," Jeb drawled, "you sure started the year off with a bang."

"Sorry about that." Patrick backed the car up and turned around.

Jeb shrugged. "Black ice is treacherous stuff."

It hadn't been ice that caused the spin; it had been his reaction to hearing Valentine's name come over the radio.

"She's pregnant, dammit," Patrick said as he started driving toward Middleburg. "She could die, stuck out here in this storm."

The fear in his voice was far from his usual controlled tone. Jeb, hearing it, cast a curious glance his way.

She was out there somewhere. Lost. Possibly hurt. She needed him. Gripping the wheel tightly, driving slower than he'd like in the name of caution—what help could he be if he killed himself rushing to her rescue like some white knight?—Patrick prayed for Valentine to be kept safe until he could find her.

OUTSIDE THE CAR, everything was dark and white. The car had stalled; there was no reassuring sound of an engine humming. Its hood was buried deep in the snow; there were no headlights to tell her exactly how much trouble she was in.

Another contraction, worlds different from the ones she'd had at the station, swept over her. Clutching her abdomen with both hands, she bent over, biting her lip as the pain intensified. Then, just when she thought she couldn't take it for another moment, it crested, leaving her weak and shaking.

This was no false labor, Valentine realized. Her babies were coming. Now. As another pain swept over her, stronger than the last, Valentine experienced a strangely calming sense of maternal purpose.

She hadn't carried these babies for nearly nine long and uncomfortable months to let them die out here in the middle of nowhere. Determined to give birth to two healthy babies, she'd given up alcohol and caffeine, forced herself to swallow the foul-tasting vitamins every morning, and exercised religiously, letting nothing deter her from her daily walks. And now, as she realized that she was on her own, Valentine vowed to keep her babies safe.

Using the controlled breathing she'd learned in Lamaze class, she managed, with effort, to ride out the next contraction. After it faded, she unbuckled her seat belt and began tugging down her panty hose. She'd managed to get them as far as her knees when a beam of light illuminated the car.

The driver's door was yanked open. "Are you all right?"

Valentine stared up, stunned at the wonderfully familiar face. "I think so. Patrick? Is that really you?"

"It's me." His heart, which had begun pounding painfully when he'd spotted the wrecked car, slowed to beat with a more natural rhythm. "Damn, you've hurt your head." He frowned at the dried blood on her forehead.

"It's not that bad," she assured him. The bleeding had stopped almost as soon as it had begun. "I can't believe it's you. After all these years." Her face paled and twisted into a grimace. She grabbed his arm tightly and closed her eyes.

"I've thought about you so many times," she gasped, pain and surprise conspiring to keep her from censuring her words—as she might have done under normal conditions. "I even tried to find you, but... Oh, God, here comes another one."

She'd tried to find him. The amazing thought ricocheted violently around in Patrick's brain until it was finally interrupted by Valentine's ragged moan.

"We'll have plenty of time to talk about all this later." And they damn well would, Patrick vowed. Valentine was no longer a child, able to hide behind her all-powerful father whenever things became too uncomfortable for her to handle.

Banking long-smoldering resentments, he pressed his gloved hands against her, massaging her convulsed abdomen. "Valentine, listen to me."

Gasping, she nodded.

"As soon as this contraction passes, I'm going to carry you to the patrol car. It's warm there. You'll be safe."

Caught in the grips of pain, she couldn't answer. But if she had, she would have told him that she'd known she'd be safe the minute the car door opened and she saw him.

"I was surprised when I found out you'd become a trooper," she said, once she'd found her voice again.

Patrick scooped her into his arms and lifted her as if she were no heavier than a pile of feathers. "Ironic, isn't it?" he murmured as he carried her through the drifting snow that was colored red and blue by flashing police lights. "The town hellion becoming a cop."

"You weren't really a hellion, Patrick."

Not that he hadn't tried damn hard to make people think he was. Her father had declared that Patrick Sullivan would end up in prison before his thirtieth birthday—if he lived that long. But Valentine had realized that the leather jacket, the motorcycle, the fights, the late-night illegal drag races on the beltway and the perpetual, undeniably sexy scowl were protective armor designed to hide a soft and vulnerable heart.

Which was why, when forbidden by her parents to ever see Patrick again, she'd rashly agreed to marriage so that no one could keep them apart.

"Not with you," he agreed gruffly, thinking how she'd seen possibilities in him that no one else had ever seen. Unfortunately, she hadn't believed in him enough. Because as soon as her parents put a little pressure on her, she'd crumbled.

As he laid her in the back seat of the blessedly warm patrol car, another contraction made Valentine grip Patrick's arms for dear life. Once again he put the hurt of the past away as a sympathetic pain shot through his groin and down his thighs.

"I think it's time we got this show on the road, Val."

Jeb, who'd been watching the exchange with interest, announced, "I called for the paramedics. They said they can't fly an evac copter in this weather, but they're sending an ambulance." His expression sobered as Patrick unzipped Valentine's suede boots and took them off, then stripped her taupe panty hose the rest of the way down her legs. "How much time do we have?"

"I don't know." Patrick was more nervous than he'd ever been in his life, but he knew he had to stay calm, for Valentine's sake. "But as close apart as her pains are, I don't think there's any way these babies are going to wait for the paramedics."

Valentine propped herself up on her elbows. "I don't suppose I could just change my mind?"

Valentine's attempt at humor reminded him how he'd once considered her amazingly plucky for a girl who'd been raised like a hothouse orchid.

If only she'd shown a bit of that spunk on that long-ago Valentine's night, things would have turned out so differently. If she'd only stood up to her patrician father and icy mother, it would be his baby she'd be having.

He pulled off the leather gloves and stroked her damp hair away from her face. "Don't worry, Val. Everything's going to be all right."

"I'm not worried." She bit her lip as the contractions swept over her, one after another, harder still. "I'm just furious with myself for driving in this storm and putting my babies at risk."

"You weren't due for another two weeks."

"How did you know when I was due?"

Valentine tried to do what she'd learned in Lamaze class—to picture the contraction as an ocean wave, gathering, breaking, subsiding. But she was discovering that it wasn't nearly as easy at it had seemed when she'd done the exercises to the soothing wavelike sounds of the relaxation audiotape.

"You'd be surprised what I know about you," he said gruffly. "I know that you married Somers at one-thirty in the afternoon. It rained that morning, but it stopped in time for the sun to be shining when you came out of the cathedral. Which rips apart that old proverb about 'Happy is the bride the sun shines on.' ''

When she experienced another contraction—the most violent so far—Valentine bit her lip, refusing to scream.

Observing the pain that swept across her face, Patrick massaged her tense abdomen with a gentleness that belied the angry passion in his voice.

''I know that you spent your honeymoon in Tahiti, although you came back after one week instead of the two you'd planned, because your damn husband needed to quell an environmental rally planned in response to his proposal to allow drilling off the Santa Barbara coast. Since your parents had moved to Middleburg, you moved into their house in Alexandria.''

His hands were strong and gentle at the same time, soothing Valentine even as his heated monologue managed to distract her from her pain.

''I know that Somers didn't know the meaning of the word *faithful,* and after the bastard finally did you the favor of setting you free, you moved out of your parents' house and bought that row house on Capitol Hill. . . .

''By the way, those rosebushes in your front yard are in serious need of pruning if you expect decent blooms this summer.''

She stopped her panting long enough to ask, ''You know where I live?''

''Of course. I also know that your public loves you, that you're bright and funny and gutsy and pregnant with twins that should have been mine—would have been mine, dammit, if you'd only hung in there and trusted me to take care of you instead of caving in to your parents' demands.

That was one helluva mistake, when you consider what a dandy husband they picked out for you."

Stunned by his passionate outburst, Valentine stared up at him. "Why?"

Patrick shrugged, feeling foolish to have let her know that he'd never gotten over her, but better now that he'd finally, after ten years, gotten it off his chest. Her parents had robbed him of more than his bride; they'd robbed him of the chance to close a painful chapter in his rocky life.

"I guess you're kinda my hobby, Val." His *obsession* was more like it, but Patrick wasn't prepared to admit to such an overpowering weakness. Especially to the only woman who'd ever possessed the power to crush his heart.

"Your hobby?"

"Some guys collect baseball cards, other guys collect vintage cars. I collect Valentine Alexander stories."

The police radio crackled static, the dispatcher periodically breaking in with indecipherable codes and instructions. Valentine could hear Patrick's partner in the front seat, quietly asking for an update on the ambulance.

"I hate like hell to interfere in this touching reunion," Jeb said, glancing back at them. "But it's going to be a while before help arrives."

"Looks like we're elected, then." Patrick frowned and brushed his thumb over the spot where her teeth had broken the skin on her lower lip. "You'll have to trust me, Valentine."

"I do." It was true, she did trust him. With her very life. With her babies' lives.

After pulling on the surgical gloves that were standard equipment in all the patrol cars, Patrick helped her out of her coat, then lifted her skirt to her waist.

His touch was brisk and professional—a far cry from the way he'd once touched her. When his hands brushed over the tender flesh between her thighs, Valentine pulled away. Murmuring something soft and inarticulate, he soothed her in much the same way he had that first time they'd made love. A gush of amniotic fluid flowed from her body and over his hands.

"Oh, God, Patrick."

Horribly embarrassed, Valentine turned her head away. As a young girl in love, she'd made certain that she had always looked absolutely perfect whenever she was with Patrick. She'd prided herself on never having a hair out of place or a chipped fingernail, or even smeared lipstick. Never, in her wildest imagination, could she have imagined allowing him to see her this way. In novels, having a child was always so wonderfully romantic. In real life, it was also decidedly unattractive.

"I'm so sorry," she moaned.

"Don't be ridiculous." He massaged her heaving stomach. "This is it. I can see the baby's head. Just push, sweetheart, and the baby will do the rest."

As she pushed with all her might, Jeb leaned over the back of the front seat and took hold of her hands, encouraging her to squeeze as hard as she wanted, not flinching as her nails dug into his flesh.

"That's it," he coaxed while Patrick's hands pressed against the insides of her thighs. "Come on, Miz Alexander. You're doin' great!"

As the two men cheered her on, Valentine pushed and pushed and pushed, her legs trembling, her teeth biting her lower lip, her hands clenching Jeb's tightly enough to cut off his circulation. She gasped as the pain built, higher and higher, and then, miraculously, the baby's head was free.

As Patrick had promised, the baby, following nature's plan, turned so that the next push succeeded in forcing out the shoulders. And then, with one last mighty effort, her child slid into Patrick's waiting hands.

"You've got yourself a girl, Val," Patrick announced, his voice husky with excitement.

"And she's every bit as gorgeous as her mama," Jeb said.

While Jeb cleaned the mucus from the infant's mouth, Patrick cut the umbilical cord that had been the lifeline between mother and daughter for so many months.

Valentine was gazing down at her baby when another contraction ripped through her.

"As much as I'd love to let you rest on your laurels, Valentine," Patrick said, "I'm afraid you've still got a bit of work to do." He handed her daughter to Jeb, who wrapped her in a blanket.

Ten minutes later, as she lay drenched in sweat, listening to the sound of her son and daughter crying, Valentine was exhausted. But happier than she'd ever been.

"I always knew you were a trooper," Patrick said. *Except for the one time he'd really needed her to be.* But this was definitely not the time to throw her desertion in her face.

"She sure is," Jeb agreed. He held out his hand. "I'm afraid in all the excitement I forgot my manners, ma'am. Jeb Stuart Longstreet, at your service."

She shook his hand, frowning at the deep, half-moon indentations in his dark skin. "Did I do that?"

He grinned. "Don't worry about a thing. I can't remember when I've had more fun just holding a lady's hand. You done good, Miz Alexander."

She smiled a faint, weary but warm smile. "I think, under the circumstances, you should call me Valentine."

"Valentine, it is," he agreed, his grin growing wider. "Hot damn, this is one helluva swell way to start the year."

They gazed down at the babies, who were still screaming their heads off. Valentine was thinking that the sound of her children crying was the sweetest music she'd ever heard, when a shrill, familiar sound cut through the night.

"Looks like your ride is here, Valentine," Jeb announced.

She looked up at Patrick, loathe to leave him. As if reading her mind, he said, "I think I'll ride along to the hospital with Val. Why don't you follow us?"

"I'll be right on your tail," Jeb answered agreeably.

As the ambulance slowly made its way through the drifting snow, back to the city, an exhausted Valentine, after being assured by the paramedics that her babies were perfectly healthy, felt herself drifting off to a much-needed sleep.

But there was one more thing....

"Patrick?" she whispered.

"Yeah?"

She licked her lips. "When you suddenly appeared like that out of the storm, I thought I was dreaming. Then I thought maybe I'd died."

"Died?" He didn't tell her that while he'd been driving through the dark, looking for her, he'd been afraid of the same thing. More than afraid. He'd been terrified.

"I thought maybe I was in heaven—you know, like what all those people who have a near-death experience talk about." Exhaustion had clouded her mind, softening self-protective instincts that on any other occasion would have kept her from sharing such an intimate admission. "And you were there. And we were together again. For always."

For always. Until death us do part. Ten years ago she'd spoken the words in a soft, trembling voice. Six hours later, she was gone. Out of his life.

"Patrick?"

"I think you should go to sleep, Valentine." The glow from delivering her babies was beginning to wear off as harsh reality set back in. Patrick didn't know how much rehashing of the past he could take for one night.

"I will. I just wanted to thank you."

He squeezed her hand in response. Then, unable to keep her eyes open another minute, Valentine allowed blessed sleep to carry her away.

Beside her, Patrick held her slender hand in his. As his thoughtful gaze moved back and forth between mother and children, he realized he'd been fooling himself to think that he could ever put his past—the fleeting, bittersweet part of it he'd shared with this woman—behind him.

Chapter Four

THE STORM HAD PASSED and the sun was shining brightly, creating diamonds on the newly fallen snow when Patrick returned to the hospital eight hours later. After last night, if he never saw the damn white stuff again, it would be too soon. He still got chills whenever he thought about what might have happened to Valentine and her babies—if he and Jeb hadn't found her.

He took the elevator to the maternity floor, ignoring the amused glances of the other passengers. Exiting the elevator, he made his way to the nurses' desk.

"Gracious!" The nurse on duty looked at him with overt amusement. "Aren't you a sight."

She had the same snickering expression the people in the elevator had worn. "What's the matter?" he growled. "Haven't you ever seen a stuffed animal before?"

"Of course. I've just never seen so many of them in one place," Susan Copeland, R.N., remarked. "What happened, Patrick? Hit a lucky streak at the carnival?"

A blue elephant fell to the floor. As he bent to pick it up, a yellow duck with an orange rain-hat tumbled free, causing a passing candy-striper to giggle.

"They're for a friend, okay?" he ground out as he secured both animals under his arm and stood up again. "For her babies."

"Babies?" The nurse lifted a blond eyebrow above the red plastic frames of her glasses. "As in plural?"

"That's right. Surely, being in the baby business, you've heard of twins."

"Of course, I have. But there's only one pair of twins in the nursery right now. And they belong to Valentine Somers."

"Alexander," he corrected. He steadfastly refused to think of Valentine by her married name. With the exception of the six short hours she'd been Mrs. Patrick Sullivan, she'd always been Valentine Alexander to him.

"You're friends with Valentine Alexander?"

"That's right. So, if you'll just tell me what room she's in—"

"Why didn't you ever tell me?"

"It didn't have anything to do with us."

"Didn't it?" She folded her arms. "All those nights—two years of nights, Patrick," she stressed, "we lay in bed together, watching the late news and you never, not once, thought to tell me that you and Valentine Alexander were friends?"

His affair with Susan Copeland had ended when she'd finally given up trying to coax him to the altar and married an internist at Georgetown University Hospital. Although her desertion had stung, Patrick had never blamed her. She'd always been outspoken in her desire for a husband and children; unfortunately, Patrick had been unwilling—or unable—to provide her with the family she'd always dreamed of.

"I honestly didn't think it mattered," he muttered. "Could you just tell me her room number?"

"Sorry, I can't do that."

A sleek purple seal popped out of the clutch of animals, skidded across the floor and went ignored. "Why the hell not?"

"Because I've been instructed to keep it a secret," she told him. "The press was crawling all over the place today, trying to get a picture of the new mommy with her babies. Since she had a pretty rough delivery, the doctor didn't want her disturbed.''

"I know exactly how rough the delivery was," Patrick countered, "since I'm the one who delivered them."

"You?" She smiled knowingly. "Aha, the plot thickens."

"Come on, Susan," Patrick urged. "Would you just tell me the damn room number?"

"If you'd ever looked that eager to see me, Patrick, I probably wouldn't have left you, marriage or no marriage." She sighed. "Room 615. It's down the hall and to your left."

"Thanks." He scooped up the seal. "You're a peach. I owe you."

"Tell me about it," she muttered as he turned away and headed down the hall. "Oh, Patrick?"

He glanced back over his shoulder. "Yeah?"

"She's already got a visitor."

He stiffened visibly. Shoulders, back and neck. "Not her husband."

"No. We called him right after she came in, but he still hasn't shown up. It's—"

"I believe the nurse was referring to me," a cool, all-too-familiar voice behind him offered.

He turned slowly to find Valentine's mother standing there, her pale blue eyes like chips of ice. Eleanor Alexander was wearing a full-length silver-fox coat that Patrick figured must have cost more than his annual salary. Considering the current wave of animal-rights activists, it was a good thing her husband had gotten out of politics, Patrick considered. Because he doubted if this woman had ever owned a good Republican cloth coat.

"Hello, Eleanor." It was the first time he'd ever used her first name, and Patrick couldn't deny that he got a sense of satisfaction at the way she flinched to hear it on his lips. "You're looking well." Actually, thanks to an obvious face-lift, diet and a clever hand with a makeup brush, she looked exactly the same as she had ten years ago.

She didn't bother acknowledging the compliment. "Hello, Patrick," she said in that same cool tone that had always frustrated him. Her gaze raked over him in a way that gave Patrick the impression that she'd love to be measuring him for a shroud. "Isn't this a coincidence? That you, of all people, should show up at the same hospital in which Valentine is a patient?"

"It wasn't exactly a coincidence, Eleanor," Patrick said levelly, looking her straight in the eye. "As soon as the call came in that you'd reported her missing—"

"I reported her overdue," Eleanor corrected. "Not missing."

Her daughter could have died and the damn woman was arguing semantics, Patrick thought. "When the call came in reporting Valentine missing," he said in a slow, measured tone, "I wasn't about to quit looking until I found her. Which I did."

"Well." She tucked an errant blond curl back beneath a fur hat that matched her coat. "I see that some things haven't changed. You are every bit as stubborn as always."

"You should be thankful I am." An orange-and-black-striped tiger slipped from the stack and fell onto the gold metal toe of Eleanor Alexander's gray suede boot.

"Yes, I'll give you that," she acknowledged reluctantly. Without even glancing down, she kicked the stuffed tiger away with a barely perceptible flick of her foot.

"This was, admittedly, one of the rare occasions when your unyielding tenacity proved useful. And I suppose you should know that Gerald and I are both extremely grateful to you for helping Valentine bring our grandchildren into the world.

"However," she said, coming to the part that Patrick had been waiting for, "if you think that doing your duty, as a state policeman, gives you the right to infiltrate yourself back into my daughter's life, I'm going to have to warn you, Patrick, that it isn't going to happen."

"Valentine is a grown woman," he pointed out quietly. "Capable of making her own decisions."

"Under normal conditions, I would grant you that," Valentine's mother agreed stiffly. "However, these are not normal conditions. After what she's been through, Valentine is bound to be in a vulnerable state. Neither her father nor I will allow you to take advantage of her temporary weakness."

"I'm well aware of Valentine's weaknesses," Patrick responded. "All of them." He let the implications of that statement hang on the air. "I am also aware that she is a far different woman from the seventeen-year-old girl I knew. Just as I am a different man. And this time there isn't any place for you in the equation, Eleanor."

Furious color rose in her cheeks—a dark, scarlet stain beneath the expertly applied rose powder blush. Her eyes flashed both ice and heat at the same time, reminding Patrick all too well that Valentine's mother was, in her own way, more formidable than her powerful husband. She was also not accustomed to being crossed. Especially by someone she considered an obvious inferior.

"There is no place for you, either." She practically spat the warning at him. "In case you've forgotten, Valentine is a married woman."

Patrick glanced around, appearing surprised. "So, where's the adoring husband?" His expression revealed none of the cold fury he was feeling as he looked this woman straight in the eye. "What's the matter, Eleanor? Couldn't Somers take time away from his teenybopper mistress to visit his wife and children?"

"She is not a teenager," Eleanor Alexander countered, her words tinged with acid. "Despite what the more unsavory members of the press have been reporting, Jennifer Nichols happens to be the same age Valentine was when she married Hamilton."

"So that makes it all right?" Patrick asked incredulously. "That the woman Valentine's husband is committing adultery with is of legal age?"

"He's not exactly committing adultery."

"Oh?" Patrick arched a black brow. "And what do you call sleeping with a woman who isn't your wife?"

"It's merely a case of midlife crisis," Eleanor hissed. "And although it's absolutely none of your business, Patrick Sullivan, once Hamilton comes to his senses, he'll return to Valentine. And his children. Where he belongs."

And you don't. She'd left the words unspoken, but her meaning was crystal clear. She turned away and marched toward the elevator, her stride long, her head held high, her back as straight as if someone had dropped a rod of cold steel down the back of her fur coat. She entered the elevator and turned around, giving Patrick one last warning glare as the steel doors slowly closed.

"Wow!" Susan came from around the desk, picked up the stuffed tiger and handed it to him. "What a barracuda!"

"Thanks." Patrick shoved it in with the others. "And watch your tongue, woman. You happen to be talking about my former mother-in-law."

"You're kidding."

"You've no idea how I wish I were."

"You were married? To Valentine Somers?"

"Alexander. And yes, we were married. For a short time." He didn't add that they'd been man and wife for a full six unforgettable hours before Eleanor and her husband had arrived at the Maryland motel with the sheriff in tow.

"Wow," Susan repeated. "How come you didn't ever tell me? I know," she said impatiently, "you didn't think it had anything to do with us." She shook her head in a way that threatened to dislodge her starched cap. "For an intelligent man, you can be a real dope when it comes to women, Patrick Sullivan."

"Why don't you tell me something I haven't figured out for myself?"

"So, when were you two married?"

"Susan, if you don't mind, I'd rather not talk about it."

"Don't you dare clam up, Patrick Sullivan," she warned, wagging an unpolished fingernail in his face. "After all we've shared, you owe me the truth."

She had a point, Patrick supposed. "It was a long time ago," he said. "When we were in school."

"You were college sweethearts?"

"High school."

Her eyes widened behind the tinted lenses of her glasses. "Wow," she repeated. "So, how long did it last?"

"Not long enough."

"Well, that explains what you're doing here with your menagerie." She tapped the same fingernail she'd waved in his face against her lips. "Valentine," she mused aloud. "That's it!"

"What's it?" The back-and-forth motion of his jaw suggested Patrick was grinding his teeth.

"That's why you refused to celebrate Valentine's Day, isn't it? That's why, in two years, I didn't receive a single red rose or a box of chocolates, or a puffy satin-and-lace greeting card. It was because of her. Because of that woman's name.''

"That's ridiculous." He refused to admit that the reason he'd never celebrated Valentine's Day was because February 14 represented both the best and worst day of his life.

"Is it?" Her intelligent gaze studied him thoughtfully. Then, as if making a decision, she put her hand on his sleeve, went up on her toes and brushed a kiss against his firmly set lips. "Good luck."

He covered her hand with his and wondered if her husband knew what a lucky bastard he was to have won this kind and caring woman by default. "Thanks." He gave her a crooked smile. "I think I'm going to need all I can get."

VALENTINE WAS SHAKING. This was ridiculous, she thought, dabbing her wet eyes with a tissue. So what if Patrick was kissing that nurse? It was certainly his right. He wasn't married to *her* any longer. And he hadn't been for a long time.

But that didn't stop her from hating the overendowed blonde. And Patrick for smiling at her the way he'd once smiled at her. Her irritation immediately dissolved when the object of all her consternation walked into the room, loaded down with his zooful of stuffed animals.

"Hi." He greeted her with the cocky grin that had nearly made her swoon when she was a girl. Although she'd given up swooning, his smile was still pretty devastating. As was the rest of him.

He'd changed into a pair of jeans, a cream fisherman's-knit sweater and a leather bomber jacket that, while in better condition than the one she remembered him wearing, still succeeded in making him look like the dashing rebel he'd once been. Valentine remembered thinking, during their short and fiery courtship, that if Hollywood had ever wanted to make a movie about James Dean, Patrick would have been perfect in the starring role.

"Hi, yourself," she said softly, feeling ridiculously like a love-struck seventeen-year-old girl.

"You look terrific."

She dragged her hand through her lank hair, wishing that she'd ignored the doctor's orders to stay in bed and had washed it. "Liar."

"It's true. But then again, you could never be anything but gorgeous to me." He glanced at the row of butterfly tape on her forehead.

"Lucky. No stitches."

"The doctor told me there shouldn't be a scar, but he can't promise."

Patrick shrugged. "I wouldn't worry about it. You're lovely enough that a scar would only make you look more interesting. So, how's the new mother?"

"Sore," she admitted, fighting down the unbidden surge of pleasure his compliment had caused. "And tired. But happy. Are all those for me?"

"They're for the kids." He tossed them onto the extra bed. "I brought something else for their mom." Reaching into the pocket of his jacket, he pulled out a small box.

Her hands trembled as she slowly opened the box. "Oh, Patrick." Lying on a bed of white satin was a silver charm proclaiming her to be a number one mom.

"I realize you probably don't have the bracelet anymore," he said. "But I figured you could wear it on a chain or something."

He'd given her the silver charm bracelet on their first date, proclaiming it to be a belated Christmas and New Year's present. At the time, the bracelet held only a silver fir tree and a replica of a bottle of champagne in a silver bucket. On Valentine's Day morning, he'd given her a silver heart.

Later that night, at the Sweethearts' Ball, although forbidden by her parents to be with Patrick, Valentine was swaying in Patrick's arms on the polished floor of the Old Dominion High School's gymnasium when he had surprised her with a second box containing a slender gold-lattice wedding band. Valentine had flung her arms around his neck and tearfully agreed to be his wife.

Three hours later they were married by a sleepy justice of the peace, the man's equally sleepy but enthusiastic wife serving as a witness. Six hours after that, Valentine's parents had arrived on the scene. Eight weeks later, the marriage was quietly and efficiently annulled.

"Oh, Patrick," she repeated. Her eyes misted, then brimmed over.

"Damn. I didn't mean to make you cry." He grabbed a handful of tissues from the bedside table and dabbed at her tears.

"It's j-just so b-beautiful…. And th-thoughtful and—"

"Hey." He brushed his knuckles up her cheek in a slow, warm sweep. "You earned it, sweetheart."

She managed a teary smile. "Thank you." She sniffed. "It was a v-very sweet th-thing to do."

When she took a deep breath, struggling for control, Patrick tried not to look at the way her swollen breasts moved against the front of her cotton nightgown, but he did anyway, then felt like a dirty old man for the thoughts he was having.

"I'm amazed you put up with me in those days," she said.

"Why?" He shot her a surprised look.

"I never should have let you give me that expensive bracelet, but at the time I was so used to having all the money I needed, I never really thought about you having more important things to spend your hard-earned money on."

Along with the heart-shaped charm on that long-ago Valentine's Day, he'd given her a red-rose wrist corsage, a flowered bottle of Anaïs Anaïs perfume—not cologne—a box of Swiss chocolates, a poem written by himself and penned inside an enormous lace card, which had made her cry, and a wonderfully indecent, sheer red nightgown that had made her blush.

"I doubt if you could have stopped me from doing any thing I wanted. But it wouldn't have mattered," Patrick said, "because you were the single, most important thing in my life in those days."

Although she knew that it was absolutely none of her business, Valentine found herself wondering who was the most important woman in Patrick's life these days.

"Where on earth did you find a jewelry store open on New Year's Day?" she asked, deciding the time had come to change the subject.

"I didn't break into one, if that's what you're thinking."

"That never crossed my mind!" But now that he'd brought it up, she couldn't help thinking that there had been a time when he might actually have considered such an action.

Patrick knew he'd overreacted to her innocent question. That's what came from locking horns with Eleanor Alexander. The woman had a way of stimulating old, defensive attitudes and behaviors he'd thought the navy had knocked out of him.

"I'm sorry I overreacted, Valentine." He sighed and combed his hands through his hair. "For the record, about six months ago I was called out on a hostage negotiation in Falls Church. A robbery had gone bad and some scared kid was holding a gun on the jeweler and his wife.

"After I talked the kid out, the jeweler told me that if he could ever do anything for me, just to ask. So, this morning I decided to take him up on his offer. He was more than happy to open the place so I could buy you a present."

Valentine recalled that particular hostage case all too well. She'd led both the six- and eleven-o'clock newscasts with it, and when Brandon MacGregor had stood outside a store surrounded by members of the SWAT team to report that Patrick Sullivan had taken the place of the jeweler's wife and was negotiating with the robber face-to-face, she'd been terrified.

"I remember that," she said. "I was amazed when Brandon reported who the negotiator was."

"A couple of years ago, the department was looking for someone to attend an FBI hostage school, so I volunteered. That was the first time I had to use what I'd learned."

Remembering exactly how persuasive he could be, Valentine was not terribly surprised. "Obviously, you're very good at your work," she said. "I also remember the jeweler calling you a hero."

"I'm not a hero. I was just doing my job."

"You were very brave." She smiled. "I almost told everyone in the newsroom that you were my high-school sweetheart."

He noticed she hadn't mentioned being his wife. "Your mother would have loved that story getting out," Patrick said dryly, "since she hasn't changed her opinion of me one iota."

"Oh, dear. You've seen Mother?"

"We talked. Out in the hall."

The grim expression on his face spoke volumes. Having been on the receiving end of Eleanor Alexander's disapproval on more than a few occasions herself, Valentine knew how it felt.

"I'm sorry," she murmured.

He shrugged. "She didn't say anything I hadn't heard before."

"I'm still sorry. You saved my life last night, Patrick. And the lives of my babies. If Mother can't put the past behind her, she should have at least thanked you for that."

"Oh, she did," Patrick allowed. "Right before she warned me not to get any ideas. Because Somers would be coming back."

"She's wrong." Valentine folded her arms. "He's not."

A rush of cold relief that he had no right to feel flooded over him. "How do you feel about that?" he asked carefully.

"Relieved," Valentine answered. "Have you seen the twins?"

It was a not-very-subtle attempt to change the subject. But a welcome one, since Patrick wasn't eager to discuss Hamilton Somers, either. "Not yet. I wanted to see their mother first."

"Well, then, let's go."

She pushed back the sheet and slid out of the high bed. Her white cotton nightgown, embroidered at the ruffled neck and hem, reminded Patrick of something from *Little House on the Prairie*. When the hem caught momentarily on the bed rail, allowing an intriguing flash of smooth thigh, Patrick was struck by a sudden urge to press his lips against what he knew to be the very sensitive flesh at the back of her knee.

"The doctor told me that the more I walked, the faster I could go home." She'd been taking such a walk when she'd turned the corner and witnessed Patrick kissing that nurse.

"When do the kids get to go home?"

"As soon as they reach five pounds," she said. "But they're ravenous little things, so the doctor thinks we're only talking about three or four days."

As she put on the ivory silk-brocade robe that was lying over the back of a nearby chair, her breasts swayed gently with the movement. An image flashed behind his lids—an image of Valentine nursing a baby. *Their* baby. Patrick sighed.

She slipped her feet into cotton slippers, but not before Patrick noticed that her toenails had been painted a soft peach color. A familiar floral Valentine scent exuded from her pores.

"You haven't changed your perfume."

She glanced up at him, surprised. "No."

"It's nice to know that some things stay the same."

Like the way being in the same room with him could make her heart treble its beat? Valentine wondered. Unwilling to deal with her unruly emotions right now, she took hold of his hand.

"Let me show you my family."

Minutes later, they were standing in front of the glass window of the nursery. "The incubator's only a precaution," she assured him when she saw his worried frown. "They should get sprung by tonight." The babies' faces were beet red and wrinkled, and their waving arms and legs looked like bright purple prunes.

"They're beautiful," he said softly. "Just like their mother."

She flushed prettily, not believing him but needing to hear the words just the same. When she'd gotten up to go to the bathroom this morning, she'd been depressed by her slack stomach, dry skin, lank hair and painfully swollen breasts.

"I thought I was prepared," she murmured. "But every time I stand in front of this window, the thought of how frighteningly dependent they are on me comes crashing down. All the stories about children drowning in toilets and swallowing gasoline and all these other horrors start flashing through my mind, and I can't help wondering how any of us make it to adulthood."

He put his arm around her. "You'll do fine. Better than fine, Valentine. You're going to be a great mother."

"I'd settle for adequate."

Patrick leaned forward, reading the cards taped to the side of the incubators: pink for the girl, blue for the boy.

"You named her Mara?"

Valentine saw the pleasure and surprise in his eyes and knew she'd made the right decision. "Well, it seemed only proper to name them for the two men who brought them into the world," she said. "Since they weren't both boys, I was thinking of naming one Jeb and the other Patricia. I figured I could always call her Pat, because there's certainly no way to feminize Jeb. But then, I knew that I'd always think of her as Mara, so that's her name."

His mother's name. The name Valentine had decided to give to their first daughter after learning that his mother had died when he was twelve—ten years after his father had taken off, causing Patrick to grow up fast and hard.

Emotion became a hard, tight ball in his throat, blocking his words. But as they exchanged a look fraught with intimate memories, no words were necessary.

"Sounds like they've inherited their mother's temper," Patrick said.

"The doctor says crying is good for their lungs. And I don't have a temper."

"Funny, that's not how I remember it."

"All right," she admitted. "Perhaps I did have a slight temper, back when I was young." *But only with you,* she tacked on silently. There had been so many tumultuous emotions that she'd first experienced with Patrick Sullivan, then never felt again.

"If that was a slight temper, sweetheart, the Grand Canyon is only a slight hairline fracture. I still have the scar from the blade of that ice skate you threw at me."

She'd been furious when she'd seen him laughing with some redheaded older woman in tight pink ski pants. Only later, after his cut had been stitched up in the emergency room, had Valentine learned that the redhead was his juvenile probation officer. That was when she'd also learned that Patrick had been thrown into the juvenile court system after running away from what he'd told Valentine was an abusive foster home.

When she'd expressed surprise that his foster father—a prominent D.C. businessman—would risk publicity by beating him, Patrick had shocked her by revealing that the businessman's wife had been the guilty party. And although he'd admitted finding the older woman's sexual advances exciting in the beginning, by the time Patrick had turned sixteen, he'd begun to feel dirty. And used.

"I didn't throw it at you," Valentine said now. "You stepped in the way."

He grinned down at her in a way that let her know he hadn't believed her excuse back then and he damn well wasn't going to buy it now. "Funny how memory is selective, isn't it?"

Her most vivid memory of that night was how after they'd left the hospital, he'd told her the story of his youthful seduction, and then, weeping with remorse for this misunderstood boy who had gone so long without anyone to love him, Valentine had surrendered her virginity in an attempt to soothe his emotional pain.

Valentine was not the only one remembering that first time they'd made love. Patrick was thinking how the first time he'd made love to Valentine, he'd felt reborn. That overwhelming experience—so different from any of the others he'd known—had taught him the difference between sex and love.

They stood there, hand in hand, looking at Valentine's babies, lost in thoughts both forbidden and exciting.

Valentine wondered if she hadn't let her parents break them up so many years ago, would they still be together?

Patrick knew they would.

Valentine wished that Patrick was Jeb and Mara's father.

Patrick wished the same.

Valentine wondered if it was possible to turn back time.

Patrick vowed to give it his best shot.

She thought about the look in that nurse's eyes, right before she kissed Patrick.

Patrick wondered if Valentine knew that despite all the women he'd been with, she was the only one he'd ever loved.

Thoughts and dreams, wishes and regrets—all went around and around in a widening gyre, and although both knew that the past would have to be faced—if for no other reason than to put it behind them—each was content to bask in this one, shared, stolen moment.

Chapter Five

VALENTINE'S HOUSE was on Capitol Hill, where delicate old town houses shared valuable space with marble government buildings. Historic landmarks stood beside starkly modern edifices. The row homes on The Hill had been quietly crumbling for half a century, but now, due to the outrageous prices of houses in the suburbs, the attraction of the vast, remodeled Union Station—part of which had been turned into a vibrant mall—and the fact that Capitol Hill provided some of the most exciting scenes the city had to offer, the neighborhood had experienced an energetic surge of regeneration.

One week after that memorable New Year's Eve, Patrick was standing on Valentine's front porch, shifting from foot to foot, waiting for her to answer her doorbell.

When she finally appeared—her silky blond hair pulled back from her face with a navy headband, and wearing an oversize navy blue Georgetown sweatshirt, faded jeans and high-topped sneakers—he felt a slow, sexual pull.

"Hi."

The pleasure shone in her face. "Hi."

In the silence that followed, Patrick gave her a thorough appraisal, from the top of her blond head down to those ridiculous shoes and back up again. He noted, with satisfaction, that she was wearing his charm on a silver chain around her neck.

"You don't look old enough to be a mother."

She flashed him a smile. "You really are a liar."

"It's not a lie. You don't look any different than you did ten years ago."

Valentine pressed her hand against her breast, as if hoping to stop her pounding heart. It had started hammering away the minute she'd opened the door and found him standing there.

Although he'd called every day to see how she was doing, she hadn't seen him since that first day in the hospital. While Valentine told herself that he had better things to do than to visit an old flame, that hadn't stopped her from missing him.

She wanted to tell him that she was different now. She wanted to tell him that she was no longer the foolish, pampered girl who hadn't had the nerve to stand up to her parents' stony displeasure. But words failed her and she could only stand there, looking up into the face she'd dreamed about too many times over the intervening years.

Patrick glanced over her shoulder. "Are you going to invite me in? Or have I come at a bad time?"

"Oh." She blushed. "I'm sorry, I'm a little slow on the uptake these days."

He frowned and traced a dark circle under one eye with his index finger. "You look tired."

His light touch was like a sparkler against her skin. It was starting all over again, her romantic side said. But how could it? her stronger, pragmatic side answered.

There was no such thing as starting over again; there was only picking up from where they'd left off. But so many years had passed and they were both so changed, and she had Jeb and Mara to think about; and how many men would want to take on the burden of another man's children?

"You know how it is with new babies," she said. "I was up and down all night." She didn't add that memories of Patrick had stolen what little sleep the children had allowed her.

"You don't have any help?"

"I grew up with nannies," she reminded him. "I want Jeb and Mara to have a very clear idea of who their mother is."

Even as he admired her attitude, Patrick couldn't deny that she really did look exhausted. "Still, with twins—"

"I'll hire someone when I go back to work," she said. "Until then, I want to keep them all to myself."

"I guess I can understand that."

"Come on in. I'll show you around."

The house was bright and sunny and smelled like springtime. The wood floors glowed in the colorful sunbeams slanting through the stained glass of the front door. Wainscotted walls had been adorned with a collection of Williamsburg samplers; a cozy fire crackled in the red brick fireplace.

"You've done a great job."

She smiled as she glanced around the room, remembering how excited she'd been the day she'd yanked up the olive-green wall-to-wall carpeting and had discovered wood floors darkened from years of abuse.

"Thanks. It's the first house I've ever owned that was really mine, and there's still a ways to go. I've been putting off hanging the wallpaper in the kitchen for months."

"Good. Standing on a ladder in your condition would've been dangerous."

"That's what my contractor told me. He wanted to take care of it for me, but I want to do as much myself as I can."

"Isn't that taking on a lot, what with work and babies?"

"Probably. But you can't imagine how much satisfaction I get from painting woodwork or hanging wallpaper."

That was a surprise. The young girl he'd known had worried about so much as chipping a fingernail. She'd grown up surrounded by servants; the Alexanders had people to cook their food, clean their house, mow their law, make their beds and launder their underwear.

Her parents drove around in a chauffeured limousine, while Valentine had received a tomato-red Mercedes two-seater sports car for her sixteenth birthday. Naturally, she hadn't had to worry about keeping the tank full or the gleaming red finish waxed. All the unpleasant, petty chores of life had been done for her.

Patrick tried to imagine this woman up on a ladder, slapping pasted paper onto a wall—and failed.

"Want to see baby Jeb and Mara?" she asked, wondering at the reason for his slight frown.

"I thought you'd never ask."

He followed her up the narrow stairs to the nursery, where bright yellow ducks carrying red-and-white-striped umbrellas frolicked on cream wallpaper. The stuffed animals Patrick had brought the babies covered every shelf and much of the floor.

"Eric—he's my contractor—found the flooring," she said, pointing out the nursery-rhyme vinyl tile. "Isn't it darling?"

"Darling," Patrick muttered, picturing some young, suntanned hunk wearing a tight white T-shirt and jeans, tool belt hung low on his hip. Something that felt uncomfortably like jealousy surged through him. "Nice of good old Eric to take such a personal interest."

There was a new edge to his voice—one that made Valentine wonder if Patrick could actually be jealous. "Not that it's relevant, but Eric Pederson is seventy-five if he's a day. He's also married, with three children, nine grandchildren, two great-grandchildren and another one on the way."

If Patrick was uncomfortable with the unruly feelings he'd been having lately, he was definitely disconcerted by how good he felt to discover his mental image had been way off-track.

"Like I said," he repeated with studied casualness, "it's nice of him to take such a personal interest in a client."

So he hadn't been jealous. Obviously her imagination had been running rampant lately. *Hormones,* Valentine decided.

"He feels sorry for me. Which is ridiculous, of course. I think he's been watching too many black-and-white movies about the trials and tribulations of pregnant single women."

Patrick decided not to mention that he'd been having a few worries along the same lines over the past few days. Although he'd been going crazy, he'd forced himself to stay away, giving her time to adjust to motherhood. Giving her time to accept the idea that he'd come back into her life.

There were two white wicker bassinets placed where the afternoon sun, slanting through the window, could warm the babies. When he gazed down at Valentine's daughter, seeing a face that was a tiny replica of her mother's, he felt a wave of emotion so strong it almost buckled his knees.

"Hey," he said, his voice roughened with feeling, "she's not red anymore."

Patrick ran his finger down the baby's satin cheek with a gentleness he'd been unaware of possessing. Mara was looking up at him with sober blue eyes. When a tiny hand reached up and curled its dimpled fingers around his, holding on with a strength that surprised him, Patrick fell in love.

"She's so beautiful, Val."

Watching the emotions move across his face, Valentine realized, not for the first time, what a mistake she'd made in letting her parents force the annulment. Although she'd left a message with his secretary, Hamilton still hadn't managed to make it to either the hospital or the house to see his own children. While Patrick was grinning foolishly at Mara as if he found her to be the most amazing, scintillating female in the world.

"She's also quiet for the first time today," Valentine answered. "Why don't we take advantage of the lull and have some coffee?"

Giving the twins one last tender look, Patrick returned downstairs with Valentine. He was sitting in the kitchen, admiring the bleached oak cabinets and ivory ceramic tile when she dumped a load of clothing on the kitchen table.

"What's this?"

"Clean laundry. I haven't had a chance to fold it."

"Sit down." He plucked a cloth diaper from her fingers. "I'll do this."

"Really, Patrick—"

"I said, sit down and drink your coffee."

Something about his quiet tone rankled. "This isn't your jurisdiction, officer," she said. "You can't throw your weight around and expect everyone to snap to attention."

"Is that what you think I was doing?" he asked, honestly surprised.

"No." She shook her head. "I overreacted. It's just that this seems so strange."

"I imagine it takes time to get used to the idea of being a parent," Patrick allowed.

"It's not that." She sank down onto an apple-green ladder-back chair, braced her elbow on the maple table and rested her chin on her palm. "You know I always wanted children, Patrick. I've dreamed of how it was going to be for so many years, that being a mother seems perfectly right.

"It's *us* that has me a little edgy," she admitted, feeling that after all the mixed messages they'd traded in the past, she owed it to him to be absolutely honest this time around.

"Us?"

Oh, God, perhaps he wasn't experiencing these same unruly feelings. Perhaps, after delivering her babies, he felt some sort of obligation to keep tabs on them. Perhaps, she thought, he was only doing what he perceived to be his duty.

She took a long drink of coffee, unnerved by Patrick's unwavering gaze. "Forget I said anything.... I told you, Patrick, new mothers get crazy from time to time."

The last time he'd heard so much bottled-up stress in a voice was when he'd spent six long hours talking that jewelry-store thief out of killing a sixty-two-year-old man.

"Val—"

"It's simply hormones," she said shakily as she began to fold the clothes again. "I've tended to get a little over-emotional lately, but the doctor assures me it'll pass. In the meantime, don't pay attention to anything I say."

"Dammit, Valentine."

Patrick snatched a bra from her hand. The utilitarian white cotton undergarment was nothing like the skimpy lace-and-satin confections he remembered her wearing—yet another reminder that she was no longer that young girl he'd fallen in love with.

"You can rattle on about hormones all you want, but we both know that it's more than that. Of course, there's an *us*.

"There's always been an *us*—even when you were married and I was trying to see how many women it took to drive you out of my mind. You can't deny that what we had doesn't just go away because we—or anyone else— might want it to."

He caught her downcast chin in his fingers and held her nervous gaze on his. "We're going to have to deal with these feelings, Valentine," he said. "If for no other reason than to let us both get on with our lives."

Over the past week, he'd come to realize that the reason he'd never gotten over Valentine was because he'd never actually accepted her leaving in the first place. Somehow, he'd managed to convince himself that she would come back. In the beginning, such deception had been necessary for survival—it was either that or go mad. As the years passed, it had become instinctive.

Before she could answer, one of the babies began to cry.

"That's Jeb," Valentine said, having learned to distinguish the individual cries. "He's probably wet again." She groaned when Mara started crying along with her brother. Mara's cries were higher, and a good deal more strident. "Terrific. Now he's got his sister going."

When she started to rise from the chair, Patrick put a firm but gentle hand on her shoulder. "I'll go."

"But—"

"Val, I'm perfectly capable of changing a diaper."

She didn't have the strength to argue. He went upstairs, leaving her to sip her cooling coffee and enjoy the rare chance to rest. The house became blissfully quiet again. Finally, growing curious at what, exactly, Patrick was doing, she went upstairs to the nursery where she found him sitting in the bentwood rocker, a baby in each arm, rocking and crooning softly.

When he saw her standing in the doorway, he put Jeb and Mara back into their wicker bassinets. Pressing a warning finger against his lips, he crept out of the room.

"You're a miracle worker. It takes me forever to get them quieted down."

A thick strand of blond hair had come loose from her headband. Patrick tugged on its end. "You'll get the hang of it."

She sighed. "I hope so."

"You will." Instead of going back downstairs, Patrick took her by the shoulders and turned her in the direction of her bedroom. "First rule of motherhood," he said. "Whenever the kids sleep, you sleep."

Too exhausted to argue, she slumped on the edge of the bed and unprotestingly let him take off her sneakers. He pulled back the quilt and she snuggled under it, nearly asleep already. Bending down, Patrick pressed a light kiss against her temple, then turned to leave.

"Patrick?"

He turned in the doorway. "Yeah, Val?"

"May I ask a question?"

"Sure."

"How many did it take?"

"How many what?"

"How many women?"

He hadn't meant to tell her about the other women. Frustration had made him rash and it had just come out. "How many did it take to make me forget you?"

She nodded, color staining her cheeks, her heart open and vulnerable in her eyes.

"I don't know."

Before she could respond to that intriguing answer, he was gone. Seconds later, Valentine had fallen asleep.

She dreamed that they were a family—she and Patrick and Jeb and Mara. They'd spent the day at the zoo, laughing and playing, and after they'd returned home and put their babies to bed, she and Patrick had made love. All night long.

But it was only a dream, Valentine reminded herself when she woke an hour later. She warned herself not to make the mistake of allowing old feelings to color this new and fragile relationship with Patrick. Hadn't she already learned the hard way that dreams very seldom come true?

Enticed by the aromas coming from the kitchen, she went downstairs and found Patrick standing in front of the stove. "Is that what I think it is?"

"Sullivan's famous chili." He greeted her with a grin. "I made extra for you to freeze."

He held out a spoonful for her to taste. She took a bite, breathing in a deep, cooling breath as the chili threatened to take the top of her head off. "What makes you think it won't burn its way through the freezer bag?"

"Too hot?"

She swallowed. "Just right. Although I hate to think how Jeb and Mara will react."

"Oh, damn. I didn't know you were breast-feeding."

She shrugged. "They'll have to get used to their mother's bad habits sooner or later. It might as well be sooner."

"Are you calling my chili a bad habit?"

"Never," she said, returning his smile.

"Exactly what you're supposed to say." He opened the oven door.

"You baked corn bread, too?"

"I saw the frozen-food boxes in the garbage, Val," Patrick said. "You need to eat properly to get your strength back."

"It's a little difficult to cook chili with a baby in each arm," she pointed out. "Besides, cooking isn't my strong suit."

It had been a joke between them that since Valentine could burn water, Patrick would have to do all the cooking once they were married.

At the time, she hadn't thought much of his willingness to take on what was traditionally a woman's role. Now, looking back on it, she realized that Patrick's steadfast refusal to cave in to any role forced on him by society was yet another reason her parents had found him so utterly unacceptable.

"I figured necessity might have forced you to pick up a few skills over the years." From what he'd heard of Hamilton Somers, Valentine's husband's area of expertise was not in the kitchen, but the bedroom. Other women's bedrooms.

"For your information, I've picked up a great many skills. But cooking isn't one of them."

"No problem." He cut the crumbly yellow corn bread into squares, slathered an impossibly fattening amount of butter on a piece and handed it to her. "I'll take care of the cooking."

"What?" Butter dripped off the corn bread onto the floor.

"I said, I'll do the cooking." He wiped the butter up with a paper towel. "I'm still on the night shift, but I can fix your dinner before I leave and prepare breakfast after I get off."

"Breakfast?"

"It is the most important meal of the day."

"I can't let you do that."

He scooped the chili into a deep white bowl and put it on the table. "Don't be ridiculous. You're an intelligent, competent woman, Valentine. But it's more than a little obvious that right now you've gotten yourself in over your head.''

He took her hand in his, linking their fingers together. ''And since you refuse to hire anyone to help out, and your husband and the father of your children seems to be conspicuously absent, I figure the least I can do, as an old friend, is fill in the best I can.''

This had happened before. Ten years ago, he'd stormed into her life, swept her up and changed the world as she'd always known it. When it was over, Valentine thought that her heart would never heal. But it had. She'd recovered and gotten on with her life, the same way she had when she'd learned of her husband's adultery. She couldn't allow anyone—even Patrick—to take her hard-won independence away from her.

Valentine knew that Patrick wanted a great deal more from her than mere friendship. What she didn't know was whether she had anything left to give.

Her throat was horribly constricted. ''I don't think it's such a good idea,'' she managed. ''So much has happened, Patrick. And we've both changed.''

''Have we?'' he asked, his eyes on hers as his thumb stroked the sensitive skin on the inside of her palm. ''I wonder if things have really changed as much as we thought?''

He bent his head for the kiss, bringing his face close—too close—to hers. ''Patrick... Please, don't.'' She pressed her hands against his chest.

It would be so easy, he thought. One little kiss, just to prove that he didn't really need her. One brief, unemotional touching of lips to satisfy his curiosity.

His gaze moved over her face like a caress. ''You can't tell me that you haven't been wondering.''

His breath was warm and minty against her parted lips. "Of course, I've wondered," she whispered. "But then I remind myself that I'm not ready."

She'd been through a rough nine months, Patrick allowed—the publicity surrounding her husband's infidelity, the impending divorce, her pregnancy, the dangerous situation of the babies' birth, and now, trying to take care of twins all by herself. What right did he have to pressure her into a relationship she was not yet prepared to handle?

No rights, he admitted, reluctantly. *None at all.*

"You're right." Releasing a long, slow breath, he straightened and raked his hand through his dark hair. Although he was wearing it shorter than she remembered, it was still as black as pitch and looked as soft as silk. "It was a stupid idea."

"Not stupid." Her fingers itched with the urge to comb his ruffled hair back into place. "Just a bit premature."

Okay, Patrick decided, they'd play it her way. He'd rushed her into marriage once before, and look how that had turned out.

"I still want to cook you dinner."

She was sick of microwave meals that tasted like cardboard. "I may be a little confused right now," she admitted, "but I'm not stupid. I'd never turn down home cooking, Patrick. Especially yours."

It was, Patrick told himself, a start.

Chapter Six

As PROMISED, Patrick began dropping by every afternoon before work. After giving her a quick, impersonal peck on top of her head, he'd move into the kitchen. Valentine noticed that although his work was constantly interrupted by the twins, he took them in stride, unruffled by the daily problems that were part and parcel of having two vocal infants under one roof.

As the days went by, Valentine was surprised at how comfortable she'd come to feel with Patrick. When they'd been younger, their relationship had been an emotional roller coaster—in constant danger of careening out of control. But now, being with him was so natural that by the time the twins were a month old, there were occasions when she would actually forget that the babies weren't his; that they weren't really a family.

They talked about everything—his work, her work, current theories on child rearing, the world. He told her about the book he'd written, and the one he was currently working on; and when she asked to read them, he simply shrugged and said, "Sure."

The self-protective barriers she'd put up around herself at the first sign of attraction to him slowly, gradually lowered. She was ready for him to kiss her. *More than ready,* Valentine decided one afternoon while she watched him chop a handful of dark green chives to add to the hearty potato soup bubbling away on a back burner. She was dying for him to kiss her, to touch her, to drag her down to the kitchen floor and make mad passionate love to her.

At first, she'd waited on tenterhooks for him to reinitiate that kiss they'd almost shared in the kitchen the first day he'd visited. But to her dismay, Patrick steadfastly avoided any romantic or sexual situations. And although she found him as stimulating as ever—even more so, with his added maturity—he treated her not like a prospective lover, but like a pal.

One afternoon, as she gathered up a pile of wet towels that had been quietly growing mold for the past week, she glanced at herself in the bathroom mirror and stopped abruptly. No wonder Patrick hadn't made a pass at her.

She'd washed her hair this morning, but before she could blow it dry, baby Jeb had begun yelling for his breakfast. Then Mara had chimed in, the shrill noise making Valentine's nerves screech. Grabbing up the rubber band that had been wrapped around the morning *Washington Post,* she'd pulled her hair back into a lopsided ponytail and forgotten all about it.

Now, unattractive hunks of hair had fallen out of the elastic band to hang limply down her neck, her lips were chapped, and she hadn't worn a smidgen of makeup in days. She glanced down at her watch. Ten minutes until Patrick was due; enough time, if she hurried, to remind him that she was still a woman.

Plugging in her hot rollers, she pulled her sweatshirt—a ragged one with cut-off sleeves, white script on faded gray proclaiming it once to have belonged to the George Washington University's athletic department—over her head, took off her nursing bra, sweatpants and cotton briefs and, without giving the water time to heat up, popped into the shower just long enough to run a soapy cloth over her body, finishing up with a wild dusting of talcum powder that covered the floor like a light snowfall. As a final, hopefully irresistible touch, she spritzed on the Anaïs Anaïs cologne Patrick had always liked.

She wrapped her hair on the hot rollers, and eschewing the time it would take to sponge on foundation, she brushed some pink blush on her cheekbones, a touch of misty mauve shadow on her eyelids, a sweep of pencil liner, a dash with the mascara brush. She lined her lips with dark rose and filled them in with a softer pink. She ran into the bedroom, yanked a royal blue silk blouse off its padded satin hanger and slipped it on. After buttoning it wrong, she cursed and started all over again, growing more and more frustrated as her fingers fumbled with the small pearl buttons.

Finally the blouse was buttoned. She stepped into a pair of black silk pre-baby panties that were still too tight but made her feel sexy, and tugged on a pair of panty hose, which promptly ran. Since they were her last pair, Valentine decided that the unsightly ladder running from knee to thigh would be covered by her pleated, black wool slacks.

Sucking in a deep breath, she turned this way and that, observing herself judiciously in the mirror on the back of the closet door. The slacks were unflatteringly snug, so she tugged the blouse from the waistband, allowing it to hang loose.

Three more minutes. Valentine was on her knees, looking in the back of the closet for a misplaced pair of black shoes when she heard the familiar sound of the key she'd given Patrick in the door.

Success! She jammed her feet into the flat suede shoes and raced down the hall, then descended the stairs with a casualness that belied the fact that she was out of breath and her heart was pounding in an out-of-control rhythm.

"Hello, Patrick," she greeted him. "You're early."

He was carrying several brown paper grocery bags. "Am I?"

"Three minutes."

He decided he liked the idea of her knowing exactly what time he arrived each afternoon. Perhaps she had been waiting for him. "I don't want to get too predictable," he said with a grin. "You'll start taking me for granted."

"Never." Disappointed when he didn't seem to notice all the trouble she'd gone to on his behalf, Valentine followed him into the kitchen.

"I brought you something," he said. Reaching into a bag, he pulled out a bouquet of flowers wrapped in green tissue.

The flowers were a portent of the spring that on this cold, gray February day seemed very far away: sunny daffodils, snowy daisies, tulips in primary colors reminiscent of a child's crayons.

"They're lovely." She reached into a cupboard and pulled down the Waterford vase that had been a wedding gift from her parents four years ago. "And they smell wonderful."

"Not as good as you," he said easily as he dug into one of the bags and took out a blue box of spaghetti, some cans of tomato sauce and various bottles of spices. He glanced over at her. "You going out somewhere?"

"No? Why?" Was it that unusual for her to look halfway decent?

"I thought you might have those curlers in your hair for a reason."

It was with frantic dread that she reached up and felt the forgotten fat plastic rollers that stuck out all over her head, making her look as if she were trying to pick up radio waves from outer space. Well, at least she'd accomplished one thing: she'd finally gotten him to notice her.

"I was sick and tired of looking like a harried new mother."

"But you *are* a harried new mother."

She yanked the rollers from her hair, slamming them down on the table, one at a time. "I wanted to look nice for you, Patrick."

He was digging around in a drawer, searching out the can opener. "I told you, Val, you could never be anything but gorgeous to me." Finding it, he took a block of Parmesan cheese from one of the bags, put it on the tile counter and started another search. "Where's your grater?"

She didn't want him to cook for her. She wanted him to seduce her. Or at least try. "In the bottom drawer, to the right of the sink."

Her flat tone earned a concerned glance. "You okay?"

"Of course."

"You look wrung out. Are you getting enough sleep?"

"I'm a new mother, Patrick," she reminded him. *Wrung out. Terrific. What had happened to gorgeous?* "Sleepless nights come with the territory."

"I told you, Val, the idea is to fit your naps to their schedules." He opened the refrigerator, pulled out a glass bottle of tomato juice he'd bought yesterday and poured them each a glass.

"I would if the little devils would agree to sleep at the same time."

"Still the relay kids, huh?" On cue, Jeb began to scream, demanding his dinner.

"I'm not going to jump right up," she decided with uncharacteristic firmness. Usually, the faintest squeak would send her running into the nursery. Unfortunately, uncommon silence also brought its own fears; she couldn't count the times she'd gone in and wakened one or both sleeping babies, to assure herself that they hadn't expired from crib death.

"I'm going to stay right here and talk with you about your book and drink my juice and go upstairs when I feel like it."

"Good for you," Patrick said agreeably, pulling up a chair beside her.

Afraid she was being a terrible mother, but having decided to show Patrick that she could still be desirable, Valentine concentrated solely on him for a full five minutes; she didn't take her eyes from his as he told her that his agent had reported a nibble on the book making the rounds in New York.

"How exciting."

He shrugged. "I've learned not to get too hopeful."

"But it's going to sell." She leaned toward him, enveloping him in a fragrant cloud. "And when you're a regular on all the bestseller lists, I can tell everyone I knew you before you were rich and famous."

She'd put her hand on his knee and although he was sure it must be his imagination, he thought he could feel the warmth burning its way through the thick wool of his uniform slacks. "You haven't even read it."

"Only because you keep forgetting to bring it with you."

That's what he'd told her. It was also a lie. What Valentine had no way of knowing was that Patrick was irrationally afraid of her opinion.

What if she didn't like it? he often wondered as he drove through the dark streets with Jeb. Of course she'd love it, Jeb insisted every time Patrick brought the subject up, which was often.

Still, Patrick couldn't be sure. And until he was, he couldn't make himself share what was, admittedly, a fictionalized account of their past romance. Past experience had made him extremely cautious where this woman was concerned.

"I have faith in you," Valentine insisted.

He didn't want to talk about his book any longer. "You know," he said finally, "I really like that blouse." He ran a hand up her arm, feeling the silk beneath his fingers, remembering that Valentine's skin was softer.

"Thank you."

"It makes your eyes look even bluer, if that's possible."

Feeling a great deal more confident, she fluttered her lashes in a way Vivien Leigh had flashed hers at Clark Gable in the *Gone With the Wind* rerun she'd seen on cable at three o'clock this morning while pacing the floor with Mara. By the time baby Jeb had demanded a turn, little Bonnie Blue had fallen off her pony and died, and Rhett was trying to drown his grief, which reminded Valentine exactly how fortunate she was to have two such healthy, albeit loud, babies.

"What a nice thing to say." Upstairs, Jeb's crying drifted off to ragged sobs, and his sister was left to pick up the slack.

"I only hope it's washable."

"By hand. Why?" She followed Patrick's chagrined look to the front of her blouse, where a dark wet spot was spreading across the royal blue silk. "Oh, no."

Some femme fatale she was! Pressing her hand over the stain, Valentine jumped up from the table and left the room in tears.

Hormones, Patrick reminded himself as he waited what he hoped was an appropriate amount of time before following Valentine upstairs.

He found her in the nursery, feeding a now quiet Jeb. The tears had stopped, leaving behind raccoon circles of black mascara around her damp eyes. Her lashes were wet and spiky, her complexion splotchy from crying and her hair hung in tangled, unbrushed curls against the nape of her neck.

She'd undone the buttons of the milk-stained blouse, allowing her son access to her breast. Patrick watched the baby's cheeks puff and pull as his rosebud mouth drew sustenance; he tried to remember a time when Valentine had looked more beautiful, and came up blank.

"You don't have to be embarrassed, Valentine," he said when she turned away from what she took to be his pitying look. He crossed the room and crouched down beside her. "What you're doing is natural. And beautiful."

Although baby Jeb's eyes were closed, he sensed the movement beside him and curled his small fist against Valentine's blue-veined flesh, as if claiming it for his own. Patrick brushed his knuckles against the baby's satiny cheek.

"And you're beautiful."

His knuckle moved from Jeb's pink cheek to her creamy breast. It was so hard to back away. For weeks he'd been going crazy, fantasizing about making love to her. Not the young and impressionable Valentine of his youth, but this woman who impressed him daily with her intelligence and stamina, and remarkably—considering what a strain he knew the twins to be—her patience and tenderness.

There'd been so many times when he'd wanted to finish that kiss he'd almost begun in the kitchen. But although he'd always prided himself on his control, Patrick feared that if he gave in to the temptation to kiss her, he wouldn't be able to stop. He didn't want to hurt her. But, dear Lord, how he wanted her!

The room was quiet. Mara had drifted back to sleep and there was only the soft sound of Valentine's son sucking and swallowing—and the hammerlike beat of his heart, pounding so hard and so loud, Patrick was amazed that Valentine couldn't hear it.

"I'd better go start the spaghetti sauce." Reluctance was in his eyes, his voice. He could easily stay here and watch this tender scene forever.

Her embarrassment had faded away. Because just as it felt so right for Patrick to have delivered her babies, it felt amazingly right for him to sit beside her now.

"I'm really not all that hungry."

Did she whisper to keep from disturbing the baby? Patrick wondered. Or because she was experiencing the same tumultuous feelings currently creating havoc within him?

"Neither am I. But I've got a trip coming up and I want to leave you with enough food that I won't have to worry about you not eating."

"You're going away?"

Patrick felt like singing the "Hallelujah Chorus" when he saw the uncensored distress in her remarkable blue eyes. "Just for a couple of days. Three at the most. I have to transport a prisoner to Boston."

"What kind of prisoner?"

"I guess you'd call him a bank robber."

"A bank robber?" Fear replaced the earlier distress. "Isn't that dangerous?"

"Only if I eat the airline food."

"This isn't anything to joke about."

He loved the idea of her worrying about him. "Val," he said, tugging at the corners of her downcast lips, coaxing them into a reluctant smile, "I was only joking. The guy's a Savings and Loan Association president."

"Oh." Relief was a cooling wave. "I'll miss you."

Unable to resist, he leaned forward, reached under her hair and cupped the back of her neck with his fingers. "I miss you already.'' Finally, he kissed her—a quick, hard meeting of lips that ended too soon and left them both wanting more.

Patrick stood with a weary sigh and was almost to the nursery door when he turned and gave her a long look rife with frustration and hunger and a host of other emotions too numerous to catalog.

''You really are so damn beautiful,'' he murmured. Then, flashing her a weary smile, he left.

She heard his footfalls on the stairs and soon there was the now familiar sound of pots and pans banging in the kitchen. She leaned her head against the back of the chair, closed her eyes and allowed herself the pleasure of basking in the memory of his wonderful, too-brief kiss.

Chapter Seven

SHE MISSED HIM. Terribly. Although the twins kept her running, the first day of Patrick's absence dragged on interminably. During whatever scarce moments of peace she was blessed with, Valentine sat in the treasured quiet and read Patrick's book, which he'd finally given her.

Having expected a police thriller, she was surprised by the obviously autobiographical story of a teenage boy who'd fallen in love with a girl beyond his reach.

Turning the pages, Valentine realized, for the first time, exactly how threatened Patrick must have been by her family's wealth and power, and how intimidated by what he took to be her "sophistication"—really a polished veneer designed to enhance her father's public image.

All her life, her actions had been geared to "what people would think." She'd heard those words so often while growing up, they'd become so much a part of her that only lately had she begun thinking about not what she *should* want, but what she *did* want.

And she wanted Patrick.

But it seemed that she hadn't been the only one putting on an act that long-ago winter. At the time, she'd thought Patrick to be so strong and self-assured. He'd never behaved as if he possessed a single doubt about himself, or about their future.

But now, as she read on, Valentine understood that those hurtful, scathing accusations Patrick had flung at her when she'd reluctantly succumbed to her parents' pressure to return home with them, had been born not of anger, but despair.

She was sitting with the manuscript pages on her lap, reliving that horrible day, when the phone rang. She scooped it up on the second ring. "When are you coming home?"

"I hope you don't ask that of every man who telephones you," the deep, wonderfully familiar voice said.

"Only the sexy ones." She held the receiver closer to her ear, as if she could lessen the distance between them. "I miss you."

"Not as much as I miss you," Patrick answered. "How are you and the Terrible Twins getting along?"

"We hit a milestone. They both slept through the night."

"Good. Then you finally got some sleep."

She decided against telling him that she hadn't slept as well as she should have. Because she couldn't stop thinking about him. "I've been reading your book."

He drew in a sharp breath, leaned his head against the wall and closed his eyes. "And?" He wondered if she knew how much it took out of him to ask that question.

"I love it. It's wonderful, Patrick. Rich and warm and bittersweet. I cried when Vanessa left with her parents."

He wondered what Valentine would say if he told her that he'd cried when she left with her parents.

"Patrick?"

He dragged a hand over his face, scrubbing away painful memories. "Yeah, Val?"

"There's something I've never told you. Why I left."

He knew why she'd left. Because her parents could offer her a far more comfortable and secure life. Never having had any of his own, Patrick had always understood the lure of security.

"You were only seventeen, Valentine," he said, deciding to finally let her off the hook. "You weren't really old enough to know your own mind."

She'd been afraid he'd thought that. Over the years, whenever she thought about that disastrous day—which was all too often—she'd realized he'd undoubtedly thought her to be a pampered, spoiled brat.

"I was young," she allowed. "But I still knew exactly what I wanted, Patrick. And that was to be your wife."

"Then why did you leave? Why did you get that damned annulment?"

The day the official, impersonal document had arrived in the mail, Patrick had drunk his way through a bottle of rotgut whiskey, trying to drown the pain. Unfortunately, the booze hadn't worked then and although the bourbon was more expensive the second time around, it hadn't proven any more helpful after he had watched the television coverage of her marriage to Hamilton Somers.

Valentine's weary sigh was easily heard over the hum of the long-distance wires. "Remember when my parents sent you out of the hotel room so they could talk to me alone?"

"I remember." How could he not? He'd paced the parking lot, heart in his throat, chain-smoking the unfiltered cigarettes he'd foolishly thought at the time made him look cool. Rebel without a clue, he thought now.

"When I refused to leave you, my father reminded me that I was only seventeen. He threatened to have you arrested for taking a minor across state lines."

Patrick knew that the former vice president never would have followed through on such a threat—because the press would have had a field day with such a powerful man admitting that he'd lost control of his own daughter.

"That's why you left?" If only she'd told him.

"I was trying to protect you, Patrick. Besides," she said, a small lingering hurt creeping into her tone, "I never expected you to give up without a fight. After all, I was nearly eighteen. In two more months my father couldn't have done anything to stop me from being with you.

"But then when you didn't come back to school, Mary Anne Martin told me that you'd joined the navy and left town."

Mary Anne had been a former girlfriend who admittedly wasn't known around Old Dominion High School for being very selective with her sexual favors. Patrick knew how hard it must have been for Valentine to go to her. He also knew how much pleasure Mary Anne would have gotten from watching Valentine squirm.

"I didn't think there was anything to stick around for." *Or anyone.* Pride, he thought. His foolish, damnable pride had cost them both so much.

"I tried to find you, but my father had already gotten to the navy and they refused to tell me anything. Finally, I decided that Mary Anne must be right—that you'd only wanted to prove that a boy from the wrong side of the tracks could talk his way into a debutante's bedroom. That hurt," she admitted softly. "A lot."

"I imagine about as much as it hurt me," Patrick countered, "thinking that you were simply an uptown girl who'd gotten her kicks slumming, and then called Daddy when things got out of hand and you found yourself married to a guy who'd never be allowed in the country club." His voice was tired. "I guess I blew it, huh?"

"I think we both did, Patrick," she answered honestly.

There was another long silence, and Valentine knew they were both thinking the same thing—that perhaps they'd been given a second chance.

"I suppose that whole fiasco ended up doing me some good," Patrick said, admitting the conclusion he'd come to a long time ago.

"How?"

"If I hadn't gone off the handle like that and joined the navy, I wouldn't have gotten assigned to the Shore Patrol, which means I wouldn't have ended up a cop, which undoubtedly came as a helluva surprise to a great many people, since everyone but you figured I'd end up on the wrong side of those bars."

"Are you going to miss police work? When your book sells and you can become a full-time writer?"

Patrick liked the way she'd said "when," not "if." "I suppose part of me will miss it," Patrick considered. "I mean, there are some terrific perks to the job."

"Like free doughnuts?"

"Real cute, Valentine," he growled on a low, rumbling laugh that had thrilled her at seventeen and still had the power to weaken her knees. "Remind me one of these days to tell you how much we cops love doughnut jokes. No, I'm talking about delivering babies in snowstorms."

She smiled. "And rescuing their mothers."

"That, too." She heard the answering smile in his voice. "But things have gotten a little crazy out there and I have to admit that I won't miss worrying about getting my head blown off every time I make a routine traffic stop."

It was something Valentine had worried about every night while she paced the floor with the twins and thought of Patrick out on the streets at the mercy of every criminal and lunatic with a gun.

"Speaking of work," she said in a not-very-subtle attempt to change a subject that was too upsetting to contemplate, "I stopped by the station today."

"How did it go?"

"I had a nice visit. Everyone cooed over the babies and said all the right things. Management also wanted to know when I'm coming back to work."

"What did you tell them?"

"That I'd stick to the agreement I made last fall for an eight-week maternity leave."

"You don't sound very thrilled with the idea."

"Part of me wants to get back to work," she admitted. "If for no other reason than to have an excuse to put on a dress and makeup, for a change. The other part of me doesn't want to put Jeb and Mara in day care."

"You can afford a private sitter, can't you?"

"Yes. And the woman next door has already asked to stay with them, but it just isn't the same, is it?" She gave another sigh. "Oh, well, I'm probably not the first mother who thinks she's irreplaceable."

"All mothers are irreplaceable," Patrick answered, speaking from experience. "But there's undoubtedly someone who could at least take care of the basics for you."

"I suppose." She sounded unconvinced. "I started weaning the twins to a bottle today. You've no idea now guilty that made me feel."

"May I make a suggestion?"

"Of course."

"How about me?"

"You what?"

"How about me staying with the kids? At least half-days. Your neighbor could take the morning shift and I could take over around noon or so."

"But you'd be exhausted when you went on patrol."

"That's a moot point," he said with studied casualness. "Since before I left, I turned in my resignation, effective as soon as I get back to town."

"You resigned? But, why?" Comprehension dawned. "You sold your book?"

"Guilty."

"Oh, Patrick. I'm thrilled!"

"That makes two of us. I was thinking, since your birthday is the day after tomorrow, what would you say to a double celebration?"

"I'd say yes," she replied immediately.

There was a slight pause as they both considered the significance of celebrating Patrick's book sale on what should have been their tenth wedding anniversary.

Valentine was remembering how happy she'd been on that long-ago Valentine's night, standing in the middle of the crowded dance floor, red confetti in her hair, her heart pounding in her throat when Patrick proposed.

Nearly four hundred miles away, Patrick was remembering how that night had ended, setting the stage for ten years of avoiding anything to do with Valentine's Day.

He'd never bought another woman red roses, he'd never purchased a box of chocolates, and he steadfastly avoided anything but fast-food restaurants on February 14. Last year and the one before that, he'd volunteered for patrol, preferring to spend the night in the squad car rather than face Susan Copeland's obvious disappointment.

"I went to the doctor today," Valentine told him.

"What's wrong?"

"Nothing's wrong," she said, soothing the alarm he hadn't tried to hide. "It was my six-week checkup."

"Oh." He exhaled a breath of relief. "It doesn't seem like it's been that long." On the other hand, it had seemed like an eternity. "Is everything okay?"

"Better than okay. The doctor says I'm fit as a fiddle. She also says that I can start living like a normal person again. I can go back to work and exercise. And make love.''

That provocative statement lingered on the air for a long, nerve-racking time.

"Well, I'm glad you're all right," Patrick said finally.

From the way his voice had deepened and turned un-mistakably husky, Valentine knew that Patrick intended to take her up on her implied invitation.

"When are you coming home?"

"Not soon enough." He combed his hand through his hair, frustrated. "I was going to fly out tonight, but the airport's closed and from the way the snow is falling up here, it doesn't look that good for tomorrow, either."

"Oh." It had already been three days. Three very long and lonely days. "Well, we'll be waiting for you."

That idea was inordinately pleasing. "I'll be there as soon as I can," Patrick promised.

They talked for another hour, both of them reluctant to sever the contact. They talked of nothing important and their words were often interrupted by long, evocative pauses, but that didn't stop either one from understand-ing that tonight had marked an important milestone in their lives.

The following morning Patrick called again with the news that it was still snowing and nothing was moving in or out of Boston. Sharing his disappointment that their reunion would be put off for another day, Valentine told him that she'd rather have him back safe and sound than have his plane crash because of bad weather.

She'd no sooner hung up when the doorbell rang. When she opened the door and saw Hamilton Somers standing on the newly renovated front porch, the pleasure she'd re-ceived from talking with Patrick instantly dissolved.

"Oh. It's you."

"Gracious as always, I see."

She'd always hated Hamilton's supercilious attitude. "I assume you're here to see Jeb and Mara."

He lifted a blond eyebrow in disdain. "Jeb and Mara? What kind of names are those?"

"They're the names I chose," she said with what she thought to be remarkable calm, considering she wanted to throw something at his blond head. "I would have conferred with you on the matter, Hamilton, but you weren't around."

An embarrassed flush rose from the fur collar of his cashmere coat. "We'd agreed that we wouldn't have children, Valentine," Hamilton reminded her.

"That was your decision," Valentine argued. "I was foolish enough to hope I could change your mind."

That was one thing she'd learned from staying home. Day after day, the television talk shows were populated by women who'd believed they could change a man's behavior and mold him into something other than he was. Although it was demoralizing to view her fatal miscalculation in the cold, clear light of the television screen, Valentine had garnered some solace from the idea that she wasn't the first woman to have made such a mistake and unfortunately, wouldn't be the last.

"Could we possibly discuss this inside?" he asked. "Or do you feel the need to let the neighbors know everything about your private life?"

He had always worried about what people thought. In that regard he was exactly like her parents. In fact, now that she thought about it, there had been several times during her marriage when she'd believed the reason her parents had urged her to marry Hamilton was that they considered him the son they'd never had. Especially since he seemed to fit into their lives far more easily than she ever had.

He was chilly and intellectual and marriage to him had been like living in a desert. Which was why his affair with that legislative assistant had come as such a surprise; she never would have suspected her husband of possessing enough passion to commit adultery.

"If you were so worried about people knowing our private affairs, you shouldn't have had one," she pointed out. Moving aside, she let him step into the foyer.

He glanced around the room with an air of disdain. "I still can't figure out what you're doing in this place."

"This place is my home."

"You had a perfectly good home. I didn't force you out."

"No. I left of my own accord when I discovered that you'd been entertaining guests in my bed. *Our* bed."

"Let's not rehash all that again, Valentine." He pulled off his leather driving gloves. "Don't you think it's time we quit living in the past and moved on with our lives?"

"On that we definitely agree," she said, thinking of Patrick. "I assume you want to see the children."

He nodded. "If it's not inconvenient."

If he'd hung around, he would have known babies were one continual inconvenience. On the other hand, they were an awfully nice one.

"They're sleeping, but I can wake them."

"Oh, that isn't necessary. Why don't I just creep in and take a look at them?"

Creep being the operative word, Valentine thought. "Whatever you want, Hamilton." He followed her up the stairs and entered the nursery without a single compliment about her decorating. As Hamilton stood beside the cribs the twins had just graduated into and looked down at them, his face remained devoid of anything resembling paternal emotion.

"They don't look anything like me," he said after he and Valentine were back in the hall again.

And you have no idea what a relief that is. She shrugged. "They look like themselves."

"Are you sure you won't take any child support?"

She might have, if she'd thought he intended to play any type of fatherly role. But considering the fact that it had taken six long weeks for him to pay a visit to his children, she wanted nothing more than to sever all emotional and financial ties with this man.

"I'm perfectly capable of taking care of my children by myself."

He didn't argue her singular-possessive pronouns. "If you're certain."

"I am." Her tone implied subject closed.

"Well . . . There's something else—something I felt you should, uh, hear from me."

"What's that?"

"Well, you know our divorce is final today."

"Is it?" Amazingly, the date that had once loomed before her so painfully had totally slipped her mind.

"Yes. Don't tell me you've forgotten?"

Strange how he could sound so much like her mother. "I've been a little busy. Is that what you came to tell me?"

"No. Actually, there's something else." He ran his finger around the starched collar of his white Brooks Brothers shirt. "Is there a possibility we could discuss this over coffee?"

"Sorry, I'm all out," Valentine lied. Although she knew it was petty, she found herself enjoying his obvious discomfort.

"We could go out."

"I'm afraid that's impossible. The children," she elaborated at his blank look.

"Oh, yes. I forgot."

Terrific father this guy would have made, Valentine considered. "Why don't you just spit it out, Hamilton?"

"Well, you know I've been interested in doing some international consulting for the Pacific Rim countries."

"Of course. That's why you were working in the Interior Department. So you could parlay your government service into big bucks down the road."

It was an accusation he'd heatedly denied whenever she'd brought the subject up. Now he didn't bother.

"I've been offered a vice-presidential spot in a major Japanese brokerage firm," he divulged.

"You're moving to Japan?"

"No. California. Specifically, San Francisco."

"Nice city," she said agreeably. "I've always liked their bridge. Does this mean you won't be asking for regular visiting privileges?"

"Visiting privileges?"

"To see Jeb and Mara."

"Oh." He nervously transferred his gloves back and forth from one hand to the other. "It would be quite a long trip."

She wondered how many jaunts he planned to make to Japan in his new career. "I guess it would." She gave him a cool smile her mother would have been proud of. "Don't worry, Hamilton. I'm sure we'll muddle through quite nicely without you."

"You've always been very competent," he allowed. "Although you have been known to suffer occasional flights of fancy."

She crossed her arms. "I'll work on that."

"Good, good." He ran his fingers distractedly through his blow-dried blond hair.

"Is there something else?"

"Well, yes. Jennifer and I are getting married. Tomorrow."

She waited fatalistically for the bombshell to shake her. When nothing happened, she realized that she had truly put this mistake behind her. "You didn't waste any time."

"Well, I'm due in California in two weeks," he said. "And we wanted a decent honeymoon."

"Of course. Well." She held out her hand. "Good luck, Hamilton."

"Thank you." He brushed his fingers against hers in the barest semblance of a handshake. "Are you all right with this, Valentine? Really?"

"I'm fine." Just when she was trying to figure out how she was going to get this stranger she'd been married to out of her house, Jeb and Mara started crying in unison.

Hamilton pushed back his cashmere sleeve and glanced down at a gold Rolex wristwatch he hadn't owned when he lived with her. "Well, I'd like to stay and chat, but I'm afraid I'm due at a meeting."

"Well, we certainly wouldn't want you to be late, would we?"

Putting her hands on his shoulders, she turned him around and practically marched him to the door. "Have a good life, Hamilton. And best wishes to your bride."

He was on the porch. "Do you mean that?"

"What do you think?" she asked sweetly, right before she slammed the door in his patrician face.

Chapter Eight

As SHE SAT in the nursery, rocking and feeding her babies with the bottle they'd finally decided to accept, Valentine considered that although the news of her now former husband's impending wedding had come as a surprise, she could honestly say that it didn't hurt. Because she honestly didn't care what Hamilton did or with whom he did it.

How ironic that she had so easily put a four-year marriage behind her, while a union that had lasted a mere six hours had never stopped haunting her.

"It's because I never really loved Hamilton," she told her daughter. She brushed her fingers through the soft blond fuzz that felt like dandelion fluff and drank in the sweet scent of powder and baby oil.

Mara looked up at her with eyes that had begun to turn a blue-green hazel but she didn't cease her avid suckling. "Of course, I suppose it's not exactly Hamilton's fault that I couldn't love him," Valentine decided. "Since I'd never truly fallen out of love with Patrick…. But I am angry with Hamilton for not wanting to be a father to such a pretty little girl," she said, softening her voice.

"Yes," she continued, smiling down at her daughter, "you are such a pretty girl. And you have a very handsome brother," she added as Jeb began making cooing noises from his crib.

Feeding the babies always calmed her, but after she'd put them down for their late-afternoon naps, when the phone began to ring incessantly—word of Hamilton's marriage obviously having gotten out—Valentine's temper flared.

Taking the phone off the hook, she went into the kitchen and decided to work off her irritation by hanging the wallpaper she'd put off doing for too long.

Five hours later, she was trying to ignore the twins who were lying in a white-mesh playpen four feet away, seemingly determined to break the sound barrier. Having fed them, then burped them and changed them and carried them on her hip for the past forty-five minutes, Valentine had laid them down with the scant hope that they'd cry themselves back to sleep.

They didn't.

She was sitting on the floor, a baby in each arm and crying herself, when Patrick suddenly appeared in the doorway, laden down with packages.

"W-what are you doing here?"

"I told you I'd be back as soon as I could." He put the red roses he'd bought on the counter, the champagne in the refrigerator.

"But the airport's closed in."

"I rented a car."

"You drove on those icy roads? You could have been killed."

"Never happen," he said easily. He located the crystal vase, filled it with water and began arranging the roses. "Because I was coming home to my girl."

"They're beautiful," she said.

"They are kinda nice, at that." He leaned back and gave them a judicious look. "Red roses always remind me of you."

"Then we're even," she admitted in a small voice that was barely audible over her son's strident screams. "Because they always reminded me of you."

Patrick sat down beside Valentine and took Jeb from her arms. Valentine's aggravation increased tenfold when her purple-faced son immediately stopped crying.

He bounced the baby on his lap. Jeb started making happy, gurgling, cooing sounds. Mara, in Valentine's arms, had run down to hiccups. "I wish I knew how you do that," Valentine said with grudging admiration. "I've been trying for ages to get him to stop crying."

"You're upset. They probably picked up on that." He traded babies with her. Mara, on cue, made soft little pigeon noises.

"I'm not upset."

He gave her a long, probing look that she decided probably worked wonders when he was interrogating a prisoner. "Aren't you?"

"Not really," she hedged.

"I heard the news about Somers and his bride-to-be on the car radio."

Her shoulders slumped. "Oh."

"I'm sorry." It tore at him that Valentine would be so stricken by the news of her husband's remarriage.

"I'm not upset about his marriage. Really," she insisted. "It's just that he doesn't give a damn about Jeb and Mara."

Patrick chose his words carefully, afraid that if he came down too hard on the bastard, he'd make her feel the need to defend him. "Some men aren't cut out to be fathers, I guess."

Hamilton had warned her of that, all along. He'd always been quite specific about the fact that he considered children an inconvenience to his carefully planned-out lifestyle.

"I suppose not," she agreed. "Still, it would have been nice if he'd at least pretended to show some interest. He's moving to California."

"I heard." He didn't mention what good news that had been.

"Do you know," she said thoughtfully, "my divorce was final today, and I didn't even remember."

"Perhaps it's because in your own mind, your marriage was already over," he suggested carefully.

"I think you're right." She sighed, looking down at her bare legs, covered with wallpaper paste. "I'm a mess." Damn him, anyway. Why hadn't he given her advance warning?

He reached out and brushed a bit of dried paste off her cheek. Her shorts were a pair of tight, faded cutoff jeans, slit up the thigh to her hips to facilitate movement. "I think you look kind of cute."

Valentine's bleak gaze circled the room, taking in the scraps of wallpaper scattered over the floor. "I'm a mess, the house is a mess, the babies are a mess, and if you've got any sense, you'll take off running right now."

Her T-shirt had pulled loose of her waistband. When she lifted her arm to comb her fingers through her tousled hair, he was treated to an enticing glimpse of skin.

"I'm not going anywhere." He plucked Jeb from her arms as well, and stood with a cooing baby propped on each lean hip. "Why don't you go upstairs and take a long hot bath?" he suggested. "I'll take care of things down here."

"No. I made the mess, it's up to me to clean it up."

"I'd almost forgotten how damn stubborn you can be," he said without rancor. "Go upstairs, Valentine. And let me help."

A bubble bath sounded wonderful. Valentine tried to recall the last time she'd allowed herself anything but a brief, rushed shower and realized it had been before the twins were born.

"I'm really taking advantage of you."

"Don't be ridiculous. I like taking care of you." He bent his head and brushed a chaste kiss on her forehead. "Go relax."

Unable to resist the seductive lure of a hot bath, she allowed herself to be persuaded.

Ten minutes later, she was luxuriating in the warm, perfumed water when Patrick knocked on the open doorjamb. "I thought you might like something to celebrate passing your checkup with flying colors." He was holding a champagne flute in each hand.

"I'd love it."

After a quick glance to make certain that the frothy white bubbles concealed the changes in her body, she accepted the glass he held out to her. "Mmm," she said, taking a sip and enjoying the way the golden bubbles danced on her tongue. "I think I've discovered heaven."

"Heaven?" The room was hot and steamy. A fragrant cloud rose from the water, carrying her scent. Discarding his own glass on the marble vanity counter, Patrick sat on the edge of the tub, picked up the blue washcloth, took hold of her free arm and began gently rubbing away the paste.

"Absolute heaven," she repeated. "A bath, champagne, sleeping babies and a very sexy man. What more could any woman want?"

Patrick didn't answer. There was no need. When he lowered her arm to the water, she switched the glass to the other hand and sighed with sheer pleasure as he began the marvelous treatment to the other.

He moved on to her neck, her shoulders. When he squeezed the washcloth, causing rivulets of water to cascade over her breasts, Valentine closed her eyes.

"Why is it you always see me at my worst?"

He ran the cloth over her breasts, brushing away the bubbles, enjoying the way her plum-hued nipples puckered beneath his light touch. "If this is your worst, sweetheart, I'm not certain I can handle your best." When he brushed a soapy finger across her nipple, he felt her shiver.

The cloth moved down her abdomen at a treacherously slow speed, creating an alarming tingle between her legs.

"But I'd planned such a special homecoming...." Her voice trailed off on a sigh as his hand brushed the sensitive flesh at the insides of her thighs. She thought of the sheer red nightgown—reminiscent of the sexy one he'd bought her so long ago and so unlike anything else she owned—hanging in her closet, bought specifically for his return.

"Knowing that you were waiting for me is all the homecoming I need."

"Oh, Patrick," she said suddenly, remembering the reason for the champagne, "I forgot to tell you how happy I am about your book."

"You told me. On the phone." He lifted one of her slender legs, and then the other—washing, caressing, driving her crazy. Then he moved to her back. "I think that's all the paste." His fingers trailed down the delicate bones of her spine, creating a sizzling white heat. "But perhaps we'd better check." He took the glass from her hand, placing it beside his untouched one.

"You haven't had any champagne," she whispered, excited by the lambent flame gleaming in his dark eyes.

"I don't need any alcohol when I'm around you, sweetheart." He ran the back of his hand down her face, around her jaw, her throat, his fingers lingering at the hollow where her heart was beating frantically. "I've waited a long time for this night."

She swallowed, suddenly mute. But her eyes gave him the answer he wanted. They came together, Patrick dragging her from the velvet cling of water, not caring that he was getting drenched in the process.

Water streamed off her. When he plucked the pins from her hair, it fell against her cheek and curved around her jaw. Lifting her into his arms, he carried her to the adjoining bedroom, pulled back the comforter and laid her on the crisp sheets she'd managed to change just before Hamilton had shown up to break the news of his impending marriage.

When he reached out to turn on the bedside lamp, Valentine caught his hand. "No," she whispered.

He lifted her hand to his lips. "I've never made love to you in the light, Valentine. In the beginning, there were only those quick desperate couplings in my truck, and even that night we got married, when you wanted to make love in the dark, I gave in because I could tell that you were shy. . . .

"But we're adults now, sweetheart." Softly, with a reverence he'd forgotten he could feel, he pressed a feather-soft kiss against each of her fingertips. "This time we know all the consequences of what we're doing, and I want to be able to see the woman I'm making love with."

How could she deny such a heartfelt request? "I've changed."

"We've all changed." He switched on the lamp, bathing her in a circle of warm light. "You are so beautiful you take my breath away."

"Flatterer." She wished she were young again. No, that wasn't true. She wouldn't want to go through those tumultuous years again for anything. What she wished was that her body was young again. "I've had children, Patrick," she reminded him unnecessarily. "Childbirth takes its toll."

Her breasts were still weighty with milk; her enlarged nipples looked as if they'd been rouged. The stomach he remembered as being girlishly flat was rounded, its fair skin marked with faint white lines. These changes were evidence of her motherhood, and not for the first time since that frightening night six weeks ago, he marveled at both Valentine's unselfishness in carrying those two precious babies inside her and the bravery she'd shown bringing them into the world.

"Jeb and Mara made those changes." Bending his head, he kissed the stretch marks she'd been so afraid he'd think were ugly. "And I couldn't love you—or them—more if they were mine." His breath was soft and warm against her stomach.

Valentine curled her fingers in his dark hair and coaxed his face to hers. Their eyes met, their lips touched, they smiled.

"I'm afraid," she admitted in a whisper.

He framed her sober face between his palms. "Of me?" His expression was so caring, so tender, that she almost started to cry again. Not wanting him to think that she was always so weepy, she struggled against the threatening tears.

"Not you. Never you." She took a deep breath, closed her eyes and said, "It's just that I don't know what you like anymore," she admitted. "What you want." When his lips nuzzled her neck, she gave a low, drugged sound of pleasure. "I don't want you to be disappointed."

"Disappointed? With you?" He traced her quivering lip with a thumbnail. "Never."

She was everything he'd ever dreamed of, without knowing he'd been dreaming. She was everything he'd ever longed for, not knowing he'd been longing. Now, having waited ten long years for this night, Patrick was determined to do it right. He started by kissing her damp hair, behind her ears, at the nape of her neck, drinking in the scent that had been driving him crazy for weeks.

"I want you, Valentine Alexander," he murmured. "More than I ever thought possible." His lips brushed her cheek before making a leisurely journey to her mouth.

He wasn't the angry young boy he'd once been; he'd grown into manhood and in doing so had witnessed insane things that told him this was a far-from-perfect world. But driving through the snow, too impatient to wait for the New England weather to clear, he'd vowed to give Valentine this one very perfect night.

"You are so lovely," he told her, weakened by the power of his desire for her and stunned by his weakness.

She wanted to be. For him. "So are you."

With trembling hands she began to undress him, but her fingers were too numb, her mind too clouded. Desperate for the touch of her hands on his flesh, Patrick yanked his shirt open; white plastic buttons ripped loose, skittering unheeded across the waxed-oak planks. The torn shirt fluttered to the floor, followed in turn by the rest of his clothing. The antique bed swayed slightly as he lay down beside her; the mattress sighed. Propped up on one elbow, he looked at her for a long time.

Valentine pressed her palm against his bare chest, loving the contrast of hard muscle and taut flesh beneath her fingertips. Her hand was steady; her pulse was not. Valentine offered with her eyes, wide and inviting; she took with her lips, warm and sweet. In turn, Patrick accepted and he gave.

For a long, silent time they lay together, smiling, content to simply touch. Patrick's fingers lingered at the soft underside of her breasts; her hands traced the rigid line of his shoulders and explored the baby-smooth skin of his back. His hand cupped her knee. Her lashes fluttered down. Her lips parted on a rippling breath. Her skin dried in the warmth of the room, then became moist again.

It was with a heartfelt sense of thanksgiving that he touched her soft flesh in places he'd never truly seen; it was with a suspended sense of wonder that he kissed her in all the places he'd wanted to kiss, but hadn't when he was young.

Patrick seduced her with patience, with gentleness, with murmured words and soft kisses when no seduction was needed. With each tender touch, her blood hummed; with every taste, his pulse pounded. He buried his mouth in her hair and whispered her name; his name shuddered from between her lips as she felt the nip of his teeth on her earlobe. Valentine's soft, shimmering sighs mingled with Patrick's low murmurs.

Slowly, devastatingly, he made love to her, touching off new and hotter fires that she hadn't known were there to be kindled. He pressed wet, openmouthed kisses against her stomach, setting off an inferno of sensations. Such heat. Glorious, resplendent heat. Her blood felt molten, flowing hot and thick through her veins. Then, deeper still, to the bone.

Dazzled, dazed, desperate, she clung to him as the years peeled away and she were young and he were young and the future stretched thrillingly, endlessly, before them. No one but Patrick had ever made her feel like this—warm, aching, glowing. No one but Patrick had ever made her feel truly loved.

Every time she whispered his name against his mouth, each time her lips caressed his hot moist skin, hunger rocketed through him. Was it only his imagination? Or had time spun backward, allowing them to recapture feelings that had always bound him to her more firmly than any chain?

Patrick kept the pace easy, even when her heightened pulse and shortened breath encouraged him to rush. Downstairs, the grandfather clock in the parlor struck the hour with its medley of Westminster chimes. Then came the quarter, the half, the three-quarter; followed in what seemed no time at all by the silvery sound of a new hour.

All the time, her perfumed body continued to flow beneath his caressing hands, fluid as water, heady as wine. The lamplight cast their shadows on the wall as they touched, shifted, drew apart, then came together once again. Somewhere in the winter night a siren wailed, a dog barked, brakes squealed. Around them her house settled for the night, as old houses do, with creaks and groans.

But the only thing Patrick and Valentine heard over the distant roaring of the blood in their ears were labored breaths, soft murmurs and the low, sounds of love.

He buried his hands in her tangled hair and tilted her head back. "Do you have any idea how long I've been waiting to be with you again? Like this? Me loving you. You loving me."

"Yes." The single word shuddered from between her softly parted lips as his caressing hand continued its delicious torment. Her eyes were open and fixed on his. "Because I've been waiting, too. For so long."

He brushed his lips against hers, savoring her taste, coaxing them to the shape he preferred. "Too long."

"Much too long," she agreed on a whisper against his mouth.

"And I don't want to wait any longer, but there's something I have to ask you."

She remembered how concerned he'd been about not getting her pregnant, and later, after he'd gone, how she'd wished that he had.

"If it's about adding to my happy little family, I already took care of that when I went to the doctor." The IUD had made her experience cramps vaguely reminiscent of labor pains, but those had passed and now there was only the low ache of desire.

He gave a quiet laugh as he nibbled and gently sucked on her swollen lips. "You were that sure?"

"Of us." She placed her hands on either side of his face and gave him a long, serious look. "I was that sure of us." She kissed him, quick and hard. "I want you." She kissed him again, lingeringly, lovingly. "I need you, Patrick."

In saying it, Valentine felt free. In hearing it, Patrick felt reborn.

He gripped her hips to pull her close, but she was already rising to meet him, to draw him in. With a yearning as deep as his love, Patrick slipped into her so easily she might have been designed just for him. They were perfectly matched—minds, hearts, bodies.

With a patience he'd been unaware of possessing, he took her slowly, coaxing her higher and higher still, to a crest that was dangerously high, forcing back his own passion until he felt the shudders ripple through her.

Even then, he continued to savor the taste of her mouth, his long fingers splayed on her hips, his mouth swallowing her soft cry as she plummeted to earth—the fall as thrilling as the ascent.

And when he resumed again—this time with a rhythm that matched precisely the wild, out-of-control beat of her heart, Valentine locked her legs around him and dragged him even closer, so filled with joy she would surely shatter.

Patrick had given himself up to passion before, but never like this. He'd made love to women both before and after Valentine, but never like this. She filled him, completed him. She made him whole.

As their warm bodies moved together and their minds tangled, time stood gloriously still.

Chapter Nine

"THAT," PATRICK SAID when he could talk again, "was definitely worth waiting for."

"Mmm." Her head was on his chest; she pressed a kiss against his cooling flesh.

"So, when are you going to let me make an honest woman of you?"

"What?"

"I want to put things right. We belong together, Valentine. And no legal gobbledegook from some judge paid off by your father could ever change that fact."

She sat up against the headboard and pulled the sheet over her breasts. "Patrick, we've changed. We need time to get to know one another again."

He sat up beside her, tautly reined tension radiating from every pore. "We've already wasted ten years. How much longer do you figure we need? Another week, a month, a year?"

His temper was in his eyes, the hard line of his lips, the jut of his jaw. Unlike Hamilton's inner coolness, Patrick's passion was always simmering just beneath the surface. Such intensity could be exciting. It could also be frightening.

"I don't know."

"Time," he muttered, dragging both hands through his hair. She had the feeling he'd love to put them around her neck right now and knew that he wouldn't. "How long did you know Somers before you married him?"

"All my life."

"You knew the guy all your life and you still didn't know what a unreliable bastard he was. That says a helluva lot for long engagements, doesn't it?"

Valentine couldn't lie to him. Not about this. "I think, deep down, I always knew what he was."

"Then why the hell did you marry the guy?"

"Because I needed to do something to quit thinking about you!" Her nerves on edge all over again, Valentine left the bed as if ejected from it and glared down at him.

"I thought if I married Hamilton I could forget about being married to you. Okay? Is that what you wanted to hear?" Frustrated by his stony, unyielding expression, she scooped up a pillow that had fallen to the floor and threw it at him, wishing it were filled with rocks rather than down. "Is your almighty male ego back intact?"

Every bit as frustrated as she, Patrick caught the pillow in one hand and tossed it aside. Then he was on his feet and his fingers curled around her trembling shoulders and he was holding her prisoner with his hands and his eyes.

"This isn't about my male ego, dammit. It's about the fact that I've never stopped thinking of you, never stopped wanting you, never stopped loving you....

"And you have just admitted you felt the same way. So, my sweet Valentine, what, exactly, is the problem?"

She wished she knew. But it was all happening so fast, and as much as she wanted to trust her heart, her head was telling her that you just didn't divorce the man who'd fathered your children, then turn right around and marry your high-school lover, even if he was the best thing that had ever happened to you—then *and* now.

"Can't we just leave things like they are?" she asked softly. "For a while, at least?"

It was not the answer he'd wanted to hear. "You mean, have an affair?"

"It sounds so tawdry when you say it."

"Because it is." His fingers tightened on her flesh. "Guys like Somers have affairs, Valentine. And, God knows, I've certainly had my share—some of which I'm not very proud of. Which is all the more reason why I don't want to have an affair with you.... I want to marry you, Valentine Alexander. I want to be your husband and I want to be Jeb and Mara's father, and I want to love you and take care of you and maybe, after a while, if you like the idea, have a baby or two of our own, although I'd never love the twins less if that did happen.

"I want to wake up every morning, knowing that you're beside me. I want to go to sleep every night with my arms wrapped around you. I want to grow old with you, Valentine."

Dear Lord, that's what she wanted, too. And there wasn't a doubt in her mind that Patrick loved her. So, why couldn't she make the leap of faith that seemed to come so easily for him?

"Patrick...I—" She was about to tell him that she needed to understand what was happening to her, to them, when the phone shattered the expectant silence.

Afraid it would wake the twins, she exchanged a regretful glance with Patrick and answered it.

"Hello? Oh. Yes, he's here." She held the receiver out to him. "It's for you."

"Sorry, I had my calls forwarded here, but I never expected to get any.... This is Sullivan," he answered.

She saw the change instantly. He stiffened, became instantly alert. "Yeah, give me about twenty minutes," he said. "Make it fifteen. The traffic's practically nonexistent this time of night." He hung up the phone and turned toward her, his expression unreadable. "I'm sorry, I know this is a helluva time to run off, but something's come up."

She was frightened by the way his eyes had hardened during that abrupt conversation. "But I thought you said you'd resigned."

"I did, but this is a special case."

"And you're the only man on the entire Virginia State Police force that can handle it?" she asked disbelievingly.

"Since they haven't assigned anyone else to take my place yet, I guess I am."

"It's something dangerous, isn't it?"

He loved her for worrying about him; he loved her for loving him, even if she couldn't quite admit it to herself yet. "Naw." He began gathering his clothing that was strewn on the floor. "You're a newslady, Val. You've reported on how budget crunches have strained manpower. They just need a little extra help."

He yanked on the white briefs without bothering to turn them right side out. That uncharacteristic oversight served to worry her even more. His jeans were next, then his socks and his shoes. He put on his shirt, forced to leave it unbuttoned, then drew her into his arms, gathering her close.

"Keep the bed warm," he murmured against her temple. "When I get back we'll continue this conversation where we left off."

"In bed?"

He ran his hands down her back in a slow, seductive sweep. "I can't think of a better place to settle an argument, can you?"

That earned a faint smile. "No," she whispered.

His head swooped down and he kissed her hard, with a desperation she'd felt once before—in that Maryland motel room, right before he gave up trying to convince her to stay with him.

"I'll be back before you know it," he promised, running his palm down her love-tousled hair.

"Be careful."

He gave her a cocky grin. "Always."

And then he was gone. She stood there, listening to him take the stairs two at a time, her heart in her throat.

Mara began to cry, then Jeb. Valentine put on her old flannel robe and answered her children's summons.

A miraculous fifteen minutes later, they'd been changed and had fallen back to sleep. Not having believed Patrick for a minute, it was with a great deal of trepidation that she tuned the radio to a twenty-four-hour news station.

When the bulletin announcing a hostage situation at an all-night convenience market in Arlington came over the air, and the announcer told his radio audience the name of the hostage negotiator called in to handle the potentially explosive situation, her heart lurched.

After throwing on some clothes, she ran next door and asked her neighbor, who'd offered to baby-sit on numerous occasions, to stay with the twins.

Fifteen minutes later, after breaking every speeding statute on both the District of Columbia's and the state of Virginia's books, Valentine was on the crime scene, flashing her press badge at the uniformed men maintaining the police line.

The parking lot was lit by a bank of klieg lights, making it as bright as day. Valentine found Patrick behind a patrol car with Jeb and several heavily armed members of the SWAT team. He'd taken his shirt off and was fastening a bulletproof vest.

"What do you think you're doing?"

Patrick exchanged a glance with his partner. "What are you doing here?"

Her chin lifted; she gave him a long, level look. "In case you've forgotten, I'm a reporter. And currently, thanks to this latest bit of grandstanding, you're the hottest story in town.''

It was more than that and they both knew it.

"Grandstanding?"

"Hi, Valentine," Jeb greeted her cheerfully in an obvious attempt to smooth tempers. "You're sure looking good. And Patrick tells me those babies are growing like weeds. Oh, and thanks a heap for naming the boy after me. I got a real kick outta that."

She didn't take her eyes from Patrick's frustrated ones. "You don't have to thank me, Jeb. Not after what you did for me. And yes, they are growing. You'll have to come by and see them."

"I'd like that."

Although her heart was pounding, she spoke calmly. "Jeb, would you mind if I had a word alone with Patrick?"

"Sure." He gestured and the uniformed men standing behind him walked away. "Go easy on him, Valentine," he murmured, patting her shoulder. "He's just doin' his job."

The minute they were alone she turned on him, hands on her hips, eyes shooting furious sparks. "Are you insane?"

"There's a pregnant clerk in that store, Val. When she started having contractions, the guy got scared. He's agreed to let her go if I take his place."

It was the same damn thing he'd done last fall. "Why you?"

"Because I'm good," Patrick answered with a calm self-confidence that Valentine knew would have seemed like arrogance in a lesser man.

Her hand was icy cold and trembled as she lifted it to his face. "What would you do if I asked you not to go in there?"

He'd willingly crawl to hell and back through broken glass for this woman. But could he turn his back on another woman—a woman who right now needed him more? He covered her hand with his.

"Are you asking?"

Valentine could tell that he was truly torn. She also knew what his answer would be. She turned her back, unwilling to let him witness her pain, her fear. "No. Not really."

"Val, look at me."

She shook her head, wrapping her arms around herself in an unconscious gesture of self-protection. "I'm sorry, Patrick. I know I should be brave, but I can't be. Not where you're concerned."

"I said, look at me." Grabbing her arm, he spun her toward him. His hands tightened on her shoulders, fingers that had only ever touched her tenderly now bruising the flesh beneath her sweater. "Do you actually think I'd risk losing you? Again? After all we've been through together?"

"Isn't that what you're doing?"

"I'm doing my job, dammit. That doesn't have anything to do with how I feel about you!"

"Doesn't it?"

He fought back the anger, the frustration. If he gave in to it, he would shout and rage and that wasn't the way. It hadn't been ten years ago and it wasn't now. "No, it doesn't. You know I love you, Valentine."

"If you really loved me..."

Her voice trailed off as she realized exactly how unfair she was being to him again. "No. I didn't mean that. I'm sorry. I know I'm behaving abominably, but I just can't help myself."

When she struggled to turn away again, he held her still. "I hate to see you like this." Ten years ago she had been the one to make the decision to leave. Now, he wondered if Valentine was going to make him choose between love and honor.

She felt her eyes fill and didn't attempt to blink back the tears. Her throat was so tight it hurt as she forced the words out. "I love you, Patrick. And I want to be your wife."

He felt the breath simply leave his body. "Oh, Val." He closed his eyes, bent his head and held his forehead to hers. "You've no idea how long I've waited to hear that. But I gotta tell you, sweetheart, you've got the lousiest sense of timing of any woman I've ever met." He smiled down at her, his fingers on her flushed cheek softening his words.

"Patrick? Would you do one thing for me?"

"Anything."

It was not quite the truth and they both knew it. But Valentine also knew that if Patrick were capable of turning his back, of ignoring his responsibility, he wouldn't be the man she'd fallen in love with.

She wanted to beg him not to go; she wanted to remind him how many years they'd already lost; she wanted to tell him that he had no right to risk the twins growing up without ever knowing the only man their mother had ever loved. Her stomach was twisted in knots that pulled tighter when she looked up into the face of a thousand desperate dreams.

"Be careful," she whispered haltingly.

He flashed her that quick, wicked smile that had always had the power to thrill her. "Don't worry about a thing, Valentine. You don't think I'd miss my lady's birthday, do you?"

Today was more than her birthday, and they both knew it. It was Valentine's Day—a day set aside for lovers. Lovers like her and Patrick. His dark eyes gleamed with a bright blend of triumph, reassurance and passion.

"I thought we might spend the day hanging around and catching up on some much-needed sleep before going out for a long, romantic dinner. And afterward," he murmured, his lips a whisper away from hers, "if the lady's willing, we'll go back to your place and have our own private celebration."

"Oh, the lady's willing, all right," Valentine said breathlessly. "But I think I'd like to skip the dinner."

Mindless of their avidly interested audience, she flung her arms around his neck and crushed her mouth to his, letting all the passion, all the emotions, all the love she felt for this man, have their way.

She pressed her body against his, trapping him between her and the hard steel of the patrol car. The horrid bulletproof vest was an unwelcome impediment, but his taste—warm and mysterious and male—seeped into her veins, entered her bloodstream and flowed thickly through her body.

His hands tangled in her hair, not gently; his morning beard was rough, scraping against her face as he tilted her head to a different angle. His fingers tightened, his breath quickened, his mouth savaged hers, causing thrills to rush up her spine.

Patrick buried his lips in the soft scent of her hair, struggling for control. He forced the breath into his lungs—once, twice, then a third deep, ragged time before he lifted his head.

"Your timing is truly rotten, Valentine. Do you have any idea how close I was to dragging you into the back seat of that patrol car?"

She laced her fingers through his ruffled hair, ran them down his neck. "We've always done some of our best work in cars," she murmured silkily. "Remember the night I lost my virginity in your truck?"

"How could I forget it?" he muttered. "I've spent the past ten years of my life kicking myself for not springing for a motel room."

"Where I made love for the first time wasn't all that important, Patrick. It was who I was making love with that mattered." She ran her hands over his shoulders, studiously avoiding the thick vest that meant he was about to risk his life.

"I hate to bring this up," Patrick said, "but—"

"I know." She pressed her head against his chest, fought for control and lost. "Duty calls."

He lifted her distressed face with the arc of one gentle finger and kissed away a tear that sparkled on her cheek. "I promise, everything's going to be okay."

She bit her lip. "I k-know."

He brushed his lips against her trembling ones softly, briefly. "I'll be back before you know it."

With one last gentle hand to her cheek, he was gone, leaving Valentine to pace on the sidelines. When Patrick reached the door of the store and the man inside insisted he strip down to his underwear to prove he was unarmed, Valentine's tentatively-held confidence plummeted.

The time dragged on. An hour turned into two. The sun slowly rose above the horizon, turning the low morning clouds the color of cotton candy. Police barricades blocked off the street, creating havoc with the morning rush-hour traffic. Across the street, the sidewalks were crowded with curious onlookers; one entrepreneurial individual began selling coffee and doughnuts from the back of his van parked at the corner. The parking lot had been taken over by the news crews.

Brandon MacGregor came over to Valentine, shoved a microphone in her face and began asking questions. Later, she would watch the tape and be amazed that she'd managed to respond with an surprising amount of clarity, considering the fact that she hadn't heard a word the reporter had been saying.

A cheer went up when the pregnant clerk came out of the store and ran across the asphalt parking lot into the waiting arms of her frantic young husband. When the reporters swarmed toward her, the police put the couple in a patrol car and drove them away.

The air grew rife with anticipation as everyone waited for Patrick to come out with the foiled robber. But he didn't. And time dragged on.

The weak February sun had disappeared behind a cloud. It began to rain—a cold, icy sleetlike rain that drove the reporters into their vans and sent the majority of the onlookers back to their homes and offices where they belonged. Valentine stayed outside, behind the patrol car, watching and waiting. Someone opened an umbrella over her head; Jeb stuck a cup of steaming coffee in her hand. It went unnoticed.

Much, much later, she remembered to have someone— the producer from her station—call her home and tell her sitter what was happening. When the young man reported that the twins were doing fine, she wanted to feel relieved, but couldn't, because Patrick was still being held at gunpoint inside that store.

She watched the SWAT team, standing beside their armored van, prepared to storm the building at a moment's notice. Their faces were uniformly stony, jaws set, eyes coldly calm, their assault rifles frightening. Other similarly armed men had taken up their positions on the roof of the convenience store, as well as the roof of the dry cleaner's next door. Valentine knew that if it came down to them being called in, Patrick's chances of survival would be slim to none.

And then, just when she thought her nerves couldn't take the suspense another second, the door opened. A moment later, an automatic rifle was thrown outside, followed by a pistol. Then a revolver.

And then Patrick was walking out of the convenience store into the slanting silver rain, dressed only in his inside-out briefs, looking, Valentine thought, absolutely wonderful. So riveted was her gaze on this man she loved that she barely noticed the man with him.

The police rushed the robber, surrounding him at gunpoint. After snapping handcuffs on his wrists, they practically tossed him in the waiting patrol car. Meanwhile, caring nothing about the television cameras pointed her way, Valentine flung herself into Patrick's arms.

"Damn you," she said on a half laugh, half sob. "I was scared to death."

He grinned down into her tearstained face. "Piece of cake."

"I want you to promise me, on your word of honor, that this was the very last time I have to wait through something like this."

"The last time," he agreed. "From now on, the most dangerous thing I'm going to be doing is changing a typewriter ribbon."

The rain fell, unfelt, over them. Their lips fused, heatedly, thrillingly. She raked her hands through his wet hair, pressed her body against his, seeking strength, seeking warmth.

"Valentine," Patrick managed against her avid mouth. "The cameras—"

"I don't care about any cameras." Her hands slid over his wet flesh. "I only care that you're safe."

"The problem is, sweetheart, I'm having a hard time remembering to be civilized, especially when I'm bucking nature."

She laughed softly as she scattered kisses over his smiling face. "I don't think anyone should ever buck nature."

She was driving him crazy. Burying his face in her hair, Patrick tried to find reason. "Valentine, in case you've noticed, I'm not exactly properly dressed."

"I love the way you're dressed." Her voice was breathless with relief and love. "Or undressed."

"That's the problem." He put his hands low on her back and pressed her against him.

She giggled unrepentantly as she felt his obvious arousal. "Did I do that?"

"Witch," he muttered. "Now, stand here quietly and keep your wickedly wonderful hands to yourself while I try to make myself presentable."

She had to press her lips together—hard—to keep from laughing, but she did as instructed. Finally he breathed a relieved sigh. "Let's go home."

Bending down, he scooped up the clothes—now wet— that he'd been forced to leave by the door of the store. After pulling on the wet jeans and shoving his shirt and vest under his arm, he laced their fingers together and began walking with her back to the car while the cameras clicked and whirred around them.

"You're still going to marry me, aren't you? That wasn't just something you said to try to get me not to go in there?"

She grinned up at him, her heart in her eyes. "Of course, I'm going to marry you."

"What about your folks?" It was a question he didn't want to ask but knew he had to.

"I love you, Patrick. And in their own way, they love me. As soon as they see how happy I am, they'll cave in. If for no other reason than to see their grandchildren."

He wished he believed it would be that easy. "And if they don't?"

"It's their loss. Because I'm going to marry you, whether they like it or not."

It was what he'd been waiting years to hear. "So, when shall we tie the knot?"

"The sooner the better," Valentine answered promptly.

"How about sooner?" He stopped again, dropping the clothes to the wet asphalt as he took her into his arms. "If you think your neighbor lady wouldn't mind staying overnight with the little rascals, I thought we might pick up some dry clothes and go for a drive in the country."

"A drive?"

"I just happen to know a certain Maryland justice of the peace who has an opening on his calendar today."

"Yes." She was laughing and crying, her tears mingling with the rain streaming down her face. "Oh, yes!"

Three hours later, on a Valentine's Day they would never forget, Patrick and Valentine exchanged vows before the same judge they'd gotten out of bed ten years earlier.

The groom was handsome, the bride radiant. When Patrick slipped the gold band on her finger—the very ring she'd returned to him by messenger after the annulment—the past dissolved and there was only this glorious present and a future of blissful tomorrows.

He'd booked a room in a picturesque country inn and when he carried her over the threshold, Valentine stared around the room in astonishment.

"Oh, I don't believe this," she said on a soft burst of delighted laughter.

Heart-shaped red balloons—hundreds of them, helium inflated and trailing white ribbons—filled the room, hugging the ten-foot-high ceiling, crowding together in scarlet profusion.

Still in Patrick's arms, Valentine took hold of one of the ribbons, drawing a balloon down. *Patrick Loves Valentine* had been painted across its red surface in bold white script.

American Beauty roses were everywhere—on the antique dresser, the end tables, overflowing white baskets placed on the gleaming wood-plank floor—their sweet, rich scent perfuming the air. And if that wasn't enough, the wedding-ring quilt had been turned back, revealing velvety crimson rose petals strewn across ridiculously romantic pink satin sheets.

The largest gold box of chocolates she'd ever seen, tied with a red velvet ribbon, shared the top of the bedside table with a dark green bottle of champagne nestled in a silver ice bucket. Flickering, welcoming flames of white beeswax candles cast the room in a soft glow.

"Oh, Patrick." He eyes grew moist with all the emotions—all the love—she felt for this man. Not wanting to ruin their wedding night, she blinked the tears away and gave him a warm, wobbly smile. "I don't know if you're the most romantic man I've ever met, or the craziest. But I love you."

"That's good to hear. Since you're stuck with me." He lowered her to the floor and, with a single finger under her chin, tilted her head for a luxurious kiss. The kiss ended much too soon for Valentine, who was left alone in the center of the room while Patrick went over to a portable stereo in the corner.

"How did you arrange all this?" she asked in wonderment. "When you were stuck inside that convenience store all morning?"

"I ordered everything from Boston," he said. "Jeb set it all up while you and I were off changing clothes and getting married." He pushed a button, causing the CD to slip into place. A moment later, the familiar voice of Eddie Rabbitt swelled from the speakers.

"I believe they're playing our song." Patrick held out his arms. "May I have this dance, Mrs. Sullivan?"

Her answering smile was absolutely beatific. "I thought you'd never ask, Mr. Sullivan."

Valentine was in heaven. As she swayed in her husband's arms to the evocative, romantic ballad, her heart seemed to take flight on gossamer wings to float somewhere above them, up with all those bright, silly, wonderful scarlet balloons.

After all the heartbreak and all the lost years, she and Patrick were finally back where they belonged. Together.

VALENTINE MISCHIEF

Vicki Lewis Thompson

A Note from Vicki Lewis Thompson

I'm a fan of whirlwind courtships like Jessie and Reid's in *Valentine Mischief,* probably because I met and married my husband, Larry, in the space of four months. We married in October and were still newlyweds on our first Valentine's Day together. I wrote him a poem; he brought me flowers. It was perfect.

However, by the second Valentine's Day we had a son, Nathan, and by the fourth a daughter, Audrey. Making time for romance became more difficult, which comes as no shock to those of you with children. We could have tried to get away for Valentine's Day, but who would have helped decorate shoe boxes with red construction paper? Who would have baked cupcakes topped with white frosting and candy hearts that said You're Sweet, and Be Mine? How could we miss those sticky lace doilies with lopsided hearts pasted in the middle and I LOVE YOU MOM AND DAD scrawled across the top?

Still, in the midst of concentrating on our offspring we managed romantic gestures for each other. I stuffed his truck cab full of red helium balloons. He tucked a valentine card behind my pillow. I left a valentine's greeting on his answering machine at work. He brought home a stuffed valentine bear for me. Through it all I had a vision of the perfect Valentine's Day celebration together—candlelight, champagne and strawberries, cuddling by the fire—alone at last.

And this year I can have it. Both children are off at college, leaving behind closets full of prom dresses, deflated footballs, airplane models, movie posters, and—I suspect, although I haven't snooped—boxes of old valentines. This year I can create my valentine fantasy with Larry, one of the best cuddlers in the business.

Yes, we can have a perfect romantic Valentine's Day for the first time in twenty-one years. And it's taken me twenty-one years to realize that, despite the difficulties, we've been having them all along.

Chapter One

"IF SEX SELLS, this should do it, Bert." Jessie Neal studied a large photograph of a well-endowed blonde, her curves tucked into a black teddy decorated with red satin hearts. With All My Love On Valentine's Day was lettered across the bottom of the photograph.

"Linda was a good sport to pose for us," Jessie added, propping the photo on an easel in the front window of the studio she shared with Roberta Mortimer. Black script on the window read Jessie And Bert's Photography, and a temporary sign advertised Hotshot Glamour Portraits For Your Valentine.

"I still say we should have used the one we took of you," Bert said from behind the counter.

"Nope." Jessie stepped back and surveyed the window, which she'd hung with white lace hearts and draped with red velvet. "Blondes attract more attention than brunettes, and besides, it would be unprofessional for me to be on display like that. Some guy might come along and get the wrong idea about what we're selling."

"Like that guy, perhaps?" Bert asked, leaning on the counter as she stared out the window.

"Who?" Jessie turned and found herself being scrutinized by a pair of speculative blue eyes. The man stood in front of the window with his feet braced and his hands in the slash pockets of his black leather trench coat. His collar was turned up against the cold Chicago wind that ruffled his dark hair. His gaze roamed over the Valentine decorations, paused at the picture of Linda, and settled again on Jessie.

Automatically Jessie noted high cheekbones and a square jaw that would photograph well from almost any angle. His face had the chiseled, rough-edged look she preferred in her male subjects—preferred in men, come to think of it. She felt an unexpected jolt as she looked into eyes that held a gleam of purpose so strong it magnetized her. With intensity like that, the guy would be a natural in front of the camera. At that moment she realized that his gaze had touched the woman in her, as well as the photographer. For a long moment he held her there, a fascinated captive. Then his mouth tightened as if he'd made a decision. He broke eye contact and headed for the studio door.

Heart pounding, Jessie wished this had been her day at the reception desk and Bert's for darkroom work. Bert was wearing a jade-green dress—one that did a lot for her red hair. Jessie's Chicago Cubs sweatshirt and faded jeans made her look like a tomboy, but she hadn't cared until now. She fluffed her short brown curls and wondered if she'd even remembered lipstick that morning.

The man pushed the door open, glanced at Jessie and crossed the room toward the counter. "I saw your Valentine's special in the window," he said to Bert in a commanding baritone. "I need a picture taken immediately."

Damn, Jessie thought. He already had a girlfriend and could hardly wait to see a poster of her in a negligee. She had no trouble imagining him as an ardent lover, white-hot passion simmering beneath the surface. Maybe *that* was what she'd seen in his eyes.

"Well, of course, we have a very busy schedule," Bert lied in her professional receptionist tone. "Jessie, is there any chance we can help Mr.—?"

"Reid Halstead," he said, turning as Jessie approached the counter. "So you're the Jessie part. Who's Bert?"

"I am," Bert said, smiling.

"I thought Jessie And Bert's Photography would be run by a couple of guys."

"It's not," Jessie said.

He looked them over. "I guess it doesn't matter."

"On the contrary, Mr. Halstead," Jessie said, bristling. "Because we're both women, we put our clients more at ease for these romantic shots. Besides that, Bert is a wizard with glamour makeup. We believe we're far better suited to this phase of the business than 'a couple of guys' would be."

"That may be true, but I don't want a picture of a woman."

Jessie coughed to cover Bert's gasp of surprise. *Wouldn't you just know it?* she thought, working to keep her expression neutral.

Reid Halstead glanced at both of them in puzzlement. Then slowly his face turned the color of old brick. "Let me be more specific, before this gets out of hand. I want a picture of a bull."

Jessie laughed, then realized she probably shouldn't have, and mumbled an apology.

"A bull?" Bert asked, wide-eyed. "For the Valentine's special?"

Jessie glanced at Bert. "Would that be in the red lingerie or the black?" she asked, and watched tears come to Bert's eyes as she tried not to laugh.

"Forget it," Reid Halstead muttered and turned toward the door.

"No, no," Jessie cried, hurrying around the counter and grabbing his arm. "I'm sorry. Please, don't go. That was very rude of me." Fear of losing him—as a client, of course, she amended to herself—made her contrite. "Please. I'm sure you have a very good reason why you want a Valentine's picture of a—" She swallowed another burst of laughter and concentrated on the studio's pitiful checkbook balance. "A picture of a bull," she said more firmly, not trusting herself to look at Bert. She released his arm and smoothed the dents from the black leather. "Tell me—" She cleared her throat. "Tell me about it."

He hesitated.

"I promise we won't laugh again, Mr. Halstead," Bert said from behind the counter.

Jessie looked over at Bert, who mouthed the words "Be nice."

Reid Halstead sighed. "All right. Here's the deal," he said, facing Jessie. "First of all, this has nothing to do with Valentine's Day. I'm not the sentimental type."

Jessie hadn't thought so, either. He was the forceful type, definitely. Perhaps even the sensual type, if coaxed in the right direction. But Reid Halstead was no sentimental sap.

"I saw your sample poster with the Valentine's Day message printed on it," he continued. "And it gave me an idea. I'm making a presentation, day after tomorrow. Can you take a picture this afternoon and have a lettered poster ready in forty-eight hours?"

"Yes," Bert assured him.

"Where's the bull?" Jessie asked, and then had to bite the inside of her lip to stifle her laughter. "What I mean is, will you bring him here, or—"

"Obviously not," he glanced around the white-walled reception area with its red canvas director's chairs and black-enameled end tables. Framed examples of the studio's work hung on the walls, and Jessie had interspersed them with red cardboard cutouts of various sized hearts. She'd also suspended red cutouts of Cupid from the ceiling. One hung over Reid Halstead's head and seemed to be pointing his arrow directly at him.

"I'll drive one of you out to the research farm," Halstead continued. "Can either of you go right away? It should take about two hours. No more than that, I hope."

Jessie glanced at Bert. The sweatshirt and jeans had become an asset instead of a liability. "Can you spare me for a while?" she asked.

Bert looked very disappointed. "I guess so."

"Then I can be ready as soon as I pack my camera equipment." Jessie glanced out the window. "We're in luck that the weather looks pretty good."

"You'll be photographing the bull inside the barn. He rarely goes outside."

"Really?" Jessie frowned. "What a shame. Maybe I'd better ask you what this is for. You mentioned lettering underneath the poster."

"Yes. I want it to say The Future Is In Genetic Engineering. This bull is one of the chief assets of a genetic-research lab located south of Chicago. I've owned stock in the company for a few years, and now I think Magnitech should buy it. We need to diversify."

"We? Magnitech?" Jessie snuck a peek at Bert, who was making choking signs with both hands around her neck. The Magnitech building took up an entire block across the street. An account with them would end the studio's financial woes. "You, uh, work for Magnitech?"

"Yes."

"In what capacity?" She'd already guessed the answer.

"Chief executive officer."

Jessie admired the way he said the imposing title straight out, no waffling. Her head was racing. With her crazy jokes she'd nearly driven away the CEO of one of the biggest corporations in Chicago. Never mind that he looked like a macho ad for musk cologne, or that she kept noticing small, intimate things about him—the shape of his earlobes, the length of his eyelashes, and the way his hair curled slightly at the nape of his neck. Such details were secondary now. "I'm flattered that you came to us, Mr. Halstead," she said, and could almost feel the heat of Bert's approving smile.

"Ordinarily I wouldn't have. We have a PR division that could have handled this, but it was your window display that gave me the idea, and besides, our PR people are working on several other projects at the moment. You're sure you can get me the print in forty-eight hours?"

"We'll work our fannies off to satisfy you, Mr. Halstead," Jessie vowed.

"I doubt that will be necessary." Something that might have been amusement flickered in his eyes.

Jessie noted what a clear blue they were. She liked the transformation when the corners crinkled ever so slightly, but he still wasn't smiling—not quite. He was impressively handsome, no matter what his expression; but he was a little too serious. She'd like to see him laugh, just once. Maybe people who attained the stature of chief executive officer didn't have time to laugh. "I'll get my stuff," she said, and left the reception area.

She packed quickly, including several speeds of film in case she could convince Halstead to let her take the bull outside. She already had some great ideas for photographing a prize bull, but they wouldn't work as well in the confines of a barn. An animal like that would look more regal against a natural backdrop.

Finally she pulled on her quilted magenta ski jacket, slung her heavy camera bag over one shoulder, picked up umbrella lights in one hand and a tripod in the other, and walked out to find Bert leaning on the counter making calf's eyes at their new client. Jessie frowned, but Halstead didn't seem to notice that Bert was flirting with him.

"Well, Mr. Halstead," Jessie said in a voice loud enough to startle Bert and make Halstead turn in Jessie's direction, "what do you say we go shoot the bull?"

ANTICIPATING THE DREAM drive of her life, Jessie settled into the silver Mercedes sedan just as the car careened away from the curb and Halstead picked up his cellular phone. He punched in a number while avoiding two taxis and a delivery truck. Jessie gasped and grabbed the armrest.

"Naylor? We need a picture of the bull," he announced into the phone. "Get him cleaned up, will you? I'm bringing a photographer out. In about forty minutes. Right." He replaced the phone.

"You could have called from the studio," Jessie said, letting out the breath she'd been holding. "In fact, I would have preferred that to having you—"

The phone buzzed and he picked it up. "Halstead. Yeah, Mike. Well, negotiate with them. I know. I'm sure you can handle it. Try for a half million. Okay." He'd barely replaced the receiver when it buzzed again. He grabbed it while veering around a stalled Lincoln limousine.

Jessie closed her eyes and recited all the prayers she knew. She would gladly have relinquished the softness of the leather, the luxurious suspension and the company of this handsome CEO to be back in her studio. Her afternoon might have been dull, but it wouldn't have been life threatening. The tires squealed as Halstead whipped the sedan through traffic and continued talking on the phone.

"I'd be glad to handle one of those jobs for you," she offered in a strained voice after he'd finished the fourth call. "I'm an excellent driver, and I also have terrific telephone skills."

"Do I scare you?"

"Yes. Let me answer the phone next time."

The corners of his eyes crinkled again. "You wouldn't know what to say."

"Sure, I would. How's this?" She spoke into the hollow of her fist. 'Good afternoon, Magnitech Corporation, Mobile Division. The big wheel is at the wheel at the moment, making sure that his esteemed passenger, one Jessie Neal, photographer extraordinaire, sees the light of another day. Please leave a message at the sound of the beep.'"

He chuckled softly.

She would have enjoyed the triumph of making him laugh except that she was too frightened to enjoy anything but the possibility of a red light. "So, have I got the job of part-time receptionist for your car?"

He shook his head. "I use every minute of the day, and the only way I can afford the time to take you out here is if I do some business on the way there and back."

"Then I could drive. In fact, I'm surprised you don't have a chauffeured limo, come to think of it."

"I'd be bored. Doing it this way is more of a challenge."

Jessie opened her mouth to debate the ethics of taking challenges that involved other people's safety, but the telephone rang again and Reid Halstead was back in business mode. Just her luck she'd hook up with Evel Knievel disguised in a three-piece suit. To be fair, he handled the car beautifully, no matter how many calls he took. He was kind of exciting to watch, but she'd rather imagine him on a video than steering the car she was riding in.

She'd heard about these high-powered, type A personalities but she'd never met one in the flesh, let alone trusted her life to one. She kept reminding herself that a guy like this could open doors for Jessie And Bert's Photography

Studio. Hell, he could open doors and roll out yards of red carpet, sound the trumpets and introduce them to the reigning business royalty of Chicago—if she lived long enough to see that day.

Deprived of conversation with her escort, Jessie relied on the only entertainment left to her—she eavesdropped. Not many of the transactions made sense to her, but she figured out that lots of money was usually involved. Several of Halstead's calls were to a woman named Rosemary, and Jessie finally concluded that Rosemary was his secretary.

Only once, when Halstead was talking with Rosemary, did his tone of brisk efficiency change. "How's Bobby?" he asked.

Jessie was so startled by the tenderness in his voice that she turned in her seat and stared at him.

He was concentrating on the road and didn't notice her scrutiny. "So it was chicken pox," he murmured. "You're sure he's okay at your sister's? Yeah, I know, but you can take a few days off it you need them. After all, Les is out of town, and you're—" He paused and listened. "That's right, but nothing's more important than getting that little guy well. Okay. Keep me posted."

Jessie looked away again as Halstead hung up the phone. He wasn't an automaton after all, she thought, the knowledge warming her. In the midst of his million-dollar deals, he'd asked about his secretary's sick child. Jessie could see how busy he was, and yet he'd told his secretary to take time off if she needed it. Jessie smiled to herself.

Gradually traffic lightened as they left the city, and Jessie unclenched her fingers from the armrests. Maybe she'd call a taxi to take her back. But Halstead might be insulted and she'd mess up this business deal and the ones she hoped to get in the future. She'd have to risk the return trip. Bert had better appreciate the sacrifices she was making for the studio.

The Mercedes left the main highway for a two-lane road that bisected fields stubbled brown with last season's crop. Jessie settled back and started to feel the magic of a powerful car driven by a powerful man. If she could just keep that combination out of heavy traffic, it would be sort of fun. Except Halstead continued to play with his telephone. She was developing an intense dislike for the thing.

When he hung up the phone and said, "That's enough of that," she foolishly expected that he intended to converse with his passenger—until he added, "We're here," and turned right. A small white sign read Malone Farms, Genetic Research. Beyond was a security gate. Halstead pushed a button to lower his window, spoke to the guard on duty, and the gate swung open.

The paved road ran straight ahead to a series of geometrically-placed white buildings. Galvanized pipe fencing divided the flat land surrounding the buildings into perfect rectangles, and the cattle enclosed within each pen were grouped by color. Jessie couldn't see a single weed, and even the dormant grass lining the road leading to the buildings and enclosures hadn't been allowed to migrate into the pens. Apparently, the cattle were fed from grain bins and weren't allowed to graze. The parking lot contained late-model sedans, not rusty old pickups. "Why do I feel as if I'm in some James Bond movie?" she asked.

"That's exactly the reaction I'm afraid the directors will have," he said, pulling up in front of a building labeled Administration. "You say the words *genetic research*, and everybody thinks of weird science fiction and spy thrillers."

"The guard at the security gate doesn't exactly dispel that feeling," Jessie said. "And I've never seen a farm like this. Where are the tractors? Where are the chickens and the little old lady feeding them from her apron?''

"The tractors are garaged when not in use, and these people don't 'do' chickens. They're concentrating on cows.''

"They've concentrated so hard they've made them look like they came off an assembly line.''

"That's sort of the idea." He switched off the engine.

"I don't know about your board of directors, but the concept certainly makes me nervous, Mr. Halstead.''

"Reid.''

His correction pleased her. Not everyone was on a first-name basis with the CEO of Magnitech. "Jessie," she said.

"Okay, Jessie, let's get started." He opened his door and a whoosh of cold February air chilled the interior of the car.

Jessie got out and started unloading her equipment. Reid helped her with a detached efficiency that she found mildly irritating. Usually men gave some indication that they noticed her as a woman. Reid seemed oblivious to everything but his business deals—except for the time he'd asked Rosemary about her little boy. Not that Jessie wanted Reid to make a pass or anything. Of course not.

Jessie forced her mind back to the project at hand. The setting threw her a little. She'd hoped for some natural rural ambience as a backdrop, but Malone Farms had about as much charm as a sterile hospital examining room. Reid led her through the administration building to an office where they were each given identification badges.

"Is all this secrecy really necessary?" she asked Reid as they followed their guide, Tom, over to the barn.

"Sure." Reid shifted her camera bag to his other shoulder. Tom had offered to carry it but Reid had waved him away. "The discoveries they make here can be worth millions of dollars."

"Wow. I can see why you want Magnitech to invest in it, then."

"I hope the directors are as easy to convince as you are. They're a conservative bunch. That's why I thought if they see a large poster of Levi, that would be something concrete, a symbol of—"

"Levi?"

"The bull. That's his name. For his superior genes."

Jessie laughed with relief. "Finally, a ray of sunshine in this bleak place. 'Superior genes.' I love it. I'd like to meet the person who thought up that name."

Reid glanced at her. "You already have."

"You?"

"Uh-hmm."

A surprise. She'd always been a sucker for surprises in people. Surprises made her want to know more. To be honest, there were lots of compelling reasons to know more about Reid Halstead. He was great to look at and he had a well-hidden but wacky sense of humor, although his in-town driving left much to be desired.

Of course, he was rich—which didn't hurt anything— and considerate of the family needs of his secretary; but the fact that he'd come up with the name for Levi struck her as the most promising thing about him. That, and the intense gaze she could still recall from that first moment she'd seen him on the other side of the studio window. She imagined that intensity focused on her—for reasons other than business—and shivered with anticipation.

As Jessie walked toward the stark-white barn she made a decision: she'd work out some way to make Reid notice her—not as a photographer, not as a business contact, but as a woman.

Chapter Two

CLASSICAL MUSIC PLAYED softly in the barn. Jessie glanced at Reid as they stepped inside the doorway. "Bulls like Beethoven?"

"So the scientists tell me."

The interior of the barn resembled nothing that Jessie had ever seen, and she'd grown up in a rural community in southern Illinois, so she knew her farms. She imagined that a cattle barn in outer space might look like this. Spotless white walls were lined with wide metal stalls, each with its own ceiling fan and heat lamp. There was virtually no smell, except for the fresh pine scent of sawdust used in the stalls instead of straw. They walked down a center aisle that was swept cleaner than the photo-staging area of her studio. Jessie unzipped her jacket in the warmth radiating from the heat lamps and wondered if she should have wiped her feet before coming in.

The music seemed to be working to soothe the animals in their stalls, except for an enormous black Angus bull at the far end of the barn. He was crosstied inside a corral of white metal piping while a man and a woman tried to give him a shampoo. The huge animal bellowed and stomped, spraying lather in every direction. Jessie thought about the occasions she'd given unwilling dogs a bath. This creature was a slightly different story, though. One unexpected move could crush an attendant against the wall.

"That's Levi?" Jessie asked, glancing up at Reid.

"That's Levi. And he's not ready." Reid's voice had an edge in it.

"Sorry about that," Tom said over his shoulder. "Levi isn't feeling cooperative today. Took four of us to get him out of his stall and over to the wash rack. But we wanted him to look good for his picture." Tom introduced Betty and Duane, who barely had the leisure to glance up from their labors with the bull.

Jessie propped her tripod and umbrella lights against a stall and prepared to watch the show. Levi bellowed again and kicked with one hind leg, narrowly missing Betty, who was wiping lather away with a metal scraper.

"Look out, look out!" Betty cried, backing away. "He's not happy."

"That's an understatement," said Duane, a short, stocky man who was holding Levi's halter. "If he's this bad with the shampoo, which one of us gets to polish his hooves? And think of all the fun we'll have cleaning his sheath."

Jessie flushed. It had been a while since she'd been around farm people, but she remembered what a sheath was. She guessed from Reid's puzzled expression that he hadn't the faintest idea. He was about to open his mouth and ask; she just knew it. She touched his arm. "Could I talk with you a minute? About how to set up the shot?"

"Sure." He eased her camera bag down to the cement floor and followed her as she moved along the center aisle, away from the wash rack.

"You don't know what they mean by washing his sheath, do you?" she asked in a low tone.

"No, but I was just about to—"

"I thought so. I wanted to save you some embarrassment." She faltered. In her rush to help him, she'd put herself in an awkward position. She took a deep breath and stared at a polished hinge on one of the stall doors.

"The sheath is what covers his...male organ." Her cheeks warmed as she flicked a glance at him.

"Oh." He cleared his throat, shifting his stance. "I wouldn't have thought of that. Especially since Levi's never...I mean, they don't let him...Oh, hell. What I'm trying to say is he doesn't do it with cows."

Jessie recovered herself enough to smile. "He has test-tube lovers?"

"That's one way to put it." He chuckled. "Sounds like a good hit song for the nineties."

Jessie saw a way to ease the tension. She grabbed an imaginary mike, held it to her mouth and began to sway to a rock beat. "We never kiss," she sang. "We never touch. We cherish clean-li-ness too much." She pursed her lips and wriggled her hips. "And that is why we're test-tube lovers."

Reid laughed—a deep-down belly laugh.

Pleased with herself, Jessie smiled back at him.

"You're something else," he said, his blue eyes twinkling. "And thanks for keeping me from making an ass of myself."

"My pleasure."

"How do you know about things like that?"

"I grew up around kids who raised livestock. I guess you're strictly a city guy."

"That's right. But I'll admit I'm sort of fascinated with all this." He waved an arm around the barn.

"What you see here is pretty sanitized compared to a real farm, Reid. You can hardly smell the— Well, anyway, you wouldn't want to be in a normal barn in a three-piece suit and a black leather trench coat. Especially not in those black wing tips."

He glanced down at his shoes and back at her. "They really wash...everything on that bull?"

"I'm sure they plan to, from the way they were talking."

"Have you ever done it? The whole job, I mean?" He surveyed her with interest.

"Not this girl."

"Why not? Finicky?"

She felt the heat in her cheeks. "Particular."

He laughed again, and she grinned in response. Then, slowly, his teasing expression faded as he continued to study her. "Your eyes are the richest shade of brown I've ever seen."

With a start she realized she'd accomplished her mission. He'd noticed her. "These old things? Why, I've had them forever." She savored the way he was looking at her, with that seductive intensity that made her toes curl. All it had taken was a discussion about washing the private parts of a black Angus bull. She wouldn't have chosen that vehicle, but the vehicle seemed to have chosen her.

"Little did I dream," he began, his voice soft, "that when I decided to have this picture taken, I'd run into someone like you."

Her breathing quickened. "Is that good or bad?" she asked, lost in the magnetic pull of his gaze.

"That depends on your point of view. Bad for my concentration on business matters. Good for...other things."

Oh, yes, she thought. This was what she'd imagined lurking beneath the surface of Reid Halstead. She'd awakened his libido, and she mustn't lose her nerve now. "What things?" she murmured.

"As if you didn't know." His voice was a caress. "As if those brown eyes aren't coaxing me to—"

"The bull's about ready, Mr. Halstead," Tom called.

Reid paused and took a long, steadying breath. "Fine," he said, still looking at Jessie. "Did they clean his sheath?"

"Yes, sir!"

"Good. Then we can begin the photo session," Reid winked at Jessie.

Jessie shook her head to clear the fog from her brain. She couldn't believe this was the same business dynamo who'd spent the entire forty-minute drive with a telephone glued to his ear. He didn't seem to do anything by halves, this Reid Halstead.

With difficulty she focused on the job at hand and followed Reid back to the wash rack. Levi snorted his displeasure and pawed the cement with hooves that gleamed like obsidian. His black coat glowed in the light from the overhead fluorescent bulbs.

He was a magnificent animal, clean sheath and all, Jessie thought, but she didn't want to shoot him here in the barn. He belonged outside, against a backdrop of blue sky if nothing else. Jessie glanced at Reid and wondered if, considering recent events, her influence had grown any. "Can I take him out to the paddock?"

Reid shook his head. As if to prove they weren't going anywhere, he took off his trench coat and slung it over the door of a vacant stall.

So much for influence, she thought. "We should at least untie him. I assume you want him as a proud, arrogant symbol of perfection, a regal example of good breeding. He won't look regal if he's trussed up like that."

Reid glanced at Duane, who stood nearby, admiring his handiwork. "What do you think?"

"I think if we untie him he'll throw himself around in there and ruin everything we've tried to do. He might even lie down and roll."

"No, he won't," Jessie said. "I'll talk to him."

Duane laughed. "And you think he'll listen? This is one grumpy animal. He doesn't like anybody today."

"You wouldn't, either, if you were cooped up inside all the time and given a bath when you hadn't had a good chance to get dirty in practically your whole life," Jessie said.

Duane laughed again, more sarcastically this time. "Oh, he's had a terrible life, all right. The barn's climate controlled so he won't get sick. He listens to the best orchestras in the world on an expensive sound system. His feed's grown and mixed right here according to a special formula. His stall is mucked out three times a day and laid with fresh sawdust. This bull's got it better than I do, for crying out loud!"

"That's not true," Jessie insisted. "You're free to come and go as you please. Would you really want to trade places with this bull?"

Duane regarded her silently for a moment. "I guess I see your point," he said, his belligerence receding. "But if we untie him, he's gonna roll. He won't look very regal after that."

Jessie glanced back at Reid. "Well?"

"Take a few pictures while he's tied, and then try it untied," Reid said. "That way, we'll be sure to get something."

"We can do that." Jessie knew she wouldn't want to put her studio's name on a photograph of this bull with a halter and ropes restricting his movements. If she understood the image Reid wanted to portray, he wouldn't want that, either; but it wouldn't hurt to snap a few throwaway shots and get Levi used to the camera.

She positioned her tripod, set up her umbrella lights and asked everyone to move away. After taking her jacket off and hanging it on the stall door beside Reid's coat, she walked to the pen and climbed in.

"Jessie!" Reid called from behind her. "You'd better not—"

"Hush," Jessie said, keeping her attention on Levi. "I need a meter reading. Besides, Levi and I will be fine in here, won't we, big boy?"

The bull rolled his eyes at her and snorted. Jessie told him how famous he would be after she took his picture and promised to make him look like the most handsome bull that ever walked the earth. Slowly the wild look disappeared from Levi's brown eyes.

Leaving the pen, Jessie continued her stream of compliments to Levi as she took several placid close-ups in which the bull stared soulfully into the lens. Then she glanced back at Reid, her eyebrows lifted in an unspoken question.

"Okay. We can try it with the halter and ropes off, I guess."

The attendants stepped forward, but Jessie held up her hand. "Let me."

Duane looked at Betty and shrugged. They moved back again.

Jessie climbed back into the pen, continuing her one-way conversation with the bull. His head and hers were almost on a level, and she estimated his weight at well over a ton. Jessie knew that Reid was observing every move she made. She had to look competent and unafraid. She decided to pretend that Levi was a friendly dog—only bigger. *Much* bigger.

She unhooked both ropes from the halter while Levi watched her carefully. He seemed mesmerized by her as she crooned to him while she climbed out of the pen. She took the pictures fast, not wanting to press her luck, but Levi only turned his head slightly. Otherwise he looked like a stuffed museum piece. The effect was better without the ropes, but it still wasn't what she'd had in mind.

Keeping eye contact with Levi, Jessie spoke to Reid. "This is better, but not best. Reid, can we possibly take him outside? The poster would be a hundred-percent more effective." She listened to the indignant muttering as he conferred with the people behind her.

"Tom will call Administration and check, Jessie," he said at last.

She sighed. Something was terribly wrong when an animal like this couldn't be let into the paddock without a phone call to Administration. Jessie decided she wanted to give Levi a small taste of freedom more than she cared about the outdoor shot. But she'd take the photograph, and she knew exactly the moment she was after.

"Mr. Halstead, Administration gave the okay for five minutes in the number-one paddock. It's right outside this back door," Tom reported.

"Great," Jessie said.

"You'd better step back, Miss Neal," Tom said. "We'll need to put the halter and lead rope on him."

"Can you possibly herd him out there without doing that?" she pleaded as she unscrewed her camera from the tripod. "Can we have a semblance of freedom in this shot?"

"She's right," Reid said. "All you have to do is open the door, open the gate of the pen, and I'll bet he'll go right out."

"Yeah," said Duane. "And how do we get him back in? You ever try to make a twenty-five-hundred-pound animal do what he doesn't want to do?"

"After I take the photograph, I'll put the halter back on." Jessie felt like a traitor. She wished she didn't have to deliver Levi to his captors again; but he wasn't hers, and Reid had said he was potentially worth millions.

Reid spoke again. "Let her try it. You've all seen the empathy she's developed with that animal. I'll take full responsibility."

Jessie flashed him a quick smile as she reloaded the camera with a lower-speed film. "Thanks." She took the halter Duane handed her. "If you'll let me go out the door before you open the gate, I can be set up in the paddock when he comes out."

Tom stepped over to the wide double doors and swung one open.

Jessie gave Levi one last look and hurried into the sunshine. In her excitement she'd forgotten her jacket, and the air was cold. She shivered as she hung the halter on the fence and positioned herself where she estimated her best angle would be. She wanted to cut out the barn and shoot Levi against the horizon, if possible. "Ready!" she called.

Levi surged through the door like a locomotive, his bulk shaking the ground under Jessie's feet. For a moment she wondered if she'd been foolhardy to stand inside the paddock with such a monumental force of nature but she was committed, and she'd stay. Bracing her arms against her sides, she raised the camera.

As if on cue, Levi paused, lifted his head, and gazed out toward the horizon. Sunlight danced across his dark coat to reveal auburn highlights that had been invisible in the barn. His muscles rippled and he tensed as if contemplating a run for freedom. Jessie pressed the shutter. "Sorry, Levi," she whispered, tears in her eyes, "but this is as far as you go."

Levi didn't charge the fence. Instead he wandered around the paddock as if looking for a gap in the railings.

Jessie followed him and squeezed off a few more frames, but she knew they weren't necessary. She had her shot.

"Five minutes is almost up," Tom called from the doorway.

"Right." Jessie walked to the edge of the paddock and set her camera outside the fence. She wasn't as sure of Levi's reaction as she'd sounded back in the barn. When she straightened and turned back to Levi, she discovered that although the others had stayed safely inside, Reid had stepped into the enclosure with her. She'd never seen a man wearing a three-piece suit standing in the same paddock with a black Angus bull. *Magnificent bull, magnificent man.* She wished she still had her camera.

"Thought you might need some help," he said softly.

Jessie glanced at Levi, who was watching them both warily. "You forgot your cape."

"I'll fake it."

"I don't know, Reid. Messing around in this paddock might not be good for those wing tips of yours."

"I'll worry about the wing tips."

She smiled at him. "You're pretty brave for a city boy."

"Maybe just dumb. But at least we're even."

"I don't think facing a belligerent animal fits in the same category as saving you from social embarrassment, but I'm glad you're here."

"I thought you might be. So what do we do first?"

She picked up the halter that was hanging on the fence. "Let's both walk slowly toward him. Maybe with two of us coming at him he won't know which way to run. But listen, Reid, if he starts charging you, jump over the fence. No heroics."

"That goes for you, too."

"You bet. Now, let's go." Jessie started her monologue again as she edged closer to Levi. She tried to keep her voice calm. Reid approached from the other side.

The bull pawed the ground and snorted, sending twin clouds of steam into the cold air.

Without changing the pitch of her voice, Jessie said, "Watch him, Reid. Watch his eyes."

"I'm watching."

"Can you run?"

"Varsity letter in track."

"Glad to hear it." Jessie could almost touch Levi's muzzle. "Just stand still, Reid. We almost have him. I'm going to ease the halter on, now." Jessie kept her movements smooth and steady. "Sorry to have to do this to you, Levi, but you brought it on yourself, by being such a handsome specimen." She clicked the halter in place.

"Good job," Reid murmured.

"Thanks. Now we lead him in," Jessie said. "You first, and I'll follow with Levi."

"All right." Reid slowly turned his back on the bull and started toward the open door.

Jessie admired his unhesitating stride, the confident set of his wide shoulders. He didn't look back once. "Come on, sweetheart," Jessie crooned, starting after Reid and pulling gently on the halter. "At least it's warm inside." To her amazement, the bull plodded along beside her. His trust was touching.

Once she and Levi were inside the barn, the attendants directed them to Levi's king-size stall. She walked him in, gave him a kiss on the nose, and left the stall.

"Want a job?" Duane asked, closing the stall door and latching it securely. He handed her the camera she'd left outside.

"Thanks, I already have a job," she said. All at once, reaction to handling a potentially dangerous animal set in, and Jessie's knees wobbled. She stumbled and reached toward the stall door for support, but Reid was there, steadying her with one arm around her waist and a hand at her elbow.

"Easy," he murmured.

Warmth flooded through her. She glanced up and almost forgot to breathe. His lips were so close. "Thanks," she whispered.

"Wouldn't want you to drop the camera," he said, but his eyes said so much more, and he released her slowly, very slowly.

She could still feel the imprint of his arm around her waist, still catch the scent of his after-shave. The contact had left her dizzy, and if the intense blue of Reid's eyes was any indication, he'd been affected, too.

She cleared her throat. "I guess if you want that poster within forty-eight hours, we'd better be going."

"Right."

This time, Jessie looked forward to a two-hour ride with Reid Halstead. The interior of a car could be very intimate, especially when two people were thinking about the same thing....

Chapter Three

AFRAID TO BREAK the spell she and Reid had created, Jessie didn't speak as they loaded her equipment in the Mercedes. He helped her into the car, his hand at her elbow, and she felt the contact all the way to her toes. The atmosphere inside the car was as cozy as she could have wished. She glanced over at Reid and smiled. He smiled back and switched on the ignition.

Halfway down the drive of Malone Farms, the cellular phone buzzed. *Ignore it,* Jessie willed. The phone buzzed again, and still Reid didn't pick it up. She glanced at him and saw his jaw tighten. The phone buzzed a third time. With a muttered oath, Reid answered it.

Jessie sagged against her seat. He hadn't been able to shut out the business world, after all, she thought, staring out the window in discouragement. She listened to his curt conversation, which duplicated all the others he'd had on the drive out to the farm.

"I'm on my way," Reid said. "Yes, it took a little longer than I'd expected. The photographer was very thorough. She—" Reid paused. "Yes, a woman. Did a great job."

Jessie looked over at him. He'd taken his attention from the road and was regarding her intently.

"A great job," he repeated, meeting her gaze.

Her resentment softened and the feeling of intimacy returned. *Perhaps now*—but Reid's attention returned to the road and his conversation.

After that one moment, he never gave her that look again. Halfway back to downtown Chicago, Jessie yearned to toss Reid's cellular telephone out the window. Perhaps she'd imagined his interest in her. She could ask him out-right about his very leading comments in the barn, and risk looking more stupid than ever if he said that he hadn't really meant anything by them. But she thought he had. In twenty-seven years on this earth she'd learned a thing or two about men, and Reid hadn't been making idle chit-chat when he'd mentioned that her presence distracted him from business. If so, however, he seemed to have over-come that particular distraction rather quickly.

As they neared the studio, Reid hung up the phone and paused at a stoplight. He unbuckled his seat belt and turned.... Jessie held her breath, wondering if he'd take her in his arms. Instead, he reached into the back seat and grabbed his briefcase.

"There's a file in here I need," he said, as the light turned green. "Would you please take it out for me?"

She had no choice but to accept the briefcase and open it as he barreled into the intersection. *A file, indeed!* She wished she'd never offered to be his car secretary. "Which one?" she asked, glancing at the accordian section con-taining computer printouts, memos and faxed messages, all neatly filed in labeled manila folders.

"Reichert," he said. "I promised to call him before three this afternoon and give him some figures."

Which are probably the only figures you care about, Jessie thought. She jerked the file out with more force than was necessary and a brochure came out with it. She handed the file to Reid, who promptly opened it on his lap and picked up the phone. Jessie started to return the brochure to its place, but she paused when she noticed it was an ad-vertisement for hang gliding in La Jolla, California.

When Reid hung up the phone and gave her the folder, she waved the brochure. "Is Magnitech diversifying into hang gliding, too?"

He glanced at the brochure as if he'd never seen it before. "Hang gliding? No. Where'd you find that?"

"It fell out. It was stuck between two files, I guess."

Reid frowned. "Oh, yeah, I remember. I picked that up in an airport last week. Thought it looked like fun, but I doubt if I'll ever take the time."

"Why not?"

"Too busy." He whipped into a parking space two doors down from the studio. "I'll drop you here. I'm not going back to the office yet. Can I help you with the equipment?"

"I think you're too busy." Jessie slammed the briefcase closed. She opened the car door.

"Jessie, you seem upset."

She glanced back at him and the words she wanted to say stuck in her throat. How could she ask him why he'd seemed so interested in her back at the farm and now seemed so detached? She hadn't known him long enough to ask those things, and besides, he was a client—an important client who could possibly be the answer to her and Bert's financial prayers. She couldn't afford the risk of alienating him now.

"I'm not upset," she replied. "In fact, I'm in quite a hurry, myself. I can carry everything. We'll say goodbye here."

"If you're sure..." He shut his door again, obviously satisfied with her response.

"Absolutely sure." She hopped out to the curb, opened the back door and began retrieving her gear. "I assume you'll want to drop by tomorrow and look at the proofs before we have the poster made up for the following day?"

"Yes. I'll work it into my lunch hour—that is, if you'll be there at—"

"Of course. I never take lunch, either," she said, setting her camera bag on the sidewalk. "See you then, Reid."

"Goodbye, Jessie. See you tomorrow."

"Right," she said, copying his brisk attitude. She swung the back door shut and shouldered her camera bag while carrying the lights and tripod. She trudged toward the studio, not even watching as the silver Mercedes pulled into traffic. She didn't want to see Reid pick up the cellular phone again as if she were already out of his mind.

THE NEXT DAY Jessie was in charge of the reception desk and Bert handled the darkroom and photography work. Jessie was glad for the switch. Maybe if Reid saw her in her white wool miniskirt and blue angora sweater he'd forget about business for a few precious minutes. She'd decided in the intervening hours since she'd seen him that she hadn't imagined his interest. Unfortunately, poor Reid had a one-track mind, and she'd have to figure out some way to jolt it from that track—business—to another: romance.

She'd talked to Bert about the whole thing the night before. They'd been sitting on their apartment floor amid cartons of Chinese food and the proofs Jessie had made of Levi. Bert's advice had been to forget Reid Halstead, who was obviously ruled by his job. But Jessie couldn't forget him. He was a challenge. She wondered how she could make his blue eyes light up again the way they had when he'd kept her from falling in the barn.

The proofs—especially the photographs taken outside—were good. She'd been right about the shot in the paddock. She hoped Reid would like it as much as she did, but she also hoped he'd pay attention to something besides her talented photography.

At twelve-thirty he walked in, his hair and the shoulders of his trench coat sprinkled with the light rain that had been threatening all day to turn into snow. He smiled at her, and she forgave him every blessed minute on the cellular phone. She didn't know if she'd read his emotions correctly the day before, but hers were becoming pretty obvious.

"Hi," he said, walking toward the counter with his hands in his pockets. "You must be the receptionist today."

"That's right." She looked into his eyes, and yes, the glimmer was there. She hadn't imagined anything. Somehow she'd fan that flame today so that it wouldn't go out so quickly. "I have the proofs here." She reached under the counter and pulled out an envelope. "Why don't we sit down and go through them?"

"Sure." He shrugged out of his coat, which she considered a good sign. Underneath it he wore a dark blue suit— no vest this time. His tie was shades of blue, one of which perfectly matched his eyes. He looked crisp and efficient. *Too crisp,* she thought, longing to loosen his tie and ruffle his damp hair.

She walked out from behind the counter and enjoyed the way his gaze traveled to her legs. *Take that,* she challenged and sauntered over to the red director's chairs. She sat down and crossed her legs.

His glance burned hot for a moment before he lowered himself into the chair beside her.

She handed him the inside shots first, making certain that she brushed his hand each time she gave him another photograph. The contact made her whole arm tingle. Better yet, she noticed his hand tremble ever so slightly as he glanced at the proofs and handed them back.

"What do you think?" she asked.

"Not bad."

"I'm saving the best for last." She shifted in the chair so that her skirt inched up a little higher. "That builds suspense," she murmured, aware that his attention lingered on her thigh. She'd never taunted a man this way in her life, but with Reid, strong measures were necessary. "I suppose in your position you understand the value of that," she said, her heart thumping erratically.

He cleared his throat and looked into her eyes. "I certainly do."

She loved nurturing that hot flame in his eyes, and she held the moment for as long as she dared. "You need something spectacular to impress your board of directors." She handed him the last photograph in her hand—the shot of Levi with his head up, staring out at the horizon. "Provocative, wouldn't you say?"

Reid took the photograph without looking at it. "Yes," he replied in a strained voice.

Now that she had him, she couldn't resist teasing him a little. "I meant the shot of the bull."

As if she'd snapped her fingers, he jerked and looked down at the proof in his hand. "Oh. Yeah. Sure is. Good work."

She knew she'd just made a terrible mistake with that chiding remark. She tried to regain the mood. "I wouldn't have that shot if you hadn't interceded for me, Reid. And I was impressed that you walked out in that paddock, while the rest of them cowered in the barn, afraid to—"

He broke into her recitation, his words laced with enthusiasm. "However you got it, Jessie, this is a great shot. Perfect for the poster. The board of directors will be sold, once they see this. In fact, I have an idea."

She hoped the idea had something to do with her, but somehow she doubted it. She had a feeling that his excitement had nothing to do with her, either.

"The poster ought to be covered. Then I'll throw back the covering sheet when I make my announcement about the acquisition plans. Can you design something like that?"

"Of course," Jessie said, mentally kicking herself. Yep, she'd blown it. Just as quickly as she'd jarred him off his one track, she'd jarred him back on it.

"This concept of genetic engineering is amazing," he said, absorbed in the photograph of Levi. "Did you know that one superior bull like this can service a hundred thousand cows a year?"

"Tell that to Levi. He should be excited."

"Just think of what that could mean to the beef and dairy industry." He turned to her, his expression animated, but not for the reason she'd hoped. "With the new genetic research in progress, we can pass all his superior traits on to generation after generation of animals. Profits will go up accordingly, and Magnitech will have a piece of the action, if I have anything to say about it. How soon can you have this ready?"

Jessie sighed. "Noon tomorrow?" She stood. Maybe Bert was right and this was a lost cause. Business would always come first with a man like Reid.

"Good." He glanced at his watch. "I have to go." He got up, put on his coat and started toward the door. He opened it and turned back to her. "Great outfit," he said, and left.

Jessie groaned.

"What happened?" Bert stood in the doorway to the photo-staging area. "I've been dying to know."

Jessie threw both hands in the air. "I don't get it! I thin
he's interested. In fact, I know he is. But then he'll sna'
back into that strictly-business mode of his and I might a
well be one of these easels."

"Give up, Jessie. Leave him to his mobile phone and hi
fax machine. Besides, we have this Hotshot special to ge
your mind off him."

"I would, except he keeps doing little things that mak
me think there's hope. When he first saw my outfit, h
couldn't take his eyes off me. But when we got on the sub
ject of his precious bull, and he... Wait a minute, wait
minute! Do I have an idea!"

"Jessie, don't look like that. I get really worried whe
you get that look in your eye. The last time you—"

"No, Bert, trust me. This is good. Foolproof."

"It's some sort of practical joke, isn't it? You always us
the word *foolproof* when you're thinking up a practica
joke. But Jessie," Bert said, crossing her arms, "I don'
remember even one time when your jokes worked the wa
they were supposed to."

"This one will. And I *have* to do it. Remember how
told you he loosened up when I sang that silly song fo
him? If I can get him laughing, I stand a chance."

"He's an important client. I don't want you messin;
around with—"

"Just listen," Jessie interrupted. "Here's my idea. Re
member the Valentine's shot of me, the one you wanted t
use in the window for the special?"

"Jessie, I don't like the sound of this."

"Nothing will happen, trust me. I'll order this bul
poster, and I'll also order that one of me in the red tedd'
on the white hearth rug, with Reid's caption under it—Th
Future Is In Genetic Engineering."

"You wouldn't."

"Why not? I'll have the real one ready to go. I'll hand him the one of me first, and after I get his reaction, I'll give him the right one." Jessie laughed. "Isn't that great?"

Bert shook her head. "No, it's insane. What if you antagonize him?"

"I won't. He has a good sense of humor. Look, you don't know as much about him as I do." She paced in front of the counter. "I'll make him laugh and he'll have his bull poster. Best of all, he'll have the poster of me, too. I'd be willing to bet he takes it with him. Then he'll have this sexy image of me to remind him that life isn't all business."

"I don't know, Jessie. I don't feel right about his."

Jessie paused and faced her. "Look at it this way, Bert. If I start dating him, he'll introduce me to all sorts of people. One of our problems is that we're unknown. A contact like Reid Halstead could be really good for the studio."

"Is that why you're doing this?"

"To be truthful, no. I'm intrigued with him and I think he's interested in me. I just thought the business argument would convince you that we should take this tiny risk when we have so much to gain."

"'Tiny risk'? I thought you said this was foolproof."

"All right, no risk. No risk at all."

Bert laughed. "Come on, Jessie. After all, I've known you for ten years, roomed with you for five and been in business with you for more than a year. I've been through these things before. I know what can happen."

"You're a worrywart," Jessie said. "What could possibly go wrong?"

Chapter Four

"DAMMIT!" Jessie leaned into the winter wind and walked faster, pushing her way through the pedestrians on Michigan Avenue. A nearby clock tower had just chimed the quarter hour. Noon was fifteen minutes away. What i Reid arrived at the studio before she did?

She'd finished one shoot at ten-thirty and had though she'd have plenty of time before Reid arrived to run ou and buy a red feather boa on sale at Marshall Field's. On of the two clients coming in for the Hotshot special tha afternoon was definitely the feather-boa type, and Jessi couldn't resist having one on hand as a prop.

On the way back she'd noticed a boutique having a sal on silk scarves and had stopped to pick up a red and white one as additional props. She hadn't expected th clerk to be new or the store to be so crowded. Shopper were out in such force that it seemed more like the wee before Christmas instead of the week before Valentine' Day.

At five minutes before noon Jessie pushed the studic door open and glanced around. No Reid. She sighed with relief and smiled at Bert standing behind the receptior desk. "Looks like I made it back in time, after all."

"Not exactly," Bert said. "This guy, Halstead's assis tant, just picked up the poster."

Jessie's smile disappeared. "Which poster?"

"And well you might ask." Bert's expression was dis approving. "I didn't know what the heck to do—which i why I don't like to get into these escapades of yours, Jes sie."

"Never mind that. Which poster did you give him?"

"I thought about it as quickly as I could, considering that I had no time to think, really. I ended up giving him the poster of you. The bull's still here."

Jessie released her held breath. "Good. You did the right thing. Otherwise all my efforts would have been wasted."

"I probably shouldn't have done it, Jessie. I should have given him the bull, and we could have forgotten about the whole incident. I gave him the wrong poster against my better judgement."

"I know you did, Bert, and I appreciate it." Jessie walked around the counter, set down her packages and gave her partner a hug. "You know, this might work out better, anyway. I'll take the bull poster up to his office and explain that there was a mix-up. He'll have had time to absorb the pose of me on the white rug. He'll know it was a joke. I'll bet you anything he asks me to lunch."

"Let's hope so, after all this. But don't be too long, okay? While you were gone we had three phone calls about our Hotshot promotion. I took the appointments, even though we're getting tight on time before Valentine's Day. We're going to be really busy this next week, and we'll need both of us here most of the time."

"Don't worry." Jessie reached under the counter and pulled out the covered poster of Levi. "Reid Halstead doesn't seem the type to take a long lunch. If I get a half hour of his time, I'll consider myself making progress." She started out the door.

"Good luck, Jessie," Bert called after her.

Jessie paused in the doorway. "You're terrific, Bert. At one point you seemed interested in Reid, and here you are helping me."

"You're right. I'm terrific. Plus, I'm not interested in Reid—he's too immersed in his business deals to suit me. Now, if I could just get the guy who moved into our apartment house to realize how terrific I am . . ."

"The blonde across the hall?" Jessie asked, vaguely remembering a jock type in gray sweats. "Hey, yeah, he is pretty cute. Let's plan some way to make him notice you."

"On second thought," Bert said, laughing, "I'll handle it myself. I can just imagine what you'd come up with."

Jessie grinned. "I can see it now. A glamour shot of you, pasted to our front door."

"Not on your life! Get out of here, Jessie Neal, and take your bull with you."

Laughing, Jessie closed the door. Then she turned and waved at Bert before she crossed the street. Good old Bert. She was always so nervous of Jessie's crazy schemes, yet she'd played along with this newest idea. Bert was a one-in-a-million friend.

The lobby of the Magnitech building arched upward three stories and a waterfall tumbled down one wall into a shallow pool surrounded by tropical plants. Jessie surveyed the magnificence of the marble floors and polished brass elevator doors with new appreciation now that she knew Reid was in charge of it all. Gazing around at this impressive lobby, she wondered briefly if she'd overstepped her bounds with the poster joke. Then she remembered how Reid had reacted to her song in the barn, and she was reassured. He needed another good laugh. Responsibilities like his required moments of fun to give balance to life.

Jessie pushed the Up button and scanned the glassed-in directory beside the bank of elevators. Magnitech corporate offices were listed on the fifty-third floor—as high as the elevator went. But then, she'd expected Reid to be on the top floor.

A soft "ping" announced the arrival of the elevator in front of her. Fifty-three floors later, the elevator doors opened onto a huge expanse of gray carpeting that felt like a mattress under Jessie's feet. She gasped at the view of the Chicago skyline displayed by the floor-to-ceiling windows of the reception area.

When Jessie stepped off the elevator, a young woman seated at a large walnut desk looked up. Rosemary. "Can I help you?" she asked, fingering the pearls that looped under the collar of her white silk blouse.

Jessie hesitated. Maybe her poster idea wasn't so great. The man who ruled this empire might consider her prank mere childishness. She could leave the correct poster with Rosemary and retreat to her little studio where she belonged. She'd probably never hear from Reid Halstead again.

But then she'd miss the chance to see that look in his eyes that gave her goose bumps. She tried to align this plush reception area with her image of Reid in the barn at Malone Farms as she'd explained about the sheath of a bull. *That* Reid didn't intimidate her in the least, but the Reid who worked in this office overlooking most of downtown Chicago did.

"Perhaps you're on the wrong floor," Rosemary said. "I'd be glad to redirect you."

Jessie squared her shoulders. She'd started this, and she might as well finish it. "Thank you, but I'm on the right floor," she said. "I'm looking for Mr. Halstead. I have an item here that he ordered."

"I'm sorry, but you've just missed him."

Jessie's balloon of anticipation deflated. Reid wasn't here, after all. "I suppose he's at lunch," she said, bidding goodbye to all her lunchtime fantasies.

"No, actually he's out of town until day after tomorrow. I'll be glad to take a message for him, or if you'd like to leave your package?" Rosemary's voice swirled upward and she smiled expectantly.

"Out of town?" Jessie felt dizzy. "But he has an important board meeting tonight."

"That's true." Rosemary eyed Jessie more carefully. "That's where he's gone, to the board meeting. Did you need to contact him about something?"

"Yes." Jessie fought her rising panic. "Yes, I do. How long ago did he leave? Perhaps I can catch him."

Rosemary glanced at her watch. "He should be boarding the company jet for Detroit by now."

"Can you reach him on that plane? I know he's crazy about being hooked up by telephone all the time. Surely there's a phone on the plane."

"Well, yes, there is a telephone, and I suppose I could contact him." Rose was obviously reluctant to indulge this person who wore a decidedly unbusinesslike ski jacket and jeans. "What is this in reference to?"

Jessie thought quickly. Detroit was only a commuter hop from Chicago, and it wasn't even noon yet. Calling Reid would do no good unless he also had the second poster for tonight's meeting. Obviously he hadn't looked at the poster his assistant had picked up, or he'd have called the studio. He had trusted her to provide him with what he needed, and she couldn't violate that trust. She'd fly to Detroit this afternoon and take him the right poster. Bert would have a fit, and the cost of a ticket would clean out their reserve cash, but Jessie would pay it back, somehow.

She looked Rosemary in the eye. "I've changed my mind about contacting Mr. Halstead by phone," she said. "I have a poster here that he needs for tonight's presentation. It was delayed in production. If you'll tell me where he's staying I'll have this couriered to him."

Rosemary looked relieved. "Fine. He did mention using a poster tonight. He'll be at the Plaza Hotel in the Renaissance Center. If you mark the package to Mr. Halstead's attention, I'm sure the bell captain will see that he gets it."

"Thank you." Jessie hurried to the elevator and punched the button. She wouldn't even trust a bell captain with this package. She was going to deliver it in person.

In the elevator she unzipped her ski jacket as adrenaline pumped through her body, making her warm. Beneath the jacket she wore her best sweater—a red cashmere that she'd chosen in case she'd had lunch with Reid. Now the sweater would have to be adequate for a business trip and an evening at the Plaza Hotel. Jessie smiled. Perhaps this practical joke of hers could turn out well, yet.

LATER THAT AFTERNOON Jessie wished she'd asked what time the board meeting began. It had taken her nearly an hour to convince Bert that this was the only reasonable plan, and another half hour to set up the shots for the two clients who had appointments for that afternoon. Phone calls about the Hotshot promotion came in while she was still there, and when she left, taking with her a sizable chunk of cash for a ticket to Detroit, Bert was scowling.

Seeing no other way out of the mess, Jessie fought down her guilt feelings and took a bus to the airport where she managed, after some delay, to get a seat on a commuter flight with a return ticket for ten-fifteen that night. She was breathing a sigh of relief, knowing that she'd get to Detroit on time, when fog rolled in and grounded all aircraft. By five o'clock, when the fog lifted, Jessie had worn a track around the waiting area. She prayed that Reid's meeting wouldn't start until eight.

When the plane finally landed, she took a taxi to the Renaissance Center. As the taxi became snarled in rush-hour traffic, Jessie grew more frantic. The hour hand on her watch crept closer and closer to seven.

She dashed into the Plaza at quarter past seven and announced to the first available desk clerk that she had to know where the Magnitech Board of Directors was meeting. She mumbled something about a financially important matter concerning the presentation and held up her covered poster. Her desperation must have convinced him, because he sent her up to the forth-level Raphael meeting room.

The circular design of the hotel with its eight-story atrium in the center was a photographer's dream. As Jessie ran up the escalators to the forth level, she made a note to come back someday with her camera.

The door to the Raphael was closed. Jessie put her ear against it and heard Reid's voice. He sounded calm, so perhaps he hadn't unveiled the poster yet. Opening the door an inch, she peeked in. Reid stood at the head of a long table, and the covered poster rested on an easel beside him. The board of directors—all men—lined both sides of the table, which was set with pitchers of water, glasses, and ashtrays.

Reid was engrossed in his presentation as he explained his belief in diversification. Jessie swallowed. She had no choice but to interrupt him. Her explanation foremost in her mind, Jessie took a deep breath and started into the room.

Just then, Reid threw back the cover of the poster without glancing at what was underneath. "Gentlemen, let me present my first diversification proposal," he announced.

Jessie froze in midstride.

Chapter Five

As IF SOMEONE HAD HIT the Pause button on a VCR, all action in the room stopped. Jessie stared at herself stretched out on the white rug, her breasts nearly spilling out of the red teddy and her mouth curved in a come-hither smile. Beneath her languorous form marched the words The Future Is In Genetic Engineering.

One of the board members cleared his throat. "Interesting concept, Halstead."

"I think so," Reid said, still smiling as he turned toward the poster. He glanced at it, and his smile faded. Color slowly drained from his face.

At that moment Jessie knew that announcing herself and replacing the poster would only make things worse. She would be recognized as the woman in the picture. She fled. Halfway around the circular walkway she noticed a sign for a women's rest room and raced for the door. Once inside, she stood there panting. This couldn't be happening! Her practical joke couldn't have gone so far astray that now her seductively posed body was on display for the Magnitech Board of Directors.

But it had happened. She'd seen it with her own eyes. She hated to think about what Reid must be going through right now. Or what Bert would do to her when she learned what had happened. The studio's reputation would be a shambles; and as for her relationship with Reid, she could forget that completely. She'd made him look like an idiot in front of his board. He'd never forgive her.

She had to figure out some way to repair the situation for Reid. The receptionist had said Reid would be in Detroit until day after next, so maybe other board sessions were planned. She could leave the bull poster at the front desk for him so that he could present it the next day and blame the photo studio for the mix-up.

Jessie eyed herself in the rest room's large mirror. Leaving the poster at the hotel desk was the coward's way out. A real woman would face the music and deliver the poster in person. She glanced at her watch. Her return flight wouldn't leave for almost three hours. If the meeting broke up within the next hour and a half, she could catch Reid before he went upstairs, give him the correct poster, and take a taxi out to the airport.

She'd have to lurk near the meeting room, however, and she'd need to hide her face so that none of the board members would recognize her when they came out. She pulled up the hood of her ski jacket and tucked her hair inside. Then she put her head down and peeked at the effect in the mirror. With the hood pulled forward, her face was in shadow. She wouldn't be recognized. Besides, she doubted many of the board members had paid attention to her face, with the rest of her hanging out like that.

She eased out into the walkway and glanced toward the meeting-room door. If she lingered in an alcove near the women's rest room, she could see the door without being noticed. When Reid came out, she'd follow him and choose a moment when he was alone to apologize.

Her plan in place, Jessie waited as the minutes dragged by. Her legs began to ache from standing in one spot so long and she began to perspire under the ski jacket, but she had no reasonable alternative except to stay there. It served her right to be uncomfortable, anyway. If she'd listened to Bert in the first place, she wouldn't be in this predicament.

Finally the door opened. Jessie's heart began to pound faster and she longed to run away, but she held her ground. Two men came out. Both were laughing. Then another came, and three more. Everyone seemed to be having a great time. She figured out from their conversation that they were all going up to The Summit at the top of the hotel for a drink.

"Hey, George," someone called as he headed away from her, "is Halstead coming?"

"Naw. He says he's tired and he's going back to his room."

Another man chuckled. "After seeing that poster, I'm not surprised," he said. "Didn't think Halstead had time for a social life, but he's obviously working it in somewhere."

The others in the group laughed and made bawdy comments as they moved out of earshot. Jessie closed her eyes. *Poor Reid.* She felt embarrassed for both of them.

Then Reid came out of the meeting room, alone. He carried the poster of her on the rug, but the picture was carefully covered. Not giving herself time to think, Jessie hurried over to him. She pushed her hood back. He glanced in her direction in surprise. Then his eyes narrowed.

"I have the poster of Levi," she said, holding it toward him. "Reid, I can explain. I—"

"Not here, for God's sake!" He grabbed her arm and propelled her across a concrete bridge leading to the elevators in the center of the building. "Two of the board members are still in there." Keeping a firm grip on her arm, he jabbed the Up button with the hand holding the poster. "Come on, come on," he muttered, staring at the elevator doors. When they opened, he dragged Jessie inside with him and hit the button for the sixtieth floor.

"Where are we going?"

"To my room, where I can say what I have to say in private."

"Then you can let go of me," she said, shaking off his restraining hold. "I'm sorry about the mix-up, but that doesn't give you the right to manhandle me."

"Doesn't it?" He jerked his tie loose and unfastened the top button of his crisp white shirt. He glared at her, his eyes as blue as the center of a gas flame, and just as hot. "I could push and pull you six ways to Sunday and not a jury in the world would convict me, once they got the whole story. Don't talk to me about rights. I have half a mind to—" He stopped speaking as the elevator paused and the doors opened to admit a man and a woman dressed in evening clothes.

Jessie wondered if she should use the couple's presence to escape. Reid had his second poster now—or would have, once she handed it to him. From the expression on his face, she doubted anything she could say would mollify him, and she wasn't in the mood to listen to his tirade. Besides, she had a plane to catch. Then she thought of Bert. Bert would want her to try and make things right; to offer unlimited photographic services for the rest of Reid's life, if he'd overlook this one little mistake. Okay, this one big mistake. Jessie decided to stick it out.

They left the elevator and marched down the hall. Reid shoved his plastic key in the door, turned the knob and swore.

"You put it in wrong," Jessie said.

"How nice of you to point that out." He reinserted the key and flung open the door. "Get in there."

"Stop ordering me around," she shot back, but she went into the room. She'd expected opulence, but still the grandeur of the suite overwhelmed her, reminding her of the stakes she'd been gambling with when she'd planned her prank. She was standing in the living-room portion; the bedroom was through double doors to her left. In front of her, floor-to-ceiling windows, with the drapes wide open, looked over the river and the lights of Detroit.

"Now, let's get to the bottom of this." Reid tossed his suit coat on a chair and crossed the room to stand in front of her. Outlined against the light-spangled window, he looked like an avenging god demanding retribution. "What in hell happened with those posters? What was *my* slogan doing under your body?"

"It was a mix-up," Jessie said. That was her safest line of defense. The room seemed very warm. She leaned the poster of Levi against a lamp table and unzipped her jacket.

"A mix-up? I'm totally humiliated in front of my board of directors, and that's all you can say?"

"Was it... Was it pretty bad in there?"

"Bad?" He paced in front of the windows and dragged his fingers through his hair. "Depends on whether you call 'bad' being the laughingstock of men you hoped to impress with your business savvy. Do you call that bad?"

"Well, I—"

"You tell me," he interrupted, stalking over to the poster of Jessie and picking it up. "Is it bad when you call a special meeting of your very conservative board, ready to guide them into the high-tech concept of genetic engineering with a poster of a prizewinning bull, and when you unveil your display, you wonder why everyone has such a funny look on his face, and you turn around and see—" He ripped off the covering and threw it on the floor. "A red-hot babe on a white rug? Is that bad?"

Jessie pictured the scene, and without warning she began to laugh.

"You think this is funny?"

"Yes," she managed, wiping her eyes. "I'm sorry, but yes, it is funny, Reid."

"The board members thought it was funny, too." Reid obviously didn't agree. He propped the poster against the back of a chair and turned to face her. "They *liked* the slogan with this picture. When I explained that I'd ordered a shot of a bull and not some sex-crazed woman in a teddy—"

"I am not sex-crazed!"

"They didn't believe me," he continued, as if she hadn't spoken. "They thought I'd planned all this as some sort of gag. In fact," he added, approaching her menacingly, "I don't know if they'll ever take me seriously again."

"They liked the poster?"

"They loved it. But that's not the point, is it?" His angry gaze burned into her. "I wanted them to admire the concept and approve the diversification. Do you suppose they're thinking about genetic engineering and Magnitech's part in it? Or do you suppose they're busy gossiping about their CEO's sex life?"

"Reid, if you had an ounce of spontaneity in you, you could play off this instead of making it into some disaster." Jessie's patience was wearing thin.

"Play off it? You must be out of your mind. I've lost all my credibility and now you want me to—"

"B.S.! You haven't lost anything." She'd obviously been mistaken about his sense of humor, she realized. "Your board of directors isn't upset with you. They just think you're a swinger."

"Terrific! That's certainly the image I want to project—of some playboy who has all sorts of women dressed like that—" he gestured toward the poster "—hanging around his neck while he handles his multimillion-dollar deals."

"Come off it, Reid. You're exaggerating."

"I'm a businessman, dammit!"

She'd had it. If he could yell and be insulting, so could she. "I'd agree with the business part, but I wonder if you're really a man!"

"And what's that supposed to mean?" he shouted back.

"It means that you're like that bull. You like everything clean and safe and predictable. One little hitch in the plan, like this poster, and you're a raging maniac. Nothing can be messy or unscheduled, can it? You don't have time for hang gliding. You don't even have time to notice a nice pair of legs!"

"Oh, yeah? You think I didn't notice that miniskirt yesterday?"

"Not once you started concentrating on your precious genetic engineering," she flung back at him.

"Well, you're wrong," he said, his blue eyes flashing as he advanced toward her. "I noticed every creamy inch of thigh you displayed for me. I'll bet you did that on purpose."

"What if I did? Maybe I wanted to see if I could pierce that all-business, no-pleasure exterior of yours."

"You'd better be careful with maneuvers like that, Jessie. When you paraded around in that miniskirt yesterday, it took all my willpower to restrain myself from doing something—" He stopped abruptly and swung away from her. "Something we'd both regret."

"Would we?" she taunted. "Why? Because you might act impulsively? Heaven forbid that you'd ever do that. Heaven forbid that you'd ever do something without working out every little detail in advance, and calculating the final effect of—"

"I told you to watch it," he rumbled, turning to face her and stepping closer.

Her heat beat faster. The anger in his eyes had been replaced by a new emotion—one she recognized. He wanted her. And the devil had her tongue. "Watch what?" she challenged. "Nothing's happening."

He grabbed her. "Oh, yes, it is," he muttered, and captured her mouth with one swift movement.

She squirmed in his arms, but he held her tightly and took what he wanted. Then gradually his lips softened against hers and he coaxed her mouth open to begin a leisurely exploration with his tongue. Anger ebbed out of her, to be replaced by an incoming tide of warm desire. She wound her arms around his neck and urged him closer.

He moaned and slowly lifted his lips from hers. "You're playing with fire, Jessie," he whispered, his breath hot against her face. "You might get burned."

She opened her eyes. "You don't scare me, Reid Halstead."

"No?" He cupped her bottom and scooped her in tight.

She trembled with excitement as he pressed her against his aroused body. She didn't think for a minute he'd go through with it. He was only toying with her, paying her back for humiliating him in the boardroom. That was all. "I don't scare that easily," she said, looking straight into his eyes.

"Is that right?" He slid his hand under her sweater and expertly unhooked her bra.

"You're bluffing." Her words trembled.

"Am I?" His touch on her bare skin was gentle, but his gaze burned into hers. "Maybe I'm proving to you that I *can* act on impulse." Pushing the bra aside, he cradled her breast and rubbed his thumb across her nipple.

She held back the moan that rose to her lips as he continued the relentless caress. Her breathing grew ragged and she licked her dry lips.

"What's the matter?" he murmured. "Cat got your tongue?" He lowered his head and brushed her lips with his. "Let's see," he said, and settled in for a deep kiss.

Jessie's will began to dissolve. She knew that at some point he would stop this seduction and leave her begging for more. No doubt he was punishing her, but she couldn't pull away. Kissing Reid and feeling his caress was more than wonderful; it was better than she'd ever dreamed. Soon enough, Reid would return to being a business tycoon and forget all about this episode with her. Until then, she seemed to have his complete attention. He certainly had hers. She wanted his loving—wanted it more than anything in her life.

He raised his head again and looked into her eyes. "Well? Had enough?"

Somehow she found her voice. "If you're waiting for me to run screaming from the room, I won't do it."

"All right." He moved his hand away from her breast. *This is it. He's had his revenge. Now he'll tell me to leave, and I'll be strong. I won't beg. I'll tell him to go to—* Her thought ended as Reid picked her up and carried her through the double doors to his bedroom. "What are you doing?" she demanded.

He gazed down at her, his eyes hot with desire. "Giving you exactly what you deserve."

Chapter Six

JESSIE STILL COULDN'T believe Reid was serious, but he certainly looked serious as he tumbled her on the king-size bed and kicked off his shoes. She lay there and watched, wide-eyed, as he discarded his tie and unbuttoned his shirt.

"Still think I'm bluffing?" he asked.

"Yes." She didn't sound quite so sure of herself.

"I'm not bluffing, Jessie," he said quietly, peeling away the snowy-white shirt to reveal a muscled chest sprinkled with dark hair.

She told herself to stop wanting him, that any minute now he'd end this charade. Still, with every minute he kept it up, longing built inside her.

He unzipped his slacks and unbuckled the belt. Jessie swallowed. As the slacks slid to the floor he kicked them away. With deliberate motions he pulled off his dark dress socks, and at last his thumbs hooked in the waistband of his white shorts. He gazed at her as he stripped them away.

She trembled at the sight of him, magnificent in his arousal. Whatever game he was playing, he wanted her as much as she wanted him. She had the satisfaction of knowing that when he called a halt, he would feel as deprived as she.

"Your turn," he taunted. "Are you woman enough to undress for me?"

Jessie met his bold glance. So this was it: a challenge, a test of courage. Had he guessed her natural response to a thrown gauntlet? Slowly she sat up and nudged her shoes off onto the floor. She struggled out of her jacket and pulled her sweater over her head. The unfastened bra came with it. She glanced at Reid and was startled by the hunger in his eyes. His chest heaved, as if he had trouble getting his breath. *Good,* she thought. *He started this game.* Except that she knew he really hadn't. *She* had, by wearing a miniskirt, by switching posters. And she couldn't back down now.

Keeping her gaze trained on his face, she pulled off her socks. Then she unfastened her jeans and wriggled out of them. At last she hooked her thumbs in the waistband of her panties, as he had done with his shorts. A muscle twitched in his jaw but he said nothing, made no motion to stop her. She took them off.

He stared at her in silence. Then he sighed.

"What is it?"

"You're beautiful." He walked toward the bed. "That's all. Just . . . beautiful. It seems that instead of being angry with you, I should be thanking you." He put one knee on the bed and guided her back against the pillows. "You've goaded me into what may be the most satisfying night of my life." The scent of his after-shave mingled with the musky aroma of his aroused body as he leaned down and cupped her face in his hand.

"I thought . . . You mean, you really aren't kidding about this?" she stammered. The heat of his naked body, poised above her, fueled the fires burning within her. He was really going to love her. She throbbed with a longing more intense than she'd ever experienced.

He fixed her with his piercing gaze. "Are you going to chicken out?"

"No." *No. Come to me.*

"Neither am I." He lowered his lips to hers.

With the searing force of his kiss and the possessive way his hands roamed over her body, she knew the bargain was sealed. Once, she might have stopped this from happening, but no longer. She placed her hands on his shoulders as she arched under his caresses. Fleetingly she wondered if she should have played hard to get, now that he'd made it so obvious that he wanted her as much as she wanted him.

But it was too late for wondering; she was too far gone. Reid's mouth found her breast, his hand slid between her thighs and he discovered how far gone she really was. She gripped his shoulders as his moving fingers coaxed a whimper of need from her lips.

He returned to kiss her mouth while he continued to work the wonderful torture that made her writhe against the bedspread. "I don't want to be controlled and sexless like that bull," he murmured, kissing his way to her earlobe.

"I may have been wrong about that," she gasped as his tongue flicked around the sensitive inner curve of her ear.

"Sometimes I am like him, though. Sometimes I restrict myself too much. But not now. Tonight I'm going to love you, Jessie Neal."

Love. The word burrowed deep inside her and took root, almost without her realizing it.

He moved away and opened the bedside drawer.

"Reid?" She couldn't be without him, not for a second.

"Compliments of a full-service hotel," he said, producing a small package and ripping it open.

Shamelessly she watched him sheath himself.

"Do you still think I'm bluffing?"

Slowly she shook her head. A challenge had brought her here, but more was at stake now. Much more.

"I never bluff," he said, moving between her thighs and bracing his arms on either side of her head, looking into her eyes. "Never," he whispered, and thrust forward.

Jessie took him inside with a kind of wonder, for the joining felt so natural, as if she'd been waiting all her life for this man who moved with such controlled passion.

The wonder was reflected in his expression as he gazed down at her. "Jessie," he murmured, withdrawing slightly and pushing forward again. "Oh, Jessie. I didn't expect this to feel so right."

"What . . . what did you expect?"

"I don't know. But not...this," he said, closing his eyes and pushing deeper. "I feel as if I'm drowning in you, Jessie, and I never want this feeling to stop."

She moved with him, caressing him, kissing him, glorying in the way they sensed each other's rhythm. She'd never felt this unity before or this passion that filled her. Never. He paused, and she knew he was restraining himself for her sake. There was no need. "Let yourself go," she whispered.

"As if I could help it." He increased the tempo. "Stay with me," he begged, moving faster.

"I'm with you, Reid." Jessie held nothing back, moving with him as he propelled her to an incredibly powerful release. His cry of pleasure joined hers, and they sank back on the thick mattress and held each other tight.

Jessie lay still, dazed by her unbridled response to this man she hardly knew. Her natural impulsiveness had never carried her so far into uncharted territory. Perhaps this sort of encounter was commonplace for Reid, but not for her. Her last serious relationship—only the second one of her life—had ended a year ago. Since then, the photography studio had claimed nearly all her interest. Until now. Until Reid. Until this powerful attraction that had blurred her focus. Gently she stroked Reid's back.

He nuzzled closer with a sigh. "I think I always knew we'd end up like this, from the first moment I saw you."

Jessie smiled. She felt warm and secure. "You looked so sexy, standing outside the studio window. I was sorry I'd worn an ordinary sweatshirt that day."

"Are you kidding?" He slid his hand under her bottom. "Those snug little jeans drove me crazy. I wanted to do just what I'm doing now." He squeezed gently.

"And I thought you were standing there thinking about Linda," Jessie laughed.

He lifted his head to look at her. "Who's Linda?"

"The blonde in the poster in the window."

"Didn't really notice," Reid said with a grin.

"Liar."

He leaned down to kiss her. "Well, I wouldn't notice now."

Jessie's heart swelled. Reid was talking as if this were more than a chance happening. "You're not angry about the poster anymore?"

He studied her, his expression soft and open. "Do I look angry?"

"No. You look ... happy."

"I am, Jessie."

Jessie lay in Reid's embrace until, with a reluctant groan, he levered himself away from her and went into the bathroom. Chilled by the absence of his warm body covering hers, she rolled up in the bedspread and waited for his return. She'd probably miss her flight, but it didn't matter. She'd find some way to get home first thing in the morning. Although she hated to leave Reid, she had to get back to the studio.

He returned, standing in unashamed glory before her, but he looked sober, uncertain. "I thought of something while I was in there," he said. "We have some things to discuss."

"About the poster?" She wished he'd smile again, the way he had when he'd left the bed.

"In a way. I assume you have a boyfriend."

"What?" Jessie couldn't have been more surprised. She'd expected almost any comment but this one. "Why would you think that?"

He gestured toward the other room. "The poster. You said it was a mix-up, but I wasn't thinking very straight then. Now my head's a little clearer and I put two and two together. You had that poster made for someone else and borrowed my slogan. My assistant got the wrong poster by mistake. He picked up the one you made for some other guy, someone you're involved with. I want to know how important he is to you."

Now it was her turn to smile. He wouldn't be asking questions like that unless he was taking their relationship seriously. "I don't have a boyfriend," she announced, and waited for his grin of relief.

It didn't come. Instead he frowned. "I don't get it. Then who was the poster for?"

"You."

"Me?"

"Oh, Reid, you big dope. Don't you see what I was trying to do? I thought you would pick up the poster yourself. I had the sexy one of me printed, and I planned to hand you that first, to get your attention. It was a harmless joke. Then I was going to give you the real one. Except I had to be out of the studio longer than I expected, so Bert gave your assistant the poster of me, thinking I could go up to your office and exchange it and surprise you there. Only you'd already left for Detroit—without the bull poster."

He stared at her. "Then it wasn't a mix-up?"

"Well, yes, in a way. But I—"

He strode toward the bed. "You planned this?"

"Not *this*," she said, gesturing toward the bed. He was beginning to irritate her with his questioning. "I just wanted to shake you up and make you laugh, force you to see that there's more to life than car phones, and genetic-engineering labs. And I think I succeeded."

"Let me get this straight." His eyes narrowed. "You played this little game, potentially jeopardizing a multi-million deal and maybe even my job, *on purpose?*"

"Reid, I think you're overreacting. It was just a joke."

"A joke, Jessie?" He glared down at her and his voice assaulted her like a battering ram. "Magnitech is a multi-national corporation. That means we have business interests all over the *world*. Our net assets are greater than certain small *countries'*. By some miracle the board has entrusted the running of this corporation to me. At thirty-six, I'm the youngest CEO of any company this size, and I'm damned proud of the fact! I'm not about to let some two-bit photography-studio owner screw up my hard-won reputation and dismiss it all as a *joke*."

Jessie was stunned by his reaction. Hurt changed swiftly to anger, pushing her out of bed. She grabbed her clothes and struggled to put them on as fast as possible. "I had you all wrong, Reid Halstead. I thought you had possibilities of being a real human being, with a sense of humor about yourself. But I see you have none." She hopped on one foot while she crammed her shoe on, tears spilling down her cheeks.

"You don't know what you're talking about!" he shouted. "You've never been close to having the kind of responsibilities I handle every day. You couldn't possibly know the pressures involved, and yet you accuse me of having no sense of humor. Now *that's* a laugh!"

"No, it isn't," Jessie choked out, grabbing her ski jacket. "It's a crying shame!" Her vision blurred by her tears, she rushed out of the bedroom and through the sitting room. It took her two tries to unlock the door into the hallway, but at last she was out and running toward the elevator.

She glanced back once, but of course Reid wouldn't follow her. In the first place she'd left him stark-naked, and in the second place he was furious with her. He'd never want to see her again. And for that matter, she never wanted to see him again, either.

Still looking backward, she collided with a man on the walkway. "Oh, I'm sorry!" she cried, new tears springing to her eyes. "Excuse me. I'm in a hurry and I wasn't watching. Excuse me," she said again, edging toward the elevators.

"Hold on, there, young lady." The man blocked her path and took her by the shoulders.

"Please let me go."

"Go where?" he asked, studying her with concern. "You don't look in any shape to go anywhere."

Jessie blinked away her tears. He reminded her of someone's grandfather, with his white walrus mustache and metal-rimmed glasses. He was about her height, and as round as a pumpkin. His three-piece suit fit him perfectly, despite his substantial belly. Jessie's professional eye told her that the suit was custom-made. He smelled faintly of cigars and brandy. "I have to go . . . to catch a plane," she mumbled.

"What time is your flight?"

"Ten-fifteen."

Releasing her, he pulled a gold pocket watch out of his vest and snapped it open. Then he turned the face around so that Jessie could see.

"Oh."

"All the running in the world won't get you to the airport in five minutes." He closed the watch and repocketed it.

"Great," Jessie wiped her eyes. "Now I've missed my plane. A perfect ending to this miserable day." Tears welled again.

"Is it a matter of life and death that you get out of Detroit tonight?"

Jessie swallowed. This old gentleman was really nice, except that the nicer he got, the faster her tears spilled onto her cheeks. She shook her head.

"You know what? I think you could do with a cup of good, strong coffee. Let's go downstairs and find one. Then we can talk about your travel alternatives."

"That's all right," she managed. "I'm sure you have other things to do. I can—"

"Nonsense." He took her arm and led her to the elevator. "My name's Andrew Gentry. What's yours?"

"Jessie Neal."

"Jessie. Is that short for Jessica?"

She nodded, feeling about five years old. Yet his solicitous behavior calmed her raw nerves. A hot cup of coffee sounded terrific, and she needed some time to figure out what to do. The woman who'd sold her the ticket had mentioned that the ten-fifteen flight was the last one that night.

Gentry didn't ask Jessie any other questions as they rode down the elevator and found a booth in the coffee shop.

"Two cups of coffee and an order of sausage and eggs for the young lady," Gentry instructed the waitress.

"Oh, you don't have to feed me, too," Jessie said, although she hadn't eaten since breakfast. Now that she was calmer, she realized she was also very hungry.

"Don't you like sausage and eggs?" Gentry asked.

Her mouth watered. "Yes, but—"

"Scrambled or fried?"

"Scrambled, but—"

"Done," he said, waving the waitress away.

"Well, now that you mention it, some food does sound good," Jessie said. "But I'll be happy to pay for it." She tried to remember how much she had left. Probably not enough for this meal and a bus ticket, but she'd figure something out.

"You're my guest." Gentry smiled. "Besides that, you remind me of my granddaughter. So, do an old man a favor and accept this small gesture, hmm?"

Jessie gazed at him and wondered what he must think of her—a woman rushing down a hotel corridor with no luggage. Perhaps he thought she was a call girl trying to get away from an abusive client. She cleared her throat. "Perhaps I should explain what I'm doing here."

"Oh, that's not necessary," Gentry said.

"Well, I'd like to. You see, I'm a photographer. My partner and I run Jessie And Bert's Photography in Chicago." She fumbled in the pocket of her ski jacket. She remembered shoving a couple of business cards in there last week. "Here," she produced the card and pushed it across the table.

"What a coincidence," he said, taking the card. "I'm also from Chicago."

"Oh, really?" Jessie guessed that he was a man of prestige. "Are you in business there?"

"I'm an investor," he replied, taking a card from the gold holder in his inside breast pocket and handing it to her. "Had business in Detroit this week. What brings you here?"

Andrew Gentry was president and CEO of Gentry Investments, Inc., whose address was even more prestigious than Magnitech's.

Jessie hesitated. After all, he had seen her crying. "Business, also."

"Oh?" His glance was skeptical. "What sort?"

"Well, you see..." She gazed at his kindly face and knew that he would understand. Her battered ego desperately needed someone to understand. Omitting Reid's name and that of his company, she began telling Gentry about the marvelous practical joke that had backfired. Her meal arrived and she ate absently. She poured out her tale, only leaving out the part about making love to Reid.

When she had finished, Gentry shook his head. "Such a pity this young man with his big title has no sense of humor. Makes me wonder if he should be running a large company, if he can't appreciate a good joke."

"Oh, I'm sure he's wonderful at running a company," Jessie hastened to add. "And to be fair, I did make him look foolish. I guess nobody likes that."

"I think someone like you, someone with spunk, is better off without a stick-in-the-mud like him."

Jessie sighed. "I guess so."

"You don't sound very convinced of that."

She picked up her fork and pushed the last bit of sausage around her plate. "I wish he'd been able to take my joke in stride, but I sort of understand why he didn't. There's something about him that really... What I mean is, in spite of everything, I still..."

"You're falling in love with him, aren't you?"

She glanced up. He was very perceptive. "Kind of, I guess," she admitted.

"Kind of?" Gentry snorted. "That ungrateful man has your heart in his hand, and he doesn't even have the good sense to know it. He should be thanking his lucky stars that you've come into his life—not sending you out of his room in tears. It's my opinion that a man like that needs a woman like you, Jessie.''

''That may be, but I'm sure he doesn't think so.''

''Then he's a damn fool.''

''Oh, well. Nothing to be done, now.'' Jessie pushed her plate aside. ''Thank you for the meal and the chance to unburden myself, Mr. Gentry.''

''Call me Andy.''

''Thanks, Andy.'' She smiled. ''And now I need to see about getting back home.''

''Let me take care of that. I won't be needing my car immediately. Fred can drive you to Chicago and be back here before noon tomorrow.''

''Fred?''

''My chauffeur.''

''Mr. Gentry—Andy—I couldn't possibly accept an offer like that.''

''Of course, you could,'' he said with a wave of his hand. ''I tremble to think what you'd have resorted to in your determination to leave tonight. It wouldn't surprise me if you decided to take the bus.'' He shuddered.

''Even if I did, I'd be fine. You're sweet for trying to help, but I can take care of this.''

He reached across the table and took her hand between both of his. ''Perhaps you can, at that. Forgive me for doubting your abilities, which I believe are considerable. Don't do this for yourself, then. Do it for me. I'm an old man with far too much money for my own good, and it isn't often I'm fortunate enough to be able to rescue a beautiful young woman in distress. It would give me great pleasure to know that you're safely on your way home.''

Jessie appreciated the sincerity of his offer. She wasn't so sure about the bus herself—brave as she'd tried to sound. "All right," she said slowly. "But please let me do something for you in return. Call me any time you want free portrait work done, for any member of your family."

"I just might do that." He picked up her card and tucked it in his vest pocket. "Be forewarned that I have lots of grandchildren," he said, chuckling. "Now, if you'll excuse me, I'll call Fred."

ANDY'S "CAR" TURNED OUT to be a fully-appointed limousine, and Jessie rode in luxury back to the apartment she shared with Bert. Yet thoughts of Reid kept her awake during the six-hour trip. Bert must have taken pity on her exhaustion, because she was far more understanding than Jessie had expected.

The next day, ignoring her weariness from lack of sleep, Jessie threw herself into her work. Business had picked up even more. The Hotshot special was a success, which helped explain why Bert was so understanding about Jessie losing Magnitech's business. For her part, Jessie tried to disguise her anguish as she dealt with clients who all seemed to be in love. The Valentine's Day season was definitely not a good time to have your heart broken.

THE FOLLOWING MORNING, Jessie was working the reception desk when the door swung open to admit the last person on earth she'd expected to see again. Reid covered the distance to the counter with quick strides. One look at his face and Jessie braced herself for a fight.

"I'll bet good money that you knew!" he said, pointing an accusing finger at her.

"Knew what?"

"Don't play innocent. You knew that Andrew Gentry was the most influential member of Magnitech's board o directors!"

Chapter Seven

"HE'S WHAT?" Horrified, Jessie stared at Reid. "No, he can't be!"

He folded his arms and gazed at her, his expression grim and accusing.

"But— But surely Andy would have told me something like that."

"Andy?" Reid raised an eyebrow. "You work fast."

"I do not work fast!" She rounded the counter and approached him with such ferocity that he retreated a step. "And don't you dare imply that there's something sleazy or shady about me and that wonderful old man," she said, shaking her finger under his nose. "I most certainly did not know that he was a member of your precious board. I would never have confided in him if I'd known. For God's sake, Reid, what sort of person do you think I am?"

He frowned. "I'm trying to figure that one out."

"Well, go figure it out somewhere else. I have work to do. If you have any more insults to hurl my way, put it in a memo!" She turned away, furious.

Bert hurried in from the staging room. "What's the shouting for? I— Oh, hello, Mr. Halstead."

Reid nodded.

"Mr. Halstead was just leaving," Jessie said. "I'm sorry if we interrupted you, Bert."

Reid shifted his weight, like a boxer waiting for the starting bell for the first round. "Actually, I'm not leaving." He gazed up at the ceiling and recited the next words as if they were memorized. "I'm here to ask Jessie out for the night of February fourteenth."

Jessie gasped and turned to face Reid. Bert looked at them both in disbelief.

"It's strictly business," he added, shoving his hands in his pockets and looking everywhere but at Jessie.

"What else could I expect?" she muttered.

"Gentry and his wife are having a Valentine's Day party, and he's made it very clear I'm to bring you. He's implied that my failure to do so will put my position with the company in jeopardy."

"Then I guess your position *will* be in jeopardy," Jessie stated flatly. "Because I'm *not* going."

"Fine." Reid turned on his heel.

"Wait," Bert said before he made it to the door. "Wait, Mr. Halstead. Please. Let me have a word alone with Jessie."

Reid turned back. "I think she's made herself clear, Bert. And I'm sure as hell not going to beg."

"Neither am I. I just want to talk with her. I don't believe she's thought of all the ramifications."

"Wait a gosh-darn minute," Jessie sputtered. "I—"

"Be quiet, Jessie." Bert turned back to Reid. "I think you'll agree with me that Jessie is a little . . . impulsive."

Reid snorted.

"Roberta Mortimer, you are stretching the bonds of this partnership. I want that man out of here. Now."

Bert took her arm. "Come in here a minute, Jessie." Her grip was unyielding.

"I'm not changing my mind."

"Okay, you're not. Just come and talk to me."

"Only because I'm a reasonable person." Jessie glared back at Reid as Bert led her away. "Unlike some people I know."

Bert waited until they were inside the staging room with the door closed. Then she released Jessie's arm. "Now, listen to me. You're going."

"What? After the way he treated me the other night? I'd rather shoot office furniture for the rest of my life."

"Well, I wouldn't. And I'm half of this happy little operation. I went along with your practical joke—very reluctantly, as you may recall—and sure enough, it turned out rotten. I don't care whether you ever see Reid Halstead again after February fourteenth, but I'm not letting you throw away this chance to make valuable contacts."

Jessie had never seen Bert so determined before. "I guess you have a point."

"Damn right, I do. Can you imagine who will be at that party? If Andrew Gentry likes you so much, and he really seems to, he'll make sure you're introduced to the right people. The studio could have *tons* of work from this one night alone."

"You're right, as usual, Bert." Jessie sighed. "All I could think about was spending the evening with a guy who hates me."

"The thing is, you don't hate him back."

Jessie hesitated while she sorted through her feelings. She was upset with Reid for suspecting her of plotting against him; and hurt—very hurt. But he wouldn't have the power to hurt her that much, unless... "No, I don't hate him," she admitted. "I can't forget the other night. We... It was magic, Bert. We might have had a chance for something special if the poster mix-up hadn't happened."

Bert put her arm around Jessie. "You still have that chance."

"You're kidding. He had to be threatened with losing his job in order to come over here."

"Which is the other side to this. Because you started thi whole mess by switching the pictures, you owe it to him t go. Imagine how you'd feel if he really did lose his job be cause you didn't go to this party."

Jessie shook her head. "Andy wouldn't do that. I'll be he's just playing around."

"If that's true, it only proves my point. Reid may no really believe it, either. But he's asking you to the party anyway. I say Andy's ultimatum gives Reid a convenien excuse to see you again. One that saves face."

"You've got holes in your head, Bert." But Jessie be gan to wonder if Bert could be right. Reid didn't seem lik the type to be intimidated into doing anything. Still, she didn't want to get her hopes up. "Maybe Reid's just too straitlaced to imagine a man like Andy could be teasing Maybe he really thinks he might lose his position if I don' go with him."

"If you do go, you'll find out which of us is right."

Jessie gazed at her. Then she walked toward the close door and opened it. Reid stood where they'd left him, hi hands now in the pockets of his black leather trench coat He looked at her when the door opened. "Okay, I'll go t the party with you." She watched his expression.

Something flickered in his blue eyes and was gone be fore she could identify the emotion. "Fine," he said "Dress is formal."

"Damn." Jessie mentally ran through her wardrobe "Maybe I should have asked that before. I don't have anything formal to wear. As you might guess, I don't trave in the circles that require it."

Bert spoke up from behind her. "Don't worry, Jessie We may be able to find something. Besides, there are lot of sales this time of—"

"I'll take care of it."

Jessie lifted her chin. "Oh, no, you won't, Reid Halstead."

He stepped toward her, his voice low and threatening. "Oh, yes, I will."

"Over my dead—"

"Goodness, what a generous offer." Bert slipped between them. "Size 6."

Reid blinked. "What?"

"She's a size 6. You are planning to shop for a dress, aren't you?"

"Well, I hadn't... Yes," he said more firmly. "Yes, I'll get something."

Jessie tapped Bert on the shoulder. "Listen, what if I don't want Reid buying my clothes? What if I don't care for his taste? What if—"

"I'll have the dress sent over the morning of the party," Reid continued, speaking to Bert and ignoring Jessie's protests. "Cocktails begin at six, so I thought I'd pick Jessie up here about five-thirty, if that's all right. I'm planning to change at the office."

"Terrific," Bert said. "While you're shopping, you might come across some shoes to match the dress. Size 7, narrow."

"Shoes?" Jessie cried. "I can't have him buying me shoes, Bert. This is ridiculous."

"Size 7, narrow?" Reid asked as if Jessie hadn't spoken.

"Right."

Jessie stepped around Bert. "Are you two quite done?"

"I think so," Bert said, smiling at her. Then she turned back to Reid. "Do you want a recommendation on color?"

Reid scrutinized Jessie for a long moment. "I think I can handle that decision," he said confidently. "See you on the fourteenth, Jessie.'' Before she could think of anything more to say, he'd left.

FEBRUARY 14 WAS a hectic day at the studio. All the women who had ordered Hotshots came to pick up the finished posters, and they spoke with giddy excitement about romantic plans for the evening. Jessie had reception duty, but she had to call on Bert occasionally when clients showed up two or three at a time. Besides, Bert was much better at sharing the women's enthusiasm for the holiday. Jessie had a cold lump in her stomach, which lurched every time she thought of the evening ahead.

"My, how I love to hear that cash register ring!'' Bert said during a lull midway through the morning.

Jessie leaned against the counter. "It may be nice now, but I wonder how many of these women will come back again, or recommend us to other people. If they don't, we'll be back to square one after this income is gone. We'll be the same as before, limping from month to month, wondering how long we can keep the business going without making enough profits to expand the way we want to.''

Bert glanced at her. "You've been Gloomy Gus all morning, and I know why. But trust me. Tonight will be fine.''

"That's easy for you to say.''

"He offered to buy you a dress. That means he's personally involved.''

"Wrong. He was about to give me money to buy a dress until you suggested he pick it out. There's a big difference.''

"Not a huge difference, Jessie. And don't forget the way he jumped on the idea of picking it out himself. I saw the look in his eyes. He was delighted.''

"That's because he's buying something hideous that I will then be forced to wear and look stupid in," Jessie muttered. "I'll bet you five dollars the dress will be a disaster—either accidentally or on purpose, and probably on purpose."

"That's your guilty conscience talking, Jessie."

Jessie sighed. "Probably. At times I think I deserve whatever I get from Reid."

"He might surprise you. And if you feel like losing money, I'll bet you five bucks the dress will be beautiful."

"Wait and see, Bert. He hates me. His revenge for the poster business will be watching me spend the evening in an outfit that'll be one of two extremes—either covered in frills to make me look like a girl going to her first prom, or cut down to my navel so that I'll look like a tramp. Mark my words: Reid Halstead has good reason to get even. I can't believe he won't grab this chance to do it."

Chapter Eight

AN HOUR LATER, Jessie turned from the full-length mirror in the staging room and handed Bert five dollars.

"Stunning," Bert proclaimed.

"Not bad." Jessie pirouetted in front of the mirror and the cocktail-length white satin skirt billowed around her, caressing her legs. The white bodice was fitted; her arms and one shoulder were bare. Outlining the bodice and the hem of the skirt was a border of red that, on close inspection, turned out to be a row of interlocking hearts.

"So, you say she's not the sentimental type?" Bert peered at the hearts trimming the gown. "That's a Valentine dress if I ever saw one. Uh-oh, there goes the phone, and I think I heard someone come through the door. I'll be back in a sec to help you get out of the dress."

Left alone in front of the mirror, Jessie stared at herself. She never remembered looking or feeling so elegant and sexy in her life. If Reid had indeed picked out this dress, she had hopes for this evening. If he'd asked Rosemary to do it, then the dress carried no special meaning. She was tempted to believe the first explanation, but leaned toward the second. A man as busy as Reid wouldn't wander around in women's dress shops. He'd pick up the phone—his cellular phone—and delegate the task.

Bert appeared in the doorway holding a large box with a smaller one on top. "A deliveryman brought these. The small one's shoes, I guess. Don't know what the big one could be. And there goes the phone again. Here, Cinderella," she said, thrusting the packages at Jessie.

"I should be helping you, not trying on stuff," Jessie called after her.

"You keep that contact with Andrew Gentry," Bert called back. "That's help enough."

Jessie set the boxes on a table behind the staging area and opened the smaller one to find a pair of white satin pumps that fit perfectly. Putting the box aside, she pulled off the lid of the second one and gasped. Inside was a white ermine cape. Reid's first tactical error, she thought. She loved animals too much to approve of the fur industry. She'd have to send the cape back.

A folded piece of paper lay on top of the cape. Thinking it might be the receipt, she unfolded it. "Dear Jessie," the note read, "This is not real ermine. I knew you wouldn't wear animal fur because of the way you treated Levi. This cape is synthetic. See you tonight. Reid."

"What was in the big box?" Bert asked, coming back into the room.

Jessie pulled the cape out and swirled it around her shoulders.

"Wow! Too bad you don't approve of furs."

"It's fake. Reid figured out I wouldn't like a real one."

"Double wow. Now will you believe me that he's interested in pursuing this relationship?"

Jessie shook her head. "He doesn't want me wearing a ski jacket over the dress and embarrassing him, that's all. I'll return this after tonight. I'd return everything, but I doubt he could take the dress and shoes back."

"Well, brace yourself. This box just arrived from Cartier jewelers."

Jessie stared at the long black velvet box in Bert's hand. Slowly Bert flipped it open and Jessie stopped breathing. A necklace of diamonds and rubies sparkled under the overhead lights. A pair of matching earrings rested in the center of the oval created by the necklace. "They can't be real," Jessie said, dazed by the magnificent jewelry.

"Want to bet?"

"Come on. They're fake like the ermine."

"I asked the delivery woman. They're real, all right. She said Mr. Halstead had already had them insured."

"Good Lord. Now, these are *definitely* going back tomorrow. Why would he do all this? The dress and shoes were one thing, but a fur cape and expensive jewelry? Is he *that* concerned about my making a good impression?"

"I think you already have. On him. Most women would consider this a sign of deep affection."

Jessie shook her head, unwilling to lay herself open to the hurt of rejection once more—especially on the most romantic day of the year. The gifts were beautiful. If only she could appreciate them as tokens of love... But she dared not. "He's got something up his sleeve, Bert. He's plotting revenge for my switching the posters. I just know it. These things are supposed to soften me up for the kill." Her heart ached as she said the words, but she forced herself to say them, trying to believe they were true.

BY FIVE TWENTY-FIVE, Jessie was so nervous her hands shook as she tried to fasten the ruby necklace.

"Here, let me." Bert pushed away Jessie's fumbling fingers. "My God, your hands are cold as ice. Want me to turn up the heat?"

"No." Jessie rubbed her hands together and blew into them. "The temperature in here isn't the problem."

Bert fastened the necklace and stood back to admire the total effect. "When Reid sees you, the temperature in this studio will jump, believe me. You look sensational, Jessie."

"I'm sure it's your makeup talents. I've been meaning to tell you what a great job you did on all those glamour shots."

"It's not the makeup this time. It's not even the dress or the necklace and earrings, although they look wonderful on you. You're glowing."

"I'm scared spitless."

"Don't be. Reid is not going to sabotage you."

Jessie rubbed her bare arms. "I wish I could believe that. What I really want to do is stay home and have pizza tonight with you and Linda, like we did last year."

Bert rolled her eyes. "Yeah, right. Romantic pizza with the girls. Listen, if I'd been able to wangle a chance meeting with the guy across the hall, I wouldn't be eating pizza and watching old movies with Linda tonight, either."

"We'll fix that situation when this is all over," Jessie promised. "I—" She paused as the unmistakable sound of the front door opening told her the time had come. Reid was here.

Bert handed Jessie the ermine cape and ushered her out of the staging room as if she were a bride about to march down the aisle—or a prisoner going to the gallows. Jessie's stomach churned.

Reid stood in the reception area, his cashmere coat unbuttoned to reveal a black tux, black bow tie and snowy pleated shirt. A black cummerbund defined his narrow waist. Jessie caught her breath at the sight of him.

He gazed at her without speaking.

"It fits," she said in a rush, her heart pounding. "Everything fits."

"I—" He paused and cleared his throat. "I see it does." He cleared his throat again.

"Is anything wrong?"

"Not at all." His voice had a funny catch in it. "You look wonderful."

She searched his expression and found no trace of mockery there. "Are you coming down with something?"

"I'm fine." He held out his hand for the cape. "Can I help you with that?"

"Umm, sure." She gave him the cape and turned so he could settle it over her shoulders. His nearness brought the scent of his after-shave and with it, an instant memory of holding him, loving him. His fingers grazed her bare skin and she shuddered in reaction.

"Have fun, you two," Bert called.

Jessie glanced toward the staging-area door and saw Bert standing there with a wide smile on her face. "Thanks for all your help, Bert."

"Yes, thanks." Reid's voice was steadier than before.

"My pleasure."

Reid took Jessie's elbow. "She may be in late," he commented over his shoulder to Bert.

"I hope she is," Bert teased.

Jessie cast one glance back at Bert and wished they were both home in the apartment ordering pizza and waiting for Linda to arrive. When Bert made a circle of her thumb and forefinger, Jessie reminded herself that she was doing this for the sake of their studio. Taking a deep breath, she went out the door.

The Mercedes waited at the curb, its engine idling.

"Lucky that you found a parking space so close at this time of night," Jessie said as he hurried her through the cold air and opened the car door.

"I paid somebody to hold it for me."

The gesture amazed her, but no more than the beautiful clothes and jewelry had. She was still waiting for the other shoe to drop.

The car's stereo was tuned to soft instrumental music. Jessie looked around for the cellular telephone and couldn't see it. She wondered if he'd tucked it into the pocket of his coat. She'd forgotten until this moment about her wild ride on the day she'd photographed Levi. Now she'd have another one, this time in rush-hour traffic. What fun.

Reid climbed in behind the wheel, shut his door and eased into traffic. He glanced at her. "Are you warm enough?"

"I'm fine," Jessie said. "But I do have a favor to ask. I know how much you love to do business on the phone while you drive, but this is rush hour, and I'd appreciate it if you'd—"

"I left the phone at the office."

"You *what?*" She stared at him. "Reid, there *is* something wrong, isn't there? Are you feeling okay?"

"Nothing's wrong with me, Jessie. At least, nothing physical."

She waited for him to deliver the punch line, and when he didn't, she decided to do it for him. "I see. You have a mental problem, and I'm the cause of it. Now that you have me captive in the car, you're going to tell me about the agonies you've suffered as a result of my prank. Maybe you've had to hire some high-priced shrink or something. Okay, I deserve whatever you lay on me, I guess. Get it over with."

He kept his eyes on the traffic and drove with amazing care, considering their last journey together in this car. "So, you think you deserve whatever I dish out?" he asked.

Jessie swallowed. "Look, I know you're planning some big revenge move, and the clothes and nice driving and soft music are just to soften me up so I won't be on my guard. But I'm on to you, Reid, so don't think I'm going to be surprised by whatever you've cooked up."

"Now, there's a challenge if I ever heard one." He swung the car into the drive of an elegant restaurant.

"Where are you going? I thought this was at Andy's house."

"No, we're having dinner here."

"I smell a rat, Halstead."

"Keep your voice down, or the valet will think you're talking about him," Reid cautioned as a man in a top hat and tails opened the passenger door.

Inside the restaurant Jessie noticed red tablecloths covered with white lace and centerpieces festooned with hearts and red satin ribbons. A woman in a short red dress and black fishnet stockings appeared, carrying a basket full of long-stemmed red roses. She handed one to Jessie. "Happy Valentine's Day," she murmured.

Jessie thanked her and glanced at Reid. He smiled and gestured for her to follow the maître d'. The tuxedoed man, who seemed to know Reid quite well, showed them to a secluded table for two and held Jessie's chair for her.

"Wait a minute." She remained standing. She was starting to panic. "Something is definitely going on here. We're supposed to be attending a party with lots of people. Where are they?"

"I'll explain in a minute," Reid said. "Just sit down, okay?"

"No, not okay! For all I know, you're planning to serve me a meal laced with hot sauce. If you think I'll go meekly along with whatever you've dreamed up, you have another think coming, Reid Halstead."

Reid glanced at the maître d' and shrugged. "Will you xcuse us a minute, Tony?"

"Certainly, Mr. Halstead." The maître d' bowed and valked away.

"I'm warning you, Reid." Jessie put down her rose and lutched her cape around her for protection. "I'm not noving from this spot without an explanation."

"All right." With lightning reflexes he pulled her into his irms and captured her mouth just as she uttered a sur-rised cry. He took advantage of her open mouth to plunge is tongue inside, taking possession of her so thoroughly hat her knees buckled from the onslaught of sensation. He lifted his head. "That's the first part of the explana-ion." He was breathing hard.

Slowly Jessie remembered where they were. Her cheeks varmed as she struggled to free herself, but he wouldn't let er go. "What do you think you're doing?" she whis-ered, glancing around at curious diners who had turned o watch them.

"Acting on impulse. It felt so good the first time with ou, I've decided to make a habit of it."

"You *do* have a mental problem."

"Yes, and you're the cause of it. But you can also be the ure. Stop struggling and listen to me, Jessie."

"I think you've messed up Bert's makeup job."

"I'm sorry, but if you don't stop squirming around, I'll ness it up some more. And don't try to tell me you don't leserve this, because you do."

Her heart hammered against her ribs and she gazed into is eyes, blue and smoldering with heat. "What are you alking about?"

"I'm talking about giving you what you've been asking or, all along."

She licked her lips nervously. "Where are the Gentrys" What about their party?"

"I told them we wouldn't make it."

"You told him that? But I thought you were set on going to preserve your job."

"I never seriously thought Gentry would oust me on a pretense like that, even if he did call me an inane blind fool. But I played along, because it served my purpose."

"Which is?"

"To be with you one more time, Jessie Neal."

"And give me what I deserve, right?" Despair clutched at her heart.

"Yes."

She closed her eyes against the pain. He'd send her home now, in a cab. After making her feel like Cinderella, he'd get rid of her as if she were the wicked stepmother.

"And here's what you deserve." He kissed her gently on the brow. "A man to love you forever, a man who cherishes that playful nature of yours, a man who can put aside his preoccupation with worldly things to enjoy the simple wonder of your touch." He paused. "Let me be that man, Jessie."

She opened her eyes. She was dreaming this. She'd been expecting a tirade, and here was a symphony instead. This couldn't be real.

He gazed into her eyes. "Beautiful, beautiful Jessie. Gentry was right. I've been a blind fool not to scoop you up the minute you showed the slightest interest in me."

She tried to say something, but no words would come out.

"After I stormed into your studio and accused you of setting up that deal with Gentry, I was so ashamed of myself that I drove out to the farm and watched Levi for a while. I thought about what you said—that I wanted my

lfe to be as regulated as his. I don't really want that, Jes-
ie." He smiled. "And by the way, I asked them to let Levi
»ut in the paddock more often. Now that Magnitech is
»uying Malone Farms, I have more say about how he's
reated."

"The deal's going through?"

"Sure. Your prank may have helped, not hurt. But even
f it had hurt, how could I forget why you did it? You paid
ne a wonderful compliment, pursuing me the way you did,
nd I threw it back in your face. Forgive me, Jessie."

She gazed up at him in confusion. "Shouldn't I be ask-
ng you to forgive me? I'm the one who caused all the
rouble."

"But I'm the one who was blind. Gentry told me I was
missing out on the best woman I'd ever find, but it took a
vhile for the message to penetrate my thick skull. Even-
ually it did, though. I may be dazzled by you, Jessie, but
'm sure as hell not blind anymore. I need to know that I
aven't ruined everything for us."

If this was a dream, Jessie never wanted to wake up.
"You haven't ruined everything," she murmured.

He took a deep breath. "That's probably more than *I*
eserve, but I want even more. I want you to marry me."

The room began to spin but he held her tight, keeping
er from falling. "Marry you?" she repeated. She could
ardly believe that she'd heard the words.

"I know it's a shock, and you'll need time to think. And
fter the way I've treated you, you may not want me as a
usband, but I can change. I've already started. Next
nonth I fly to California for hang gliding lessons. If I have
o, I'll hire you as my photographer for the trip, just to get
ou there with me. But I'd rather you came willingly. I'd
ather you came as my wife. I love you, Jessie."

"Do it!" called a woman from the table behind them "Marry him!"

"After all, it's Valentine's Day!" cried someone else followed by a chorus of encouragement and catcalls.

"Please, Jessie. Can you love me back, just a little?"

"I already do," she confessed, her heart overflowing "More than a little. I started loving you from the firs moment I saw you outside the studio window."

He closed his eyes and sucked in his breath. "What jerk I've been, what a bullheaded—"

"Don't insult Levi," she teased softly, cradling Reid' face in both hands.

"You're right," he murmured, looking deep into he eyes. "That bull recognized quality right away. Oh, Jes sie, I'll make it up to you. I'll spend my life making it u to you."

Jessie felt as if she were soaring as she smiled at Reid "Perhaps the future is in genetic engineering, after all."

"The future is us," Reid said. "Happy Valentine's Day Jessie."